## "WHAT CAN YOU DO WITH YOUR HANDS?"

Grant braced his forehead against Victoria's shoulder, adding, "Show me. . . ." His hands splayed across her back, holding her loosely to him. Victoria's palms, roaming restlessly, explored every warm inch of him from his throat to the hair tapering into his unbound jeans.

He thought he was strangling. He sat paralyzed, eyes slits of dark passion. Then his kisses rained over her mouth, her cheeks, her eyelids. Eagerly he filled his hands with her breasts, gently kneading —still it wasn't enough.

"Grant," Victoria moaned. "I wish this was the first time for both of us. I wish I were brand-new."

"Hush, lover, hush. Just love me like new. . . ."

GW00691730

# COME SPRING

Barbara Kaye

A *SuperRomance from*
**HARLEQUIN**
London · Toronto · New York · Sydney

All the characters in this book have no existence outside the imagination of the Author, and have no relation whatsoever to anyone bearing the same name or names. They are not even distantly inspired by any individual known or unknown to the Author, and all the incidents are pure invention.

The text of this publication or any part thereof may not be reproduced or transmitted in any form or by any means, electronic or mechanical, including photocopying, recording, storage in an information retrieval system, or otherwise, without the written permission of the publisher.

This book is sold subject to the condition that it shall not, by way of trade or otherwise, be lent, resold, hired out or otherwise circulated without the prior consent of the publisher in any form of binding or cover other than that in which it is published and without a similar condition including this condition being imposed on the subsequent purchaser.

First published in Great Britain in 1985 by
Harlequin, 15–16 Brook's Mews, London W1A 1DR

© Barbara K. Walker 1984

ISBN 0 373 70124 1

11–1185

Printed and bound in Great Britain by
Cox & Wyman Ltd, Reading

# *PROLOGUE*

THE NOISE WAS UNMISTAKABLE. Grant Mackenzie
had just stepped out onto the front porch spanning the entire width of Arroyo Grande Lodge,
and was in the process of zipping up his pile-lined
jacket, when he heard it—a distinctive whop-
whop-whop. He stopped dead in his tracks,
cocked his head and squinted into the distance.
His fourteen-year-old daughter, Rita, who was
only a few steps behind, paused also.

"What is it, daddy?" she asked, buttoning her
own heavy jacket to ward off the January afternoon's chill.

"Listen, hon."

A few seconds passed. "It's a chopper!" Rita
exclaimed.

Grant's ruggedly handsome features took on a
granite-hard cast, and the dark eyes narrowed
under the brim of his Stetson. The grim expression
transformed his face and made him look older
than his thirty-five years. "No doubt about it,
young'un. No doubt about it."

"Close, too," the girl observed.

"A couple of miles away maybe...but still well
within Arroyo Grande's boundaries."

Rita Mackenzie hooked her thumbs into the pockets of her well-worn jeans in an unconscious copying of her father's stance. "You think it's the same one?"

"Has to be," Grant said. "I know of only one chopper in Reyes County."

"I thought you told them you didn't want any helicopters on our place."

"So did I, Rita. So did I." In a flash Grant's long legs carried him off the porch in the direction of a tan Ford pickup parked in front of the lodge. "Come on. . . let's investigate."

Father and daughter jumped into the vehicle and headed toward the noise. The road they took led through a winter-bare landscape of shinnery and live oak, past scattering herds of whitetail deer, over two shallow stream crossings, across flatlands strewn with slabs and shards of rocks. Finally they drove onto a grassy slope falling away from a steep bluff. Grant stopped the truck, and he and Rita scrambled out. Instinctively both of them lifted their eyes.

A magnificent golden eagle swept out of the sky. As usual, its aerial acrobatics couldn't have been more awesome. Grant smiled, immediately recognizing the bird as one of their Canadian visitors. He couldn't have explained how he distinguished the wintering eagles from the nesting birds that lived on Arroyo Grande all year; he just did. And he was fiercely protective of them. It was his fondest wish that, come spring, this fellow would find his way safely back to Alberta or Saskatchewan or wherever his aerie was located.

Then Grant froze, and the smile faded from his face. The bird, he realized, wasn't engaged in frolicsome acrobatics at all. He was employing evasive tactics, feinting toward the bluff, then away from it. An ominous sound sent a chill up and down Grant's spine, and he tore his gaze away from the spectacle of the soaring eagle. Directly behind it, at a higher elevation, a helicopter droned through the sky. It was in pursuit of the eagle, and the bird knew it.

"Daddy!" Rita cried in wide-eyed, youthful fright, her tone imploring her father to *do something*.

Cursing viciously, Grant jerked open the door of the truck and hit the horn, again and again. The sound rent the winter air. With his free hand he gestured wildly at the helicopter. "Get away from here, damn you!" he yelled. "You're on private property! Get the hell out of here!"

But even as he shouted he could see a man in the helicopter holding a high-powered rifle. If the gunner saw the man and the girl, he apparently didn't care. While the two spectators on the ground looked on in horror, the man raised the rifle to his shoulder, and four shots rang out in rapid succession. The noise of the helicopter drowned out the girl's scream.

Grant and his daughter watched helplessly as the eagle's wings collapsed against its sides; the wings stretched out again as the bird plummeted to earth. Rita whimpered, slipped her arms around her father's waist and buried her face against his chest.

Grant stood for a moment in impotent rage, watching the helicopter disappear behind the surrounding hills. With a struggling sigh, he patted his daughter's shoulder and led her back to the truck. "Let's go, Rita. There's nothing we can do here. . . and I've got a phone call to make."

IN HIS CORPUS CHRISTI OFFICE, Chuck Singleton listened, tight-lipped, as Grant Mackenzie related the afternoon's events over the phone. Chuck and Grant were friends of long standing and had briefly roomed together at Texas A&M University. As a senior investigative agent for the U.S. Fish and Wildlife Service, Chuck had supported Grant's efforts to turn Arroyo Grande into a wildlife refuge and game preserve. He shared his friend's outrage at the eagle slaughter.

"Violation of federal law," he stated emphatically when Grant had finished speaking. "The Bald Eagle Protection Act specifically prohibits the killing of golden eagles, too. Know who did it?"

"I've got a pretty good idea. Some of the sheepmen around here have organized and hired a guy with a helicopter. They tried to get me to go in with them. They claim it's for coyote control, but coyotes aren't a real problem at Arroyo Grande, and I told them if I saw that chopper on my place I was going to shoot it! Unfortunately, I didn't happen to have a gun with me at the time."

"Hold on, friend. Don't go shooting anything. So. . . I take it you've never signed a permit allowing aerial hunting on your place?"

"Are you nuts? On a wildlife refuge? There's no telling what they'd hit. No way!"

"Then they violated state law, too. Tell you what. You get out there and recover the eagle's carcass as evidence."

"Will do."

"And I'll send an agent out to your place tomorrow. Don't talk to anyone about this in the meantime."

Grant snorted. "Don't worry. To tell you the truth, Chuck, I'd as soon folks around here didn't find out I'm the one who blew the whistle." He paused, adding, "It's not for my sake. I don't give a damn what they think of me, but...well, it's kinda hard on Rita. And I doubt that your investigation will do any good, anyway."

"So why did you call me?" Chuck asked reasonably. "You leave this up to me. I'll keep your name out of it if I can," he promised. "Can you put my agent up for a few days?"

"Sure. There aren't any paying guests due until the weekend."

"Good. You'll be hearing from me, Grant."

After he hung up, Chuck sat at his desk awhile, idly making notations in a small notebook. Then he punched the button on the desk intercom. When a soft feminine voice responded, he said, "Victoria, can you get in here right away?"

"Of course."

Chuck released the button, tugging on his chin. For years he had resisted the government's attempts to place a female agent in his office, and when Victoria Bartlett, all twenty-six years and one hundred fifteen pounds of her, had first reported for duty with her brand new ID card and shiny badge, he had been appalled. Although her shapely figure and that fantastic mass of chestnut hair improved the office scenery considerably, he could think of nothing else good about having here there. Learning that she came from one of Corpus Christi's most high-toned families had only intensified his feeling that she didn't belong. To date he hadn't seen fit to send her out alone on an assignment.

But like it or not, he had her, and this eagle killing was a tame enough thing. The chances of its amounting to anything were slim to zero. She could go up to Reyes County, ask a few questions, suffer the resentment of some old ranchers who despised government "interference" anyway and would doubly resent a female agent. Then she could come back and file her reports. He had to do something with her, and this might give her some confidence. Kick her out of the nest, see if she could fly.

There was a light knock on his office door. It opened, and Chuck found himself looking into those gorgeous green eyes.

"Yes, Chuck?" Victoria Bartlett said.

Chuck cleared his throat. "Sit down, Victoria. I have something I want you to look into."

# CHAPTER ONE

THE FOLLOWING AFTERNOON, a sparkling-clear afternoon crisp with below-freezing temperatures, the limestone hills of the Edwards Plateau stretched ahead for seemingly endless miles. Behind the wheel of the government car, Victoria viewed the landscape through owl-round sunglasses. The hillsides were covered with cedar, and the flatlands rolling out from under them were strewn with rocks of all sizes, from huge slabs to small stones. It was sheep country, although she saw plenty of cattle and goats, and more deer than anything.

Certainly it was lonely country. The farther down the winding country road Victoria traveled the lonelier it became—no towns, few people. She had passed only two vehicles since leaving the main highway, both of them dilapidated pickups, and both times the drivers had gawked at the lovely young woman behind the wheel of the government car. A shudder swept through her as she dwelt on the possibility of car trouble on this remote stretch of highway.

"Isolated," Chuck had warned her when he gave her the assignment. Definitely an understatement.

Thinking about her supervisor brought a frown to Victoria's face. Chuck hadn't accepted her yet, and she didn't know what she could do about that. He doubted her abilities, distrusted her motives for becoming an agent. She could recall with amazing clarity every word of her initial interview with him.

"This is not a nine-to-five job, do you realize that, Victoria?"

"Yes, of course."

"And days off are not necessarily Saturday and Sunday."

"I'm aware of that."

"And if I call you out at midnight to sit in some godforsaken deer blind all night, I don't want to hear that it's too cold or too wet or you're having your period or anything like that, is that clear?"

"Yes."

Her supervisor, Victoria had noted more than once, was something of a chauvinist, who preferred working with men. Regretfully, she didn't think his opinion of her had changed all that much. His unspoken but unmistakable attitude was still, "this isn't for you."

Well, Victoria disagreed; to her mind her career was the most logical thing in the world. Her father was a biologist, a Ph.D. who taught at Del Mar College and had written several scholarly books on wildlife conservation. Her high-society mother was an inveterate bird-watcher and espouser of conservationist causes.

Victoria's childhood summers had been spent at

her family's house in the hill country, surrounded by wildlife, cattle and horses. Her earliest ambition had been to become a veterinarian, an ambition she had cast aside when she married her high-school sweetheart. But always she had harbored the feeling she would one day work with animals.

Yet Chuck Singleton withheld approval and refused to believe she was serious about her work, because of the way she looked and because she had moved in some fairly lofty social circles.

Victoria knew she shouldn't let him bother her so much. She was a special agent now. Her training had been a snap for her, since she already knew so much about wildlife from living so close to it. She had opted for the outdoorsy life, knew her way around firearms and was stronger than she looked. Plus she was committed to her work. Someday she would prove to her supervisor that she wasn't just a bored society divorcée out looking to put some spice in her life.

She straightened and flexed her shoulders and fingers, stiff from the long drive. She could have saved some time by flying to San Antonio and renting a car, but she honestly didn't mind driving and she hated flying. She glanced at her watch for the dozenth time.

A late start hadn't been part of her plans, but she had telephoned her mother before leaving town, and once her mother started talking there was no tactful way to terminate the conversation. Rachel Carpenter loved to "visit" over the telephone. Though Victoria despised the habit, she tolerated her mother's gossip for the simple reason that Rachel was the only soul on earth she felt close to. And, Victoria forcibly reminded herself, her mother was just as alone as she was and didn't have the solace of an interesting job.

But this morning's conversation had been a bad way to start the day. "Oh, Victoria," Rachel had trilled once the pleasantries had been exchanged. "I was just going to call you. Guess who I just spoke to."

"Who, mom?"

"Steve."

His name. Good Lord, they had been divorced for over a year, and she still couldn't stand to hear his name. "What did he want?" she asked harshly.

"He remembered that my birthday is coming up, but he said he would be out of town on the actual date, so he called to wish me a happy one in advance. I thought that was sweet."

"Oh, mom, he's probably on a guilt trip."

There was a pause. Rachel added, "Your father called, too."

"This really was your day for bastards, wasn't it, mom?"

Another pause. "Victoria, I wish you wouldn't be so. . .unyielding, so unforgiving. Your father's chief reason for calling was to inquire about you. He said he hasn't heard from you in the longest time."

Victoria's voice was brittle. "He has my phone number."

"Dear, don't wring every drop of misery out of problems. It will only make you old before your time."

"Honestly, mom, you kill me, really you do! Dad left you for another woman, and my darling husband left me for the same reason. How can you even give either one of them the time of day?"

Rachel's response to that was a very heavy sigh before she moved on to other topics—the museum fund drive, her church work, her garden club—finally concluding with, "Well, I suppose I should let you get on your way. Do be careful, Victoria. I just hate having you driving on those awful country roads."

"Mom, I'm probably a lot safer on 'those country roads' than I am driving here in the city."

"Perhaps. Please...call your father."

"I'll think about it," had been the best Victoria could do.

Now she gripped the steering wheel so tightly her knuckles turned white. For a time after hanging up the phone she had grappled with her conscience, until the old resentment surfaced, as it invariably did. Adam Carpenter had willingly left Rachel, just as Stephen Bartlett had willingly left her. So why the hell didn't they just stay away?

Peering ahead, Victoria saw the road sign she'd been waiting for. Arroyo Grande Lodge, it read, and a huge arrow instructed her to turn left onto a farm-to-market road. That was even more deserted than the state highway, if possible. On either side of the road the high-fenced pastures stretched to the cedar hills. The fences spoke of human habitation, but she saw nothing but livestock. When Victoria finally spotted the massive wooden arch with the lodge's name painted on it, she breathed an audible sigh of relief.

Swinging her car onto the long narrow drive that led to the lodge, she felt as though she had somehow entered another world. Unlike the grazed-clean countryside she had just passed through, the Arroyo Grande refuge was dense with vegetation, even in the dead of winter. Victoria could imagine how lovely the place would be during spring and summer, and the autumnal colors would be breathtaking.

Ahead of her, at the side of the drive, another sign read, Warning! You Are Entering a Private Wildlife Refuge. Rules Regarding the Use of Firearms Are Strictly Enforced.

Nearing her destination, she quickly recalled some of the things Chuck had told her about the lodge's owner. An old friend from college, her boss had said, so that would put Grant Mackenzie in his mid-thirties. "And he's a loner," Chuck had added. "So be careful when you start snooping around. Grant's not anxious for his neighbors to know he's the one who asked for the investigation."

"He sounds like a man without the courage of his convictions," Victoria had remarked.

"Aw, it's not that. Some of those old ranchers have taken a fit over his plunking a wildlife refuge in their midst. Even though he's a loner,

I imagine he tries to get along whenever he can.''

She drove on, and it was a few more minutes before she spotted the lodge, standing on a small rise, an imposing structure of native stone and cedar shingles. Several chimneys pointing skyward and the wide front veranda immediately caught her eye. The cedar-and-oak forest marched right up to the sides and rear of the building. The refuge looked wild and untouched; in short, the perfect place for wildlife to flourish, exactly the kind of country where migrating eagles would choose to spend the winter.

But what kind of people would choose to live out here in the back of beyond? Only a puff of smoke from one of the chimneys suggested anyone or anything stirred in this far-out place.

Then Victoria spied a tan Ford pickup parked to one side of the veranda. She braked and pulled in behind it, reached for her heavy camel-hair coat, grabbed the door handle and braced herself for the blast of wintery air she knew would greet her. Leaving her luggage behind for the time being, she got out of the car almost at a dead run—good grief, it was cold!—sprinted up the steps and hurried into the welcome warmth of the lodge.

The size of the main room was overwhelming, its decor rustic, its aroma definitely masculine— old leather and stale tobacco. A native stone fireplace, in which an inviting fire now crackled, dominated the far wall, with game tables set up in front of the picture windows. Wood paneling covered the walls; oak beams crisscrossed the ceiling. Accented by several large rugs of geometric Indian design, well-worn wood floors gleamed from countless polishings. It was a room meant for men, no doubt about it.

The heels of Victoria's pumps tapped out a staccato rhythm as she crossed to stand in the center of the room and listen for some activity. She heard nothing.

She waited a few minutes, then noticed a reception desk in one corner of the room. She walked to it and lightly tapped the small service bell. In the deathly quiet room the ensuing ping was startlingly loud.

Seconds passed. She heard a door open and close; heavy footsteps sounded in the hallway, and behind her a throaty masculine voice asked, "May I help you?"

Victoria turned. A man stood in the doorway, his eyes squinted in curiosity. He was tall—somewhere around six feet, she guessed—and powerfully built, with broad shoulders and chest, muscular arms. His hair was thick and chocolate-colored, his skin a deep tan, even this late into winter. He was wearing a plaid flannel shirt, sleeves rolled to the elbows and faded jeans that had seen better days. Yet the very ordinary clothing seemed to highlight his extraordinary masculinity.

Victoria lifted her gaze to his face, and found herself staring into the most intriguing pair of eyes she had ever seen. Dark brown, as dark as his hair, they assaulted her, roamed over her in candid curiosity, and from his expression of wonder one would have thought she was the first woman he'd ever seen. Men had been looking at her with varying degrees of interest since she was sixteen, but she didn't think any of them had ever stared at her so openly. The most peculiar, unfamiliar, yet oddly pleasant sensation stirred inside her. Awareness. And it had been a very long time since she had looked at a man with anything but detachment. Victoria couldn't have known what an appealing picture she presented, standing with her coat cinched around her waist, the fake fur collar pushed high around her face, cheeks rosy from the cold. Her large green eyes had widened farther, and her full red lips were slightly parted. She was a pretty woman in a healthy, wholesome way, but more than pretty. Her coloring and flawless skin, her finely shaped patrician nose and full sensitive mouth combined to create a face that would be hard to forget.

Nor could she have known how long it had been since the man in the doorway had seen a woman of such obvious class, or what an incongruous sight such a woman was at Arroyo Grande.

Under his scrutiny, Victoria nervously shifted her handbag on her shoulder and stuffed her hands deeper into her coat pockets. This slight movement seemed to break the spell between them. The man propped one shoulder against the doorjamb and hooked his thumbs into the pockets of his jeans. "May I help you?" he repeated. "Are you lost?"

"Are you Mr. Mackenzie?"

He nodded. "Grant Mackenzie, at your service."

Victoria stepped toward him, withdrew her right hand from her pocket and offered it to him along with a small smile. "Then I'm not lost. How do you do, Mr. Mackenzie. I'm Victoria Bartlett from Fish and Wildlife."

For a moment Victoria thought he hadn't understood her. Until his dark eyes widened, and Grant Mackenzie straightened, staring first at her face, then at her outstretched hand, back to her face. "You're kidding!" he exclaimed.

Victoria smiled wryly. A year ago she would have been incensed, but she had become so accustomed to this reaction that she was almost disappointed if it wasn't forthcoming. Since the man appeared to be too stunned to shake her hand, she dipped it into her handbag, withdrew her billfold and deftly flipped it open to reveal her identification.

Grant looked down and back up. "Well, I'll be damned! *You're* the agent Chuck sent me?"

"Yes, I am."

Grant guffawed. "Is this some kind of joke? Chuck always did have a weird sense of humor."

Now Victoria bristled. "It's no joke, Mr. Mackenzie, I can assure you of that. I'm here to investigate a possible violation of the Bald Eagle Protection Act. Since you were the one who reported the violation, I assume I will receive your complete cooperation."

Grant tugged thoughtfully on his chin and struggled, unsuccessfully, to wipe the grin off his face. He took a step closer to her, and once again Victoria felt the impact of those compelling eyes. "I'm sorry, Miss Bartlett. You were just a surprise, that's all. Here, let me take your coat and get you some coffee or something."

"Thank you. I'd like that." Victoria turned her back to him and slipped out of her coat; Grant folded it across his arm. Perhaps she only imagined his quick intake of breath as she turned around, but she didn't imagine his appreciative gaze as his eyes raked her from head to foot. She was wearing a soft shirt of cream-colored silk and a pleated skirt of varying shades of brown—simple, sensible garments, she had thought. Grant Mackenzie's expression made her think again. Perhaps the blouse did cling too seductively to her breasts; perhaps the skirt showed off her small waist and hugged her trim hips. The moment she got the chance she would change.

"I'll just hang this up and go in the kitchen and get that coffee," Grant said. "Have a seat by the fireplace."

Victoria nodded, crossing the room to do just that. The space immediately in front of the fireplace was several degrees warmer than the center of the room, and it felt marvelous. She held her hands closer to the firescreen, rubbed them together briskly, then clasped them tightly in her lap. Only a few minutes elapsed before her host was back with a steaming cup of coffee.

"Sorry," he said. "I forgot to ask how you like it."

"Black is fine." She took the cup from him. Grant took a seat opposite her, leveling an inquisitive look at her. Victoria knew that look so well. He was burning with questions, and the first one would be something like, "How did a pretty thing like you get into this kind of work?" She waited.

He surprised her. "So, Miss Bartlett, do you live in Corpus Christi?"

"Yes, and it isn't Miss Bartlett."

"Oh?" He glanced pointedly at her ringless left hand.

"I'm not married. . . anymore." It was the closest she could come to saying, "I'm divorced." The word *divorcée* still sent a shudder of revulsion through her, possibly because it was a word she had never expected to be associated with her. She lifted the cup and took a sip of the hot coffee.

"Oh," he said again. "Any children?"

"No, thank heavens!"

He seemed surprised. "You don't like kids?"

"I love them, but I wouldn't want to have to raise one by myself." How had the conversation strayed to the personal, she wondered. Setting her cup on a nearby table, she reached into her handbag for her small notebook and a pencil. "Now Mr. Mackenzie, I—"

"Grant, please," he interrupted.

"All right, Grant—and please call me Victoria. I'd like you to relate to me yesterday's events, exactly as you recall them."

Succinctly Grant told her of his witnessing the eagle killing, concluding with, "What are you hoping the outcome of all this will be, Victoria?"

"I can't say at this point, Grant. It depends on what I find out while I'm, as Chuck puts it, 'snooping.'"

"Then I can save you a lot of time. Nothing will come of it."

Victoria frowned. "Why do you say that?"

"Because when you start talking to folks around here, you're going to discover none of them has ever seen a helicopter or an eagle in their entire lives, much less a man in a helicopter shooting an eagle right here in Reyes County."

"You saw it. And your daughter saw it."

Grant nodded. "But neither of us thought to get the chopper's ID number. All we have is an eagle's carcass with thirty-ought-six bullets in him. . . . If you search every ranch in Reyes County you're gonna find thirty-ought-six rifles on every one of 'em."

"But the carcass proves there was a slaughter. And your daughter's having seen it is a plus," Victoria insisted.

"I don't want her name mentioned," Grant snapped. At his altered tone, Victoria's head jerked up, and immediately he tried to explain. "I'll be honest with you, Victoria. . . . We're not the best-loved people around these parts, and we do have to try to get along."

Victoria remembered the things Chuck had told her. But that, she decided, in no way absolved

Grant of the responsibility for aiding the investigation. "Grant, whoever hired that helicopter, whoever piloted it, whoever fired that gun broke federal law."

"I know that and I'm as against it as anybody. Six years ago I decided to devote my life to the propagation of wildlife and to protecting endangered species. But I don't want to make things any more difficult for Rita than they already are."

"Rita is your daughter?"

He nodded.

"How old is she?"

"Fourteen."

"Old enough to tell what she saw." Victoria glanced around. "Is she here?"

"No, she's not home from school yet." He grinned lopsidedly. "And I'll spare you having to ask. No, my wife isn't here, either. Like you, I'm not married...anymore. Mrs. Mackenzie also flew the coop."

Victoria stiffened. Perhaps he had meant nothing by the remark, but she was overly sensitive to any assumption that she had been the one to terminate her marriage. She was constantly amazed at how many strangers, almost always men, assumed that.

She opened her mouth to say, "I'm sorry," then quickly shut it. It was a pitiful remark, usually insincere, and one she herself hated. Instead she pretended absorbed interest in the shorthand notes she had taken, before shutting the notebook and slipping it back into her handbag. "Now I'd like to see the recovered carcass,'' she said, all business. ''But first I'd like to change.''

''That reminds me. I'm afraid this lodge was designed for male guests. Weekend hunters require little in the way of creature comforts. The rooms are definitely masculine and a bit Spartan.''

''Don't give it a thought. I have to move around the state quite a bit, and I'm rarely afforded luxurious accommodations.''

''I just wanted to warn you.''

Without seeming to, Victoria studied her host. Chuck had classified Grant Mackenzie as a loner, and the label fit him to a T. But what on earth did a fourteen-year-old girl find to do here when she wasn't in school? No mother, no nearby neighbors. Trying to envision Grant's daughter, Victoria came up with a picture of the quintessential tomboy.

The picture had no more than formed in her mind when there were footsteps on the porch, and the front door opened to admit the girl, bundled to the nose, her small face flushed with the cold. She entered the lodge with normal adolescent exuberance, then stopped when she saw Victoria. Quickly she whipped off her muffler and dumped the rather formidable stack of books she had been carrying under her arm.

''Oh, hi!'' she said, her gaze focused on Victoria.

''Hi.'' Victoria smiled back.

''Come here, Rita,'' Grant said. ''I want you to meet our guest.''

Rita Mackenzie advanced shyly, slowly unbuttoning her coat, never taking her eyes off their guest. Looking at her, Victoria thought Grant's daughter was surely the loveliest young girl she had ever seen in her life.

"Rita, this is Victoria," Grant said.

"How nice to meet you, Rita."

"How do you do," Rita said self-consciously.

Even in jeans and a plaid shirt, Grant's daughter didn't look like a tomboy. There was a Dresden-doll quality about her, making Victoria think what a lovely woman she would one day be. The girl had a heart-shaped, elfin face and enormous dove-gray eyes, hair the color of ripened wheat and a delicate little body that had formed hips, a waist, breasts. Fourteen could be a singularly unlovely age for a girl, but it had been kind to Rita.

Nothing about her suggested she was Grant Mackenzie's daughter, so Victoria had to assume Rita had inherited her looks from her mother. The woman who "flew the coop" must have been stunning.

Rita plopped into the chair next to Victoria. "That's a pretty blouse," she said admiringly, in a wistful voice.

"Why, thank you, Rita."

"Are you staying with us?"

"Yes, I am."

"Victoria is here to investigate the eagle killing we saw yesterday," Grant explained, his tone indicating he still found it hard to believe she was what she was.

Rita's eyes widened in astonishment. "Really?"

"Yes, really," Victoria said.

"Gosh, how neat! I figured they'd send out some kind of cop, or a game warden."

"I'm sort of a cop," Victoria told her with a smile. "A game warden, too."

"Neat! Where do you live?"

"Corpus Christi."

"Daddy keeps saying he'll take me to the coast sometime, but...." Rita's voice trailed off.

"Well, there's plenty to see. If you ever make it down there, give me a call and I'll show you the sights."

It was one of those offhand remarks, not meant to be taken seriously or literally, but Rita latched on to it immediately. "Did you hear that, daddy?"

Grant cleared his throat and got to his feet. "I heard. Tell you what, young'un. Victoria wants to change, so why don't we get her settled in? I'll see to her luggage, and you take her to room 12—"

"Oh, daddy, let her have my room," Rita pleaded.

"Rita, I wouldn't think of taking your room!" Victoria exclaimed.

"Please," the girl said. "The other rooms are all so yucky and meant for men, but I have a nice room...and I think you should have a pretty room."

Victoria was touched. "Rita, that's awfully sweet of you, but I...."

"Please—"

Victoria looked at Rita's earnest young face; instinct told her to accept the expansive offer. To do otherwise might hurt Rita's feelings.

Grant's impatient voice interrupted. "Okay, okay, we'll put Victoria in your room. I trust it's presentable."

"Spotless," Rita assured him proudly. "I changed the sheets before I went to school this morning."

Grant turned to Victoria. "Your luggage?"

"There are two small suitcases in the back seat." She rummaged in her handbag for her car keys, which she handed to him.

"I'll be right back," he said, striding away.

Rita took Victoria by the hand. "Come on, Ms...." She paused, then timidly asked, "Can I really call you Victoria?"

"I wish you would."

"It's such a pretty name."

"So is Rita."

The girl led her down a long hallway. "Daddy and I have rooms down here. Upstairs is for the paying guests."

"Are there many of those?"

"Lots sometimes. Depends on what daddy calls 'conditions.' There's a bunch due in for weekend, bird-watchers from San Antonio, I think."

"Surely you and your father don't run this place by yourselves."

"Nope." Rita pushed open the door to her room. "There's Jake. He's sorta daddy's assistant. He ought to be around somewhere. And then there are two other men who help lead the hunts and take care of all the animals. And there's Maria; she's the housekeeper. Mrs. Guilford is the cook. They live in, but today's everybody's day off. You'll meet them tomorrow.'' She looked at Victoria hopefully. ''You will be here tomorrow, won't you?''

''Yes, I'm sure the investigation will take a couple of days at least.''

''I wish you could stay a long time. We never have a woman staying here.''

Rita's room turned out to be a girlish haven in the midst of all the rustic masculinity. A four-poster bed covered with a patchwork quilt was the focal point. There were ruffly curtains at the windows and a hooked rug on the floor. ''It's charming, Rita,'' Victoria said sincerely.

''Mrs. Guilford helped me decorate it. We had to order most of the stuff from the Sears catalog.''

Victoria's eyes were caught and held by a lovely woven tapestry hanging over Rita's bed. ''You didn't get that out of the Sears catalog. What a lovely piece of art!''

Rita turned to her with bright eyes. ''Do you really think so? I made it.''

''You made it? Why, Rita, it's beautiful!'' Victoria walked to the bed to get a closer look. She touched the tapestry gently and felt its soft texture and tight weave. ''You're very talented. How on earth did you learn to do such work?''

Rita looked as though she might explode with delight. ''There used to be an Indian woman living here. Her husband worked for daddy for a while, but then they went back to New Mexico. She taught me. She learned weaving from her Navaho grandmother. The Navahos are the best, you know."

"I know. You have real talent, Rita. Your father must be enormously proud of you."

Surprisingly, the girl's face clouded, and she shrugged. "Oh. . . you know how fathers are."

Peculiar remark, Victoria thought. Most parents almost burst with pride over their children's accomplishments, no matter how small, and to Victoria's mind, Rita's weaving was no small accomplishment. "Well, I hope you do something with it."

"Someday I'm going to buy a really good loom, but good ones cost a lot of money." The "a lot" was accompanied by much rolling of the eyes.

Victoria grinned. "What's a lot?"

"Oh, anywhere from five hundred to five thousand dollars."

"That's a lot," Victoria agreed. Once more her eyes swept around the room. "Well, you have a lovely room. I'll bet you enjoy living in it."

"And I have my own bathroom, too," Rita announced. "It's over there."

"But where are you going to sleep?"

"There's an extra bed in daddy's room. I'll sleep there."

At that moment Grant appeared on the threshold with Victoria's garment bag and makeup case. "You travel light," he said approvingly.

"You learn to with practice." Victoria relieved him of one of the cases.

"I'll put this one in the closet for now," he said, indicating the other suitcase. On his way across the room, he looked at his daughter over his shoulder. "Okay, hon, run on and get the homework done."

"Aw, daddy, can't I do it tonight? I want to visit with Victoria."

"Victoria, is it? Nope...you won't want to do it any more tonight than you do right now. Get on with it."

Rita made a face, then lifted her slim shoulders resignedly and left the room. Victoria smiled after her retreating figure. "She's such a darling girl, Grant."

He closed the closet door. "Yeah, I guess she is."

"She's going to be a real beauty when she grows up."

He had crossed the room to stand in front of her, but he stopped dead-still the moment she uttered those words. The most peculiar expression crossed his face. Victoria was at a loss to interpret it. The look, which lasted only a second, was almost menacing. It disappeared, and he ruefully ran his fingers through his dark hair. "Lord, I hope you're wrong!"

Victoria frowned. "What a strange thing for a father to say!"

"Is it? I want Rita to be happy, and it's been my observation that beautiful women are seldom happy."

"That's an absurd generalization."

He stepped forward, lessening the distance between them. Not many men could make her feel petite, but he did. And he was too close, so close she could smell his clean masculine scent. His eyes, deep and intense, so dark they seemed to have no pupils, held her transfixed, and in that one breathless, suspended moment of time, Victoria was more aware of Grant Mackenzie than she had ever been of anyone. It was a nerve-rattling sensation.

"Absurd?" he asked huskily. "Has your beauty made you happy, Victoria?"

"I . . . I think there's a compliment lurking in there somewhere." She sounded out of breath.

The barest suggestion of a smile quirked the corners of his mouth. "All women like to be told they're beautiful."

"Another generalization. How do you know what all women like?"

He chuckled. "Did your beauty help you find whatever it was you were looking for when your marriage split up?"

Victoria set her chin defiantly. "I had everything I was looking for *before* the marriage split up. And my husband left me for a woman a lot of people might describe as Plain Jane," she said evenly, at a loss to explain why she was telling this man these things. "Does that answer your question?"

Apparently he had expected anything but that kind of frankness, and for a moment he looked completely nonplussed. He recovered quickly, and his tone mellowed. "Yes, I can see it...the pain. In your eyes. Forgive my rudeness."

She suspected his humility was out of character. Stepping back, she effectively switched off the current that sizzled between them. "I'll change now, and then I would like to view the remains."

Grant stared at her for a second longer. He gave himself a little shake and moved toward the door. But before leaving he stopped and turned to her. "Tell me something, Victoria. How on earth did a pretty woman like you get involved in this kind of work?"

Victoria put her hand to her forehead and laughed lightly. "Well, at least it wasn't the *first* thing you asked me."

## CHAPTER TWO

THE GRIM REMAINS OF THE SLAUGHTER were in a small shed to the rear of the lodge. Grant handled the carcass carefully and pointed out the two bullet holes that had done the bird in. Victoria's mouth set tightly. "We can certainly rule out death due to natural causes," she said bitterly.

"There were four shots fired," he told her, looking up from where he squatted on his haunches. "Whoever did it was going to make sure the bird was dead."

Victoria huddled deeper inside her ski jacket. The sun was rapidly disappearing below the horizon, and it was cold! "You don't have the slightest idea who it was?"

"I don't know who pulled the trigger," he said, pushing himself to his feet. "Nor do I know who was piloting the chopper. But—"

At that moment the door to the shed squeaked open. Grant glanced at it and said, "Hi, Jake, come on in. There's somebody here I'd like you to meet."

Victoria turned to see a wiry, spare man of indeterminate age enter the shed. He was dressed much like Grant, in well-worn jeans, scuffed boots, heavy jacket and the inevitable Stetson, dipped so low in front it obscured his eyes. As he came closer she saw the pleasant weathered face of an outdoorsman, craggy and deeply colored from years in the sun. He didn't attempt to conceal his surprise at seeing her.

"Jake, this is Victoria Bartlett," Grant said.

The man whipped off the Stetson for a second, then replaced it. "Pleased t'meetcha, ma'am."

"Victoria's with Fish and Wildlife."

The small man's eyes widened in a predictable reaction. "Do tell!"

"Victoria, this is Jake McGrath. Jake is my... well, now, let's see... my right-hand man, my overseer, my foreman? What's your official title, Jake?"

"Slave," the man said without hesitation, and all three laughed.

Grant slid a hand under Victoria's elbow. "Are you finished, Victoria? It's getting damned cold out here."

She nodded. "I'll want to photograph the carcass, as well as the shooting site, but there's not enough light for that. It can wait until tomorrow."

"Come on, Jake. Let's go up to the house and see what's for supper."

The three of them walked briskly back to the welcome warmth of the lodge. Using the back door, they stepped into the kitchen, where Rita was busily working at the sink.

"How's it going, hon?" Grant asked.

"Fine, daddy. Hi, Jake."

"Hi, young'un. How's school?" Jake asked.

Rita wrinkled her nose. "You ask me that every day, and every day I tell you it's awful."

Jake cackled. "That's what I like, a young'un with a thirst for knowledge."

"Ladies, we'll see you later," Grant said. "Jake and I will be in the office."

The men left the kitchen, and Victoria shrugged out of her coat and draped it over the back of a chair. She surveyed the big room. The kitchen looked rustic but wasn't, equipped as it was with an industrial-sized refrigerator, an eight-burner restaurant stove and a heavy-duty dishwasher. In fact, Victoria had noticed the lodge's rusticity was all for show. It possessed central heating and air conditioning, and all the plumbing she had seen was completely modern.

From the sink Rita shot her a smile. "Oh, I like that sweater!" Victoria had changed into slacks and a soft cowl-necked sweater, both in a shade of dusky blue that complemented her russet hair.

"Thanks, Rita. What are you doing?"

"Since it's Mrs. Guilford's day off, I'm in charge of supper. We'll have what daddy and I always have on Wednesday night—steak, baked potatoes and salad. Even I can cook that."

"I can pan-broil a pretty mean steak myself. Or toss a salad. Give me something to do."

"Then you cook the steaks. That's the hard part. Daddy and Jake like theirs well-done."

"I would have bet on it," Victoria said dryly. "And you?"

"Pink in the middle."

"And I like mine medium rare. This ought to test a cook's mettle. But that's a last-minute job. First I'll set the table."

"We usually eat in here at the kitchen table, if that's all right with you."

"It's fine with me. Just show me where everything is."

While Victoria was setting the table Rita asked, "How long have you been...doing what you're doing?"

"A little over a year."

"What did you do before that?"

"I had an office job for a while, but mostly I ran a home."

"You were married?"

Victoria nodded.

"Any kids?"

"No."

"Do you like living in Corpus Christi?"

"I love it. I've spent most of my life there, and I love being close to the water."

"It must be fun to live somewhere like that and have an interesting job," Rita said wistfully as she tore chunks of lettuce into a wooden bowl.

Yes, Victoria could see how a young girl would think so, particularly one who led such a solitary life. She cast a glance at the girl. Not a thing had been done to highlight her striking youthful beauty. She was dressed for all the world like a fourteen-year-old boy. Her honey-colored hair was left to fall pretty much the way it pleased. How adorable she would have looked with a shorter cut that flattered her elfin face. Watching the girl, Victoria tried to recall herself at fourteen. Nothing much came to her except that adolescence had been filled with people, things to do, places to go.

"Have you always lived here, Rita?"

The girl shook her head. "I was born in Houston. We lived in River Oaks. Ever hear of it?"

Victoria nodded. Indeed she had heard of it, a Houston suburb where million-dollar mansions were commonplace.

"We lived there until my mother left. Then daddy bought Arroyo Grande, and we moved here. That was six years ago."

Victoria pursed her lips. When Grant had said his wife had flown the coop, she had assumed he meant this coop, that it had been a classic case of a wife unable to cope with a solitary existence. But Mrs. Mackenzie had left not only a River Oaks mansion but a child, and even in this day and age that was unusual. It was only natural to speculate that another man had been involved. That might account for Grant's having Rita, and it would explain his instant empathy earlier. Arroyo Grande was a place for him to hide from unpleasant memories. But how unfair to the girl!

"Do you miss Houston, Rita?"

The girl shrugged. "I really don't remember a lot about it, and daddy says we'll never go back. To tell you the truth, I'm not sure he'll ever take me to the coast. Sometimes we go shopping in Kerrville, but mostly daddy says anything he can't find in Kierney he doesn't need.''

Victoria smiled sadly to herself. Arroyo Grande might suit Grant fine—from all appearances it did—but Rita needed more. She was fast approaching a time in her life when peers and an active social life would mean everything. Plus, she seemed to be a talented girl who needed artistic stimulation, something she was unlikely to find here.

That, however, was none of Victoria's business. ''Well, maybe he's right,'' she offered brightly.

Rita threw an amused look over her shoulder. ''Have you ever been to Kierney, Victoria?''

''No, no, I haven't.''

''It...is...the...pits!'' Her young face sobered. ''And I'm going to leave it just as soon as I'm old enough.''

## CHAPTER THREE

"RITA, YOU DID A FINE JOB," Grant said. Victoria glanced up to see the men getting to their feet. "My steak was delicious."

"Victoria cooked them," Rita told him.

"You did?" Grant asked, shooting Victoria a chagrined look. "Well...thanks. But I'm sorry you had to draw kitchen duty."

She smiled. "It was nothing, and I'm glad you enjoyed your steak."

"Mine was perfect, ma'am," Jake said politely. "Now if y'all just excuse me, I'll be going to my own place."

"Jake has a cabin out back," Grant explained. "He refuses to move in here with us."

Dinner had passed in a blur. Victoria could hardly remember consuming the meal at all, and she realized she had been lost in a private reverie. For some inexplicable reason she hadn't been able to tear her thoughts away from her host.

He intrigued her, and that was a new experience. The reason for that went far beyond his rugged good looks. Steve was far better looking in the classic sense, but she couldn't say her ex-husband had ever intrigued her. Having known Steve since she was sixteen, she supposed he had simply been too familiar. Grant was another matter. Behind his lighthearted banter and charming grins lurked a haunting melancholy that somehow touched her. *Eyes don't lie,* she thought. Grant had seen her pain in her eyes, and she saw his in those dark orbs that held such fascination for her. They had a lot in common, and that, she decided, had to be the source of the fascination.

His looks were of the lumberjack-of-the-north-woods, cowboy-of-the-western-plains variety. Try as she might she couldn't envision him in a River Oaks mansion. What kind of work had he done that had allowed him that life-style?

Ah, what did it matter? Once she left Arroyo Grande, Grant Mackenzie would fade into the background just like every other man she met.

"I'll be in the lobby," he announced, and the comment was directed squarely at Victoria.

She watched him saunter out of the room before helping Rita clear the table. The two of them made for the sink and dishwasher. When the kitchen had been cleaned up, Rita turned to her with an exaggerated sigh of persecution. "I wish we could just talk, but I've got a dumb history test tomorrow, and daddy will be furious if I don't come up with a good grade."

"I understand, Rita, really I do."

"But I'm going to study in daddy's room 'cause he's got a TV in there." She grinned.

Victoria grinned back. "Then do you mind if I

borrow your bathroom? I'd like to soak for a long time."

"Help yourself. I'll talk to you later."

Victoria crossed through the dining room and into the lobby. Grant was seated in front of the fireplace, puffing thoughtfully on a pipe. The spicy tobacco scent filled the room. He glanced up when she entered and got to his feet. "Will you join me, please?" he asked simply.

She was only too happy to, for there was a question that had been on her mind all evening. Settling into the chair next to his, she leaned forward and spoke earnestly. "Grant, just before Jake came into the shed this afternoon you said something...something to the effect that you didn't know who piloted the helicopter or who fired the shot, but.... But what?"

"Victoria, Reyes County is run by two men. Sheriff Cody Thornton and a man named Martin Rumbaugh. Of the two, I'd say Rumbaugh has the most power."

Victoria frowned. "Who's Rumbaugh?"

"A stockman with influence that goes far beyond simply owning the biggest spread in the county. His family's been here for generations, and his connections stretch to Austin and Washington. Damned little takes place in the county that he doesn't either take an active part in or sanction. As far as he's concerned, Reyes County is his, and not too many people have seen fit to disagree with that. Certainly not Sheriff Thornton. He owes his lofty status to Rumbaugh."

"And you think Rumbaugh's behind the eagle episode?"

"I'm sure he's responsible for the helicopter's being in Reyes County, and he's an old line stockman. As a group they traditionally resent eagles. They're absolutely convinced the birds are as big a threat to their lamb crops as coyotes are, and all the wildlife experts in the world aren't going to change their minds. Before we had legislation to protect eagles, those old boys damned near annihilated the resident population. But if Rumbaugh's responsible, there's no way on earth you'll ever prove it. You're up against a closed shop; the ranchers around here despise the federal government. I just thought I'd warn you." He paused. "You might save yourself some leg work and the taxpayers some money if you just sashayed on back to Corpus Christi."

Victoria's eyes flashed green fire. "Without even attempting an investigation? That certainly would impress my supervisor."

Grant shrugged. "Don't say I didn't warn you." He settled back in his chair, sucked on his pipe a moment, then said, "You never really answered my question about what prompted you to get into this line of work."

She raised her eyes to the ceiling. "I don't know why that fascinates people so. In my case it was just a natural extension of the way I was raised." She related the pertinent details of her family and her childhood, adding, "But after I got married, Steve's architectural career came first. We did a lot of entertaining, and I had a lot of civic and social obligations. But a few years ago I found myself with time on my hands and decided to get a part-time job. I heard about one at Texas Parks and Wildlife, a clerical position, so I applied for it and got it.''

"What was your husband doing all this time?"

"Oh, he was building a fabulous career, so busy I scarcely ever saw him." *Busy getting acquainted with his secretary,* she thought bitterly. "I really liked my job, and it seemed to require just the right amount of time. But when...my marriage broke up, I wanted something more challenging, time-consuming. There was a move afoot to hire female agents for U.S. Fish and Wildlife, but the ones who had applied weren't especially happy about the odd hours the job required. They suited me perfectly, though. If ever there was a foot-loose, fancy-free person, it was I." She lifted her shoulders and spread out her hands in a "so there you have it" gesture.

Silence descended for a moment before Grant quietly observed, "The divorce still bugs you, doesn't it?"

Victoria expelled a ragged breath. "It bugs the hell out of me."

"And you persist in asking yourself why, don't you? You can't imagine how you could have lived with him and not known there was someone else, right?"

How could he know these things? He was so right. Steve's announcement that Nancy Bergman, his secretary, was pregnant, that he wanted a divorce so he could marry her, had stunned Victoria. She had stormed and raged, had threatened to drag Nancy's name through every court in Texas, to make Steve wish to heaven he had never set eyes on the woman.

Of course, she hadn't done any of the dreadful things she had vowed she would. In the end she had merely signed the papers and stepped aside so Steve could marry Nancy. Today her ex and his new wife lived in a lovely home in Corpus Christi. Their son was five months old. On several occasions Victoria had chanced to meet one or both, and each time the meetings had been cordial. Friends spoke admiringly of the way she had handled "things."

Still, Victoria wasn't too proud of the way she had behaved in the beginning, but she had been totally irrational, heartbroken, feeling abused and strangely inadequate. She might have behaved less hysterically had the whole miserable scenario not been so achingly familiar. She was nineteen when Adam Carpenter left Rachel for another woman, and it had taken Victoria longer to accept it than it had her mother.

Shaking free of her somber thoughts, she forced her attention back to Grant. His gaze was deep and penetrating. "Right?" he repeated.

Somehow Victoria knew it would be useless to lie to him, even if she wanted to, which strangely she did not. He saw too much. He seemed to see things she had never revealed to another soul, and she thought she knew the source of his perception: he had been there himself. He must have.

"Yes." The word fluttered out on a defeated sigh.

"Give it up, Victoria. It's a waste of time. It befuddles the mind and clouds the judgment. How long were the two of you together?"

"We were married five years, but I'd dated him since I was sixteen."

"Was he a good-looking guy?"

"Yes, extremely so."

"Then maybe he couldn't stand the competition. Didn't you say he married a Plain Jane?"

Victoria's brow furrowed. "I beg your pardon."

His voice was low, almost seductive. "It's been my observation that really good-looking men like the limelight all to themselves. With a wife who looks the way you do by his side, a man would have to share it."

An astonishing flush of pleasure rippled through Victoria; then she chided her feminine susceptibility to what was nothing more than a glib male tongue. Was he flirting with her? Good Lord, she hadn't flirted in years. Come to think of it, she couldn't ever remember flirting. It hadn't been necessary. Steve had been the only man in her life.

"Will a simple 'thank you' suffice as a response to that?" she asked, hating the flutter she heard in her voice.

Grant rubbed his chin and chomped down on

his pipe. "Tell me, has anyone ever called you Vicky?"

Briefly her face clouded. Only Steve. She didn't know why, but in all her life only Steve had called her Vicky. "Not many."

"I didn't think so."

Victoria's head shot up. "Now what the devil was that supposed to mean?"

"You're not the Vicky type. Victoria suits you perfectly."

She wondered if she should be feeling flattered or insulted. Nothing about this disturbing man prompted normal reactions from her. Not having the slightest idea what to say to him next, she quickly got to her feet. "If you'll excuse me, Grant, Rita has offered me the use of her bathroom for a long soaking bath. It sounds irresistible."

"Of course." He uncurled from his chair and stood up. "Good night, Victoria."

"Good night, Grant." And she hurried away from him, down the hall and into Rita's room. Closing the door behind her, she leaned her head back on it a moment and waited for her heart's erratic dancing to stop. Then she went into the bathroom to draw water for her bath. After soaking for a luxurious time, she dusted herself liberally with powder, slipped on her long-sleeved, lace-trimmed nightgown and shrugged into a burgundy velour robe. She was sitting at the dressing table, brushing her hair, when Rita timidly knocked and peeked in.

"Can I get my stuff now, Victoria?"

"Of course, Rita, come on in. How did the studying go?"

"Bor-ring, as always. Why do I have to know the causes of the Spanish-American War, anyway?"

Victoria tried to think of a good answer. "I was always told that we study history in order to prevent the mistakes of the past."

Rita thought about this a second. "Do you suppose we'll ever have to fight Spain again?"

"Lord, I hope not—or anyone else, for that matter."

"True. War's stupid. I'm just going to get my stuff out of the bathroom."

Victoria continued brushing her hair, gazing absently at her reflection in the mirror, until Rita emerged. She was holding Victoria's box of bath powder. "Oh, Victoria, this is yummy! The whole bathroom smells like it."

Victoria turned and smiled. "Why don't you use some of it?"

"Can I?"

"Of course you may. Come to think of it, why don't you take the box and keep it? I have several kinds at home."

Rita stared down at the box, her eyes alight, looking for all the world as though Victoria had just presented her with diamonds and gold. "Can I really have it?"

"Of course. I'd love you to."

"Oh, wow, thanks!" In a swift, exuberant motion, Rita crossed the room, threw her arm around Victoria's shoulders and kissed her on the cheek. "You will be here when I get home tomorrow, won't you, Victoria?"

Victoria was truly moved. How long had it been since anyone had so appealingly clamored for her presence? The girl, she sensed, was starved for feminine companionship. "If I'm not here when you get home, I'll be along shortly thereafter," she promised.

"Oh, good!" Rita clutched the bath powder to her chest. "Good night, Victoria."

"Good night, Rita."

The girl turned and had reached the threshold when a towering figure appeared in the doorway. Grant's eyes settled on Victoria. "So this is where you are, Rita. What are you ladies up to?" He looked down at his daughter, and his expression altered dramatically. "What's that?" he demanded, indicating the box in her hand.

"Bath powder," Rita said delightedly. "Victoria gave it to me." She lifted the lid and held the puff near her father's nose. "Doesn't it smell heavenly?" Giving Victoria a smile, she went off happily down the hall.

Grant stood at the threshold for a moment, scowling darkly, for whatever reason Victoria couldn't imagine. She expected him to say goodnight and follow his daughter. Instead, in a surprising move, he stepped into the room, closed the door behind him with a precise click and crossed to stand beside the dressing table.

"Don't give Rita any more of that junk," he said sharply.

Victoria pulled the brush through her hair, uttering a little laugh. "Junk? If you had bought any nice bath powder recently you'd know it isn't junk."

"I don't want her to have it!"

With deliberation Victoria set down the hairbrush and turned to him, folding her hands in her lap. "For heaven's sakes, why not? Grant, it's only bath powder. All girls love it. It's not as though I'd given her makeup or perfume."

"Don't give her any more of that stuff!"

Victoria was at a loss to understand his attitude, and his manner was insufferable. Under other circumstances she would have been furious at anyone who, for little reason, spoke to her so harshly. But he was, after all, Rita's father, and his wishes couldn't be ignored. Her gesture seemed so harmless, though perhaps she should have asked first. Not being a parent, she possibly didn't understand the protocol involved in strangers' giving gifts to children.

Poised, mildly contrite, she looked at him. "I'm sorry. It never occurred to me that you would object, or I naturally would have asked if it was all right."

She stood up. . . but she had misjudged his nearness. They were only inches apart, and he loomed over her, forcing her to tilt her head to look up at him.

Warmth, enticing warmth, emanated from his

body. She could smell the tempting aroma of shaving lotion and pipe tobacco, and a series of tiny explosions erupted within her. One step and the tips of her breasts would have been brushing his chest. One step and their bodies would have been pressed together. Victoria knew how perfectly she would fit against him. At that moment her own femininity seemed a blatant, flagrant, tangible thing. A melting weakness invaded her limbs.

Hoping to mitigate his dark mood, she spoke to him softly. "She's a girl, Grant, and she needs soft, feminine things. You wear after-shave, and don't you appreciate fragrance on a woman?"

Grant's expression was like nothing she had ever seen. Victoria trembled under the onslaught of his gaze. She couldn't think, she couldn't breathe, she couldn't do anything but stand there entranced, her lips parted, staring up at this man who had such a mystifying effect on her.

He looked stunned, agitated; his breathing came in short, quick, uncontrolled puffs. Her heart thudded against her rib cage. For one terrifying, exhilarating moment she thought, hoped she was going to be kissed. Grant raised one hand, poised at her shoulder, and Victoria's throat closed completely.

His hand dropped to his side as though weighted by lead. He closed his eyes briefly, stepping back, and the moment had passed. She heard his struggling sigh. "Good night, Victoria," he said in a voice that didn't sound like his. Pivoting, he left the room.

Victoria's body sagged. She sank back to the chair and placed one hand on her breast, as though that would slow her heartbeat's runaway course. *I wanted him to kiss me,* she thought in astonishment.

Most women, she guessed, would have considered that normal, but she wasn't most women. In this marvelously enlightened age of sexual awareness, she normally recoiled in horror at a man's touch. She had even laughed confidently when Chuck had warned her that she would be working almost exclusively with men—and every one of them would make a pass at her. "That won't be a problem, you can be sure of that," she had told him. To date it hadn't been. She had become expert in the art of the rebuff.

But a few moments ago, had Grant Mackenzie taken one step closer to her, she wasn't sure she wouldn't have willingly gone into his arms.

Such a strange man.... Troubled, moody... yet warmly human. Unlike anyone she had ever met before. Possibly that explained the attraction. Yes, she was irresistibly drawn to Grant Mackenzie, and that was something she neither wanted nor knew how to handle.

ACROSS THE HALL Grant braced himself before entering his bedroom. Taking several deep breaths, he quietly opened the door and stepped inside. In the spare bed Rita sat up.

"Good night, daddy."

"Good night, hon."

"I left a light on for you."

"Well, you can turn it off now. I can undress in the dark." He crossed the room and bent over the bed to place a light kiss on his daughter's cheek. He jerked back as though he'd tasted poison. Damn! Rita smelled like *her*! How was he supposed to sleep with the smell of Victoria in the room? Shaken, he switched off the lamp, moved away from Rita's bed and viciously pulled his shirt free of his jeans.

He felt foolish, and it was an unfamiliar sensation. He had overreacted to the powder, just as he seemed to overreact to everything concerning Rita. Yet tonight's response had been especially uncalled for.

What was the matter with him? He had been grappling with some sort of inner confusion ever since... ever since Victoria Bartlett had stepped into the lodge. Try as he might he could not be indifferent to her. Sensations he thought long dead sprang to life every time he looked at her. At the dinner table tonight he had imagined his hands full of that shimmering hair of hers, and he kept thinking of the shape of her mouth, imagining the way it would taste....

*Idiot,* he berated himself. Good God, she was only a woman, and he knew the havoc a woman could wreak in his life. There was nothing all that unusual about Victoria...unless it was her eyes, the way she had of looking at you, all wide-eyed Little Mary Sunshine. Over there in that room a minute ago she had, just for a second, looked like a girl on the verge of receiving her first kiss. She had reminded him of a startled fawn, intensely fragile. If it was an act, it was a damned effective one. How could a woman have been married for five years and still radiate innocence? What had her husband been like?

Rich, no doubt. Was she well-off, too? Victoria's clothes were expensive—he knew that much—and she wore them with the casualness of a woman accustomed to fine clothes. Normally he never noticed what anyone wore, but he could describe in detail what Victoria had had on when she arrived, what she had worn at dinner.

Grant stepped into the dark closet to strip. In deference to Rita, he put on pajama bottoms, though he preferred to sleep naked. And he cursed his masculine weakness where Victoria was concerned. Surely she didn't think changing into those slacks and that sweater had done anything to disguise that appealing body of hers.

Grant closed the closet door and moved to stand in front of the window and stare out over the moonlit grounds of Arroyo Grande. Victoria was the kind of woman who could invade a man's life, entrench herself, fill up all the empty spaces. The kind of woman you could like as well as—he paused to rub a hand wearily over his eyes—as well as love. He wondered how long it had been since she had been loved. Her husband—her ex-husband—was a fool.

Rita was already enchanted with her. Dammit, he didn't need any of this, didn't want it! Somewhere in the dim recesses of his mind warning bells were clanging.

Well, with luck maybe she'd be gone quickly and he could put her out of his mind, Grant fumed. He could have kicked Chuck's butt up between his shoulder blades for sending Victoria to Arroyo Grande.

# CHAPTER FOUR

VICTORIA STEPPED INTO HER JEANS and zipped them up, slipping a dark green velour shirt over her head. Deftly securing her hair at the nape with a silver clasp, she inspected her appearance in the dressing-table mirror. Neat and unspectacular, she decided; precisely the way Chuck liked her to look.

Wednesday morning had dawned clear and bright. It was now nearing eight o'clock, a late hour to be getting started when she had gone to bed so early, but it had taken her a long time to get to sleep the night before. Tossing and turning for two hours or more, she had persisted in thinking about Grant and trying to analyze all the confusing emotions he had aroused in her.

Peculiar how one person, one out of hundreds, could come along and make you sit up and take notice. Victoria marveled at the abrupt disorganization of her mind, which had always been so tidy and well-ordered. Even in those first awful days following Steve's request for a divorce, she had been remarkably lucid. She had vacillated between cold fury, self-pity and resentment, but under the circumstances she thought those reactions had been perfectly normal. Far more normal than her reactions to Grant Mackenzie. They were contrary and unmanageable. Especially unmanageable.

It had to be physical attraction in its most basic form, she decided; what else could account for this odd feeling? And she had thought herself immune.

Gathering up her jacket and handbag, she left the bedroom, heading for the kitchen. A gray-haired, sweet-faced woman in an apron turned from the sink to smile at her. "Good morning. You must be Victoria."

"Yes, I am."

"I thought so. I got an earful of Victoria-said-this and Victoria-does-this from Rita this morning. I'm Bess Guilford, dear. Grant said to tell you he'd be out back. Sit down and let me get you some breakfast."

"Thanks no, Mrs. Guilford. Not just yet. I guess Rita's already left for school."

"Oh, my, yes. The school bus comes around bright and early. It has a lot of territory to cover before eight-thirty."

Victoria pushed open the back door and stepped outside. Though the morning was bright with sunshine, promising a much warmer day than yesterday, the air was still a bit nippy. She hugged herself and rubbed her arms briskly, then raised one hand to shield her eyes from the morning glare. Two figures emerged from the shed where the eagle's carcass was kept. Grant and Jake. They lingered in conversation a moment. Then Jake took off in one direction and Grant moved toward the lodge.

Again that queer fluttery sensation rose inside her. Tall and dark, he moved with a kind of quick-silver grace, like a leopard. He was wearing his work clothes—jeans, boots, Stetson, a faded denim jacket. Victoria could just picture him swinging up on a stallion and galloping off into the sunset—leaving the pining heroine behind, like in those old Westerns. Dear God, what had made her think of that?

She waited until he was nearer before calling to him. "Good morning!"

"Well, good morning!" Grant advanced on her, and when he was close enough for her to see the crinkling corners of his eyes, he shot her a lop-sided grin. "Sleep well?" he inquired, tapping the brim of his big hat with one finger in a kind of salute.

"Yes, thanks." It wasn't much of a lie. Once she had fallen asleep, she had slept soundly.

"That's good." Gently he touched her on the shoulder, his hand seeming to move there of its own volition. He was glad one of them had slept; he had spent a miserable night and had finally fallen asleep vowing to keep his distance from this woman. Yet here she was, looking so damned fresh and energetic. The mere sight of her made him feel as awkward as a schoolboy. "Jake and I took the liberty of photographing the bird for you, and he's on his way to the shooting site now.

We have a small photo lab next to my office. Jake's something of an artist with a camera.''

"Thank you, Grant. That was thoughtful of you.''

"Don't mention it. What are you going to do this morning?''

"Ask around, I guess. For courtesy's sake I should begin by calling on the local law-enforcement officer and telling him what I'm doing.''

"Cody?'' Grant scoffed. "You won't get anything out of him. He owes Martin Rumbaugh everything. Tell you what, Victoria. I'm going to do you a favor.''

"Oh?''

"I'm going to let you take my pickup into town. If you show up in Kierney in that government car, you're not going to find anyone who'll tell you what time it is.''

Victoria bit her lower lip. She was sure he was exaggerating. "They'll have to talk to me, Grant. I'm the law.''

"Humph! You've got a lot to learn. Cody's not going to take you seriously. You don't *look* like a law-enforcement officer.''

Victoria flushed hotly. "The way I look has nothing to do with my authority, which is considerable, I assure you.''

He smiled down at her with the condescending air of an adult indulging the whims of an impulsive child. "And another thing...if I wanted to find out what's going on around here, I'd go sit in

Sally's Café for a while and just keep my ears open. It's sort of an unofficial town hall for the locals.''

"Thanks. I just might do that.''

Grant paused a moment, and his eyes swept around, looking at nothing in particular. Victoria could see his jaw muscles working, until finally he looked at her probingly. "I guess you're not in any danger. I guess you know what you're doing.''

He was worried about her! It was a satisfying realization. "Yes, I do.''

He scuffed at the ground with the toe of his boot. "I don't suppose you know when you'll be getting back.''

"No...no, I don't.''

"Then I'll look for you when I see you coming.''

"Yes. How far is it into town?''

"Not far. A few miles.''


"A FEW MILES" turned out to be twenty of them— twenty of the loneliest miles Victoria had ever traveled. But Kierney, surprisingly, proved to be a neat little town built around a courthouse square. The Victorian courthouse was the only two-storied structure in the community. Clustered around it on four sides were a dozen or so commercial establishments, one of which was Sally's Café.

Traffic and parking had yet to become problems in Kierney. Victoria eased the pickup into a slot immediately in front of the café; she entered and took a seat at the long counter. There weren't many customers, but every head in the place turned to stare at the newcomer.

A woman hurried out of the kitchen to wait on her. Thirtyish, trim and pretty in a homespun way, she smiled. "Hi, I'm Sally Anderson, the owner of this place. What'll you have?" She spoke while placing silverware rolled up in a napkin in front of Victoria and, without asking if she wanted it, poured her a cup of coffee.

Victoria wasn't in the least hungry, not being a breakfast person, but she had no idea when she would next get the chance to eat. And a meal would give her an excuse to linger awhile. If the café was the local gathering place, Sally herself was probably privy to plenty of information. "Bacon and eggs, soft-scrambled," she said.

"Hash browns or grits?"

"Hash browns."

"Coming right up."

The woman scurried back into the kitchen, and Victoria's eyes idly swept the surroundings. The little café was neat and plain and spotlessly clean. The lunchtime menu was scrawled in chalk on a big blackboard. She would have been willing to bet the food was not only delicious but served in huge quantities, and if the breakfast Sally Anderson placed before her was any indication, she was right. Had Victoria not eaten in three days she wouldn't have been able to do justice to the amount of food staring back at her from the plate.

Sally was curious about her new customer, so

while Victoria ate she talked. "You just passing through Kierney?"

"Not really. I'm staying at Arroyo Grande Lodge for a few days."

"Oh?" Sally's interest was clearly piqued. "Grant's place. I didn't know he catered to transients. I thought he only rented out to hunting parties and things like that."

"Well, Grant and my boss are old friends. When he—my boss—discovered I was going to be traveling this way, he arranged accommodation for me at Arroyo Grande."

Sally nodded, accepting the explanation. "It's a nice place. I guess Grant gets lots of guests from places like Dallas and Houston, but few of them make their way on into Kierney. Can't say as I blame them."

"Have you been here long, Miss Anderson?" Victoria inquired politely.

"Six years, and it's Mrs. Anderson. But everyone calls me Sally, and I wish you would, too."

"How do you do, Sally. I'm Victoria Bartlett."

"Where're you from, Victoria?"

"Corpus Christi."

"Nice place." Sally sighed. "Course, I haven't been there in ages. I can't seem to get away from this café. I have an apartment in back, so sometimes it seems like I live, eat and breathe this place."

"You said you had been here six years. Where's home originally?"

"Ohio. Cleveland."

"This is a far cry from Cleveland."

"Isn't that the truth! Six years ago my husband suddenly decided he had to get out of the rat race. He was stationed in San Antonio when he was in the air force, so he knew this country. Well, before I realized what was happening, he had made a down payment on eight hundred acres near here. He wanted to be a rancher, of all things! Crazy, huh? We worked the land for two years, and then he took sick, and. . .when he died, I sold the ranch and bought this café."

"You didn't want to go back to Cleveland?"

"No, not really, not after I saw what happened when Jeff died. Everyone for miles around pitched in and helped me. I mean, they came for *miles* to bring food, to lend a hand with the housework. The men went out and took care of the livestock until I could get it sold. People I didn't even know! Back home, no one but relatives and real good friends would do such a thing. And since my parents were gone. . . ." Sally shrugged. "Anyway, I stayed, and I can't say I've ever been sorry. Once folks around here accept you, you have friends for life. That's what I keep trying to tell Grant—if he would only work a little harder at fitting in."

Victoria's attention was instantly arrested. "Do you know Grant well?"

"I guess you could say we're friends."

"He's, ah, an interesting man, don't you think so?" Victoria prodded.

"If strange is interesting, then he's interesting."

Sally giggled. "I think he honestly enjoys being different. I mean, putting a wildlife refuge right in the middle of folks who think all animals should turn a profit! I suppose if that life suits Grant, it's all right, but I feel kinda sorry for that kid of his, stuck out there at Arroyo Grande, away from kids her own age. And I've noticed that since the ranchers around here don't much cotton to Grant, their kids don't have much to do with Rita. What kind of life is that for a young girl? And she's such a pretty little thing."

"Yes, she's lovely," Victoria agreed, and joined Sally in feeling sorry for Rita. She hadn't realized the Mackenzies were such outsiders.

"Poor thing. Grant's too protective of her, as I've pointed out to him a hundred times. I feel damned sorry for Rita when she gets to be dating age. No, come to think of it, I feel sorry for the young fellows who want to date her."

Apparently Sally was losing her enthusiasm for the conversation. She looked at Victoria's plate. "Are you finished?"

Victoria had eaten as much of the breakfast she could. Pushing her plate away, she dabbed at her mouth with a napkin, then took a sip of coffee. It was time she got to work. Instinct cautioned her against announcing her real business in Reyes County—not yet. So she searched her brain for a plausible reason to inquire about the availability of a helicopter.

"Sally, Grant tells me there might be a helicopter for hire around here. You see, I'm a photographer, and I've been commissioned to do a layout on Reyes County for a national magazine. I'd like to get some aerial shots if possible."

Sally looked impressed. "Really? Why on earth would a magazine be interested in Reyes County?"

"Well, ah...." Victoria faltered. "The... topography and flora and fauna of the county are quite... diverse."

"Yeah? You don't say! Guess you'd have to know a lot more about that kind of thing than I do to see that. Well, listen, the helicopter Grant must have been referring to is usually kept parked behind Miller's Feed Store at the west end of town. I think it's been hired by some of the ranchers around here to kill coyotes and bobcats and stuff like that, so I don't know if you could hire it for a couple of hours or not. But I tell you what... see that fellow in the back booth there, the one wearing the old air force jacket?"

Victoria swiveled on the stool, her eyes following the path of Sally's gesturing finger. "Yes."

"His name is Frank Oakley. He pilots the chopper. Why don't you ask him?"

Victoria couldn't believe her luck. "Thanks, Sally. I'll do that." She fumbled in her billfold and paid the check. Sliding off the stool, she smiled at the woman behind the counter. "It was nice meeting you, Sally. And that's the best coffee I've had in a long time."

"Yeah, I make it fresh every thirty minutes all day long. I couldn't stay in business five minutes if

I didn't serve good coffee. Will you be around here long, Victoria?''

"I really don't know. Possibly a few days. I'll try to make a point of stopping in again before I leave."

"Do that. Be seeing you."

Victoria threaded her way through the tables and chairs toward the back booth, acutely aware of the eyes trained on her. She was almost upon him before Frank Oakley glanced up from the newspaper he was reading. When it became obvious the attractive young woman wished to speak to him, he jumped to his feet and flashed her a broad grin.

"Mr. Oakley?"

"At your service, ma'am." He was thirtyish, tall with a trim build, sand-colored hair and pale blue eyes. Freckles were sprinkled lightly across his nose, and he had an amiable expression on his face.

"My name is Victoria Bartlett, Mr. Oakley. May I have a few moments of your time?"

"Shoot, you can have a whole lot more than that. Sit down. Would you like coffee or something?"

"Thank you, no. I've just had breakfast." Victoria slid into the booth across from him and waited for him to be seated. She indicated the café owner with a nod of her head. "Sally tells me you pilot the helicopter I've seen parked behind Miller's Feed Store," she said, hoping this would make her sound less a stranger to the area.

"Yeah, that's right."

"I wondered if it was for hire. I'm a photographer and I'd like to get some aerial shots of the surrounding terrain."

"Sorry, ma'am, you've come to the wrong guy. Mr. Rumbaugh has the helicopter pretty well tied up."

"Mr. Oakley, I would only need to hire the helicopter for a couple of hours."

"Well, you'd have to talk to Mr. Rumbaugh about that. Some of the other ranchers use it, too, but it's Mr. Rumbaugh who decides when and where. I don't know if he'd turn it loose for a few hours."

"I see. Mr. Rumbaugh...."

"Yeah. As long as he's paying for it we take our orders from him."

"We?"

"Jim Nelson, my gunner."

"Gunner?" Victoria affected a fluttery laugh. "Good heavens, that sounds so violent...and dangerous."

Frank Oakley grinned. "Naw, not really. We only shoot animals. They don't shoot back."

Everything inside Victoria surged and boiled with anger, and it was all she could do to keep a bland expression on her face. "Isn't that against the law?"

The man shrugged with total unconcern. "Not to my knowledge. Even if it is, who's going to complain?"

"Indeed," she said stiffly. "Well, Mr. Oakley,

perhaps you know of another helicopter I could hire.''

"Not in Reyes County. I think I'd know if there was. But tell you what. . . .'' He reached inside his jacket, fumbled in his shirt pocket and withdrew a business card. "If Mr. Rumbaugh doesn't want to turn over the chopper to you for a few hours, you might want to contact my company.''

Victoria took the card and glanced at it. "Dawson Helicopter Service,'' she read aloud.

"It's about fifteen miles the other side of Kerrville. They'll be glad to rent one to you. And I'd appreciate your mentioning my name. Never hurts to let the company know you're out drumming up business for them.''

Victoria slipped the card into her handbag and got to her feet. "I might do that, Mr. Oakley, but first I'll talk to Mr. Rumbaugh. I do thank you for your time.''

Frank Oakley also stood up. "My pleasure, ma'am. Maybe I'll be seeing you again. If Mr. Rumbaugh gives his okay, I'll be more than glad to take you any place you want to go.''

"I'll remember that.'' Victoria gave him a small smile, then turned and marched purposefully out of the café.

HAD SHE HAD HER WAY, Victoria would have dispensed with the courtesy call on the sheriff. From what Grant had said, she expected nothing but hostility, but regulations were regulations. Chuck insisted no agent engage in investigative work without first letting the local law know what was going on.

Cody Thornton, sheriff of Reyes County, regarded her with interest across the expanse of his oak desk. He was an unimposing man of about forty, lean with a weathered face, neither the strong, flint-eyed sheriff of legend nor the paunchy buffoon depicted in so many television situation comedies. Without the khaki uniform and the badge, he would have gone unnoticed in a crowd.

His curiosity about Victoria, though evident, was contained. Idly tapping the top of his desk with a pencil, he gave her a cool, speculative smile. "So, Miss Bartlett, my deputy said you're with the federal government. In what capacity?"

"I'm a special agent with U.S. Fish and Wildlife."

Cody Thornton appeared to have some difficulty accepting that. "And what can I do for you?"

"I simply wanted to announce my presence and tell you I'm in Reyes County to investigate a violation of the Bald Eagle Protection Act."

"Oh?" The pencil stopped in midair; the sheriff's expression altered. A tight set came to his face, an openly suspicious look. His eyes raked over her in a much more thorough appraisal than she had received on entering his office.

"Yes. My office got a complaint from a local citizen who chanced to witness the shooting of an eagle on his property." She smiled meaningfully.

"You, of course, are aware this violates federal law."

"Of course."

"And since the citizen in question had never signed a permit allowing aerial hunting on his property, state law has also been violated."

"I see," Cody said, his eyes narrowing. "Who is this citizen?"

"I'm afraid, for the time being, I'll have to plead privileged information, sheriff. At this point I don't believe your office will have to become involved. As I said, this is merely a courtesy call."

The sheriff dropped the pencil and hooked his forefinger over his upper lip. "Do you have any leads...or is that 'privileged information,' too?" His tone, Victoria thought, stopped just short of being offensive.

"Actually, no. I've learned that the only helicopter in Reyes County is leased by a man named Martin Rumbaugh. Do you know him?"

Did Sheriff Thornton visibly blanch? Victoria thought so. "Yes, I know him," Cody said. "He's a prominent man in the state. And he has some powerful friends in Washington."

Whether it was meant to or not, the remark came out like a warning. "So I understand," Victoria said, watching the man intently. "I'm hoping he'll be able to give me some more information about the helicopter's activities."

"Surely you're not going to accuse an important man like Martin Rumbaugh of breaking the law!" Cody exclaimed.

"Why, the thought hadn't crossed my mind, sheriff," she said with wide-eyed innocence. "But if Mr. Rumbaugh has allowed someone else the use of the helicopter, or something of that nature.... Anyway, it's a place to start. Can you tell me how to find the Rumbaugh ranch?"

For a moment she thought he was going to refuse, but then somewhat reluctantly, the sheriff swiveled in his chair and pointed to a county map on the wall behind him. "Here's Kierney," he said, tapping the map. "Go down south about ten miles and you'll see a ranch road on your right. Take it another ten miles or so, you'll come to the ranch's gate. The house is a mile or two from there. This—" he made an arc with his hand "—is the Rumbaugh spread."

The area was immense, even for west Texas. It began considerably south of Kierney and swept north almost to Arroyo Grande. No wonder Martin Rumbaugh considered Reyes County "his"; a good part of it was.

Victoria got to her feet, waiting for Sheriff Thornton to do the same. When he did, she extended her hand and gave him her warmest smile. "Thanks so much for your time, sheriff, and if I come up with anything I'll be sure to let you know."

"You do that, Miss Bartlett."

"By the way, it's Ms Bartlett."

"I might have known," he said dryly.

Victoria noted that he didn't show her to the door, something he probably did routinely.

Nor did he offer her the services of his office, which would reasonably be expected of a law-enforcement colleague. Something stirred inside her then. For lack of a better description, she would call it a "gut" feeling. Grant had doubtless been right; she was up against a closed shop. She squared her shoulders and prepared, with a mixture of trepidation and anticipation, to drive to the Rumbaugh ranch.

A DIMINUTIVE, DARK-HAIRED WOMAN in a maid's uniform admitted Victoria into the impressive Rumbaugh ranch house. She showed the inspector to a large study, where she was requested to wait while the maid informed Mr. Rumbaugh of her presence.

The room was predictable—heavy leather furniture, gun racks, mounted deer heads over the fireplace. The paneled walls were covered with family photographs, plaques and commendations from various stockmen's organizations, as well as numerous autographed pictures of well-known political figures. Victoria had ample time to study all of them; whether by design or not, Martin Rumbaugh kept her waiting an excessively long time.

Finally the door to the study flew open, and Martin Rumbaugh not so much entered the room as charged into it. He was a big man—barrel-chested, thick arms and legs, large hands. His tufted white hair curled slightly at his shirt collar; his eyes under bushy white brows were set in a permanent squint. Years in the Texas sun had burned a thick layer of bronze into his skin. His air was authoritarian, and displeased.

"Mr. Rumbaugh?" Victoria began.

"Yeah," Martin Rumbaugh growled.

She stepped toward him to extend her hand. "I'm—"

He ignored her hand, which she immediately withdrew and clenched at her side. "Sit down, Ms Bartlett," he said contemptuously. "I know who you are, and I know why you're here." And he clomped across the room to take a seat behind a massive mahogany desk that dominated the far end of the study.

*So,* Victoria thought bitterly. *Sheriff Thornton has been on the phone.* If she couldn't count on the local law, she had her work cut out for her. Seething, she slipped into a chair facing the desk and clasped her hands in her lap.

Martin Rumbaugh launched into a tirade. "Damned if the federal government can't think of the damndest ways to spend our money! How much you figure it's costing the taxpayers to send you down here because of some bird's untimely demise? If you think I'm going to talk to you, you're crazy! What's the government doing hiring a little filly like you for this kind of work, anyway? Damndest bit of nonsense I've ever heard!"

"Mr. Rumbaugh, I—"

"Look, Ms Bartlett, I'll tell you one thing and one thing only. Yes, I lease a helicopter, and yes, I hunt coyotes with it. End of interview. You know, twenty years ago I personally went to Washington to try to get this Eagle Act killed 'cause I figured it was only a matter of time before this would happen. Things have come to a sorry pass when a man can't take care of his land and his livestock the way he sees fit. You conservationists slay me, you really do. You come down here crying crocodile tears 'cause some poor bird got killed, but no one sheds a tear when I lose twenty percent of my lamb crop to the varmints.''

Victoria took a deep breath. "Mr. Rumbaugh, I'm sure you're aware of the doubt surrounding that issue. Biologists and even some stockmen now believe an eagle will not attack a live lamb if there is any other food available to it. In fact, eagles show a distinct preference for jackrabbit, and I'm sure you'll agree the Edwards Plateau has an abundance of jackrabbits.''

Martin snorted. "Another fairy tale the bleeding hearts have circulated. You know Ms Bartlett, the problem is the laws are made by people who've never been west of the Mississippi River. They need to come out here and talk to those of us who live with the predator problem day in and day out. Then we might get some legislation that would help the stockmen, instead of putting another stumbling block in our path. You want something to cry about? Cry about wool that never reaches the market. The federal government's got no business meddling in things it doesn't understand.''

"Mr. Rumbaugh, this debate has been going on for generations, and I hardly think you and I are going to decide the issue today. Stockmen feel the government always sides with the conservationists; in turn the conservationists say that in spite of the law, the stockman on the range does as he damn well pleases. That's not the point of this visit. There is a law stating an eagle cannot be killed. An eagle has been killed. Therefore, it's my job to find out who did it and to bring the offender, or offenders, to justice. It's as simple as that.''

"Well, you won't find out," Martin Rumbaugh stated emphatically with a thrust of his chin. "Folks around here stick together. Have to, 'cause we don't have anybody looking out for us. Anyone around here who kills an eagle is apt to get a medal.''

"Even though he's broken the law?"

"It's a law we don't believe in."

"But that doesn't give you the right to break it.''

"It's a law that can't be enforced," Martin said with a malicious smile. "Go back and tell your government friends that.''

It was obvious to Victoria she was wasting her time. She could question Rumbaugh about the helicopter, but he would have all the pat answers. If she persisted, she might be accused, with some justification, of harassment. She stood up. "I will find out who was responsible for the shooting, Mr. Rumbaugh—make no mistake about that. I have all the time in the world and the government to back me up.''

Rumbaugh didn't get to his feet. He stared at

her stonily for a moment before saying, "Why aren't you home raising a passel of kids?"

Victoria clenched her teeth. "Good day, sir," she said icily, pivoted and walked to the door. She had opened it, when Rumbaugh's voice detained her.

"Ms Bartlett, do yourself a big favor. Take your cute little tush back to wherever you came from and leave us the hell alone."

Victoria closed the door behind her with more force than was necessary.

# CHAPTER FIVE

"CUTE LITTLE TUSH, INDEED!" Victoria fumed, pacing back and forth in the Arroyo Grande lobby.

From a chair in front of the fireplace, Grant chuckled. "I'll give Rumbaugh credit for having a good eye."

Victoria whirled on him. "My God, I have stumbled onto the very epicenter of male-chauvinist piggery!"

Grant laughed heartily this time. "Relax, Victoria. I warned you how it would be. Reyes County is run like your average medieval serfdom."

"It just infuriates me, because if Rumbaugh himself didn't kill that eagle, I *know* he knows who did."

"But you can't prove it."

"No, not yet."

"So what now?"

A deep V formed between her brows. "The helicopter company, I guess. How far is it to Kerrville?"

"Too far to drive there and back this afternoon. Leave it till morning, and I'll go with you. I'm overdue for a shopping trip. You can drop me in town, go do whatever it is you have to do, then come back and get me."

Victoria sighed. "All right. I feel as though I've already driven hundreds of miles today. I can't get used to these west Texas distances."

Grant shoved himself out of the chair. "How about letting me give you the grand tour? We have a great afternoon for it. The weatherman says it might reach the mid-sixties today. Have you had lunch?"

She shook her head.

"I'll have Mrs. Guilford pack us some sandwiches and coffee."

"That sounds like fun. I'm anxious to see everything."

Grant briefly reflected on the caprice of human nature. He suspected he should keep his distance from this woman, for his reactions weren't running true to form. Yet here he was, arranging a way for them to spend the afternoon alone together. "Bundle up," he said. "If you're going to see everything we'll have to take the Jeep, and it might get chilly. I'll meet you out in front in fifteen minutes or so."

SITTING BESIDE GRANT, snug in her hooded ski jacket, her gloved hands holding on for dear life as the vehicle bounced over the rough terrain, Victoria swiveled her head, trying not to miss anything. They had been traveling over Arroyo Grande refuge for over an hour, and now they descended into a steep gully. Its dry rocky bottom was lined with sycamore and Spanish oak. Wildlife abounded. Ahead of them, an orange-and-black rock squirrel scampered away; another ran up a tree and flattened out on a branch. Victoria spotted a couple of ravens, and deer were everywhere.

"Whitetails are marvelously adaptable," Grant told her when she commented on the heavy concentration. "They can survive almost anywhere, given some cover, water and a reasonable amount of food. In fact, the whitetail is a textbook example of what wildlife management can do. In 1928 there were fewer than one hundred thousand of them in all of Texas; today there are well over three million." He made a triumphant clicking sound with his tongue. "And management did it. When the herd gets too large for the habitat to support, we allow controlled hunting, but here at Arroyo Grande, any species not designated as game is protected."

Grant halted the Jeep and handed Victoria a pair of binoculars. "For instance. . . I want you to look into that thicket over there and tell me what you see."

Victoria took the glasses, studying the brush he had pointed out. Several moments passed before she exclaimed, "Oh! Oh, I've got something! It's a quail—or is it?" She lowered the glasses, blinked several times, then raised them again and focused. "Yes, I think it's a quail."

"You're right. There should be several of them. At least six or seven."

"Yes, yes, there's another one. Very well camouflaged."

"Look and tell me what's different about them."

"I thought I was something of an expert on quail, but these little fellows— Oh, I think I see! It's the markings on the head...all black and white, as though they were wearing masks." She lowered the glasses. "Right?"

Grant nodded. "You're an observant lady. They're harlequins—very rare. The books will tell you they're restricted to the Davis Mountains and the western edge of the plateau, but we introduced the little fellows to this section two years ago."

"How are they doing?"

"I'll tell you in three more years. I give any introduced species five years, and in the meantime they're pampered like visiting royalty. I have a mountain of data on them already. In three years I ought to be able to write a book on the harlequin quail."

"If they survive."

"Even if they don't, I'll have information biologists all over the world can use. But they seem to be adapting well to their new habitat. Maybe someday we'll be able to take them off the rare list."

Victoria stared at him with open admiration. "You're very serious about your work, aren't you, Grant?"

"Completely."

"Isn't it very solitary work?"

"Maybe. Certainly it's never-ending. Not a day goes by when there isn't something happening that needs to be observed and recorded. But it suits me." He started the Jeep. From there they drove across a shallow river crossing, coming out onto a grassy slope. "This is where Rita and I saw the eagle come down," he said, halting the vehicle. "If luck is with us, you might see quite a sight."

Something moved in the trees ahead, and a large shadow fell over the ground. Victoria lifted her eyes in time to see a golden eagle taking off. Even as she watched its soaring flight, another eagle appeared in the sky over a distant bluff. Joining the first bird, it sailed directly overhead, so low Victoria could clearly see the splotched undersides.

Grant quickly handed her the binoculars, and just as she got the birds in view, he tapped her on the shoulder and pointed. Another eagle soared above the gully ahead of them, then another and another.

Victoria was thunderstruck. How many people, she wondered, would ever witness such a spectacle? And while she was marveling at the sight, another bird emerged from behind the hills. "Oh, Grant," she said. "It's breathtaking!"

"And these babies are only a fraction of the entire population. Some winters we host as many as thirty eagles. No one seems to know why the plateau is such a favorite wintering spot for them. We say they're from Canada, but we don't really know that, either. Surely some are, but others might be from Montana or Wyoming. Come spring, the older birds will scurry on back to their northern breeding grounds, but the youngsters linger awhile. An awful lot of those get killed every year. You know, it takes an eagle five years to reach sexual maturity, and that's one reason it's such a damned shame to lose a young one.''

"They seem to epitomize freedom, don't they?"

"I guess they do," Grant agreed. "No doubt what the Founding Fathers had in mind when they made the eagle our national bird. But they aren't free at all, you know."

Victoria quizzed him with her eyes.

"Nope. Once an eagle mates, he's forever tied to his aerie."

"Too bad it's not that way with people."

"Isn't that the truth!"

THE GRASSY SLOPE was a perfect place for them to eat the lunch Mrs. Guilford had packed. Victoria accepted the sandwich and mug of coffee Grant handed her, then settled back in the seat to enjoy the bright day, the delicious sandwich and the stimulating man next to her.

She was alive with interest. "What prompted you to get involved in this kind of work, Grant?"

"Oh, I found myself with a lot of land, and I knew I didn't want to ranch. And, too, I spent most of my childhood at my grandparents' place in the country, where wildlife was as much a part of the scene as grass and trees. I just liked that sort of thing, I guess. When I bought Arroyo Grande I remembered Chuck and the work he was doing, so I got in touch with him and. . .one thing led to another.''

''I spent a lot of time in the country when I was a kid, too. Where did you live?''

''Not far from Fredericksburg.''

''Our place was near Bandera. We were almost neighbors.''

''You would still have been in pigtails when I left the country.''

She smiled at him. ''How could you possibly know I wore pigtails?''

He reached out and took a handful of her hair, fingering it gently, something he had been itching to do. It did feel like silk! ''Isn't braiding hair supposed to make it grow in full and thick?''

Victoria felt the rise of color in her cheeks. ''Well. . .'' she said nervously, contemplating her sandwich so she wouldn't have to look at him. He had the most unfortunate knack of making her feel awkward and flustered. ''You're going to have to tell me everything about what you do. I've only been with the service a year, and working in enforcement, I'm concerned mostly with violations. I have some vague idea of the way a refuge is run, of course, but I don't understand too much about the nuts and bolts. How does a wildlife manager operate?''

Grant dropped his hand from her hair, pursed his lips and gave it some thought. Victoria, he knew, was genuinely interested, not just making conversation, so he tried to give her a well-considered reply. "I suppose you could say I observe and record. I like to think of myself as a professional fact finder. I have to have fairly extensive knowledge of the species here on the preserve, their habits, their approximate number and distribution, how productive they are and what their mortality rate is. Does the habitat support them, and if not, what can I do to improve it? Then I make this information available to anyone who wants it. Until I got the computer, just keeping data was a full-time job. We host tour groups, too—schoolkids, bird-watchers, wildlife enthusiasts, even hunting parties when the game is too abundant for the habitat to support. Regulated taking of wildlife is a management tool, as well."

Victoria was fascinated. Here was wildlife conservation at the grass roots. "How did you come to own Arroyo Grande? What did you have to do to turn it into what you have now?"

"Lord, you could write volumes about making over a run-down sheep ranch."

"Arroyo Grande was once a sheep ranch?" she asked in some surprise. It was so lush and wild, and she had seen what sheep could do to land.

He nodded. "Sorriest piece of real estate you ever saw. The first couple of years we mainly worked on the lodge, gave the land a chance to renew itself."

"How did you come to buy it?"

"I was looking for something, somewhere to move, and a fellow I knew told me about it."

"In Houston?"

Grant turned to her abruptly. "How did you know I lived in Houston?"

"I believe Rita told me."

"What else did she tell you?" His tone was harsh.

Victoria frowned. Grant was the most mercurial person she had ever met. "Nothing...only that you used to live in River Oaks and that the two of you moved here six years ago." His expression was so dark that she quickly added, "Honestly, Grant, that's all she told me. Why do you care that I know you're from Houston?"

He turned from her, and his rigid body slumped in the seat. For a few seconds he stared blankly into his mug of coffee. "I don't," he finally said. "Not really. It's just that...I sometimes wonder how much Rita remembers."

They munched their sandwiches in silence for a minute. Then Victoria quietly offered, "I wouldn't worry, Grant. When I asked Rita if she ever misses Houston, she told me she doesn't remember much about it."

"I hope to God she was telling the truth...but kids have minds like sponges. I'm willing to bet Rita remembers a lot about Helena."

"Your wife?"

He nodded. "Rita's the living image of her."

"Then Helena was—is a beautiful woman. You loved her a great deal?"

"I guess so."

Silence descended again. Victoria felt so drawn to him; apparently it was true that misery loved company. She tried to picture a son the living image of Steve. A child would have made everything so much harder. There was a lot she would have liked to say to Grant, but she didn't know where to start. He might not be a man who welcomed such confidences. She finished the last of her sandwich, wiped her hands with a napkin and sipped her coffee.

She was thinking of a way to start the conversation again, when Grant suddenly asked, "Would you like me to tell you about her?"

She couldn't have been more startled. "Your wife?"

He nodded.

"Only. . . only if you want to."

He pondered a moment, then shifted in his seat. "Let's take a walk."

They confined their walk to the clearings where the sun could beat down on them. Casually Grant took her hand, holding it warmly in his rough palm, and absurdly, Victoria thought how right it felt there. They strolled in compatible silence while she waited expectantly, feeling oddly gratified that he wanted to talk to her.

Finally he asked, "Have you ever heard of Mac's Auto Parts, Victoria?"

"Of course." One could hardly avoid hearing about the huge chain with stores all over the South, from Florida to Texas. The airwaves were saturated with its commercials.

"Mac was what everyone called my grandfather. He opened a small store in Houston, selling Model T parts. That was in the early thirties. By the time my brother and I came along, it was one of the largest family-owned businesses in the country. We had our pick from a Houston mansion, a Gulf Coast apartment and a ranch in the hill country.''

That explained the River Oaks mansion. ''You have a brother?''

''His name's Jordan. He's four years older than I am. When our folks crashed in their light plane, they were killed.... I was only twenty and suddenly Jordan and I owned the family business. We were millionaires. We were too young for that kind of responsibility but we didn't do a half-bad job of it, if I do say so. I dropped out of college to devote my time to the business...and about then I met Helena and fell in love. At least that's what I called it. I was too young for that, too.''

Victoria, sensing he was on the verge of a badly needed soul-purging, didn't prod or probe. For a minute the only sound was the crunching of leaves beneath their feet. Grant continued. ''She was two years older, an artist, a bit Bohemian for our social circle, but I thought she was the most beautiful woman I'd ever seen.'' Again he lapsed into silence.

That cleared up one thing. From what Rita had said, Victoria guessed Grant was less than enthusiastic about her weaving. Was her artistry a constant reminder of the wife he had obviously adored? Why had they split up? And why did Grant have Rita? There must have been another man.

Well, whatever it was he wanted to say, he was having a damnably difficult time of it. The words sounded as though they were being wrenched from his very soul.

They walked on. A twig snapped beneath Victoria's foot with the crack of a pistol shot. Never would she have dreamed the world could be so absolutely quiet. Abruptly Grant dropped her hand and began pounding his fist rhythmically into the palm of his other hand.

His voice was almost emotionless as he said, "I think Helena hated being married. She said I smothered her, that I was too possessive. Perhaps she was right. She said I didn't understand the creative mind, and she was probably right about that, too. I told myself I loved her too much, but I think...I didn't love her enough, tried to turn her into something she couldn't be—a 'correct' society matron—when what she was was a free spirit who didn't give a flip about society."

Pain pierced Victoria's heart. She often thought she had loved Steve too much, and he had also accused her of possessiveness. She had taken a job in an effort to loosen her hold on him, only to have him go straight to Nancy Bergman. Sympathetically she looked at Grant.

He sighed deeply. "I know now that Helena rebelled the way some women do...with other men. Yet while we were living together I didn't suspect other men." A pause, then.... "Jordan was one of her lovers."

Victoria had been poised, waiting for almost

anything, but she hadn't expected a jolt like that. How awful for him! Could anyone ever get over such betrayal, by his own brother? At least Nancy Bergman had meant nothing to Victoria; she had barely met the woman.

Her breath oozed out of her slowly. At that moment she would have given anything to have known Grant better, for she could have put her arms around him, comforted him in some way. He looked so vulnerable, and she would never have imagined associating that word with Grant.

He was the one who slipped an arm around her waist. "Would you like to sit down?"

There in the clearing, beside a shallow gully, a huge slab of stone protruded from the earth. Grant led Victoria to it. Picking up a stray twig, he used it to poke at the dry ground. "I discovered her adultery in the old trite way—returning home unexpectedly from a trip. I was violently angry and threatened a lot of things, but the only threat I carried out was to demand sole custody of Rita. Helena didn't argue the point too strenuously— not that she wasn't fond of Rita," he admitted in a grudging tone. "Other things, like her art and life in the city, were more important to her. She was definitely unconventional mother material. She hasn't even pressed to see Rita since...."

Victoria tentatively placed her hand on his shoulder and closed her eyes. His tone was both bitter and hurt—he didn't want Helena's influence on their daughter, yet he resented his ex-wife's cavalier attitude toward Rita. Grant's reaction wasn't logical, but it was human. And as for threats.... When Victoria thought of all the dreadful things she had threatened to do to Steve and Nancy.... She was hardly one to pass judgment.

"I left everything—the house, the cars, everything. I took Rita, our personal possessions, and we moved to our old place in the hill country for a time."

"Then Rita hasn't seen her mother in six years?"

He shook his head.

"And Helena...and Jordan?"

"I have no idea what they've done with their lives. I assume Helena still lives in our old house. I sold out to Jordan, brought Rita here. It was a long time ago, and she was awfully young, but I still worry that she might have seen her mother and her uncle together."

"Grant, it seems to me that Rita has no serious emotional problems. She's delightfully normal."

Again he jabbed at the ground with the stick. "I suppose you think it's not right for me to keep her from Helena, to bury her out here in the hinterlands."

"It's not my place to think anything, Grant."

"I know we're outsiders and I know sometimes it's rough on Rita. The old-timers around here don't think too kindly of me, so their kids leave her alone. But I'm convinced she's better off here. I don't want her influenced by the kinds of things that influenced her mother."

Victoria removed her hand from his shoulder. "You won't be able to keep her forever. You know that, don't you?"

"I know. It scares hell out of me that she's so much like Helena. That weaving she does—she just picked it up on her own. I'm the least artistic person on earth. It just scares hell out of me. . . ."

"Does that have something to do with the powder episode last night?"

He nodded. "Helena was addicted to paint, powder and perfume. It took her an hour to put on her face every morning. It was the most important part of her day." His voice dripped with scorn.

"Grant—" Victoria bit her lip, trying to choose her words carefully "—Rita is fast approaching an age when she'll be very interested in makeup. Teenage girls love the stuff. It's quite normal. There's nothing wrong with cosmetics per se. You can't fly off the handle every time you see her powdering her nose."

He stared at her for a second, then expelled his breath painfully and raised his eyes skyward. "I hope to heaven I live through it."

Victoria managed a light laugh. "You will, if you keep your sense of humor."

"How come you know so much about young girls?"

"I was one once."

"Were you a nice one?"

"I think so," she told him in all seriousness. "I don't think I ever gave my folks anything to worry about, not seriously."

"Somehow I believe that. Victoria...I don't have the slightest idea why I decided to unload on you like this."

"Everyone needs to talk to someone sometime. Maybe you knew I would understand. After all, we have something in common."

"Does it bother you to talk about your husband?"

"Not anymore, not really. But I've never actually talked about Steve with anyone except my mother. Now there's a sympathetic ear. My father ran out on her, too."

"And you've never forgiven him." It was a statement of fact.

She looked at him with some surprise. "How did you know?"

"I just knew."

"You're right. I've never forgiven him."

"I think that's the worst part of it...when you can't forgive and forget."

Their shared mood was pensive. Grant was an astute man, Victoria thought. Of course that was the worst part, the inability to forgive. It kept the wound festering. Was she, as her mother often claimed, one of those people who enjoyed wringing every drop of misery from problems?

Grant slapped his knee, effectively dispelling the mood. "Well, Victoria, between the two of us we must have enough hangups to keep a roomful of psychiatrists scratching their heads for hours." He grinned. "One might almost get the idea the institution of marriage is in trouble."

"True. We Carpenter women certainly botched it."

His expression was difficult to describe, though Victoria thought she saw communion and sympathy there. "Do you think you'll ever try it again? Marriage, I mean?"

She lifted her shoulders. "I don't know. Right now it doesn't seem likely, but how do I know how I'll feel in five or six years?"

"Have you made any attempts to get back into circulation?"

"Oh, a few dates with old acquaintances, but...."

"But it's not easy because the rules have changed since you were last single."

"It's even more complex than that for me, Grant, because...I never understood the rules to begin with, not really. I started dating Steve when I was sixteen. I never knew anyone else."

His expression changed dramatically; something she couldn't define blazed from his eyes. Victoria was transfixed, and she knew with absolute certainty she had said the wrong thing. She had unwittingly offered an invitation.

Her eyes widened. She honestly meant to move away from him. She didn't mean to sit there paralyzed and expectant, watching as his head bent and came closer to hers. She didn't mean to part her lips invitingly as his warm mouth closed over hers.

At the first touch of his lips, warmth spiraled through her. Her heart began drumming an exotic beat, and jumbled sensations assaulted her from all directions, transmitting crazy impulses. She experienced a wild desire to have him touch her all over.

He didn't. He didn't touch her with his hands at all, and she had to restrain herself from reaching for him. His mouth did all the work, moving lazily against hers, sipping and savoring. She couldn't even protest when his tongue hesitantly slipped beyond her teeth to explore the sweet private hollows of her mouth. She merely accepted the caress as the most natural thing in the world, and gave him a too-eager response of her own.

The enticing masculine aroma of him filled her nostrils, and the thrill coursing through her body was an exquisite torment. She wished only that the kiss could go on and on and on. . . .

It was over much too soon. When Grant lifted his head, it was to stare at her dazedly for a moment, then to smile warmly.

Everything inside her fluttered like a butterfly's wings. Victoria was stunned that he had affected her so profoundly. When Grant stood and pulled her up with him, her legs were decidedly unstable. While they retraced their path to the waiting Jeep, she had to struggle to regain her composure. She reflected on her unreliable nature during the drive back to the lodge. The last thing she wanted was to be attracted to a man; she wasn't over Steve yet. Certainly she didn't want one who had plenty of problems of his own, whose path she was destined to cross only briefly. But. . . .

She chanced one glance in Grant's direction. In spite of everything, she had to admit he was a perplexingly desirable man. How interesting it would be to probe his dark depths, to find out what really made him tick.

And wasn't that something, meeting a man who interested her beyond normal curiosity! Troubling, actually. She would be relieved to finish her investigation and get back home, where she could effectively and permanently put Grant Mackenzie out of her mind.

THE MOMENT THEY REACHED the lodge, Grant took off down the hallway to his office, and Victoria tried not to notice the way he moved, the blatant sensuality of his hips and legs in the well-fitting jeans. She watched him until he had disappeared from sight; almost immediately Rita appeared from the same direction. "Hi!" the girl said.

"Hi, yourself. I was wondering if you were home from school yet."

"Yeah, I got home about twenty minutes ago." Rita shifted from foot to foot. "Victoria, would you like to see where I do my weaving?" she asked hopefully.

"I'd love to."

"Come on, it's down this way, across from daddy's office."

Rita's workroom, or perhaps "studio" would have been a more appropriate word, elicited a gasp of delight from Victoria. An upright loom stood in the center of the room, supporting a partially completed piece. Spools of woolen yarn in every imaginable hue spilled from wall shelves. In one corner of the room stood a small drafting table, where designs had been worked out on graph paper. Victoria walked to the loom and studied the work in progress.

The design wasn't yet evident, but the colors Rita had chosen were lovely—eggplant and cream, apricot and lime. What a waste if her talent wasn't encouraged and developed.

"You have a charming place to work, Rita."

Rita nodded solemnly. "The light's good, and it's cozy and warm. Heat does something to wool, softens it and makes it easier to handle."

Victoria rubbed her hand over the work on the loom. "I love the colors. How long does it take you to finish a piece?"

"Depends. Top speed's an inch an hour."

"Apparently weaving is not for the impatient."

"True, but it seems to go faster when you're actually doing it. Warping the loom is the slow part."

"Warping?" Victoria asked. "I'm afraid I'm not very knowledgeable about weaving."

"The lengthwise threads are the warp. They have to be cut and measured and put on the loom before weaving begins. Nobody likes to rewarp, but the Navahos say you should rewarp within three days after a piece is finished."

"Why?"

Rita screwed up her face. "Well...it's because if the loom is standing there rewarped and ready to go, you just can't leave it alone. You want to start a new piece. Do you understand?"

"Yes, I think I do."

Rita turned to her eagerly. "Oh, Victoria, I wish you would stay with us a long time!"

Victoria couldn't resist brushing her hand across the girl's silken wheat hair. "Rita, once my investigation is completed I'll have to go back."

"Couldn't you stall—you know, stretch it out?"

Victoria laughed. "Now that wouldn't be honest, would it?"

Rita lifted her small shoulders as if to say "who cares?"

"Besides, you need your room back."

"I don't mind, honest!"

"And doesn't your father have some people coming this weekend?"

"Good! He'll be busy, so you and I can spend the weekend together."

Victoria didn't think she had ever been so touched. Taking both the girl's hands in hers, she spoke earnestly. "Perhaps you can persuade your father to let you come to Corpus Christi when school's out this summer. There's an arts-and-crafts center there, and I know the woman who runs it. She gives lessons in spinning and weaving. I understand she's quite good. Maybe he would let you stay with me, and you could enroll. . . ."

Rita's eyes grew as bright as diamonds. "Oh, Victoria!"

At that moment Victoria became aware of

someone standing in the doorway. Glancing over her shoulder, she saw Grant glaring at them. No, not at them—at her! His eyes were actually menacing. Startled, she straightened and dropped Rita's hands. The girl turned to look at her father.

"Oh, daddy!" Rita enthused. "Did you hear what Victoria said—"

"I heard," he answered coldly, his eyes never leaving Victoria. "Do you have homework?"

"Just a little bit."

"I suggest you get on with it."

There was no protest. The tone of his voice told the girl this was one time her father would tolerate no argument. Rita shot Victoria something of a desperate look, then quickly scampered out of the room, past her father's towering figure.

Victoria braced herself for the verbal lashing she was sure was coming. Grant said nothing for a second or two. Then he sighed gustily and said, "I imagine you meant well, Victoria, but don't put ideas in the girl's head. If there's one thing I'm not going to do, it's allow Rita to spend the summer in the city with a single woman. I have enough to worry about as it is." With those words he turned on his heel, clomped across the hall into his office and slammed the door.

*Damn!* Victoria's face turned crimson. He was implying she wouldn't be a proper influence on Rita. What had happened to the sympathetic stranger of this afternoon? She thought she'd given him a pretty clear picture of her life-style, but perhaps he hadn't believed her. For the past year only a nun could have led a more cloistered existence than Victoria Bartlett. It bothered her enormously that Grant might think her improper.

She gave herself a mental shake. *Oh, dumb, Victoria. Dumb, dumb! What in hell do you care what he thinks?* The man definitely had a problem; he had taken the worst of his wife's attributes and projected them onto all women. What woman in her right mind would want to fight that?

No, she didn't care what Grant thought. She just felt sorry for Rita, that was all. A nice teenager stuck out here in the boondocks with a father who suspected femininity in all its so-called guises! Outsiders, to boot. Victoria's heart went out to Rita, for she doubted the girl had any friends to confide in.

Grant was making a grave mistake. He couldn't keep the girl under lock and key forever, and if he didn't ease off, one day he would lose her for sure.

Curiously then, Victoria felt a wave of pity for Grant, too.

# CHAPTER SIX

VICTORIA LIFTED HERSELF out of the bathtub, towel-dried briskly and slipped on her gown, doing up the four dainty buttons at the bodice. But before putting on her velour robe she preened in front of the mirror, studying her body under the thin nightgown. Not too bad, she decided. Not as curvaceous as she might wish, but her waist was trim, her stomach flat, and she had firm, nice-sized breasts. She wondered how she measured up to the other women Grant had known.

Thinking about him brought a rueful sigh to her lips. She put on her robe. Tying it tightly around her, she picked up her hairbrush, switched off the light and walked to the window of the dark bedroom to stare vacantly out at the black night. She wasn't in the least sleepy yet she knew she should be in bed. She and Grant were driving to Kerrville in the morning. He would probably want to get an early start.

That would be a fun trip, she thought sourly, if tonight had been any indication. The air between them had been charged with tension, although she was sure she had been the only one at the dining table who noticed it. She had met some new people: Maria Ramos, the energetic housekeeper who also waited on table; and Sam Burchell and Roy Simpson, the two young men who helped Grant run the preserve. Of course Jake McGrath had been there, amusingly loquacious. Jake, Victoria discovered, held views on virtually every subject under the sun and was not in the least loath to voice them.

"I was just reading an article the other day," he had announced. "This fellow said to take a map of North America and draw a line from northern Manitoba down to the Gulf of Mexico—" he had paused to make certain everyone was paying attention "—and he said the twenty-first century is gonna belong to everyone west of that line. Yessir, everyone's gonna to be up to the eyeballs in concrete and neon. I'm just goddanged glad I ain't gonna be around to have to see it." He had brandished his fork at Victoria. "And let me tell you something, ma'am—when that happens you ain't gonna have to worry about them wild critters of yours, 'cause there ain't gonna be any of them around no more."

"Jake, you're just a little ray of sunshine," Roy Simpson had put in, grinning.

It was a good thing Jake had been there to keep the conversation flowing, since Grant had been notably uncommunicative. Victoria couldn't remember his addressing one word to her all evening. Moody and preoccupied, he had vanished into his office the moment the meal ended, puffing on his pipe, leaving Victoria to watch a dreadful TV movie with Rita...and to feel foolishly bereft.

She set the hairbrush on the windowsill, folded her arms under her breasts and leaned her head against the window facing. This disconsolate mood made no sense, but it existed. It seemed the only way she would get Grant out of her head would be to quit Arroyo Grande for good.

She regretted this in a way. For a few wonderful moments that afternoon she had felt the first stirrings of closeness between them. Obviously the sensation had been an illusion, only a bit of wishful thinking on her part. His behavior ever since he had kissed her so warmly—his intimation that she wasn't a proper influence for Rita, his morose silence at dinner—told her unequivocally she was an unwelcome intrusion in his life.

Victoria sighed. Why on earth was she letting it bother her so much? She didn't want him in hers, either.

She would never know just what alerted her at that moment—a noise outside? Some sort of movement? Something snapped her out of her reverie. Frowning, poised and alert, she peered out the window. It was several seconds before she saw it—a bobbing light falling on tree trunks, dim at first, growing brighter. Her window faced the side yard; the light was coming from the front of the lodge. A moment ticked by, and she thought she knew what it was—an automobile's headlights.

But who would be arriving at this hour? Certainly none of the weekend guests, for they weren't due until Saturday morning. Her eyes flew to the illuminated face of the bedside clock. It was after eleven. On impulse she quickly left the room, walking stealthily down the hall to the lobby.

At night the big picture windows were covered with heavy drapes. The lobby was pitch black. Moving soundlessly, Victoria crossed the big room and pushed the edge of one drape aside a fraction of an inch, just enough to allow her to peek outside.

Yes, there was a vehicle approaching; it looked like a truck but was larger than a pickup. As it neared the lodge the driver extinguished the lights—whoever was inside the cab wasn't anxious to announce his arrival. Victoria instinctively searched for the license plate, but there wasn't enough moonlight to enable her to read the number.

While she watched, the truck made a sweeping turn in front of the lodge and came to a halt. The passenger door flew open, and something was tossed to the ground. Continuing its U-turn, the vehicle picked up speed and drove off. Several yards down the road its lights came on again.

Victoria dropped the curtain and was hurrying toward the front door, when Grant's husky voice stopped her. "Victoria? What the hell's going on?"

She turned. . . and the sight of him. . . . He stood silhouetted in the entrance of the hallway, clad only in silky pajama bottoms that emphasized his splendid physique. Even though the lodge was very dark, she could see how wide his shoulders were, and as he advanced on her she took in the mat of dark chest hair tapering to a V and disappearing below his waistband. Her previous experience of male anatomy hadn't prepared her for the sight of Grant scantily clothed. There was something so elemental about him. She couldn't look away; she felt as though he were reaching out and physically drawing her to him.

"I...." Her hand flew to her chest, and she tried again. "I'm sorry I woke you...."

"You didn't. I couldn't sleep. I sensed rather than heard someone out here."

"I couldn't sleep, either, and I saw a light. There was a truck outside. Someone threw something into the yard."

"Are you sure?"

"Of course I'm sure."

Scowling, Grant moved past her toward the door. "Well, let's go see what it is."

"Grant, you can't go outside like that! It's too cold."

He paused, apparently agreeing with her. Without a word he went to a closet behind the reception desk and withdrew a heavy parka. Slipping it on, he joined her just as she opened the front door. They stepped into air that was, to put it mildly, bracing. Grant squatted to inspect the object that had been tossed into the yard.

"What the devil!" he muttered, then rose and turned to Victoria. "It's our sign."

"What?"

"The sign out on the road that points the way to the lodge."

"Why would someone go to all that trouble to pull up the sign and bring it up here? It doesn't make sense."

"Doesn't it?" he asked enigmatically.

"Some kind of adolescent vandalism, do you think?"

"Maybe." He bent over and picked up the board, climbing the steps to prop it against the porch railing. Victoria followed him. "But I'm thinking it wasn't adolescent," he said pointedly. "Juvenile might be a better word."

A gust of wind swept across the porch, making Victoria shiver. Even though her robe was heavy, the winter night air seeped right through it.

Noticing, Grant quickly propelled her toward the front door. "Let's get inside before you catch pneumonia."

In the lodge's comforting warmth, Grant shrugged out of the parka, tossing it on a nearby chair. Now Victoria was only inches from that broad bare chest. A longing overtook her, the longing to let her fingers crawl up through the forest of his dark hair. She gulped in some air. "You were saying?"

His expression was grave and thoughtful as they slowly walked down the hall to the bedrooms. "Victoria, think a minute.... Did you tell anyone who filed that complaint with Fish and Wildlife?"

She shook her head. "No, no one. I'm sure of

it. And since you called Chuck directly instead of going through channels, the local game warden doesn't even know about it.''

"Well, someone knows where the eagle came down. That business with the sign was just a bit of malicious mischief designed to let me know someone doesn't appreciate my bringing the government to Reyes County. Supposedly, you and I are the only ones who know where the killing took place. Don't you find that interesting?''

They had reached the door to Rita's room. Halting, Victoria looked up at him. "Sure. Interesting but worthless. Of course there are others who know where the eagle came down, but I need someone who is willing to testify in court.''

He took a step nearer and placed his hand on her shoulder. "Victoria, if I could identify anybody, even if I had the helicopter's number, I'd help you all I could. I would hate it because of Rita . . . but my conscience would demand that I go to court.''

"I know, Grant.''

"So far your trip has been such a waste of time.''

A waste of time? Victoria wondered if he really meant it had been a mistake. "You get used to that in this business. You spend most of your time chasing down blind alleys, running into stone walls, dealing with people who don't want to talk to you. You learn not to let it frustrate you.'' She had heard one of the older agents say that once, and it was a good line. True, too. Even though she had observed the truth of it more from the sidelines than in the thick of battle.

"Your work, does it satisfy you?"

"Is it personally satisfying, you mean? Yes, it is. I think it's important work. Somehow the governments of the United States, Canada and Mexico have managed to find time to pass reciprocal laws protecting the wild creatures that inhabit this continent. Someone's got to enforce them, because so few people care. When you get right down to it, those creatures don't have anyone to look out for them except people like us."

The "us" struck them simultaneously, bringing to both their minds how much they had in common—their work, their pasts. Two pairs of eyes locked, and time seemed to stop. A heavy sensation spread through the lower part of Victoria's stomach. His fingers began kneading her shoulder, and they were standing so close that his breath fanned the hair at her temples. She caught a whiff of the soap he had obviously showered with that evening. That, mingled with the natural musky aroma of his skin, was more powerful than any aphrodisiac. It was all she could do to remain motionless. She wanted to close the space between them, to lay her head on his shoulder. . . .

"Victoria. . . ." Her name came out of his mouth in a choking sound. "I—about this afternoon. I want to apologize."

She expelled her breath. "About not wanting Rita to come to see me in Corpus Christi? Grant, I was completely sincere in my invitation. And I assure you that if she were a guest in my home, she would be my first consideration. If I discovered I had to be gone for a while, for whatever reason, my mother would be delighted to look after her. Mom...well, my mom majored in motherhood. Nothing would please her more than having a young girl to fuss over again.''

Grant looked away for a moment, then back at her. ''By now you must realize how uptight I am about this business of parenting.''

''It can't be easy, alone.''

His grip on her shoulder tightened to the point of being painful; still Victoria couldn't move. His compelling eyes rooted her in place. He was looking at her in the strangest way. *What is he thinking?* she wondered.

## CHAPTER SEVEN

GRANT WAS THINKING he had never wanted a woman more, nor had he ever felt so inadequate. Victoria was different, like no woman he had ever met, and that put him at a disadvantage. Since Helena there had been the inevitable casual involvements, but only with women who were no more interested in emotional entanglements than he was. His pride had taken a severe beating at his ex-wife's hands, and he had had to prove to himself he was still a man. Once reassured, he had built a wall of stone around himself. For years he had been convinced he was incapable of genuinely caring for a woman.

So...what was this feeling? Sexual desire, of course; his loins ached with it. He imagined there was damned little but Victoria underneath that robe, and he longed to throw it open. In her flesh he could find an end to the loneliness he wore like a hair shirt.

Okay, the physical desire he could understand. She was one good-looking woman, and he was no more immune to that than any other man. But there was more...and that's what confounded him, what had made him so withdrawn all evening. He simply wasn't prepared for this sudden yearning for her companionship, for the understanding that seemed to exist between them.

His inner voice mocked him: *her mind isn't what you're coveting right now, Mackenzie!*

But he hadn't taken complete leave of his senses. Some basic insight warned him to take delicate care with this woman. If only they could have met before either of them had been wounded.

She stirred, and Grant was startled to see her warm limpid eyes misting over. "Please, Grant," she whispered. "You're hurting me."

His eyes fell to the hand clutching her shoulder. Lord, he had been manhandling her! His hand dropped to his side, and he watched as she slipped her slender fingers inside the robe to tenderly massage her shoulder. "I'm sorry. I can't imagine. . . ."

She offered him a small smile. "It's all right."

"Let me see."

Before Victoria could stop him or utter even a small protest, he had stepped into the bedroom, pulling her with him, and turned on the dressing-table lamp. With unsteady fingers he pushed the robe off her shoulder and stared at the angry red splotch marring her satiny skin. Eyes wide with wonder, Victoria clutched at her robe and watched as he dipped his head. Gently he touched his lips to her shoulder with a deliberate sensuousness that stunned her. Her insides tensed, quivered, then melted into hot liquid. If he had swept her into his arms and kissed her passionately she wouldn't have been more staggered.

His lips wandered languorously over her bare shoulder. Fascinated, Victoria laced her fingers through his thick dark hair. She experienced one brief clear-headed moment of sanity, when she knew she should back away from him. The next moment she was reveling in the feel of the kisses he was showering over her skin.

His big hands fumbled with the robe's belt; the garment fell open, his arms slipped around her waist, and his mouth moved to her throat, her chin, her cheek, her ear, and finally, finally to her eager mouth. Up slid her arms. Her hands locked behind his neck. They fit together perfectly, just as she had known they would. Drinking from her mouth, Grant slipped his hands past the small of her back to cup her round buttocks and draw her upward to the hard aching core of him.

Victoria's mind reeled and stumbled. She was drowning in a sea of sensuality. Hesitation, reluctance, gentleness—all were forgotten; they kissed with a need each had felt for a long time. It was unthinkable that she could feel so much unbridled desire for a man she barely knew. She had believed she would never feel in any other man's arms what she had felt in Steve's. Yet, here was this...this primitive compulsion.

Yes, that was the word for it. It was a compulsion to lose herself in Grant Mackenzie, to seize the moment and let the devil take tomorrow, and she had felt it from the moment she first laid eyes on him. There was nothing rational about it.

When at last they were forced to part, to gasp for air, they stared at each other with bewilderment, as though they had just discovered something unique that defied description. Grant no longer needed to hold her against him, for she was voluntarily pressing herself insistently to him. He moved his palms upward, sliding them along her hips, to her waist and up. The four tiny buttons of her gown's bodice were dispensed with, the fabric pushed aside. Full, creamy, pink-tipped mounds were exposed to his avid gaze. He filled his hands with them and thought surely he would explode.

Victoria collapsed against him. "Grant, please...."

"Please what?"

"Please, don't...."

"You don't mean that." His thumbs teased at the telltale hardened nipples, punctuating his remark.

No, she supposed she didn't, not really. There was growing within her a fierce desire to abandon all restraint and caution. It had been so long since she had felt like anything but an automaton, devoid of all the vital human emotions. New, fresh, exciting sensations washed over her. She turned her face up to Grant's, and their mouths fused again. He moved against her, giving her proof of his arousal, unleashing a hot liquid feeling in her limbs. With his mouth covering hers, she uttered a low moan.

He lifted his head and gazed down at her with

eyes glazed with passion. "I need you, Victoria," he said, hating the admission but powerless to alter the fact.

She swallowed hard, tried to find her voice. "I—" She pressed her lips against his shoulder, tasting the sweet flavor of his skin. For once in her life she didn't want to think, only to feel. Was that so wrong? "I need you, too," she heard her own voice saying.

He groaned, and one hand shot out to extinguish the lamp. He reached for the door to close it.

"Daddy?" a sleepy youthful voice called from down the hall. "Daddy, where are you?"

A siren could hardly have had a more shattering effect on the eloquence of the moment. Victoria jumped away from Grant as his body stiffened. Her heart was thudding, and her labored breathing matched his. In the dim light she saw his facial muscles working convulsively. "Damn!" he muttered. "Damn!"

"Daddy?" Rita's voice sounded perplexed. "Daddy, where are you?"

Grant struggled. "Here, hon," he managed to say.

"What are you doing?"

"I, ah, heard a noise. But everything's all right. You just go on back to bed."

"Aren't you coming?"

"In a minute. Go back to bed."

"Okay."

Victoria clutched at the front of her gown.

Good Lord, what was she doing? She didn't even know this man! Rita's interruption couldn't have been more timely. Reason replaced passion, and mortification slowly overtook her. This was precisely the sort of thing she had guarded against— physical gratification without genuine affection. She considered herself a realist. She didn't yearn for the moon, and she no longer believed in fairy tales. But lovemaking, if and when it entered her life again, would have to be based on something more meaningful than lust.

Grant looked down at her, smiling regretfully. Gently he touched her arm. "Sorry. I guess I'd better go and wait until she's settled down. I'll be back."

"No!" she said quickly. "No, Grant."

"No?" He couldn't believe it. "Dammit, Victoria—"

"No," she said again, fighting for control. "It's not right. I don't want this sort of thing— casual sex."

"It's more than that, and you know it!"

"Oh? What is it, Grant? Shining everlasting love?"

His breath escaped in a hiss. "I'm not sure I believe in that anymore."

"I'm not sure I do, either, which makes this wrong." Victoria's face grew hot. She wrapped her robe tightly about her. "Grant, we don't even know each other!"

"That didn't seem to bother you a minute ago."

"I...I wasn't thinking clearly. I won't deny you aroused me, but...."

"And I will again, Victoria." His voice mellowed considerably, and he bent his head as if to kiss her once more. "I'll be back as soon as Rita is asleep."

Victoria stepped back from him and shook her head vigorously. "No, Grant, please don't. I mean it."

He stared at her, breathing rapidly. Yes, he could tell she meant it. But a moment ago she had been alive with passion. Damn! Something wonderful had slipped from his grasp, and he wasn't going to recapture it tonight. Maybe he never would.

"All right, Victoria," he managed to say when he was mildly restored. "Whatever you say. Perhaps this way is best. I've always thought every relationship needed at least one sane, stable partner, and...and you and I are a couple of emotional cripples." He turned on his heel and was gone.

Victoria's body sagged. She felt spent, exhausted, as though she had just completed some rigorous physical exercise. Taking several deep breaths, she walked to the door and closed it, then whipped off her robe and climbed into bed. She wanted to cry.

Emotional cripple. The truth hurt. Her mind quickly relived the past year, a difficult, plodding, uncompromising year. Thankfully she had had her job, which quickly became her chief reason for existence. But on a few occasions, when common sense had told her she needed to get out and be with people, she had accepted invitations from men, usually to dinner, once to a private party. The men, without exception, had been longtime acquaintances with whom she felt comfortable, with whom she could be herself. She had managed to have a reasonably good time with each of them until.... Until the touch, the touch that informed her the gentleman was ready for a little romance. Every time, every single time she had frozen, just turned to a block of ice. And every time she had experienced a ludicrous urge to cry, "Don't touch me!"

Her divorce had left her frigid, and if that wasn't emotionally crippled she didn't know what was.

Yet... tonight, when Grant had touched her, she had been anything but a block of ice. She had melted instantly, and she still wasn't sure she didn't wish he were in this bed with her. Something she thought had died forever had stirred inside her. His mouth, his hands, his body promised such exquisite release. It would be so nice to be held....

Maybe that was the crux of the matter. She wanted to be embraced, petted, kissed... but no more, not now. And in her wildest dreams she couldn't imagine Grant's settling for that.

Oh, she was a mess! There was too much about her own emotional makeup she didn't understand, and she couldn't seem to trust her instincts. Once she had considered herself so fortunate to have fallen in love at sixteen with the man she eventually married. It had spared her so much of the mental turmoil her friends had experienced as a result of their numerous affairs of the heart.

Now she realized her early marriage had left her embarrassingly uneducated in one of life's fundamental aspects, the man-woman thing. There was a lot she didn't know. For sure she didn't know how to deal with her feelings for Grant Mackenzie.

VICTORIA AWAKENED VERY EARLY the next morning, too early to go into the kitchen for a much-wanted cup of coffee. She lay restlessly in bed until she heard the rest of the household stirring for the day. Then she dressed with special care in her most crisply efficient manner—a tailored suit of a nubby beige fabric, silky coral blouse underneath, plain bone-colored pumps. She wound her hair expertly into an elegant French twist and put gold studs into her earlobes. She left the bedroom and joined the others at the breakfast table.

She was dreading the trip to Kerrville with Grant. What could they possibly say to each other after last night? It had occurred to her, of course, that he might think her something of a tease, leading him on to great expectations, only to renege at the last moment. She still couldn't believe she had been capable of responding to him so eagerly.

Maybe, she thought hopefully, he had come up with a reason not to accompany her. Whatever happened, she would just have to brazen it out.

She needn't have worried. He couldn't have been more polite. Coolly, indifferently polite. He merely added his good morning to the others' and resumed the conversation her arrival had interrupted. Several times during the meal Victoria allowed her gaze to stray to him. Nothing special lingered in his eyes. Silently she sipped coffee and nibbled on toast and scrambled eggs, waiting to hear what excuse he would use to avoid the trip to Kerrville.

He offered none. When everyone had finished breakfast and Maria had appeared to clear the table, Rita headed off to catch the school bus. The other men left the house to tend to their various chores, and Grant got to his feet. "I don't suppose we can accomplish much in town before ten o'clock," he said. "So what say we leave in about an hour?"

Oh, Lord, this promised to be a long day! "Yes, that's fine," she gulped, avoiding looking at him. Last night hadn't been a figment of her imagination—his next words assured her of that.

"Well, I'm going to drive down to the highway and put that damned sign back where it belongs." With that he strode out of the dining room. Shaking her head, Victoria watched his retreating figure.

# CHAPTER EIGHT

THE ROUTE TO KERRVILLE took them through a beautiful, peaceful valley bisected by the Guadalupe River. The river's cypress-laden banks created some of the state's handsomest scenery, and for years the area had lured artists and artisans from all over the country. Strung along the river were resorts, children's summer camps, studios, galleries and fine homes. It was the part of the state Victoria most loved, not far from her family's Bandera retreat, and today she foolishly wished she and Grant had merely been out on a pleasure drive. They could have taken time to browse through the galleries and antique shops, stroll along the river, perhaps stop at a quaint café for lunch and not hurry back at all.

Inside the truck, they somehow managed to keep the conversation going. Never once did it stray to the personal, and Victoria chanced only two sidelong glances in Grant's direction. They both strove too hard for nonchalance, but at least he didn't appear angry or resentful.

Perhaps last night hadn't had the emotional impact on him that it had on her. A stunning, heart-stopping episode might have constituted nothing more than a normal pass at an attractive woman. A humbling thought.

It was a relief to reach their destination, to have Grant pull into the shopping-center parking lot, park the truck and hop out. "I have plenty of shopping to do," he told her. "Everyone at home gave me a list, so let's plan to meet back here at, say, one o'clock. We'll have lunch before heading back to the lodge, okay?"

"Okay."

"And if you get tied up, don't worry about me. I'll just kill time till you get back."

"Fine." Victoria scooted across the bench seat and took the wheel.

Grant touched the brim of his big hat. "Good luck," he said before walking away. It was the warmest thing he had said to her all morning.

Victoria found Dawson Helicopter Service without trouble, since it was located right on the highway. If the size of its physical plant was any indication, the operation was prosperous. She noted a heliopad, an enormous hangar with a wind gauge, or wind sock, on top, several pumps that dispensed gas and a blue-and-white prefab-type building housing the company's offices. The whole was surrounded by barbed wire.

She parked Grant's pickup in front of the office building and slid out, smoothing her skirt and wishing she had worn pants. Getting in and out of a pickup wasn't easily or gracefully accomplished in a skirt. The government car would have been more comfortable, but Victoria was very conscientious. Grant's shopping trip was personal business and therefore precluded their using the official vehicle.

Inside, the office teemed with activity. A middle-aged receptionist was banging away at a typewriter. Against one wall a man sat at a radio console and conversed with airborne pilots. Other men were at other desks, talking on telephones. Strolling through in grease-spattered overalls, a mechanic openly stared at Victoria.

The woman at the typewriter looked up with a smile. Could she help her? Victoria dutifully presented her identification; she asked to speak to the owner. The woman hurried away, returning in a moment to say Mr. Dawson would see her. Victoria was ushered into a small private cubicle, where a tall burly man in khakis introduced himself as Morgan Dawson. They exchanged a few courtesies. Dawson asked Victoria to be seated, after which she crisply stated her business.

"Always glad to cooperate with the government, young lady," Morgan Dawson said expansively. Too expansively, Victoria thought suspiciously. Something wasn't right.

What it was came to her suddenly. He hadn't quizzed her, not at all. He hadn't shown the slightest trace of surprise at seeing her. He seemed to know who she was and what she wanted before she even opened her mouth. He had been expecting her. There could be only one explanation for that. She was as certain that Dawson had been talking to Martin Rumbaugh as if she had heard the conversation with her own ears. And she had the worst feeling she had turned into another blind alley.

Nevertheless, she plunged ahead. "Mr. Dawson, I believe one of your aircraft has been leased to a Martin Rumbaugh in Reyes County. Is that correct?"

"Sure is. Rumbaugh's one of the few ranchers who pays us out of his own pocket. He's got a mighty big spread, and coyotes have given him a fit for years. But most of this company's income comes from government contracts to do predator hunting." He shot her a meaningful glance. He had all the answers before she'd even asked the questions—a reflection of his self-confidence. "So you see, ma'am, I'd hardly allow my pilots to have anything to do with killing an eagle. That's against the law. The government would jerk our contracts right away."

Dawson had touched on a bureaucratic fact of life. Fish and Wildlife was split into divisions, among them, Enforcement, Victoria's bailiwick; and Animal Damage Control, which was responsible for monitoring predators in the West, issuing contracts to companies like Dawson's. The two departments were often at odds. Enforcement accused ADC of working too hand-in-glove with the stockmen, while ADC accused Enforcement of being so concerned with endangered species that it lost sight of the very real danger predators posed to valuable livestock.

Victoria's mouth compressed into a tight line.

So, she thought dispiritedly, Dawson would hardly admit to knowing anything about the Arroyo Grande eagle incident, not with lucrative government contracts at stake.

"Mr. Dawson, what would you do if you discovered some of your pilots—without your knowledge, of course—had taken part in killing an eagle?"

"Why, I wouldn't put up with it for a minute! I'd fire 'em."

"That's it? You wouldn't turn them over to the proper authorities?"

Dawson cleared his throat. "I suppose that would depend on the circumstances," he said obscurely.

"Of course," she murmured, just as obscurely. "Mr. Dawson, regarding the helicopter that's leased to Mr. Rumbaugh. . . . I suppose you have records of its activities last Monday."

"Indeed I do."

"Would you mind my taking a look at them?"

Dawson hesitated. "I'm not required by law to do that, you know."

"I know," Victoria said calmly, giving him her nicest smile. "But I hoped you would be as anxious to get to the bottom of this as I am. As you said, killing an eagle is against the law."

The smile she received in return was crafty. "Of course. You just tell Mrs. Saunders—that's the lady you spoke to in the outer office—what you want, and I'll instruct her to give it to you."

Studying the records a few minutes later, Victoria understood his confidence. They were worthless. Monday's entry showed only that Frank Oakley and Jim Nelson had patrolled the Rumbaugh ranch for three hours. Their mission wasn't specified, so she inquired about it.

"Oh," Dawson said blithely, "those old ranchers like having someone flying around looking over things, spotting injured or straying livestock, broken fences, things of that nature. That way they can spend more time in town drinking coffee and jawing with their friends."

"And, of course, the helicopter is used for predator control."

"Sure, but only coyotes."

Victoria was tired of fencing with this man. "I wonder if I might speak to Mr. Oakley and Mr. Nelson."

Dawson rubbed his chin. " 'Fraid not, not right away at least. They've been sent down to the Big Bend to patrol the Mexican border."

How convenient! If Dawson was telling her the truth, the two men had been sent to as remote and isolated an area as could be found in the United States. "They're not working the Rumbaugh ranch anymore?"

"Nope. This Mexican-border thing is a government job, so it took precedence."

"Wasn't it awfully sudden? I spoke to Mr. Oakley only yesterday, and he made no mention of a reassignment."

Dawson didn't appear in the least surprised that she had talked to his pilot. "Well, that's the nature of the business. The pilots have to be ready to move out on a moment's notice.''

Victoria stared at the papers in front of her. She was certain state law would require more specific information than Dawson's records provided, but not being that familiar with those laws, she didn't feel she could ask the right questions. "These forms seem to be incomplete, Mr. Dawson," she commented with a frown.

Dawson waved her remark aside. "No one pays any attention to those things, anyway. Everyone's got too much paperwork to do as it is, so they're all grateful to us for keeping it simple." He got to his feet, glanced at his wristwatch, then regarded her levelly. "Now, young lady, if there's nothing else, I have some work to do."

She was being summarily dismissed, and she knew she had no right to press him further. A feeling of impotence swept through her. Momentarily she wondered if one of the older agents, someone who had been at this sort of thing for years, could have come up with the next move.

But no, she had done everything she could. She wasn't allowed to go barging into places demanding this and that of citizens who, on the surface at least, had done nothing wrong; Chuck was adamant about that. Dawson kept deplorable records, but the most she could do about that was to recommend to state officials that the company's procedures be investigated. Sloppy record-keeping was not a federal offense.

Stiffly she thanked Morgan Dawson for his

time, hating the satisfied look on the man's face, and left the office with a renewed sense of failure.

RETURNING TO THE SHOPPING CENTER, she found Grant standing where she had left him earlier, but now he was surrounded by what appeared to be half the goods from the stores inside. Since she saw him before he spotted her, she took advantage of the opportunity to slow the truck to a snail's pace and stare at him in open admiration. He lounged with his rump against a wall, his thumbs hooked into the pockets of his jeans, one ankled crossed over the other, the big hat pushed down low.

What a magnificent-looking man! Did he have any idea just how attractive he was, and did he ever use it to his advantage? For a moment she stopped smarting over the nonresults of her visit to the helicopter company and simply marveled at the peculiar sensation the sight of him aroused in her.

With his thumb Grant pushed the hat farther back on his head and scanned the parking lot. The movement brought Victoria up sharply. Quickly she, too, pretended to be looking for him and slowly inched the truck forward. He raised a hand to wave to her, and she waved back, as though only now spying him. Braking, she watched him stride toward her.

"Been waiting long?" she asked, turning off the ignition.

"Only a few minutes. I'll get this stuff loaded, and we'll be on our way."

It took a good fifteen minutes to load the bed of the pickup with his purchases, and he had to put several sacks of staples and cleaning supplies in the cab with them. Victoria slid over to the passenger side as Grant got behind the wheel.

"How'd it go?" he wanted to know.

Succinctly she told him of her meeting with the "cooperative" Mr. Dawson. Grant listened to the account, sensing her disappointment. "Did you really expect to find out anything?"

She sniffed. "Well, I certainly didn't expect the helicopter company to be in cahoots with Rumbaugh."

"Victoria, you can't say for sure it is. Dawson might very well have been telling you the truth as he knows it."

"Maybe." Her tone implied she considered that a remote possibility. She lapsed into silence as Grant drove out of the parking lot, remaining deep in thought for several minutes. "The problem is that I do know it," she said at last, more to herself than to him. "I just can't prove it. I have to accept the fact that I have nothing, absolutely nothing. I'm going to have to go back to the lodge, telephone Chuck and tell him I've come up with zero. I'm sure he'll tell *me* to get myself back to Corpus Christi."

She sighed then, deeply, and turned her head to stare out the window, so she didn't see the regret etched on Grant's face. A part of him couldn't forget last night, though he had been striving valiantly for forgetfulness. She had responded to him in a way that told him it had been a long time since she had been held and caressed. In memory, those baby-soft lips still burned on his mouth.

Another more sensible part of him said he was a fool to want her, to even think of her as a desirable woman. He had realized all along she would soon be going back to her own world.

Grant knew all about that world. Victoria's work might seem unusual for a woman, but everything about her screamed femininity. He imagined that when she wasn't trying to make the world safer for its wild creatures, she enjoyed getting dressed up, going to places where there was shine and glitter. Any woman who looked like Victoria would enjoy that sort of thing.

It was a world he had rejected and had no wish to return to. That was just one of the reasons he had awakened that morning filled with steady resolve to keep his distance. Of course, this trip together wasn't the best way to accomplish that, but he rationalized that he had genuinely needed to get some shopping done. However, when they returned to Arroyo Grande he intended staying so busy he would have no time to think about her, about the way she smelled, the way she felt in his arms. . . .

Still, his sympathies were entirely with her. He, too, wished her investigation had borne fruit. He shot her a look of communion, but she didn't see it. She continued to stare out the window.

"Cheer up, Victoria. You've done your job. No one can ask for more than that. Weren't you the one who said you couldn't let blind alleys and stone walls frustrate you?''

The remark inevitably sent Victoria's thoughts back to the previous evening. She was having a damnably hard time keeping her mind on the business at hand. It was easy when Grant wasn't around, but here in the cramped confines of the truck cab she was too acutely aware of him. For several long moments she said nothing, until finally she gave herself a little shake and turned in the seat to face him.

"You're right, of course, but somehow I just know this thing is important—I'm just not sure how. I keep going over it, and I come up with nothing except...except that too many people don't want to talk to me. That's what really bugs me. I mean, killing an eagle is a misdemeanor. It's not as though I could get them for murder. I'd like to, I hasten to add, but I can't.''

Grant gave it some thought, then slowly shook his head. "I don't know, Victoria. I suppose it's your job to think of all possible angles, but this thing might be something very simple. A couple of chopper pilots make a bet that one can't hit an eagle. Or some stockmen want to prove the wildlife laws have no clout.''

Victoria chewed on her bottom lip. She remembered Rumbaugh's saying, "It's a law that can't be enforced.'' Dammit, she wanted to prove it could.

"You know, Victoria, the old ranchers like Rumbaugh have had things their own way for so long they can't imagine that changing. If there's something on their property they want shot, they expect to be able to shoot it and not get any guff. It wasn't all that long ago that this included people, too.''

"The code of the West," she said derisively, throwing up her hands in a gesture of futility. "When I became an agent I thought I would be doing so much good. Sometimes I don't feel like I'm doing anything at all."

"Victoria, perhaps one agent, one biologist, one manager doesn't do all that much, but collectively we do a helluva lot.''

She realized he was trying his best to be encouraging, so she gave him a small, almost shy smile of thanks. His use of the word "we" was not lost on her. For one absurd moment she felt unusually close to him.

Then she remembered his indifference that morning, the abrupt way he had left her the night before, and his words rang in her ears: emotional cripples. An apt description of the two of them. Although at times there seemed to be some mysterious magnetic pull between them, they could never be close. Not even if she wanted an involvement, which she didn't. Not even if there had been time for the relationship to develop, which there wasn't.

The restaurant he chose had character—Victoria would give it that. It was a rather ramshackle building with an assortment of additions tacked onto it. What it lacked in appearance, it made up for in popularity. It was well past the noon rush hour, but a swarm of vehicles of every description were parked in front.

"Doesn't look like much," Grant apologized, "but the burgers are great. Cooked on a grill after you order them. I happen to be fond of places like this."

"So am I," she said truthfully, thinking of the dilapidated waterfront shack near Corpus Christi that was her favorite place for seafood.

The restaurant's decor was slapdash. The wooden floor sagged noticeably, none of the tables and chairs matched and wall decorations were limited to beer advertisements. Country music blared from a jukebox. Grant waved a greeting to the man behind the counter, leading Victoria to a small table for two in a far corner. Almost immediately a pudgy waitress with rouged cheeks appeared to take their order.

"Hiya, Grant," she said, smiling. "Haven't seen you around in a spell."

"Nope. Been busy as a bee in April. How's my favorite waitress, Gracie?"

Gracie simpered and shot a curious look in Victoria's direction. "What'll y'all be having?"

"The lady here has never had a decent hamburger, Gracie," Grant said, "so I think we ought to remedy that. Make it two cheeseburgers with fries, and I'll take a glass of whatever's on tap. Victoria?"

She nodded. "That's fine."

"That'll be two beers, Gracie."

The waitress hurried away, and Grant settled back in his seat, stretching his long legs in front of him. One brushed against Victoria's. She moved and tried to cross her legs, but only succeeded in kicking his boot top. Finally she placed both feet squarely on the floor. "There doesn't seem to be room for both of us under here," she remarked lightly, and he grinned.

*He has the nicest smile,* she thought wistfully, then instantly chided her foolishness. She had more important things to think about than Grant's even white teeth or the way one corner of his mouth lifted higher than the other. With so many things demanding her attention, why was she absorbed in the fact that his knee was braced firmly against hers? The rough texture of his jeans brushed her smooth nylon stocking. The touching seemed so warmly intimate. Victoria didn't think she could have moved if her life had depended on it. She refused to entertain the notion that the physical contact was a deliberate action on his part. There was nowhere else to put those long legs of his under such a small table.

Gracie brought their beers right away. While Grant quaffed his, Victoria sipped and glanced idly around the crowded café. "Charming place. A real slice of middle-class America."

"Yeah," he agreed. "It's been here for. . .oh, I don't know. . .forever. When I was a kid staying in Fredericksburg, my folks were convinced this was a den of iniquity, and I was forbidden to set foot in it. So naturally I could hardly wait to do just that. The night of high-school graduation, a bunch of us came here. What a disappointment to discover it was nothing but a place to eat and drink beer. The owners must have made a small fortune off it, yet they've never done a thing to spruce it up. I guess it wouldn't be the same if it looked nice."

His idle conversation helped Victoria steer her thoughts back on their proper course. Over the cheeseburgers and French fries—excellent ones, as he had promised—they discussed her investigation.

"I think I've got a pretty good picture of what really happened," she told Grant seriously, plucking a hot strip of potato from a napkin-lined basket. "Monday afternoon Oakley and Nelson were patrolling the Rumbaugh ranch. They spotted the eagle, gave chase. Why? Who knows? A dare, sport, or. . . . I've been told there are ranchers who will pay a bonus to a trapper who kills an eagle. Maybe Rumbaugh's one of them. Anyway, they pursued the bird and killed it, but they couldn't land to recover their quarry—"

"Because Rita and I were there."

Victoria nodded. "Possibly they returned later, but by that time you would have been out there and removed the carcass. Now I imagine they would have reported the incident to Rumbaugh, hoping he would take their word for the kill and would pay the bonus, anyway."

"Strictly conjecture, Victoria."

Her eyes narrowed thoughtfully. "I know, I

know, but let me finish. Rumbaugh wouldn't have thought anything of the incident until Sheriff Thornton telephoned to tell him it was being investigated. At this point, my friend, whether you like it or not, Rumbaugh would have had a pretty good idea who had reported it.''

"Hmm, no doubt you're right. He would have known where the bird went down, and no one else around there would have cared if twenty eagles had been shot.''

"As a matter of fact, it would appear there were plenty of phone calls flying back and forth, and one of them was to the helicopter company. The outcome was to send Oakley and Nelson down to the Mexican border so they couldn't talk to me.''

Grant pursed his lips. "Sounds reasonable. Give or take a few details, it probably happened just that way.''

Victoria chewed on her burger for a moment. She swallowed, and a deep V formed between her brows. "So much ado over one bird, that's the stickler. You know, Grant, if every one of the people concerned were to troop in here right now and say, 'All right, we did it, and we're sorry,' all they'd get would be a fine and a stern admonishment from some judge. Unless. . . .''

"Unless?''

"Unless the killing you witnessed was just one of many. Unless Rumbaugh and Dawson are engaged in a large-scale slaughtering operation. It's happened before, you know. Do you remember the rancher in Wyoming who killed hundreds of eagles before he was caught?''

He nodded.

"In a case like that, if it could be proved, Dawson would lose his state license and his government contracts—Oakley and Nelson could lose their jobs. It probably wouldn't hurt Rumbaugh too much, but he'd have to cancel his trapping operations until everything died down.''

"Fascinating,'' Grant said. "The investigative mind is a wondrous thing to behold. Trouble is, you can't prove any of that.''

Victoria sighed in exasperation. "I know...but I had a great case there for a minute. By now I'm sure everyone concerned realizes you can't identify anyone, or this whole thing would have broken wide open by now. Oh, Grant, if only you had gotten the helicopter's number! I could get a grand-jury investigation if you had.''

"I know, Victoria, and I'm sorry about that. But it all happened so damned suddenly, and I was steamed as hell.''

"I didn't mean to sound critical. It's just that I'm so blasted disappointed that apparently nothing's going to come of all this.''

"Why, Victoria? Why is this so important to you? I know you're sworn to uphold the law and all that, but you must have had dozens of more important incidents to investigate.''

Her expression was austere. "As a matter of fact, Grant, this is the first time Chuck has sent me out on assignment without one of the other agents. Surprised?''

He inclined his head slightly. "A little. You're so professional. I guessed this was old stuff to you.''

"My supervisor doesn't place much faith in my abilities, I'm afraid. He's never said a word to that effect, but I can tell what he thinks. He thinks I should be typing at a desk or standing behind a cosmetics counter or running a boutique or doing anything but what I'm doing.'' Regarding him evenly, she said, "I suppose you agree with him.''

Grant's shrug was noncommittal, but she had hit pretty close to what he felt. It had nothing to do with her capabilities; he had a notion Victoria could do anything she set her mind to. Nor did he think it odd for a woman to be involved in wildlife work.

It was the investigative aspect of her work. Dammit, it could be dangerous! If she stayed in it very long, chances were good she would get into undercover work, tracking down illegal dealers in furs, hides and what have you. Those boys weren't averse to using guns. Didn't she realize that? What in the devil was she doing letting herself in for that kind of thing?

Oh, God, listen to him! He was determined to put her out of his mind, to keep his distance, not to have anything more to do with her...yet the thought of anything happening to her made his stomach lurch.

"Do you ever carry a gun?" he blurted, not realizing what he was going to ask until the words were out of his mouth.

Her mouth dropped in astonishment. "Well, yes, sometimes. Not routinely. Unless you're dealing with big-time operators and huge sums of money, the badge is usually enough. Why, Grant? Why are you looking at me like that?"

His color changed noticeably. Leaning across the table, he spoke earnestly. "God in heaven, Victoria! Why don't you go back to Corpus Christi and open a boutique?"

The look she gave him could have frozen an erupting volcano.

IT WAS LATE AFTERNOON by the time they reached Arroyo Grande, and the moment they entered the lodge they were accosted by Maria. "*Senora*, you had a phone call. He left a message." Fishing around in her apron pocket, the housekeeper withdrew a slip of paper, handing it to Victoria.

"Thank you, Maria." She glanced at the paper, then at Grant. "Chuck's trying to get in touch with me. I'm to call him at the office before six, or at home after that. I guess he wants to know why I haven't called him."

Grant took her by the arm. "Come on. You can use the phone in my office."

Grant's office, which Victoria hadn't seen before, was a large room, furnished in a functional manner. The door was kept closed at all times, so the temperature inside was noticeably cooler than the rest of the house. She immediately recognized the need for that; one section of the big room was taken up by a complicated computer setup.

With Grant looking on, she placed a call to the Corpus Christi office. It was after office hours, so Chuck himself answered the phone. He came right to the point.

"Victoria," he barked. "What the hell are you doing up there?"

Accustomed to her supervisor's brusqueness, she didn't flinch. "I don't understand, Chuck."

"I got a call from the Washington office around noon today. Seems they were contacted by a congressman who claims one of our agents is harassing an influential constituent."

Victoria clenched her teeth. "This constituent wouldn't be named Rumbaugh by any chance, would he?"

"That's the man."

"I haven't been 'harassing' anybody. As a matter of fact, I've gone out of my way to be polite." Her spirits sagged. She thought she had a pretty good idea what would be coming next.

"Well, well, Victoria.... I turn you loose just once, and the next thing I know I've got a congressman on my ass."

She sucked in her breath. "I suppose you want me to call off the investigation and come home like a good girl."

A long pause followed; then, to her utter amazement, she heard Chuck Singleton laughing quietly. "Hell, no! If you've got someone worried enough to call his congressman, you must be on to something. Press on, Victoria. Let me hear from you if you come up with anything, and give Grant my regards, will you?''

''Of course.'' The exultation she felt as she hung up the phone would have been impossible for her to explain to anyone. It was a heady sensation, knowing she had finally begun to prove her competence.

Grant had been watching her intently. ''Well?'' he demanded. ''What is it?''

Victoria turned to him triumphantly. ''I think I've just been accepted. Chuck sends his regards— and he wants me to continue the investigation. It seems Mr. Rumbaugh has contacted his congressman.''

Brown eyes locked with green. Though neither Grant nor Victoria would have admitted it, both were thinking, *It isn't over, not yet.* For a long wordless moment they simply stared at each other.

Grant was the first to recover. Pulling himself up sharply, he managed some semblance of a normal expression, but his thoughts were in turmoil. The longer she stayed in the house the greater the chance of—

What? Of making love to her? Since when had he run from such a delightful prospect? Conflict assaulted him from all sides. This woman tantalized him in ways he didn't understand. Making love to Victoria would be the most unwise move of his life. Thoughts of her would linger inside his head for weeks, months, years. From the beginning, such a few short days ago, he had feared she could so insinuate herself into his life that he couldn't bear to be without her. No telling what she might do to him if he let her.

He didn't want any of this! Getting really close to a woman was a sign of weakness in a man. Hadn't Helena taught him that?

"Well, I'm sure you're very pleased with yourself," he said gruffly.

Perplexed by his tone, Victoria parted her lips. "Yes. Yes, I am."

"Good." He cleared his throat and busily riffled through a stack of papers on his desk. "Now if you'll excuse me, Victoria, I see Jake has left some information I need to put in the computer. From the looks of things it might take most of the evening."

She flushed. A barked "Get out of here!" would hardly have been more explicit. What was the man's problem? One minute he was so warm and human; the next he was as cold and distant as the farthest star. Half the time she thought him insufferable; the other half she considered him a confoundedly attractive man. At no time could she seem to regard him dispassionately.

For a moment Victoria was almost sorry Chuck had prolonged the investigation. The longer she stayed at Arroyo Grande, the greater the chance that Grant's problem would become hers. And it crossed her mind that she could leave, stay somewhere else—in a motel in the nearest town, perhaps. But the nearest town was Kierney, and she couldn't remember seeing a motel of any kind there. That left Kerrville, which was one heck of a long way, considering her investigation was centered in Reyes County.

Oh, what utter nonsense! From this moment on she would just keep her distance, put him to the back of her mind and concentrate on her work, something she should have been doing all along. She didn't want a man in her life, but if she had wanted one, it certainly wouldn't have been a complicated man like Grant Mackenzie.

Affecting insouciance, she coolly murmured, "Of course," turned on her heel and left his office.

# CHAPTER NINE

SALLY ANDERSON braced her arms on the café counter and looked at her customer with censure. "How's the photography business, Victoria?"

Smiling wanly, Victoria set her coffee cup in the saucer. "Sorry for the deception, Sally, but at the time I saw no reason to tell anyone who I was. How did you find out?"

Sally snorted. "The same way I find out everything—somebody told somebody who told somebody else. Most of the ranchers around here make it into this café several times a week, and all they do is gossip and talk about the weather. Believe me, lately the weather has taken a back seat to all the chatter about the female federal agent who's been snooping around." She swiped unnecessarily at the counter with a rag. "Is an eagle being killed really that big a deal?"

"It's against the law, Sally. If an incident is reported, it has to be checked out."

"And Grant was the one who reported it, of course, and of course that's the reason you're staying at Arroyo Grande." Sally sighed. "Damned if that man can't keep coming up with more ways to stay in hot water with the local citizens. Sometimes I think he enjoys having everyone mad at him. I swear I don't understand him."

*Neither do I,* Victoria thought. Grant had carefully avoided being alone with her since Chuck's phone call. Save for a few exchanged remarks at the dinner table the night before, they hadn't spoken to each other. He had excused himself immediately after the meal and remained in his office until after Victoria had gone to bed. When she appeared for breakfast, she discovered he had eaten and left the house. Rita's expressed delight over Victoria's continued presence at Arroyo Grande obviously was not shared by her father.

Well, he would be happy to learn she wouldn't be there much longer. After an entire day of traversing the county, talking to anyone who would talk to *her*, Victoria was convinced she had no case. Reyes County's citizens had been remarkably closemouthed; if any of them knew anything about eagles being killed, they weren't saying. The common sentiment seemed to be, "So what? If there was an eagle on my place, I might shoot it, too."

There was no one left to talk to, and if she returned to Rumbaugh or Dawson without new evidence, they could claim harassment and make it stick. She couldn't justify continuing her investigation.

It was disappointing, but the day had been enlightening in one respect. She had been impressed by the sincerity of the stockmen. They honestly believed the government didn't give a damn about them or their problems, so the general feeling was that they had to look out for themselves. As biased as Victoria was, she was beginning to realize there were two sides to the issue.

But not where Martin Rumbaugh was concerned. She had no use for people who thought they were God Almighty and lived accordingly. Given the chance, she would relish hauling Rumbaugh into court.

She had been passing through Kierney on her way back to Arroyo Grande when she decided to stop in at Sally's Café for a cup of coffee. It was midafternoon, and the café was deserted. Had it not been, Victoria doubted Sally would have talked to her so readily.

"How long you figure on being around here, Victoria?" Sally asked.

"I guess I'll be leaving in the morning. It seems no one around here wants to talk to me." Victoria attempted a smile.

Sally was completely serious. "Can you really blame them? What you've got to realize is that you're going to go back to Corpus Christi and forget all about this, but the rest of us have to live here. Around here, you get along...or you don't get along, if you get my meaning."

Victoria shook her head in disbelief. "Sally, does Martin Rumbaugh really have that much influence in the county?"

"I reckon he does. His family's been here longer than anyone else, and he owns the biggest spread. No one seems to want to cross him, plus

the sheriff's always in his corner. Guess that's because Cody wouldn't be sheriff if Martin didn't
want him to be.''

Victoria eyed the café owner quizzically. "Sally,
if you knew anything about the eagle episode, and
if I came in here flashing my badge, would you tell
me what you knew?"

"Probably not," the woman said. "I don't
know anything, though, honest. I hear lots of talk
about coyotes and bobcats and eagles, but I don't
pay too much attention to it, 'cause it doesn't affect me. I know there are ranchers who'll swear
eagles kill x number of lambs every year—I've
heard others swear they've never actually seen an
eagle kill a lamb. Now, coyotes are a different
matter. They all hate coyotes, and I guess they've
got good reason. Me...personally I don't hold
with killing eagles. I mean, they're our national
bird and all. Oh, I know it's the bald eagle that's
the national symbol, but an eagle's an eagle. Reyes
County is loaded with them in the winter. I kinda
like them. I don't know why...I just do.''

On an impulse Victoria reached into her handbag and withdrew a card. "Sally, I'd like to leave
my card with you and ask a favor. If there's ever
anything you'd like to...talk to me about....''
She paused and gave the woman a look filled with
meaning. "I wish you'd telephone me at this number. If I'm not there, someone will get word to me,
and I'll return the call. It would be strictly confidential. No one would ever know you made the
call.''

Sally stared at the card. For a moment Victoria feared she was going to refuse to take it. She kept it, stuffing it into her apron pocket with the furtiveness of someone receiving contraband. "Sure. But I can't imagine why I'd ever want to call."

Victoria drained the last of her coffee and slid off the stool. "Thanks, Sally. The coffee was delicious, as usual."

"Guess I won't be seeing you again, Victoria."

"Oh. . . you never can tell."

"Well, take care."

"You too." Victoria flashed her a smile and started for the door. Halfway there, she turned. "You're wrong about one thing, Sally. I'm not going to forget about this. Not about Rumbaugh, not about the helicopter company, not about anything."

And she wouldn't. All during the long lonely drive back to Arroyo Grande she mulled over the events of the past few days. She took the facts, one by one, and slipped them into the cubbyholes of her mind. This episode had reached a dead end. . . but one of these days, she was convinced, something would come of it. She had nothing to base that on. Again, it was simply a gut feeling.

Returning to the lodge, Victoria encountered a flurry of activity. Everyone was busy getting ready for tomorrow's guests. Maria strode past carrying a bundle of freshly laundered sheets; she mumbled a greeting and hurried up the stairs. Roy Simpson clomped in the front door with a load of firewood. He shot her a shy smile before stacking the logs beside the hearth. Mrs. Guilford emerged from the hall that led to Grant's office. "Had to get the boss to okay the weekend's menus," she explained, brandishing a piece of paper.

"Is there anything I can do to help?"

"Not a thing, dear. Everything's under control." The cook headed in the direction of the kitchen.

Apparently Grant was in his office, but since he had made such a point of avoiding her, Victoria certainly wasn't going to seek him out. Quickly she went down the hall to Rita's bedroom, took her suitcases out of the closet and threw them on the bed.

She would only be in the way, so she might as well leave immediately. She could make it to San Antonio before dark, then drive on to Corpus Christi in the morning. Forget that she already had driven countless miles today. Her leaving would make things easier all the way around. Grant was obviously uneasy with her there, and she didn't think she could endure another evening of being pointedly ignored. Her mind made up, she went into the bathroom and began gathering her things together.

She had returned to the bedroom when she remembered the photographs Jake had taken for her. She didn't have the slightest idea where they were, but she would have to have them. And that meant asking Grant for them.

Well, if she had to, she had to. She left the bedroom, crossing through the lodge to the door of his office. Taking a deep breath, she knocked sharply and waited for his summons.

"Come in," he called.

Victoria opened the door, stepped inside and quickly closed it, mindful of the need to maintain the room's cooler temperature. Grant was seated in front of his computer. He didn't turn around immediately. His unlit pipe was clenched between his teeth, and to Victoria's surprise, he was wearing dark-rimmed glasses. So he needed glasses for close work. It was hardly a stunning revelation, but it was something about him she hadn't known before. If anything, the glasses added to his striking handsomeness. He looked positively Clark Kent-ish. Since he was so engrossed in his work, she was afforded a moment of just looking at him.

He punched a key, then jumped to his feet, pulling the pipe from his mouth. "Damned if it doesn't irritate the hell out of me to have a *machine* tell me I've made an error!" he barked.

Victoria couldn't help the giggle that escaped. At the sound, Grant turned. Seeing her, he whipped off the glasses. "Victoria! I...I didn't know you were back."

"I got back a few minutes ago."

"Find out anything?"

"Nothing. Zero. The investigation is over. I'm terribly sorry to disturb you, Grant, but I need those photographs Jake took."

His pipe and glasses were quickly deposited on his desk. "Of course. Right now?"

"Yes. I thought I would drive to San Antonio tonight, then on home in the morning."

Grant felt as though he had just taken a blow to his stomach. His inspection of her took in the stubborn lift of her chin, the way she held her body so rigidly correct. She was leaving. He had tried to convince himself it was what he wanted, but he had been a fool to think it wouldn't bother him to see her go. Good sense quit him completely. He didn't know what his next move would be, but he had to do something. He couldn't let her leave with this charged tension between them.

Seeming to have a mind of their own, his feet carried him across the room in a flash. He gripped her upper arm so tightly she winced. "Why now, Victoria?"

"Why? I told you. The investigation is over."

"Are you absolutely certain you've explored all possible avenues?"

"Of course I'm certain! I can't continue badgering the same people over and over again. I can no longer justify spending time and money on an investigation that has nowhere to go. And since I'll be leaving, what difference does it make if I leave now or in the morning?"

His expelled breath was a harsh sound, and even Grant was surprised at his next words. "I . . . I was going to invite you out to dinner."

"You . . . were?"

He released his grip on her. "You and Rita. I told Mrs. Guilford not to bother with dinner for anyone but herself and Maria tonight. Jake and the boys are driving into town to eat at Sally's place—a little breather for them before the busy weekend starts. I thought I'd take you and Rita to the Country Store.''

"The Country Store?''

"It really is a country store, with a restaurant and dance floor in back. It's a family place and it's usually jumping on Friday night. I thought... you might enjoy it.'' Lord, he hadn't thought of the Country Store in ages!

Victoria stared at him mutely. Last night, this morning, he hadn't even wanted to talk to her, and now he wanted to take her to dinner! She stifled the urge to throw up her hands in bewilderment. He changed moods the way other men changed shirts. A puzzle wrapped up in a mystery; that was Grant. How fascinating it would have been to try to solve the puzzle. But even if there had been time, Victoria feared the finished picture might have been too appealing to resist.

"Please come with us,'' he said quietly. "There's really no pressing reason for you to leave this afternoon, is there?''

*Idiot!* Her inner voice taunted. *Don't do it. What can possibly be gained from spending another evening with this strange, disturbing man?*

Yet she didn't have anything to lose, either, did she? It was getting late, and she had already spent so much time in a car today. "Well, I...'' she faltered.

"Rita will enjoy it so much more if you're with

us. You wouldn't leave without saying goodbye to her, would you?"

His eyes, those dark brown pools that held such fascination for her, flickered over her slowly, but his expression was shuttered, guarded. Oh, if only she understood him better. If only she could fathom even the tiniest part of what he was thinking. It would have been easier to know what to do. A part of her was demanding that she go, while another more persistent part was urging her to stay. "Well, I—I guess I can leave in the morning just as well as tonight," she heard herself saying.

He visibly relaxed. A small smile played at the corners of his mouth. "That's great," he said, and sounded as though he meant it. This time when he laid a hand on her shoulder, his touch was gentle. "Now come with me, and I'll get those photos for you."

Sighing, Victoria followed him out of the office and down the hall to the photo lab. Maybe there were some people you just weren't supposed to understand. It was as good an explanation as any for the mysterious power he seemed to hold over her.

"THE PLACE WE'RE GOING TO," Grant said as Victoria and Rita climbed into the pickup, "is quite a drive from here."

Victoria laughed. "Everything in Reyes County is 'quite a drive' from everything else."

"I guess that's true. But people travel for miles to go to the Country Store, some from as far away as Fredericksburg. I usually see people I haven't seen in years.''

By accident rather than design, Victoria had climbed into the truck ahead of Rita, which meant she was sitting next to Grant. When Rita scooted in behind her and slammed the door, Victoria realized to her dismay that the quarters were close indeed. Her hip bumped against Grant's, and their thighs rubbed together. It was impossible for Victoria to move away from him, so she sat immobile, a knot of emotion forming inside her. She clasped her hands tightly in her lap, staring straight ahead.

Grant had warned her not to dress up or "you'll stick out like a sore thumb." She didn't have anything dressy with her, and since Maria had thoughtfully laundered her jeans, she had chosen to wear those with the soft cream-colored blouse she had been wearing when she arrived at Arroyo Grande. She liked the contrast between the blouse's soft fabric and the denim. She brought along a corduroy blazer, which she had tossed over the back of the seat. The clothes were simple but alluring, given Victoria's shapely figure to fill them out. Her peripheral vision caught Grant's gaze trained on her; she obviously had his full attention. Nervously he slid a forefinger over his mouth before collecting himself and starting the engine.

Their destination was a large roadside frame structure, ablaze with lights and surrounded by vehicles. It was indeed a converted country store.

The place was packed with people, the patrons ranging in age from babes in arms to senior citizens. Everyone appeared to be in the mood for a grand time.

The Country Store's homemade tamales were its main claim to fame, Grant told her, and Victoria consumed more of the delicious spicy bundles of cornmeal and shredded pork than she would have cared to admit, all washed down with ice-cold beer.

Background music was provided by five enthusiastic musicians who didn't look much beyond high-school age. Everyone danced—fathers with daughters, mothers with sons, brothers with sisters, grandparents with each other. Watching the merriment, Victoria reflected on how long it had been since she had enjoyed such pure, spontaneous fun. In retrospect, she could see that she and Steve had rarely done any socializing that hadn't been business oriented. The enormous dinners they had hosted so expertly and lavishly, the bridge parties, the golf and tennis matches at the country club—all had, in some form or fashion, been designed to further Steve's career.

Grant was more relaxed than she had ever seen him. He joked with her, teased Rita and engaged in some table-hopping in order to introduce Victoria to acquaintances, mostly older people he had known as a boy. He exuded a charisma impossible for others to ignore. She had seen brief glimpses of his charm before, but tonight it fairly oozed from him. The warm hand he kept at her waist as he led her from table to table suggested a certain intimacy, eliciting some quizzical looks from his acquaintances. His amiable manner, his proximity lulled Victoria into a state of well-being, and for a moment she dwelled on the possibility that they might continue to see each other occasionally, even though she had to go back to Corpus Christi.

That was ridiculous, and she knew it. If Grant had ever entertained any notion of coming to see her, he would have mentioned it by now.

Time passed swiftly. After the three of them had eaten all they could hold, had talked and gotten their fill of "people-watching," Rita left them to join some of her contemporaries at the video games and pinball machines. She didn't actually know any of the kids, but that didn't seem to matter at the Country Store. Victoria watched the lovely girl's progress across the crowded dance hall, then folded her arms on the table and looked at Grant. The smile he gave her was devastating.

"Having a good time?" he asked.

"Oh, yes. You are, too, I can tell. You look loose and. . .oh, unfettered."

"I don't get out and do this sort of thing much anymore." He reached across the table and took her by the hand. "Let's dance, Victoria," he said quietly.

"All right," she said just as quietly, but she followed him onto the dance floor and went into his arms in a haze of emotion.

The band was playing "Waltz Across Texas," an oldie Victoria had danced to hundreds of times.

Effortlessly they moved across the floor. Grant proved to be a smooth accomplished dancer, something she wouldn't have expected. It was so easy for her to forget his high-society background. For the life of her she couldn't imagine him in a ballroom, wearing a tuxedo, but she supposed it was something he had done many times.

The arm encircling her waist held her tightly, crushing her against him. Gradually Victoria relaxed, and their bodies melted together. The dance floor was crowded. Occasionally they were jostled a bit, but she was barely aware of the music or the other dancers, only of Grant. It was uncanny that something as simple as dancing with him could have such a profound effect on her. She rested her head on his shoulder so she could avoid looking into his eyes. The aroma that was so uniquely him attacked her senses. His hand pressed hers to his chest, and through the soft flannel of his shirt she could feel the drumming of his heart. Erratically thumping against her plam, it matched the beat of her own. Closing her eyes, she pressed her cheek against his shoulder and enjoyed a few brief moments of feeling absolutely alive and warm and feminine.

Her emotions confounded her. That Grant should be the first man since Steve to stir her was a contradiction. He was given to dark moods and sudden contrasts, stubborn prejudices and powerful urges—the antithesis of the kind of man she thought she liked. Yet in his arms she felt more like a woman than she ever had in her life.

Perhaps that was the source of her fascination with him. Steve had destroyed her confidence in herself as a desirable woman; Grant had unwittingly restored it.

The music ended. Their bodies stilled. The rustle of activity as the other dancers left the floor shook Victoria out of her reverie, and she numbly turned and made her way back to the table. Grant stayed close behind. When they reached their seats he placed both hands at her waist and turned her to face him.

"As hard as it is to believe, it's going on midnight," he said. "I'm sure Rita's almost dead on her feet, though she'd never admit it. If it's all right with you, I guess we'd better head on back home."

She reached for her handbag. "Yes, I guess so." Tomorrow it would all be over. Victoria experienced the most overwhelming sense of regret. Dear God, she was going to miss him. How had she let this happen to her?

Rita put forth only token protests to their departure, her drooping eyelids revealing that she was worn out. The pickup hadn't been traveling down the dark country road very long when the heavy head propped against her shoulder told Victoria the girl was sound asleep.

It was very cold outside. Now and then the truck's headlights would pick up patches of frost covering the low-lying areas by the side of the road. But the sky was clear black lacquer, a full moon shone and a million stars glittered. Inside the truck, the heater kept the cab so cozy and warm that neither Victoria nor Grant wore their jackets.

Soft music came from the car's radio; conversation would have been an intrusion. Victoria chanced a sidelong glance in Grant's direction. His face was implacable. The unlit pipe was clenched between his teeth, and the Stetson sat low over his forehead. Her eyes memorized his features. Images were stashed in her mind, to be recalled on demand. How long would it take her to forget him? Would she always equate rugged masculine good looks with his face?

It was safer to look at something else—his strong brown hands as they gripped the steering wheel, for instance. He flexed his fingers and gripped again, as though he was battling something within himself. The earlier relaxation was gone. Everything about him suggested the poised wariness of an animal sensing danger. What had happened? Surely it wasn't being so close to her that had him coiled as though ready to strike.

Victoria shifted in the seat, careful not to disturb the sleeping Rita. Something involuntary, something not rooted in thought prompted her to slide her left arm behind Grant's shoulders, to let her slender fingers begin a tentative massage of the tense, taut neck muscles she encountered. She heard his sharp intake of breath; then his body slumped forward slightly to give her better access. A slow loosening of muscle took place as her fingers began to work their magic.

"Ahh," he finally murmured. "That feels good."

"Left-handed, too. I can't do much with only one, but I give a mean massage when I can use both hands."

"Ahh," he repeated.

It was an oddly euphoric interlude. Absurdly, Victoria thought that she, Grant and Rita might have been any family on their way home after a Friday-night outing. She continued her soothing ministrations until the truck shuddered to a stop in front of the lodge.

Rita stirred and sat up. "Are we home?" she asked sleepily.

"Sure are, hon."

Fumbling for the door handle, the girl found it and pushed. Immediately the overhead light came on. Victoria blinked and removed her hand from Grant's neck. Rita stumbled out of the truck. "Y'all coming?" she inquired with a yawn.

"In a minute, hon. G'night."

"'Night, daddy. 'Night, Victoria." The door slammed shut, and the cab was plunged into darkness. Victoria's breath caught sharply in her throat. She knew she should follow Rita into that house... but it was the last thing she wanted to do.

A strong steady hand on her shoulder propelled her around, and she was looking into Grant's eyes. "Now," he said huskily. "You were telling me what you can do with both hands...." He dipped his head, bracing his forehead on her shoulder. "You may continue."

Automatically Victoria complied. Kneading and squeezing, she worked with his tense muscles. He uttered a sound that strangely resembled a cat's purring. Grant's hands splayed across her back to hold her loosely against him.

At some point the massaging stopped and the caressing began. Her fingertips seemed to have a mind of their own. Gradually her hands moved to his shoulders and slipped inside the collar of his shirt. There his skin was cool and smooth and pulled taut across rippling muscles. Abandoning all pretense of performing therapy, Victoria gave in to her need to feel the satisfying warmth of that skin under her palms.

Grant lifted his head, sat back, and his eyes were narrow slits of dark passion. Victoria's hands strayed to the smooth brown skin at the base of his throat. She touched the throbbing pulse point, moving lower. Impeded by his shirt, she deftly undid three buttons and shoved the fabric aside. At last her hands could wander unhindered across the broad expanse of his chest. Her fingers curled into the coarse mat of dark hair, teased at his flat nipples. Roaming restlessly, they explored every inch of him from throat to waist, followed the tapering line of hair to the point where it disappeared into his jeans. Astonished at her own aggressiveness, she nevertheless was absorbed by her need to feel him.

Grant thought he was strangling. He sat paralyzed, unable to move, unable to breathe. He tried to say something, anything, but not even her name would escape his throat. His eyes grew fever-bright, and his chest heaved uncontrollably.

Finally he couldn't stand it anymore. He reached for her, cradling her head in one hand, pulling her toward him. Holding her immobile, he rained dozens of kisses over her face—her mouth, her cheeks, her ears, her closed eyelids. Still it wasn't enough to assuage the terrible ache growing in him. He captured her mouth again and again, and still it wasn't enough. Her hands inside his shirt tantalized him. Her head was tilted back, eyes closed, kiss-moistened lips parted. Mindless with the wonder of her, he fumbled for the buttons of her blouse. He needed to fill his hands with her once more.

One by one the buttons gave way, as did the front closure of the filmy bra she was wearing. Eagerly he cupped her breasts, lifting them, pressing them against his chest. Gently he pushed her head back to rest on the seat, and he bent his head. Taking one roseate point between his lips, he sucked hungrily. His hand slipped down to her hips, then moved to rest between her thighs, and he was rewarded by the sudden arching of her body.

"Grant." Victoria moaned his name on a shuddering sigh. His quick hot breath seared her tender flesh like tongues of fire, and a hard knot of need formed in her loins. She ached for the emotional release he promised, a deliverance from the emptiness and loneliness of the past year. She wanted to take this man's body, to give him pleasure, to know she was still capable. In Grant's arms she could find peace, if only for a night, an hour.

It was then that the transience of their relationship struck her, like a dash of ice water in her face. She was leaving in the morning! What was she doing? Hadn't living with nothing but memories for a year taught her anything? If Grant made love to her he would brand his image on her mind, and then what would she have? Another memory to torture her during cold sleepless nights?

No, a one-night affair was not the answer to loneliness. She cared for Grant, perhaps more than she wanted to admit. She wouldn't use him as a sexual catharsis...nor would she let him use her.

Grant felt her body tense in his arms. At a loss to understand the sudden shift from warm pliancy to rigidity, he raised his head to look at her. Those fantastic green eyes of hers, closed in passion only a moment ago, were wide and filled with desperation. What had happened? "Victoria? Victoria?"

She raised one hand to shield her eyes from his penetrating gaze, shaking her head. "Oh, Grant." Her voice was small and quiet and full of regret. "Oh, Grant, no. This isn't the answer, for either of us."

He couldn't believe it! The need to make love to her was suffocating him, yet he had lost his chance. He didn't know how or why, but he had lost it. "God in heaven, Victoria! What are you trying to do to me?"

She placed her hands between their bodies and

fumbled with the front of her blouse. "I'm sorry, but...." The stunned expression on his face unnerved her. "Casual sex is not what... either of us needs."

Casual sex? Was that all it was to her? Grant sobered instantly. Of course it was. The lady was still in love with her ex-husband. He had almost forgotten that. Heavy with arousal, he had deluded himself into thinking he had become special to her. He even, he now realized to his horror, had begun mentally rearranging his life to make room for her.

Damned fool! Caring, loving made him feel vulnerable, and that was the feeling he despised above all others. Jerking away from her, he buttoned his shirt. Damned fool.

"Is this the way you get your kicks, lady? From now on you'd best be careful, Victoria. Didn't your mother ever warn you about what happens to little girls who try to play grown-up games?" His voice shook with contempt.

Miserable, she wanted to lash out at him; at the same time she longed to reach for him. She wanted to try to explain, but what could she say that wouldn't make things worse? Actually, she couldn't blame him for his contempt. Twice she had come on strong to him, only to call a halt. She felt physically ill.

So this was the way he would remember her, if he remembered her at all.

Oh, what difference did it make? She would never see him again.

He opened his door. "We'd best be getting in," he said stiffly. "You have a long drive tomorrow."

THE FOLLOWING MORNING, after having slept a miserable total of two hours, Victoria dressed and packed hurriedly. She left a short note, along with her address and telephone number, for Rita, who was sleeping late on Saturday morning. Then Victoria ventured into the main part of the lodge. Grant was nowhere to be seen.

Just as well, Victoria thought. She hated goodbyes, and she didn't think she could have endured seeing Grant again. She simply thanked Maria and Mrs. Guilford for their many kindnesses and tossed her things into the back seat of the government car. She had put the key in the ignition when a strong hand shot through the open window and covered the one on the steering wheel. Grant bent to come to eye level with her.

"Were you going to leave without saying goodbye?"

"Well, I assumed you were busy. I asked Mrs. Guilford to convey my...appreciation."

"I'm not that busy, and 'appreciation' isn't what I want from you, Victoria."

His face filled her vision. She couldn't see beyond his eyes, his nose, the shape of his mouth. Quickly she looked away to stare through the windshield. "Grant, there's something I'd like to say to you. You might think me presumptuous."

He sucked in his breath. "I give you permission

to be presumptuous. What is it?'' His voice throbbed with an expectant timbre.

She turned earnest eyes on him. "Grant, Rita is such a talented girl, and there's nothing inherently immoral about creativity. Please don't stifle hers.''

Apparently that was the last thing he expected or wanted to hear. He stared at her for what seemed forever but could only have been a second or two. He straightened and shoved himself away from the car.

"Goodbye, Victoria."

"Goodbye, Grant." Victoria was appalled at the tears welling. Turning the key in the ignition, she waited for the engine's purr, then tromped on the accelerator and sped away from Arroyo Grande as fast as she could.

## CHAPTER TEN

"YOU DID EVERYTHING you possibly could, Victoria." Chuck Singleton's head was bent over the reports she had submitted. "You handled the whole thing very professionally. I'm proud of you."

"Thank you, Chuck." At the moment Victoria didn't feel very professional. She should have been experiencing elation over her supervisor's marked change of attitude toward her instead of this fog of depression and lethargy. It had followed her around ever since she had returned home Saturday afternoon. Sunday alone in her solitary rooms had passed on leaden feet. Returning to work had been a blessing. "I'm just sorry there were no more positive results."

Chuck shrugged his unconcern. "That's the way these things go more often than not. Like you, I'd be willing to bet my next paycheck that Rumbaugh is paying those chopper pilots to kill eagles. I've met too many Rumbaughs in my day. Most ranchers hate the birds and half the time they don't even know why. And I'm sure the helicopter company knows about it. But we can't prove it, so we drop it and go on to something else. I will, however, sug-

gest to the proper authorities that Dawson's procedures be investigated." He shoved the report
aside and looked at her. "Tell me, what did you
think of Grant?"

Victoria straightened at the sound of the name.
"Wh-who?" she asked stupidly.

"Grant," Chuck repeated with a grin. "Mackenzie. You know, the fellow you were staying
with."

"Oh...well, he's...." How to describe him?
Dynamic, charming, attractive? Brooding, scowling, angry? All those things and more. She
thought of him too often—all the time, in fact. It
was a shock to realize she was feeling some of
what she had felt when Steve left, with far less
good reason. "He's interesting," she finished
lamely.

"Yeah." He chuckled. "We sure had us some
wild times back in college when we both were
young and crazy and didn't give a damn about
anything but right now. I always liked running
around with Grant, 'cause he had looks and
money and drew girls the way honey draws flies."

"It's difficult to picture Grant as young and
crazy," she said truthfully.

"Is it? Well, you could probably say the same
about me, right?"

She laughed lightly and shrugged.

"Time changes all of us," Chuck said. "Mostly
for the good, I hope. Just thinking about those
college days exhausts me now, but we sure had us
some fun!"

Victoria studied her fingernails. She supposed Chuck could tell her plenty about Grant, and how she would have loved to ask questions. She wouldn't, not for the world, but there was one she simply couldn't hold in check.

"Did . . . did you know his wife?"

"Huh? Oh, Grant's wife? Know her, no, but I met her once. She might have been the prettiest woman I've ever seen, and I think Grant's daughter is going to look just like her. Sure surprised me that they split up. Guess she must have been the one who wanted out, 'cause Grant was so nutty about her it was painful to watch."

*I had to ask.*

"Listen, Victoria, while I have you here. . . . You know you're overdue for annual leave."

"Yes, I know. I just haven't gotten around to taking it yet."

"Well, if it's all right with you I wish you would take it now. Everyone else is scheduled for spring and early summer. Would this week and next be agreeable with you?"

Lord, what would she do with two weeks off? That was the reason she hadn't signed up for leave; she liked waking up in the morning and having something she had to do. Most people would have given anything for two weeks on the gulf in the winter, but Victoria couldn't think of anything less appealing than long lazy days. Which spoke volumes for the sad state of her personal life. What she really wanted was for Chuck to send her out on another assignment.

"Sure, boss," she said simply. "That suits me fine."

THE FIRST DAY of Victoria's vacation passed in an orgy of housecleaning. The elegant champagne-and-burgundy townhouse she and Steve had called home for five years didn't need the attention—by habit she kept it immaculate—but the physical activity was an effective way of dispelling mental turmoil.

She went shopping the second day, attacking the chore with the same fervor she had the housework. She bought two expensive dresses she didn't need, but they gave her spirits a momentary lift. She returned home to eat a solitary supper in front of the television set and to read herself to sleep.

By Wednesday she was already bored and restless, so she spent the day at her mother's Ocean Drive mansion, where to her astonishment she found herself telling Rachel all about Grant. All about him.

"This far, mom," she admitted, pinching her fingertips together. "I honestly think I was this far from making love."

Rachel sighed and patted her perfect coiffure. A strikingly attractive woman, she looked much younger than forty-nine. She glanced at her daughter with fondness and empathy. The two women were unusually close, bound not only by blood ties but by shared pain. "Forgive me if I sound like something straight out of the fifties, dear, but it's probably a good thing it didn't happen. And I'm not talking about rules or anything like that; does anyone care about those anymore? No, I'm thinking of you, of the attack of conscience afterward, the lingering effects. A man you aren't likely to see again.... It just wouldn't have been good for you, Victoria. Sexual liberation is a lot of applesauce! How can a man and woman be equal in that sense when they don't think alike? A man can enjoy a woman like a good meal and then forget her. Women, *most* women, get emotionally involved. In my wildest dreams I cannot imagine going to bed with someone, then waving goodbye and never giving him another thought.''

Victoria agreed. As difficult as it was for her to put Grant out of her thoughts now, what would she have felt like if they had made love?

''Mom, has there been anyone since dad?''

''One,'' Rachel said without hesitation. ''Do you remember Dan Graham?''

''Of course. But I had no idea there was anything serious between you two.''

''Oh, it was quite serious for a time, I assure you.''

''But...what happened, if I'm not being too nosy?''

''Oh, I don't know. Something was missing, and I still don't know what it was. After twenty years of marriage to your father I was pretty set in my ways. I wanted exactly what I had had with him, which was ridiculous, but there it was. A woman has to do a lot of adapting to a man, and I guess I just didn't want to put forth all that effort again. It's easier when you're young. You won't have such a hard time of it.''

"Oh, mom, I don't really think there'll be another time for me.''

"Nonsense. Of course there will. This man, the one you met last week—you admitted he lit a spark. If he can, someone else can, too.''

Victoria leaned forward and spoke earnestly. "How did you do it, mom. . . get over the divorce so fast? It's always amazed me. You're even nice to what's-her-name.''

A smile tugged at the corners of Rachel's mouth. "Her name is Martina, and you know it. She's not a bad sort really. Short in the brains department, and there's your father with all those degrees, but. . . .'' She lifted her shoulders. "I didn't get over the divorce as easily as it seemed. I pretended for your sake, since you took it so hard. Oh, I was bitter! Forty years old and cast aside for a pretty young thing. I was bitter, all right, and it was eating me alive.''

"You're an amazingly good actress. I never dreamed. But you aren't bitter now, so. . . what happened?''

"I went to a friend of mine, a marriage counselor, and she snapped me out of my misery fast. You see, Victoria, I was wallowing in self-recrimination, wondering what I had done to make your father leave. I felt guilty, and my friend examined the situation with me. Though Adam and I had both done things wrong in the marriage, he was the one who had given up on the relationship—I couldn't be responsible for his leaving. Once I accepted that, I was able to cope."

Victoria sighed. It seemed to her the woman was always the loser in affairs of the heart. "It doesn't seem fair, does it? I mean, dad and Steve were the adulterers, yet they emerged unscathed. Quite content and happy, in fact. You and I were the ones who got burned."

"If you dwell on that you'll drive yourself crazy, dear." A note of confidentiality crept into Rachel's voice. "Victoria, tell me...when you think of Steve these days, what do you mostly think?"

Her mother was one person Victoria could be completely honest with. "I guess I mostly wonder if he's ever been sorry. If he ever wishes he hadn't divorced me."

Rachel smiled knowingly. "Mmm. But not wonder so much as...hope. You hope he's been sorry."

Laughter swelled in Victoria's throat. "Yes."

"Maybe miserable?" Rachel prodded impishly.

"Yes!"

"You like to picture him pacing the floor, trying to think of a way to crawl back."

"So I can throw him out!" Victoria cried.

"I know, I know. Oh, Victoria, let's have a drink!"

"Let's!" Victoria was overtaken by a fit of giggles, and she and Rachel spent a wonderful, if slightly tipsy, evening. The mild hangover she suffered the following morning was a small price to pay for the inner loosening she felt, and she thought maybe, just maybe, this would be the first step in her long climb out of the doldrums. And if she could get over Steve, she could damn well get over Grant Mackenzie.

THE TELEPHONE WAS RINGING insistently when Victoria returned from her trip to the supermarket. Quickly setting her sack of groceries down, she hurried to answer it. She couldn't have been more startled to hear the girlish voice on the other end of the line.

"Hi, Victoria."

"Rita!"

"I really don't have anything important to say. I just thought I'd call and see what you're doing."

"Oh, it's so good to hear from you, Rita! I'm not doing much of anything. I came back only to have my boss order me to take my vacation, so I'm just goofing off and being lazy. How are you?"

"Okay, I guess. I . . . miss you."

"Rita, how sweet. . . . I miss you, too." Victoria was dying to ask if Grant knew and approved of the call, but she wouldn't have inquired for the world. She hoped Rita would say something, anything, about her father. The girl didn't mention him at all. They merely chatted idly for a few minutes until Rita said, "Well, I guess I'd better hang up. It was probably dumb to call, but I was thinking about you. . . ."

"Rita, it wasn't dumb at all. Please...I wish you would call me anytime you feel the urge, provided your father approves, of course."

"Aw, he won't care."

Rita's frankness gave Victoria a momentary jolt, which she dismissed. Indeed, Grant could probably not care less now whether she and Rita kept in touch.

"You stay after him about coming to Corpus Christi this summer."

"I'll do that. I'd like to come to see you. Bye, Victoria."

"Goodbye, Rita. Thanks for calling."

But the telephone call had unpleasant side effects. Despite Victoria's resolve to the contrary, thoughts of Grant plagued her the rest of the evening and long after she had gone to bed. Hovering between dreams and fantasies, she thought of his hands on her, of his mouth devouring hers. She shifted restlessly beneath the covers and felt his compelling eyes locked to hers. A soft groan escaped her lips.

She supposed it was only natural that the first man to pierce her shell wouldn't be so easily dismissed, but dear God, was she never to know any inner peace?

Next time, if there was a next time, she would be smarter. Next time she would fall for an uncomplicated man whose only emotional problem was that he was insane about her!

FRIDAY AFTERNOON Victoria sprawled lazily on the low-slung champagne-colored sofa that dominated her living room. She was lost in a seven-hundred

page saga of tumultuous love spanning generations. A cheerful fire crackled in the fireplace,
though the coast's winter temperatures hardly demanded a fire. In the kitchen a pot of homemade
vegetable soup simmered and sent out an irresistible aroma. Victoria was beginning to come to
grips with her solitude, even to enjoy it, and what
better way to spend a solitary evening than with a
good book, a companionable fire and something
delicious to eat?

She turned the page. The heroine's monumental
emotional problems made her own pale by comparison. So engrossed was she that the doorbell's
first soft chimes barely registered with her. When
they sounded again, she sighed, grimaced and
fleetingly considered ignoring the summons. Who
could it be but Mrs. Gregory from next door, and
although her neighbor was a lovely woman, Victoria wasn't in the mood for her incessant chatter,
not this evening.

The bell rang again. Resigned, she marked her
place and set the book on the coffee table. With
luck Mrs. Gregory would only be wanting to borrow something.

Victoria's eyes widened and her mouth dropped
in astonishment when she saw the figure standing
on the front stoop. "Rita!" she cried.

"Hi." Grant's daughter stood before her,
dressed in jeans and a plaid shirt. Her quilted jacket
was thrown over one arm; under the other was a
stack of schoolbooks. She grinned sheepishly at
Victoria. "It's lots warmer here than it is at home."

"Rita, what on earth are you doing here?"

"I, ah. . . . Can I come in, Victoria?"

"Oh. Of course." Collecting her wits, Victoria quickly stepped back. "Rita, how did you get here?" Would Grant have brought her? How else could she have come to be in Corpus Christi? Victoria's heart tripped wildly.

"This morning when the school bus stopped in Kierney, I saw some people getting on a bus across the street. It had Corpus Christi above the windshield, and I remembered you were on vacation and not doing anything, so. . . . Daddy had just given me my allowance. I'm supposed to buy next week's lunch tickets with part of it, so there was plenty. Anyway, I got off the school bus and bought a ticket." She lowered her eyes. "Sure am glad you're home. I was halfway here before I thought about that." She lifted her eyes. "Are you mad at me?"

Victoria closed the door and stepped forward to give Rita a hug. "Oh, honey, of course I'm not mad at you, but dear God, what if I hadn't been here? Why didn't you call me? How did you get from the bus station?"

"I took a cab. It cost almost as much as the bus ticket." She shifted her books under her arm. "I had to bring these dumb things with me 'cause I didn't know what else to do with them."

Something occurred to Victoria; she took Rita by the shoulders. "Rita, your father. He doesn't know you're here?"

Rita shook her head vigorously. "He'll be expecting me in from school pretty soon."

"Oh, Rita!" Adultlike, she could think of all the horrible ramifications. "What if the bus had broken down? What if I hadn't been here? What if your father had called the school for some reason and discovered you weren't in class?"

Chagrined, the girl could only shrug. "I...I just wanted to see you."

"Oh, Rita." The impulsive thoughtlessness of youth. So unmindful of anything but the moment. Victoria wanted to spank her...but she wanted to kiss her, too. The child tugged at her heartstrings as no one ever had.

"I guess...I didn't think."

"No, you didn't," Victoria agreed, "but no sense worrying about things that, thankfully, didn't happen. I— Oh, Lord, Rita, we've got to call your father this minute! If that school bus reaches Arroyo Grande and you aren't on it...!"

Rita groaned. "He's going to be furious."

"Something you should have thought of before the fact, young lady!" She raced for the phone. "What's the number?"

While Victoria dialed, Rita set her books down on the nearest flat surface, then crossed the living room, her wide eyes taking in every detail of the elegant townhouse. She went to stand beside Victoria, who put a reassuring hand on her shoulder while she waited for the call to be answered.

The phone rang three times before Mrs. Guilford said, "Arroyo Grande Lodge."

"Mrs. Guilford, this is Victoria Bartlett. May I speak to Grant, please?"

"Oh, hello, Victoria. Of course. Wait a minute while I fetch him."

Victoria's stomach did several sickening somersaults as she waited. Her mouth was dry with dread. Just what she was dreading she wasn't sure. An eternity later she heard the familiar baritone.

"Victoria?" He sounded as if he couldn't believe who was on the other end of the line.

"Grant, I . . . seem to have an unexpected caller." Tersely she told him about Rita's impromptu visit. The silence that followed was deafening.

Finally he exploded. "Victoria, goddammit, what kind of ideas did you feed the kid?"

For a moment Victoria thought everything in her head had shattered into a million pieces. She clenched her teeth, and her chest heaved while she fought for control. "Now just a minute! It was a foolish thing for her to do, admittedly, but I had nothing to do with it! I called you so you wouldn't worry. She's here safe and sound, and I'll look after her until we can get her home."

"What do you mean you'll look after her? How can you watch her? You have to work—"

"I'm on vacation! I assure you, I'll look after her!"

"Let me talk to Rita!" he barked.

Victoria's hand trembled as she held the receiver to the girl. "Your father wants to talk to you."

A fearful look came to Rita's eyes. Swallowing hard, she took the phone and lifted it to her ear. "Hello, daddy. . . . Yes, I know, but I just wanted to see Victoria. I—'' There was a long pause. ''I know. I'm sorry....''

Victoria put her hands to her pounding temples. Dreadful man! She might have known. Not ''Thanks for being concerned. Thanks for taking care of my daughter.'' Just an explosion. Horrible man! Why had the mere sound of his voice aroused all those fluttery sensations? She must have latent masochistic tendencies, she decided, to give this mercurial man a second thought.

Rita's voice had taken on a wavery quality. ''No, I spent it all getting here. Okay, daddy. Yes...okay. I understand.'' She turned to Victoria with misting eyes and held out the receiver. ''He wants to talk to you again.''

Victoria's mouth set in a determined line. ''Yes,'' she said coolly into the receiver.

''She's broke,'' he growled. ''Will you lend her the money for a return ticket?''

''Of course I will,'' she spit out. ''But I don't like the idea of her riding all over the countryside on a bus.''

''I don't, either, but I didn't have anything to do with her being down there!''

''Neither did I!''

''The hell you didn't! Planned or unplanned, you're the reason she's down there. Now I've got to get her back here.''

''I'll bring her home!'' Victoria hadn't intended to say that, but once it was out, she realized she would prefer taking Rita home to putting her on a bus, even though it would doubtless mean an unpleasant confrontation with Grant.

"No!" he roared.

"No?" Was he so opposed to seeing her again that he would prefer having his fourteen-year-old daughter make the long return journey alone?

"No," he repeated more quietly. "I'll...come down there and get her—tomorrow."

"Tomorrow?" Victoria felt weak. Grant was coming here? "Well, I—"

"In the meantime, what are you going to do with her?"

"Well, we'll have supper, then watch television, and tomorrow perhaps I'll take her to meet my mother. The three of us might go shopping. Does that meet with your approval?"

"I don't suppose it matters whether it does or not. I don't seem to be in control of the situation right now."

His tone was insufferable; red fury washed over Victoria. "Will you hold on just a minute?" she asked icily, and without waiting for his reply, lowered the receiver and covered it with her hand. "Rita, the kitchen is right through that door. Would you be a dear and get me a glass of water? The glasses are in the cupboard to the left of the sink, and there's an ice dispenser in the refrigerator door."

Rita grinned, obviously feeling better now that Victoria was in command. "You want me out of here, right? Okay, I'll get you a drink."

When the girl was out of earshot, Victoria raised the phone. "Listen to me, Grant, and kindly control that acid tongue of yours! I don't in the least approve of what Rita did, but I think I understand why she did it. She telephoned me last night, did you know that?''

"No. . . no, I didn't.''

"She said. . . she missed me. But what she really missed was feminine influence.''

"She has Mrs. Guilford and Maria.''

"That's not the same. Don't be so hard on her.''

In his office, Grant swiveled in his desk chair and stared blankly across his office. His thoughts were whirling; he held the receiver in a viselike grip. Why did he invariably put his worst foot forward where Victoria was concerned? He was playing the worried-parent role to the hilt, but most of it was an act. Oh, he was furious at Rita for doing such a foolhardy thing, and he had told her precisely that when he had her on the phone. However, his thoughts weren't so much on his daughter's antics as on the results. He would see Victoria again; the thought pounded in his brain.

For a week now he had tried hard to get her out of his mind. He hadn't succeeded. He was plagued by longing. Thoughts of her sprang up at the oddest times, sometimes embarrassingly. When it had become obvious that she wasn't going to slip quietly and conveniently into the dim mists of memory, he had found himself inventing reasons to see her again. None were legitimate, most were foolish. Now Rita had handed him a perfectly plausible one.

Not wanting to care counted for nothing, he had discovered. He did care, and he wanted to see her again, this time on her home turf. Maybe then he could sort out and analyze this peculiar fascination she held for him, and find a means to eradicate it.

He cleared his throat. "Victoria, I . . . . I'm sure Rita is in good hands."

She expelled a taut breath. "Well, thank you," she said with exaggerated sweetness.

"I'll be there tomorrow, probably about sundown. Give me some directions."

For a long moment after hanging up, Victoria held the receiver, staring into space. An odd mixture of trepidation and excitement swirled through her. She hadn't expected to see him again, wasn't prepared for it. If he came only for Rita and left immediately— No, no, it was a long drive. He would have to stay in Corpus Christi one night at least, so should she plan to have dinner? With Rita here, they wouldn't have any time alone. That was a plus. . . or was it?

*Oh, Victoria, confess. You're aching to see him.*

"Here's your water, Victoria." Rita nudged her elbow, snapping her out of her daydreaming.

"Huh? Oh, thanks, honey."

Rita set the glass on the table. "I didn't figure you really wanted it. What did daddy say?"

"He's coming to get you tomorrow."

"Tomorrow?" Rita cried in dismay. "I was hoping he'd let me stay awhile."

"Well, he won't be here until tomorrow night,

so we can spend the day together. And tonight. If I had known I was going to have company for dinner, I would have made something more exciting than vegetable soup.''

"I don't care what we have to eat." Rita's eyes shone with excitement. "Oh, Victoria, your house is so neat! I've never seen anything so pretty."

She must have, Victoria thought, if she had lived in a River Oaks mansion. She had just forgotten, and that was all to the good. "Why, thank you, Rita."

"I can't believe I'm actually here." Rita hung her head, and when she again looked at Victoria it was with a somewhat sober expression. "You know, I got on that bus on purpose."

Victoria smiled. "Of course you did, honey. No one gets off one bus and onto another by accident."

"No, I mean...I've kinda been planning to come to see you some way or another. Then when I talked to you yesterday and found out you were on vacation.... And then I saw that bus this morning...well, it seemed sorta like an omen or something. And I figured you would either have to take me home or daddy would have to come get me."

Victoria's look was wary. "Rita, you didn't!"

"Victoria, I know daddy likes you. He's been a bear all week, and sometimes I've caught him just staring into space, like he's a million miles away. It has to be because you left."

Victoria's pulse began to race. Could Grant

have been thinking about her? It didn't seem likely. "Rita, you're reading something into my relationship with your father that simply doesn't exist."

"Maybe. Maybe not."

"Scamp! Come on, let's see how the soup's doing."

Rita was grinning from ear to ear, and for a moment Victoria thought the girl looked surprisingly like her father. She remembered those even white teeth of his and the way one corner of his mouth lifted higher than the other when he grinned just that way. In fact, every single aspect of his features came into focus.

Oh, Lord, seeing him again was going to be devastating!

## CHAPTER ELEVEN

"SHE'S SUCH A LOVELY GIRL, VICTORIA," Rachel said, watching Rita's retreating figure.

"Isn't she, though."

"Those clothes you bought her look wonderful on her."

The three of them were having a late lunch at a waterfront café after a morning of shopping, and Rita had just excused herself to go to the rest room. "I hope her father doesn't throw a tantrum over them," Victoria said worriedly.

Rachel folded her hands on the table, regarding her daughter with interest. "So you'll be seeing him again tonight. How do you feel about it?"

Victoria didn't even try to pretend indifference. Her mother could read her too well. "Nervous," she admitted. "I told you how changeable he is, and he's completely uptight about anything concerning Rita."

"Men don't have any business raising children," Rachel said, another of her sweeping statements. "At least not exclusively. Emotionally they're totally unsuited to the task. Too inflexible."

Victoria smiled. "Inflexible? That's a pretty

good word for Grant. But I've seen another side of him, too—warm and vulnerable, though he fights it. Oh, how he fights it!''

"Why do I have the feeling you're as skittish as a girl getting ready for her first date?" Rachel asked with a knowing smile.

"Because I am. Isn't that absurd? He blames me for this folly of Rita's, so we'll probably do nothing but snarl at each other. He sounded anything but warm and vulnerable on the telephone last night."

"Well, he's struck some kind of responsive chord in you, that's for sure."

"Oh, mom, he baffles me more than anything. I guess that's it. I've never known a man like him."

"Victoria, you've never known anyone but Steve. Something about that didn't sit right with me, that you should marry the only man you'd ever dated. And since the divorce you've been as faithful to him as if you were still married, which isn't right. It's mid-Victorian, in fact. How could I have known when I named you that it would fit so aptly? This man, Rita's father, has made an impression on you, and I consider that a step in the right direction, which I've said before. I'm thinking. . . ." Rachel's voice trailed off.

"I can see those wheels turning in your head, mom. *What* are you thinking?"

At that moment Rita returned to the table and slipped into her chair. She did look so lovely, Victoria thought. The jade-green jumpsuit with its paisley sash hugged her youthful body in all the right places, and the color was a perfect foil for her delicate beauty. The instant Rita put on the garment, Victoria had noticed a transformation in the girl. She held her head more regally, moved more gracefully. She had seemed almost thunderstruck by her own reflection in the dressing-room mirror.

Pray Grant wouldn't blow a fuse over their shopping spree. Victoria hadn't been able to resist buying Rita not only the jumpsuit, but also a skirt and matching sweater, some new shoes, and because Rita had been forced to wear one of Victoria's shortie nightgowns the night before, a ruffly feminine gown. The entire episode had been as much fun for Victoria and Rachel as it had for Rita. It would have been more fun if it hadn't been for Victoria's nagging worry that Grant wouldn't approve. She could only hope the sight of his lovely daughter would melt his resistance.

Rachel had picked up the check and now handed it, along with a twenty-dollar bill, to Rita. "Rita, dear, will you go to the cashier and pay our check for us?"

Rita jumped to her feet. "Sure," she said, scampering away. Rachel leaned forward and spoke conspiratorially.

"What I'm thinking is that I've changed my mind about you and Grant.... Victoria, I'm going to ask Rita to have dinner with me, then to spend the night."

"Oh, mom, don't you dare! I know what you're up to!"

Rachel feigned innocence. "Why, what on earth do you mean? I simply want the child to stay with me, and I'm sure she'll be delighted to. I adore young girls—haven't been around one in the longest time."

"Garbage, mom. It's not a good idea for Grant and me to...to be alone."

"Oh, how ridiculous. I think it's a superb idea. What are you afraid of, losing your virginity? Is the man given to ravishment...I hope."

"Mom!" Victoria hissed. "This is a wanton side of you I haven't seen before. If Grant shows up at my place to get Rita, and I tell him she's spending the night at your house, he might think—well, he might think I arranged a cozy little tête-à-tête, and—"

Rachel's brows arched. "So? He should be flattered."

"I don't want to become involved with anyone, mom. I failed so miserably before. I never, ever want to go through that again."

Rachel looked at her in the manner of a parent dealing with an impossibly dense child. "Dear, I'm not talking about marriage or even deep and abiding love. But some kind of relationship that means something to you would be the best medicine in the world." Rachel's eyes sparkled merrily. "You could at least give it a try."

Victoria bit her bottom lip and absently drew a circle on the table with a spoon. "I'm not too sure there isn't something wrong with me. I seem to only be able to go so far, and then...then I freeze."

"Rubbish! Frigid, you mean? Given the right man, no woman is truly frigid."

"Mom—" Victoria sighed in exasperation "— that is another one of your ridiculous generalizations, and you know it."

"Nevertheless," Rachel replied, unperturbed, "tonight you should have cocktails waiting, soft music on the stereo and be wearing something delightfully sexy. Be receptive, Victoria, then sit back and let him do all the work."

"Mom, the man will think I'm trying to seduce him!"

"More rubbish! If you play your part well, he won't be able to think."

"I absolutely refuse—"

"Don't argue with me, Victoria. I'm your mother and I know what's best for you. Ah, Rita dear, there you are! Shall we go now? I have the most wonderful idea for tonight. . . ."

FOR THE DOZENTH TIME Victoria told herself, *I am not nervous. For heaven's sake, there's nothing to be nervous about!*

She twisted her hair high on top of her head and pinned it carelessly; some wayward tendrils escaped. She stepped back and surveyed her reflection in the mirror. It was Rachel who had suggested the clothes she wore: glittery black tunic with ruffles at the wrists and a deep V neckline, tight black velvet slacks and spiky black sandals. An outlandish, spectacular "at home" outfit that belonged to the socialite Victoria of a few years ago. In it she projected an alluring image, a far cry from the understated elegance that was her trademark now. Gold nuggets shone from her earlobes, and a russet blush highlighted her magnificent cheekbones. She had used a slightly heavier hand with the eye makeup, too. The entire effect was dramatic.

*What am I trying to do?* She didn't feel sexy; she felt foolish. Grant, no doubt, would show up in his jeans and scuffed boots, wanting to collect his daughter quickly and be gone. There was no good reason to think he would want to stay. He probably wouldn't even notice what she was wearing. Why had she listened to her mother?

Because once Rachel got something into her head she was impossible to ignore, that's why.

Muted voices from the living room reached her. Rita was so excited about the prospect of spending the night with Rachel, and Rachel was captivated by the striking young girl. Her mother had wanted to take Rita home with her immediately, but Victoria had been adamant—they would stay until Grant arrived, then Rachel would ask for his permission. There was no way on earth Victoria was going to greet him alone, dressed this way. It would look too suggestive.

She gave her reflection one last inspection, turned off the bedroom light and went into the living room. Rita was stretched out on the sofa, thumbing through the latest issue of *Bazaar*.

Rachel was seated at the dining table, doing her nails. Both glanced up when Victoria came in.

"Wow, Victoria!" Rita gasped. "You look great! Better than anything I've seen in here." She indicated the magazine.

"Very nice, dear, very nice. Yes, I knew it would be perfect," was Rachel's verdict.

"Well, thank you both. I...guess I'll go see how the pot roast is coming."

"Pot roast, indeed!" Rachel scoffed. "I would have thought you could come up with something more imaginative."

"Oh, mom, honestly...." Victoria hurried into the kitchen and turned on the light. She had no idea if Grant would want to stay for dinner—probably not—but it had seemed sensible to have something to offer in case. She crossed the kitchen and lifted the pot lid. Her stomach fluttered nervously; her gaze kept wandering to the wall clock. When the doorbell rang she jumped. Pivoting, she left the kitchen.

Rita had gotten to her feet. "Will you get it, Victoria?" she asked apprehensively.

"Of course." Victoria's heart was in her throat as she hurried across the living room. When she threw open the door, a dazed feeling swamped her.

Grant lounged in the doorway. The scruffy garb she associated with him had been replaced by dark brown slacks, a camel blazer and a coordinating check shirt open at the throat. The slacks fit him so flawlessly they might have been tailor-made.

He looked urbane, sophisticated, so unlike the Grant she remembered in the dreams that haunted her. For a moment she was almost disappointed. Then her eyes locked with his, and a breathtaking feeling rushed over her, just as it had the first time she'd seen him. In all the world there was only one pair of eyes that could so hypnotize her. Her body, her senses were reawakened. A week had dispelled none of the mystique surrounding him. He was beautiful!

She struggled for composure, aware that Rachel and Rita were witnessing this exchange. "Hello." Dismayingly, her voice was hardly more than a whisper.

"Good evening, Victoria."

Grant had vowed he wouldn't let the sight of Victoria destroy his equilibrium, but it had been a useless vow. It would be easier to eradicate the moon in the sky than his desire for her. Even with all his barricades up, this woman had invaded his life. Good God, what was she wearing? He had never seen Victoria like this, with that fantastic hair tumbling all over her head, half up, half down. He had thought of that hair too often, re-membered the way it felt in his hands.

His gaze traveled downward. How had she managed to get into those pants? She looked so damned sexy! A sexy socialite, not the Victoria who haunted his dreams. Then he returned his at-tention to her face, to that silken skin, those soft lips, the green eyes he could fall into, and he knew it was the same Victoria. All the muscles in his body tightened. How could a woman make him grow taut with desire just by looking at him?

She stepped back. "Please. . . come in."

He entered the plant-laden foyer. His eyes roamed idly over his surroundings, then widened in astonishment. Rita was approaching him; at first he couldn't believe it.

"Well, look at you!" he exclaimed.

Rita pirouetted before him. "Do you like it, daddy? Victoria bought it for me."

Grant turned and gave Victoria a look she was helpless to interpret. He glanced again at his daughter. "Yes, it's very. . . nice. You look great, hon." His throat closed in on the words. Where had all the baby years gone? Why hadn't he paid more attention to the passing of time?

Rita visibly relaxed, but Victoria's backbone was ramrod straight. Grant's voice was dispassionate, his expression bland as he stared at Rita, but somehow Victoria knew what he was thinking. It was occurring to him for the first time that the day was not too far off when Rita would be grown. Wouldn't that realization affect a parent profoundly, particularly a parent like Grant? She longed to step closer to him, place a hand on his shoulder and tell him she understood.

Fortunately, Rachel chose that moment to put in an appearance. Coming to stand beside Rita, she flashed a dazzling smile. "Well, hello."

Victoria quickly stepped closer to Grant. "Grant, I'd like you to meet my mother, Rachel Carpenter. Mom, this is Grant Mackenzie."

Rachel extended a perfectly manicured hand. "Rita's father. What a pleasure to meet you, Grant! I've heard so much about you," she cooed, ignoring her daughter's warning look.

Grant took her hand and held it in both his. The dispassionate expression disappeared, replaced by one of warmth and charm. "How do you do, Mrs. Carpenter. Yes, I think I would have known you were Victoria's mother, no matter where I met you. The resemblance is remarkable."

"I'm flattered. I consider my daughter to be an unusually attractive young woman." Victoria couldn't have been more appalled, but she suffered in silence.

"So do I, Mrs. Carpenter."

"Please, call me Rachel."

"All right, Rachel."

"Now, Grant," Rachel said, coming right to the point. "I would like your permission to take Rita home to spend the night at my house. We've had such a short time together, and I think we should get to know each other better. She's such a delight! I would have spirited her away long before now, but Victoria insisted we wait and ask you."

Victoria's heart seemed to stop. Grant's answer would be very revealing. If he refused to allow Rita to go, it would mean he didn't want to spend any time alone with her, and that would be that. If, however, he agreed....

Grant faltered. "Well, I—"

"Please, daddy."

Grant's mind was racing along a wild uncharted course. Victoria dressed the way she was, this house, no one in it but the two of them.... He wished he could tell what Victoria was thinking. Did she want Rita to go? Was it even reasonable to dwell on such a delightful prospect? He could smell something cooking. Was she expecting him to stay for dinner? He had planned to ask her and Rita out, but now this.

A knot formed in the pit of his stomach. He needed a drink. Affecting nonchalance, he shrugged. "I guess it's all right."

Victoria silently expelled her pent-up breath.

Rachel clapped her hands together. "Oh, splendid! Rita dear, run and get your nightgown, and we'll be off."

It all happened very quickly. While Rita hurried away, Rachel picked up her handbag, exchanged a few more pleasantries with Grant. Rita returned, kissed her father, and within minutes Rachel and Rita were going off happily together, leaving Victoria and Grant standing somewhat awkwardly in the foyer.

He moved past her to the step of the sunken living room. Behind him, Victoria tried to view the familiar surroundings as they might look to a stranger: plush carpet, low-slung sofa, glass-topped coffee table, plants and silk flowers everywhere. Every item in the house had been selected with painstaking care; it was expensive and looked it.

Grant turned to her. "It looks like you," he

said simply. "Working for the government must pay you well."

Victoria chortled. "I had this house long before I went to work for the government. May I take your jacket?"

Grant flicked the button at the waist, gladly shrugged out of the blazer and handed it to her. "When I drove into this complex I noticed the sign over the entrance gate. Bartlett Square." He quizzed her with his eyes.

"My hus—er, my ex-husband's architectural firm designed these places."

"I see," he said obscurely.

"I'm so glad you let Rita go with mom, Grant. She wanted to so badly." Victoria hung his jacket in the closet, then turned to him. Even in her spike-heeled shoes she felt dwarfed by him. "She really did want to go," she finished weakly.

"I don't doubt that, Victoria. She probably was scared I was going to blister her butt, something that's crossed my mind more than once."

"Don't be mad at her."

"She did a stupid, foolish thing. Should I ignore that?"

"Everybody does stupid, foolish things occasionally."

Grant moistened his lips. Wasn't that the truth! Coming here was his stupid, foolish thing, for he possessed an astonishing lack of control where Victoria was concerned. He had convinced himself that because of Helena, he distrusted and disliked all women, but he had been wrong. He didn't distrust or dislike this woman; he was besotted with her.

She stepped closer to him, so close the flowery smell of her filled his nostrils, and the corners of her mouth lifted in a smile. "Would you care for a drink?"

"Sounds great."

They stepped into the living room. "What would you like?"

"What've you got?"

"Almost everything, I think."

"Scotch and soda?"

"That's easy. Coming right up. Have a seat."

While Grant made himself comfortable on the sofa, Victoria went into the kitchen to fill a bucket with ice. She was appalled to notice how badly her hands shook. How incredibly inept she was! How ridiculous for a woman her age to let a man fluster her so. Could Grant see her nervousness? Were her clothes too much? She would give anything to know what he was thinking right now. No, on second thought, perhaps it was best she didn't.

The liquor was kept in a sideboard in the dining room. Victoria mixed two Scotch and sodas, set them on cocktail napkins and carried them to the sofa.

"Here you are," she said too brightly.

"Thanks." He took the drink from her, quaffing a rather large amount of it in one gulp.

Because it would have looked odd to do anything else, Victoria also sat down on the sofa, some distance from him. "So...how've you been?"

"Fine. And you?"

"Fine."

"How's work?"

"I don't know. Chuck asked me to take a leave when I got back, so I'm on vacation this week and next. I happened to tell Rita the other night when she called, and that's one reason she came to see me."

"Can you imagine that kid pulling a stunt like that?"

"The impulsiveness of youth." Victoria managed a weak smile. "How was your weekend?"

"Hmm? Oh, last weekend, you mean. Busy. Guests always require a great deal of looking after, making sure they don't hurt themselves or the animals. But they help to pay the bills."

"I trust that Jake, Mrs. Guilford, everyone is all right."

"They're fine, Victoria. I'll tell them you asked about them." He took another long pull on his drink. "By the way, the harlequins moved."

"Moved?"

He nodded. "They just up and moved to another part of the refuge."

"Why?"

"That's what we're trying to figure out. Was it more food, better shelter? Were they running from a natural enemy, or what?"

"Is all that important?"

"Yep. Another chapter to the book I could write."

"Have there been any more ramifications of my investigation? Any more malicious mischief?"

"Nope. But Sally Anderson did tell me Martin Rumbaugh was strutting around her café the other day, bragging about 'running off' that federal agent."

Victoria bristled. "That's one I sure hated to see get away."

"Yeah, I imagine so."

A moment of awkward silence followed. She asked, "Have you had dinner?"

"No. No, I haven't."

"Well, I'm cooking a pot roast. If you'd like, I'd love you to stay and have some."

He turned to her, and one corner of his mouth quirked. "Thanks. I'd like that."

With dismay she realized he had suspected she was going to ask him. What else did he suspect?

She watched as he drained his glass. Quickly reaching for it, she got to her feet. "Let me get you a refill, and I'll check on the roast. It's probably time to put the vegetables in."

A few minutes later, she found setting the table as they talked made conversation easier.

"Nice place you have here, Victoria," Grant said from the sofa. "It suits you. I guess you lived in it when...."

"When I was married? Yes."

"I'm surprised you wanted to keep it."

She lined up the silverware precisely on either

side of their plates. "At first it did occur to me to get rid of it, but I discovered I'd have to pay so much more for what I have already. It seemed foolish to sell, so I bought it from Steve."

"You certainly live better than the average civil servant."

"A divorce settlement isn't responsible, if that's what you're thinking. My grandfather, my mother's father, left a trust fund for me. He was a terribly wealthy man."

"How did he get so wealthy?"

"He owned oil."

"That'll do it!"

With nothing left to do for a while, she returned to the sofa and sipped from her drink. A very little liquor went a long way with her, and she was beginning to feel its relaxing effects. She settled against the sofa's cushions and chanced a long level look at Grant. It wasn't fair for one man to be so blatantly masculine. Everything about him combined to form her definition of the adjective.

His eyes rambled around the room. "Yes, this place suits you perfectly. Far better than chasing eagle killers does."

She laughed. "Now don't start that! Not when I've finally convinced my boss I'm not a complete incompetent."

"Why do you do it?"

She frowned. "I don't understand what you're asking, Grant."

"Your job. Why, when you have all this?" He

made a sweeping gesture to indicate the elegant room.

"I'm surprised that you, of all people, don't understand. It fills a need in me 'all this' can't."

"But do you intend staying with the service? How long? A year or two, three or four?"

She shook her head. "I don't know. I don't like to plan too far down the road. I had my life all planned once, but plans have a way of being squelched in odd ways."

"Isn't that the truth." Grant contemplated the amber liquid in his glass. "So. . . what did you and Rita do all day?"

"Oh, mom came by. Then the three of us went shopping and had lunch. Woman stuff."

"I guess she enjoyed it."

"She seemed to. My mother's completely taken with her. Do you mind my buying her a few things?"

Grant sighed heavily. "No, not really, though I'd like to reimburse you. I guess Rita needs more of that kind of thing. . . woman stuff. She never asks for much, and God knows, I don't know what to buy her."

"Hardly unusual. Not many men would. Do I detect a distinct softening in your attitude toward Rita and. . . woman stuff in general?"

Grant shrugged. Damned if he knew what he thought about anything anymore.

Silence fell. Neither of them was saying what they wanted to, Victoria sensed. It was more difficult than she had imagined it would be. Had he stormed in the house, fussing and fuming, she could have handled it better. This was a quiet, pensive Grant, another facet of a many-faceted personality.

She thought she was fairly accustomed to his changeable nature, but his next question was a complete shock. "Do you always dress like that in the evening?"

She glanced down at her clothes as though trying to remember what she was wearing. "Well, actually, no."

"Then may I assume you're wearing that outfit for my benefit?"

She struggled to be noncommittal. "I guess so."

"Have you missed me?" he asked calmly.

She turned to him with startled eyes. He was the damndest man she had ever met! Would she ever understand him? More important, was she utterly foolish to want him the way she did, defying all common sense? Victoria didn't seem to be able to help herself; she dived headlong. "Yes."

The admission galvanized Grant. He straightened, set his drink on the coffee table and reached for hers, taking it out of her hand and setting it beside his. He closed the gap between them—just how he wasn't sure—and she was in his arms.

"Now that we've dispensed with the obligatory small talk—"

"Grant," she managed to gasp, just before his mouth claimed hers.

He drank deliciously from her lips for a moment before lifting his head to stare down at her. "Why don't we both stop hedging and admit what we want?"

She had no immediate answer to that.

He braced his hands on either side of her head and held it immobile; with his thumbs he tilted her head back so that their faces were inches apart. The corded muscles of his neck were rigid, and his eyes blazed with urgency. He dipped his head, toying with her mouth, tasting, nipping. His tongue traced the outline of her bottom lip, then captured it between his teeth and nibbled gently. Withdrawing, his eyes raked her face, and his fingertips played lightly over her cheeks, her closed lashes, down to trail along the line of her jaw.

"You are...so damned...gorgeous." His voice rumbled up from deep inside his chest.

"Th-thank you." The words came out on a suspended breath.

"Why don't we both admit this is what we've wanted since the moment I stepped through that door?" His fingers played restless havoc with her hair. Victoria could feel it slipping, falling to her shoulders in a waving cascade. Grant laced his hands through the shimmering softness, lifted several lustrous strands and pressed his lips against them.

Victoria melted. Her hands inched around and met at the small of his back. Oh, he felt so good!

Yes, this was what she wanted, to be held so close, to feel his warmth seeping into her veins. If she could have her way, they would stay like this, just like this.

Surprisingly, Grant was content for the moment, too. The trembling pliancy of her body told him what he needed to know—that he could move her. Instinct told him she needed tenderness first; the passion could come later. They had all the time in the world. They could be on the brink of something wonderful, but one thoughtless, careless move on his part could ruin it.

He propped his chin on top of her head and wrapped his strong arms around her, gently holding her to him. A few moments ticked by. Then he pulled away slightly, bent his head and gave her a long searching kiss that demanded nothing but a like one in return. Still Victoria felt its effect deep inside. Slow, deliberate, languorous, it was so much like another kiss, the one he had given her as they sat on a rock beside a shallow gully, the afternoon he told her about Helena. She remembered how close she had felt to him then, how brusque he had become later. Yet he had only been fighting the attraction, just as she had.

Fighting it didn't seem so important anymore. They parted. She buried her head in the hollow of his shoulder while his lips made a lazy foray along her hairline, stopping to nibble luxuriously on her earlobe. Though Victoria experienced a fierce desire to have him touch her all over, he didn't. His hands, splayed across her back, remained still.

She inhaled deeply, exhaled slowly. Suddenly her nostrils were assailed by an acrid smell that overpowered the pleasant fragrance of Grant's after-shave. The roast! "I guess I...should turn down the heat under the roast...or we may have to send out for pizza."

Releasing her, he sat back. His dark eyes smoldered as they rained liquid fire over her face, but he was smiling tenderly. "All right. Let's not do anything to spoil what I'm sure is going to be a splendid dinner. We can have...dessert later."

Victoria's heart knocked against her ribs. His intention was plain, his course of action charted. He was going to take his time, make her wait. And she would let him. The final realization would be so sweet, so sweet.... Where had her innate sensuality been hiding all these years?

"Do you want dinner now?" she asked tremulously.

"Anytime the chef is ready."

Bracing one arm on the back of the sofa, she pushed herself to her feet. "I'll put the rolls in the oven and make the gravy. It won't take but a few minutes. Help yourself if you want another drink."

THE FOOD WAS SUPERB and the wine perfect, but Victoria's mind was on neither. It was concentrated on the stimulating man across from her. As the meal progressed, she felt herself growing more and more disoriented, detached from the familiar surroundings. It was some time before she figured out what was happening to her. Grant was deliberately, cleverly seducing her without touching her, letting his eyes do all the work.

It was a blatant sensual assault on her nerves, most effective. His gaze caressed her intimately, silently telling her how desirable she was to him. While he ate, he chatted pleasantly about inconsequential things, but his eyes savored every aspect of her features. Lazily they wandered down the vanilla-cream smoothness of her throat, down farther to the deep V neckline and the valley between her breasts. His tongue skimmed over his bottom lip, and Victoria's chest rose in agitation.

In a strangled voice she asked him to pass the pepper; as he handed it to her his fingertips grazed the back of her hand, sensitively tactile. With some difficulty she set down her fork and raised the goblet of burgundy liquid to her decidedly trembling lips. Every cell, every nerve in her body was tuned in to his frequency, and he was transmitting some very erotic signals.

By the time the meal ended, Victoria's insides were a turbulent whirlpool. "It. . . won't take but a few minutes to clean up," she muttered, getting to her feet.

"I'll help."

"You don't have to."

"I'll just keep you company, then."

Numbly she nodded and began clearing the table, feeling Grant's eyes on her all the while. In the kitchen he propped his hip against the counter, folded his arms across his chest and watched as she scurried nervously around, scraping dishes, loading them into the dishwasher, wrapping leftovers for the refrigerator. The probing intensity of his gaze never left her. It was a relief to make a final swipe at the countertop, then reach for the hand lotion.

"All finished," she said, furiously rubbing the lotion in. "Would you like more wine?"

"Yes, I'll take another glass."

She refilled their goblets. When she handed one to Grant, he took it, capturing her hand and lifting it to his lips. In a trance, mouth partially open, Victoria watched as his tongue gently laved, one by one, each fingertip. He pressed his mouth into her palm. "A hand like this should never do housework," he said.

"A woman comes in once a week to clean, but the rest of the time it's all mine. That. . . hand has done plenty of housework."

"It doesn't look it." And he held it firmly in his as they left the kitchen for the living room.

Grant had made a total hodgepodge of her senses; Victoria felt as though she existed on some lofty plane, completely divorced from reality. Gratefully she sank to the sofa. Oh, he knew what he was doing to her! No man could affect a woman so profoundly without knowing exactly what he was doing. He was so masterful at it that she couldn't avoid wondering how many other women had been treated to his seduction.

What difference did it make? She was his victim tonight, and she might as well relax and enjoy it, since there wasn't a thing she wanted to do to break his bewitching spell.

"I can't think when I've had a better meal," Grant said, hitching his trousers at the knee, sitting beside her. "Somehow I hadn't imagined you as a good cook."

"Oh? How had you imagined me?"

He pretended to give it some thought. "Oh, a temptress, perhaps." He lifted his wineglass to his lips, sipped, lowering it. "A sorceress."

Victoria set her glass on the coffee table without taking so much as a taste. If there was anything she didn't need it was more alcohol. Inside her was a heady sensation far more intoxicating than anything wine could induce. "A far cry from my usual sensible image." She cleared her throat. "Wh-where are you staying tonight?"

The corners of his mouth twitched. "When I got to town this evening I drove straight here. I...haven't done anything about reservations. Do you suppose it's too late?"

Victoria took a deep breath. "I, ah, have a spare bedroom. I don't see why you can't stay here." Amazing how easily the words tumbled out.

With deliberation, Grant set his wineglass beside hers and reached for her. She went into his arms without hesitation, naturally, locking her hands behind his neck. He whispered her name. "Victoria." His hands began wandering over her back, stroking, rubbing, petting. His mouth moved across her cheek to capture her lips with his, and a warm yearning crept through Victoria. She parted her lips to receive his probing tongue, and the simmering heat in her loins erupted. When at last he dragged his mouth from hers, the pitchblende eyes staring down at her were fiery and determined, just as hers were.

"There doesn't seem to be anything we can do about this, does there?"

"N-no."

"Tell me you want me," he commanded softly.

Victoria didn't have to be told; the words came readily. "I want you. Surely you know I do."

"You don't honestly expect to sleep alone tonight, do you, Victoria?"

"No."

He kissed her, again and again, each kiss more urgent than the last. He kissed her until her soft trembling lips tasted of him, and still he couldn't get enough of her. He was full and heavy with desire, his breath raspy, ragged, tortured. "God in heaven, Victoria, do something with me before I lose my mind!"

She made a little sound, part sigh, part moan. Her hands left his neck, traveled down to the broad expanse of his chest, rested there to feel his pounding heartbeat, then dropped to her lap. Bending forward, she carefully undid her spike-heeled sandals and slipped them off. Standing, she held out her hand to him. "Come with me."

## CHAPTER TWELVE

VICTORIA EXPERIENCED only a moment of panic as she led Grant into her luxuriously appointed bedroom. *Please, don't let me freeze up!* she silently pleaded. Her heart hammered viciously in her chest, but otherwise she felt surprisingly normal, as though it was perfectly right that she and Grant should be here, in the room where she and Steve had lived and loved. Lost in the erotic sweetness of the moment, she only wanted to give in to the desire that engulfed her body.

Grant stood behind her and slipped his arms around her waist. She felt him kiss the top of her head, her temple. Slowly she turned in his arms and slid hers around him. For a long wordless moment they stood locked together, until Victoria raised her eyes to him. The look he gave her was one of the utmost gentleness.

"I've never known anyone like you, Victoria Bartlett," he whispered.

"Nor I like you, Grant Mackenzie."

She smiled, closed her eyes and settled her hips into the niche formed by his, feeling the hard proof of his passion. He groaned, and his restless hands wandered over her shoulders, her arms, her breasts. There they stopped, searching. "How do you get out of this thing?"

"Over my head. Here, let me do it."

Even though her hands trembled violently she managed to pull the tunic over her head in one fluid motion. The garment fell to the floor at her feet, and she stood before him.

Grant's expression was almost reverent. He hooked a finger through the front opening of her bra. "Allow me," he said thickly. "I think I can manage the rest." The closure gave way; he pushed the straps off her shoulders and down her arms. It joined the tunic on the floor.

His big hands zealously roamed over her back, then moved forward, each cupping a breast. They seemed to swell to fill his eager hands; the nipples grew erect with desire. "Dear God, Victoria, your skin feels like velvet. In my mind I've undressed you a hundred times, but. . . the fantasy was nothing compared to reality."

His hands were driving her insane, and she was filled with the first stirrings of a new emotion, something that went far beyond physical desire. She knew making love with him was going to intensify the feeling. She wasn't prepared to call it love, not yet, but it was so powerful she could only be awed by it. It was a sweeping kind of tenderness, a kind of caring she had never experienced before. This big man had confounded her from the beginning, had stirred her senses and muddled her mind. It was as though she had been marching toward this moment ever since she first set eyes on him. To her horror, a lone tear splashed out of her eye and rolled down her cheek.

Grant was looking down at her. He watched the tear as it slid to the corner of her mouth, bending his head to flick it away with the tip of his tongue. He thought he understood. For Victoria this was a momentous decision, and to carry it through she would have to shed inhibitions and past fears. "Victoria...lovely Victoria, I understand, really I do. But it's going to be beautiful, for both of us. Relax in my arms. It's going to be beautiful."

And he swept her up into his arms and crossed to the bed. Setting her on her feet, he pulled down the bedspread with a quick motion, then hurriedly divested her of the velvet slacks as Victoria wiggled her hips to aid him. When the last of her clothing was on the floor, he began a silent worship of her smooth body with his feverish hands. The fire smoldering inside Victoria spread out of control. She staggered against him. "Grant, please...I can't stand up."

Cupping her buttocks, he lifted her off the floor, helped her slide between the cool fragrant sheets. Absurdly, she remembered changing them that morning. For this?

Grant stood in full view as he undressed; Victoria was treated to a rapid male striptease. She couldn't take her eyes off him. He was powerful and urgent and supremely male, and she gloried in the sight of his naked body. But when he sank beside her, she stiffened at the touch of his heated

flesh. The tense, taut moment she had dreaded
had arrived. Closing her eyes, she tried to relax.

Grant cautioned himself not to hurry, to take
his time, astutely realizing that coming this far had
been a momentous decision for her. He murmured
endearments, promises of what was in store for
them, a new experience for Victoria. Steve had
been such a silent lover, but Grant crooned to her,
and his hands were never still. They cupped and
fondled her breasts, and when his lips lowered to
capture first one erect nipple, then the other, his
hands continued their downward journey, moving
over her firm flat stomach, her hips, to rest on the
sensitive flesh at the inside of her thigh.

Victoria's response was gradual and instinctive,
a slow awakening of dormant sensuality, and she
assisted him with a pliant yielding. Grant kept to
his deliciously torturous pace. He moved over her,
fitted his long muscular legs against her smooth
ones and gently parted them.

He entered her easily. Their bodies fused as
their mouths clung voraciously, parted, then clung
again. Grant urged her to participate, to recipro-
cate and to hold back nothing, but for Victoria,
drifting in a haze of fierce but tender enchantment, giving was the best she could do. Merely
giving herself to him was a giant leap forward for
her.

Too soon the enchantment was dispelled, when
in one tight second Grant's body stilled in her
hands; then a desperate spasm racked his body.
The sounds that filled her ears were harsh and gut-

tural, yet full of ecstasy and a kind of wonder. She stroked and petted him and waited for him to say something.

It was some time before he did. "Good God!" he muttered hoarsely.

A little chuckle escaped Victoria's lips. "Oh, you disappoint me," she whispered. "I thought you would come up with something memorable, perhaps something poetic."

"I'm too stunned for poetry." He levered himself up on one elbow to look down at her. "I'm waiting to hear what you have to say."

Her eyes raked his immensely contented face. "Say?"

"Yes. How do you feel?"

"I feel wonderful." Her eyes sparkled a brilliant hue.

Grant stared at her for a long second, trying to ascertain how much truth lay in her words. "Women sometimes lie and say it was better than it was. It wasn't. . . complete for you."

Victoria's eyelashes dipped briefly. "You know women don't always. . . ." She paused. She had never been able to talk freely about sex with Steve, so she hardly could be expected to do so with this man. "It's. . . different for us maybe, but that doesn't mean it can't be wonderful. And it was."

Grant pursed his lips thoughtfully, carefully pulled her to him. "We've just begun to know each other, sweetheart, and we have all the time in the world. It'll get better. . . and better."

Drowsily she melted against him, fitting her

length along his, noticing once more how neatly they interlocked. It was pretty good right now.

TIME LOST ALL MEANING. Victoria awakened, fell into slumber, awakened again, not knowing or caring what the hour was. With her body dovetailed into Grant's and his arms wrapped snuggly about her, she felt warm and sheltered.

She sighed, so blissfully happy. He had been magnificent, the perfect lover as far as she was concerned. Strange that this man who could be so dark and scowling could be capable of such tenderness. During the night he had reached for her again, and that time it had been... wonderful, a trite word that didn't begin to describe the joy of the union. Each love stroke had been accompanied by whispered endearments. It had seemed his only purpose was to give her pleasure. She thought they both had discovered something during those tumultuous moments—emotional cripples could do a lot to heal each other.

She basked in the afterglow of their lovemaking. It had never *been* so wonderful, not with Steve, who had been repetitious as well as nonverbal, although she hadn't given that much thought at the time. Now she had a basis for comparison. Grant's words, coupled with his sensual technique, had brought her to untapped depths of sexual delight, liberated her from all her imagined shortcomings. Knowing she had, in turn, excited him filled her with a sense of power and satisfaction. She wasn't the same woman she had been a few hours earlier.

Behind her, Grant was breathing shallowly and evenly; his face was pressed against her back, a possessive leg was thrown across her. Victoria hugged her pillow, smiling into it. She wasn't foolish enough to believe that after tonight they would walk off, arm in arm, into the sunset, joyously happy forever. One night of love would not magically eradicate their problems.

But for now they had something. Rachel had suggested a relationship with meaning; well, this had meaning, Grant had meaning for her. For now she felt very womanly, and her heart was full of this man. If he had to go back to Arroyo Grande when morning came, she would spend the remainder of her vacation there; it was as simple as that. She didn't want to think and analyze every move, to ponder her actions and wonder at their wisdom. Seize the moment. For now it was enough.

"BREAKFAST IN BED?" Grant's tone was incredulous. "I'm being seduced!"

"Past tense, love," Victoria said, smiling, as she set the tray on the bedside table. "You've already been seduced."

"Then I'm being spoiled."

"It's not really breakfast, anyway. Just juice and coffee. I need to find out what you want this morning."

Grant was propped up in bed, sheet at his waist, his broad, forested chest splendidly bare. He looked so virile he made Victoria's heart ache. The stubble on the lower third of his face only added to his appeal. His eyes were raking over her in a way that sent her pulses on a runaway course.

Grant was thoroughly enjoying her nearness. Victoria had never looked lovelier to him, so bright and energetic. She had put on a robe, and her hair was wild and tousled. What color was it? He could never be sure. Sometimes more brown than red, other times more red than brown. Always the perfect combination of both.

Without makeup her face looked so fresh and real. He wanted her, this sweet, exquisite woman whose beauty transcended any he had ever known, even Helena's. Victoria's beauty came from deep within. Burying himself deep within her had been a sacred love ritual. Remembering it brought a familiar ache to his loins.

"I'm thinking," he said seductively, "that I'd like more of what I had last night."

"You're a sex maniac!" she exclaimed softly, her eyes bright.

"I think you might be right." He reached for her. "Is there anything but you underneath that robe?"

"Not a thing." Her heart pounded furiously. Odd how much more acute the yearning was now that she had known him intimately.

He fingered the robe's lapel. "You were wearing this the night we found the sign in the yard."

"Yes."

"Lovely. Take it off."

Victoria complied. "Does this mean you don't want coffee?" she teased.

With a lusty laugh Grant threw back the sheet, and in a lightning-quick motion picked her up and brought her down on top of him. "This time... you make love to me."

"I'm...not sure I know how."

"You'll know. I promise...you'll know."

And she did. She wouldn't have believed she could be so aggressive, nor how expertly, with fingers, lips and tongue, she could bring him to full arousal. She marveled at how easy and natural their lovemaking was, as though they were longtime partners. Taking her cue from him, she talked to him while they made love, shamelessly murmuring words of endearment she had never before uttered, eliciting gasps of astonished pleasure from him. Their excitement rocked the room. She brought him to the brink of fulfillment, only to still her movements and let his tumult subside. Hovering over him, she smiled at the sensuous torment on his face, feeling every inch the conqueror.

Grant groaned hoarsely. "Victoria...good God...I think I'm dying. Please...."

His image blurred as her eyelids closed. Her own yearning overwhelmed her. She buried her face in the curve of his shoulder and felt his arms clamp around her like steel bands, and together they fell into a whirlpool of ecstasy.

"WHAT ARE WE GOING TO DO ABOUT THIS?" Grant asked sometime later.

Victoria stirred in his arms. Her limbs felt

lifeless, glutted with contentment. "I don't understand what you mean, Grant."

"I think you do. We've begun something, Victoria. Where do we go from here?"

She didn't want to think, only to savor this new bliss. "Must we make plans? Can't we just enjoy this, what we have now?"

"You mean no promises, no commitment?"

"Must we?" She felt saddened that the perfection of the moment had been spoiled. "Do we have to make promises? Promises are never kept."

"Sometimes they are." Grant propped himself up on one elbow and stared down at her. A love-induced glow radiated from her eyes. With his forefinger he brushed a damp tendril of hair from her face. "I wish you could see how beautiful you are right now, Victoria. Perhaps it's true that love's the world's best cosmetic. Love, don't you think I know how you feel? I didn't want this, either. I swore I would never care again, but I do care, and there's not a damned thing I can do about it. There never has been, not from the first moment I laid eyes on you."

"Are you trying to tell me that you. . . ."

"Love you, yes."

"You don't believe in love, remember?"

"I do now."

"Grant, how can you be sure? It's been such a short time."

"What does time have to do with anything? How long is it supposed to take, Victoria? A week, a month? Is time so important?"

No, she supposed it wasn't. She had known Steve for five years before they married, and that had guaranteed nothing. She laid her hand on Grant's chest; her fingers curled through the coarse hair. "No, it's not the time aspect. It's something more complicated than that."

His brow furrowed. "Victoria, are you trying to think of a way to tell me you don't feel the same way about me?"

"Oh, no, Grant." She hugged him furiously. "I care. I care for you deeply."

"Care for me, love? I hoped for more."

"You don't understand. Caring, feeling something for a man.... I didn't expect ever to be able to do that again. For me, this is an earthshaking development. But a commitment? Please, don't ask that of me, not yet."

"What are you afraid of?"

"Surely you know the answer to that."

"Failing?"

She nodded. "Something like that."

Grant lay down and contemplated the ceiling. Yes, he understood; he wasn't happy about it, but he understood. He, too, had sworn never to care again, but his emotions, his opinions had undergone a violent change since Victoria entered his life so abruptly. Feelings he thought had atrophied were alive and well and begging to be assuaged.

But he had had longer to get over past pain than Victoria; he mustn't forget that. A commitment to him would require sweeping changes in her life, and she would need time to get used to that. Care, caution. He couldn't honestly say he had ever regretted moving cautiously, and this was so important, so important. Slipping his arm under her, he pulled her to him and pressed his lips to her forehead. "All right, love...whatever you can give. I'll take it and be grateful. At least for now."

Victoria smiled against his neck. "You're really something, lover. Really something."

"I'm really something, all right, and it's called hungry. I'm going to need sustenance if you continue to demand such strenuous demonstrations of love."

Quickly she hopped out of bed and reached for her robe. Shrugging into it, she said, "I have another week of my vacation. Please ask me to spend it at Arroyo Grande."

"Please spend the rest of your vacation at Arroyo Grande."

"All right, if you insist."

"But let's not leave today. I want to spend today here. Maybe tomorrow, too."

"Aren't you anxious to get Rita back in school?"

"A couple of missed days won't hurt her. She's twice as smart as most kids, anyway. Besides, I have some wooing to do." He grinned charmingly. "I hope I remember how."

"Oh, I'll bet you do. Chuck told me all about your wild and wicked womanizing days."

Grant winced. "God, I hope he didn't tell you all about them!" He stood up and stretched luxuriously, raising his arms high above his head. "I didn't even bring in my shaving gear. It's still in the car with my suitcase.''

"I'll get everything for you.'' Victoria's eyes drank in the magnificence of his naked body. Stepping closer to him, she flattened her palms against his chest. "You really are gorgeous!''

He smiled down at her. "I feel used, shamed. I know your kind—you're only interested in my body.''

Laughing happily, she twirled away from him and picked up the tray she had set on the bedside table. "The juice is lukewarm, and the coffee's ice cold. I'll make fresh. By the time you've shaved and showered, I'll have breakfast ready.''

Over breakfast they talked. "I was incredibly nervous about seeing you again,'' Victoria told him with an intimate smile. "Could you tell? Among other things, I was afraid you would be furious with me for buying Rita those clothes. I haven't forgotten the powder episode. I had decided if you snarled at me, I would just ask you to leave, but what I really wanted more than anything was for you to stay. Does that make any sense?''

"Few things make sense when the heart gets involved. Love, in all my life I've never felt less like snarling than I do now.'' Grant speared a piece of ham with a fork. The ham was halfway to his mouth when he paused. "Do I snarl?''

"Magnificently sometimes.''

He thought about it. "Yeah, I guess I do. That's a defense mechanism, I suppose. Something I call upon when I find myself in a situation I can't handle. It's like cursing when you can't think of a better way to express yourself.''

Victoria smiled at him over the rim of her coffee cup. "Now when have you found yourself in a situation you couldn't handle?"

"Too many times to count, my dear."

"You seem so. . .oh, so in control."

"Victoria, I haven't been 'in control' since the day you arrived at Arroyo Grande."

Victoria stared at him across the small breakfast table. That admission seemed to unleash something in him, for he chewed thoughtfully, then swallowed, set down his fork and turned earnest eyes on her. "For years I've thought being in control was everything. It isn't. It made me aloof, and everyone around me suffered, especially Rita. I never wanted to expend any energy on making friends, on expanding my horizons. But when I woke up this morning with you in my arms, I felt completely out of control. . .and happier than I've ever been."

"I know, I know."

"Do you, Victoria? I think maybe you do. Is that why you fascinate me, why you were the one to bring out my softer emotions? The first night you were at Arroyo Grande, the first damned night, I wondered what it would be like to love you." He reached across the table and took her hand in his. "Yet if the attraction had been only a physical one, I could have dismissed you the minute you were out of sight. Making love with you last night, this morning, may have been the high point of my entire life, and God knows I'm looking forward to the next time, but if something were to happen that we couldn't...I would still want to be with you. Do you have any idea how much that stuns me?''

Her chin trembled uncontrollably. No one had ever said anything to move her so. She got to her feet and slid into his lap, winding herself around him. Half laughing, half crying, she held his head in her hands and rained kisses over his face. What was the matter with her? This was the man she wanted to be with; why couldn't she commit herself to him completely? ''Grant, I wish...I wish—''

He silenced her with his mouth. ''Hush. Don't cry. I understand you, babe, and this is all going to work out. I want everything from you, Victoria. I want you to quit your job, sell this house, come to Arroyo Grande to live with me, work with me...if *you* want to. Love me...that most of all. I wish I could promise you you'd never be unhappy, that we wouldn't fail, but I can't.''

''Oh, Grant, I know that.''

''I can promise you I'll try. Now, I won't mention the subject again until you bring it up. There's no hurry. Let's just enjoy and worry about tomorrow tomorrow, okay?''

She wiped her eyes with the heel of her hand. ''Okay. You're really quite wonderful, do you know that?''

''Of course.'' A deep chuckle rumbled up from his chest. ''The best. Remember that.''

She uncurled from his lap. "I'll clean up these dishes, then call my mother and tell her you won't be leaving today. That should thrill Rita to death. Then we'll decide how we want to spend our day. How's that?"

"Suits me. I'm a very contented, easy-to-please man."

WITH A QUIET WINTER SUNDAY at hand and the Gulf of Mexico on their doorstep, Victoria and Grant succumbed to the timeless urge to find a quiet stretch of beach all to themselves and just do nothing, or close to it. Winter had always been Victoria's favorite season on the coast. The crowds were gone, and the migratory birds from Canada were gathered in full force. Certainly it was only in winter that one could hope to satisfy a desire for a peaceful sand dune to call one's own.

Dressed in jeans and sneakers, armed with folding chairs and the picnic lunch Victoria had prepared, they boarded the jetty boat in Port Aransas for the trip to unspoiled San Jose Island. The boat could transport thirty or so people each trip, but this afternoon, to their delight, Victoria and Grant were its only passengers. Once on the island, they staked their claim to an isolated spot and spent the remainder of the afternoon doing nothing more taxing than staring at the watery horizon, snoozing, munching sandwiches and trying to catalog the bird species overhead. As knowledgeable as they both were, they gave up after twenty-eight, particularly when Victoria remembered the Texas coast was winter home to some four hundred different species.

The afternoon passed in a fog of contentment. "There are supposed to be a hundred ways to do nothing, and I think this is one of the best," Victoria said. "Nothing but wind, sand, surf and sky. I love it!" She turned to Grant, who was stretched out on a lounge beside her. His eyes were closed, and he was the picture of bliss. Nothing moody or complicated about him today. She smiled, drinking in the sight of him. In all her life she didn't think she had so enjoyed just looking at a man, and she could feel herself slipping further under his spell, reaching the point where she wouldn't want to be without him. She felt so comfortable, free of the need for guile and poses. Here was a man she could lean on a little. A comforting thought.

"This would be a good time to satisfy your urge to hunt for buried treasure, assuming such an urge exists," she said softly.

He grinned but didn't open his eyes. "It doesn't, not in the least."

"Well, I never come to the island without digging a little bit. Every once in a while someone comes up with a doubloon or two, a souvenier from some shipwrecked buccaneer from centuries ago. Guess I'll give 'er a go."

Victoria walked to the water's edge, and for the next twenty minutes or so she sifted through the sand, coming up with nothing more exciting than bottle caps. Grant watched her idly, and as she slowly walked back to their spot, a lazy smile crossed his face. She approached his lounge, stood over him and stared down. Through a veil of thick lashes he looked up. "What? No treasure?"

"Not unless you're unusually fond of beer caps. What have you been doing?"

"Communing with a great blue heron. We both agree this beats the hell out of working. And I've been thinking about getting on a plane and flying somewhere remote and romantic. Naturally I'd want you with me."

"I hate to tell you this, but I'm terrified of flying."

"You're joking! In this day and age? That's ridiculous!"

"Maybe, but it's a fact of life. Whenever I'm forced to fly, it's strictly white knuckles from take-off to landing." She paused, adding, "Just now, when I was walking toward you, you had the silliest grin on your face. What was that all about?"

He grinned again. "I was imagining you in a bikini. There's a most appealing picture forming in my mind. I wish you could see it. I trust you have a bikini."

She nodded. "Several. My newest one is emerald green."

"I hope I get to see you in it sometime."

"Well...." She smiled down at him temptingly. "I suppose I could model it for you when we get home."

Grant sucked in his breath. "Then...it might be a good idea to go home now."

"No chance until the jetty boat comes to fetch us. We're stranded."

"I don't suppose the skipper ever forgets any of his passengers."

"Afraid not, not when he makes eight or so trips a day." Victoria settled onto the lounge beside him, forcing him over. She slipped her arms around his waist and settled her head on his shoulder. "Besides, we have to watch the sunset! It's obligatory."

They lay locked together as the sunset flamed and died over the bays. Fish jumped and sea gulls called. Waves sluiced and sighed at the shore as the sea swallowed up the flaming-red ball. "Isn't it a sight?" she murmured in awe.

"That it is."

"The Karankawas—they were the first inhabitants of the Texas coast, did you know—used to become so entranced by that sight that they would stand motionless for over an hour while the sun set."

"The Karankawa trance. I've heard of it," Grant mused. "Can't say they didn't have the right idea. For all they were supposed to be cannibals and a rather unsavory bunch, they must have spent a lot of time just hanging out at the beach."

The sun took its final curtain call, disappearing behind the horizon. The day had been indescribably beautiful. Had she ever been happier? Victoria didn't think so. She stirred beside Grant and sighed. "I feel like applauding."

"So do I."

"The jetty boat's coming. We're going to have to leave."

"I know," he said regretfully. He pressed his lips into her hair. "Have I scored any points today?"

She smiled. "Many."

"You love me, you know."

"Maybe you're right."

## CHAPTER THIRTEEN

VICTORIA HEARD THE INSISTENT RINGING of her telephone the moment they pulled into the driveway. Quickly getting out of her car, she sprinted for the house.

"I'll unload all this stuff," Grant called after her. "Just tell me where to put it."

"Thanks. It goes in the garage," she said over her shoulder as she pushed open the front door. Rushing to the phone, she raised the receiver to her ear. "Hello," she said breathlessly.

"Victoria?" It was Rachel. "Where on earth have you been? I've called four times this afternoon. I was beginning to think you weren't answering your phone."

"No, nothing like that, mom. Grant and I went to St. Joe to do some bird-watching."

Rachel groaned her disapproval. "Bird-watching? I don't believe this! I'm not playing babysitter to give you time to do some bird-watching! How could a child of mine have so little romance in her soul?"

"Mom, a solitary beach in winter is the most romantic place in the world...believe me."

"Hmm. Well, I'm calling to ask Grant if Rita

can stay over here again tonight. I'm taking her to Rusty's for the best burgers in Corpus. Then there's a movie she wants to see. Some science-fiction thing that sounds perfectly dreadful to me, but I'm reminded of the time I sat through *Planet of the Apes* with you when you were young.''

Her mother, Victoria thought, had all the finesse of a sledgehammer, and was the dearest person imaginable. How different the weekend might have been without Rachel to keep Rita entertained. ''Well, Grant's outside unloading the car, but I guess it will be all right. Are you and Rita having a good time?''

''We're having a perfectly splendid time. My good manners and inherent sense of propriety prevent my inquiring about what kind of time you're having.''

Victoria grinned. ''I'll spare your having to ask. Wonderful. In fact, I'm going back to Arroyo Grande with Grant and Rita tomorrow. I'll be spending the rest of my vacation there.''

A chuckle of pleasure came from the other end of the line. ''See, Victoria—mother always knows best.''

Victoria was still grinning when she put down the receiver. Grant walked through the front door and shot her a quizzical look. ''What's so funny?'' he asked.

''My mother.''

''Your mother's funny?''

''She's a regular riot. She wants Rita to stay over another night. They're going out for hamburgers and a movie. I took the liberty of telling her it was all right. Is it all right with you?"

He winked. "What do you think?"

She gave him a seductive smile as she headed for her bedroom. "How about steaks for dinner tonight? There are five or six T-bones in the freezer. I happened on a sale at the supermarket this week. Why don't you pick out a couple that look good to you, and I'll thaw them in the microwave?"

"Sounds great! I think I'm going to be starved."

"Is the way to your heart through your stomach?" she asked teasingly.

"Victoria, you've already found your way to my heart."

Their gazes locked momentarily in a mutual expression of the easy, light-hearted familiarity they had established. Grant continued on into the kitchen, and Victoria ducked into the bedroom, peeling off her clothes as she did.

Quickly she stepped into her bathroom, turned on the shower and washed off the day's accumulation of sand. Drying, she wrapped the towel around her sarong-fashion and went to her closet to pick out something comfortable for an evening of lounging around the house. She reached for a pair of electric-blue hostess pajamas, before her hand halted in midair. She went to the bottom drawer of her dresser, where she kept her swimsuits. Retrieving two bits of emerald-green cloth from the pile, she dropped the towel, slipped into the bikini.

She was standing in front of the mirror when Grant walked through the bedroom door. "Those steaks are damned big ones, love," he said. "Can you eat a whole...."

The words died in his throat, and the smile faded from his lips. Halting in his tracks, his mouth slightly agape, he struggled for breath. The sight of her stunned him. The bikini was scandalous; that was the only way to describe it. Surely she wouldn't have been caught dead outside the house in it. Her skin gleamed ivory, and the contrast between pale flesh and the vivid hue was sharp. There wasn't a superfluous ounce of weight on her curvaceous frame he noted once more. Her stomach was flat and firm, her breasts full and high. "Good God, Victoria!" he exclaimed.

Slowly she turned and gave him her most dazzling smile. "I told you I'd model it for you. Like it?"

"Like it?" He walked toward her. "I'd have to be made of wood not to like it. You'd turn on a ninety-year-old monk!"

She fought back a giggle. "Then may I assume the reality lives up to the fantasy?"

His eyes were filled with wonder as he reached out one hand to place it on her shoulder. His hot gaze wandered over her in a way that made her pulses pound. It was like a physical caress. "What do you think? No imagination, however fertile, could conjure up you in that suit. Your body is a true work of art."

"Thank you." Victoria honestly thought she

had originally put on the suit as a playful gesture, but now she realized what a boldly suggestive invitation she was sending him. There was certainly nothing playful about Grant's expression. His eyes were searing her, sending little shivers of desire through her veins. Their intimacy was too new; the slightest provocation could arouse their passion.

Slowly, deliberately, his hands began a sensitive foray over her smooth skin, skin which had suddenly become heated and responsive. Victoria's heart beat faster, faster still as his hands slid up and down her arms, back to her shoulders, then down to her breasts, which were straining against their skimpy covering. Her arms crawled up the hard wall of his chest to lock behind his neck, and she lifted her mouth.

The first touch of their lips was light, feathery, the merest brush. Once, twice they exchanged soft kisses, sipping gently. Victoria's senses fed on the musky aroma and flavor of his skin, the slightly abrasive texture of his cheek as it pressed against hers. Grant's tongue traced the outline of her bottom lip, then slipped inside to seek the sweet hollows of her mouth. This time he kissed her with drugging force, drawing her to him, enfolding her in a hard embrace, molding her against his hips, where she could feel the turgid proof of his desire. The familiar fierceness of her own passion tugged at Victoria's stomach.

Dragging her mouth away from his to gasp for air, she buried her face in the curve of his shoulder; she was trembling all over. "Grant, I can't believe the way you make me feel. It's so... so...."

"Different. At least it is for me. It's so different with you, Victoria," he said in a shaken, gruff whisper. "So different. I can't get enough of you, never enough...."

He dispensed with her bikini effortlessly; with little more than a few flicks of his fingers he removed the top, then shoved his hands down her hips to push the bottom to the floor. Somehow he managed to shed his own clothing, even though she could only seem to let go of him for brief seconds. Scooping her up in his arms, he carried her to the bed. He knelt beside her for a moment, rubbing, petting, bringing her to a fever pitch of excitement, before covering her with his own body.

Victoria's legs moved restlessly, parting to enfold him. She accepted him eagerly, luxuriating in the feel of his long naked form crushing her into the mattress. She marveled at the ease with which their bodies melded, at the intense pleasure of their union. There was a happy abandon to their lovemaking now, unlike last night when they had been more desperate, discovering each other for the first time. Grant mumbled words of endearment against her skin; instinctively she moved her hips with his in the giving and taking of exquisite pleasure. The feeling flowing through her was like molten gold.

She trailed her lips across the bunching muscles of his shoulders, slid her hands over the slippery sweatiness of his back. She longed with all her heart to delay the climax, but knew it was impossible. Grant was entering her with relentless rhythm, his breath coming in labored gasps. This time she waited for him, waited until spasms were racking his body before allowing ecstasy to claim her. The final release, when it came, was a grand convulsion, a stunning and shattering explosion, almost unbearable in its pleasure. At the very height of their passion Victoria uttered a contented sigh.

Victoria was limp from exhaustion when Grant rolled off her to gather her into his arms and bury his face in her hair. They lay wound together for several spent moments before she said, "Pull the covers up over us, lover. We'll catch cold."

He complied, then drew her to him again. "Victoria, I never did get those steaks out of the freezer."

"It doesn't matter," she replied lethargically. "We'll have something else. For now, can we sleep for a while?"

"Of course."

Victoria was drifting on the edge of slumber when she heard him say, "Victoria?"

"Hmm?"

"I don't want you to wear that damned bikini out in public, do you hear?"

She snuggled against him, and laughter bubbled up in her throat. "You're too damned bossy."

THE FOLLOWING DAY dawned gray and overcast. Victoria awakened much later than was usual for her; still Grant slept soundly beside her. She had no idea what time they had finally gone to bed, but it had been very late. Closing her eyes, she turned her head on the pillow and smiled secretively before quietly crawling out of bed. Her mind was awhirl with erotic memories.

Last night had really been something! They had ordered pizza, drunk wine and talked for hours before going to bed, only to reach for each other again. It had been insane. . . and wonderful.

Victoria couldn't imagine where the uninhibited, wanton side of her had been hiding all these years. Steve would have been downright shocked. It had crossed her mind more than once that if she and Steve had ever experienced the sheer force of mutual, unfettered, desperate passion, their marriage might have survived. In her wildest dreams she couldn't imagine Stephen Bartlett caught in the throes of the lusty abandonment that came so naturally to Grant Mackenzie.

Married all those years, she naturally assumed she knew all there was to know about intimacy between a man and a woman. She didn't. Her body had magical places Grant knew how to touch. Odd how gentle and sensitive his big hands were. It seemed only reasonable to assume that by placing herself in those hands she would be led to a new kind of love.

She shrugged into her robe and stared down at his broad, bare back. *I have a lover,* she thought in amazement. Her first lover. She and Steve hadn't been intimate before they married. In fact, she had always harbored a rather lofty disdain for women who engaged in affairs, but that was rapidly changing. Marriage was only one of the relationships a man and woman could share. Being with Grant seemed the most natural thing in the world. Certainly there was nothing sordid about it.

She was almost sure she loved Grant; if she didn't now she soon would. And because that was so, she would have to admit Steve hadn't been the One Great Love, a belief she had nurtured for a long time. Could she shake it off and relegate Steve to the dim dark past? It was what Grant wanted. He had said so last night. "I want no ghosts between us, Victoria. I want to be all that matters to you."

That bothered her a bit. Grant had admitted to being too possessive of his wife. Well, she had been too possessive, too, and she wondered if two such adamant people could make it together. She had plenty of doubts; the main one concerned her ability to make a marriage work over the long haul. One nagging question pushed to the forefront of her mind: if she hadn't succeeded with Steve, what chance did she have with someone else? Grant, she knew, expected marriage to come out of all this.

They would be leaving for Arroyo Grande this morning. This week together would be important—a time for them to solidify their relationship and try to determine what should come next. She was anxious to get back to the place where it had all begun, although as Grant had warned, they certainly wouldn't enjoy the solitude and privacy they had known here in Corpus.

She glanced at the bedside clock. It was almost nine. Even if they hurried they would get a late start, and Grant was still dead to the world. Silently she crossed the room to the bathroom to brush her teeth and wash her face, after which she went into the kitchen to make coffee.

The pot was perking cheerfully, and Victoria had telephoned Rachel to tell her they would pick up Rita in a couple of hours, when the doorbell rang. She frowned. Who on earth would be calling on her at this hour on a Monday morning? Glancing down at her bare legs beneath the robe and thinking of her freshly scrubbed, unmade-up face, she seriously considered ignoring the bell. She couldn't think of a soul she cared to see or talk to. The bell sounded again. Shrugging, she left the kitchen, crossing through the house to answer the door.

The sight that greeted her eyes stunned her. Her entire body went rigid. "Steve!" she cried in disbelief and dismay.

The tall, light-haired man in the impeccable three-piece suit gave her an anxious smile. "Hello, Vicky. I hope I'm not disturbing you. I called your office and was told you were on vacation. I happened to be passing near here, so I took the liberty of stopping by."

She felt paralyzed. She struggled to find her voice. "I . . . well, Steve, ah, how are you?" He looked fine, she thought absurdly. He had gained a few pounds, but that was all to the good, since he had always been on the gaunt side. Nancy was taking good care of him. He was wearing his hair a bit longer, but otherwise he looked...the same. What was he doing here?

"Fine, thanks. May I come in?"

"Come in?" she repeated stupidly.

"Yes, please," he said, giving her a quizzical look. "This will only take a minute. I just need your signature on some papers."

Victoria couldn't believe it. She hadn't set eyes on him in months, and he hadn't stepped foot into this house since the day he had requested a divorce. Why now? Papers? What papers? She couldn't possibly have looked worse!

*Dolt!* she berated herself. *That can't make any difference. This man doesn't give a damn how you look. He doesn't give a damn about you!* "Does it have to be right now?" she asked stiffly. "I'm busy."

His brow lifted in mild surprise. "It will only take a minute."

In a feeble attempt to salvage some of her composure, she straightened, cinched the robe more tightly around her waist and stepped back. "Of course," she said coolly, sending up a silent prayer that Grant was still soundly sleeping.

Stephen Bartlett crossed the threshold of the townhouse he had designed, and his eyes dispassionately surveyed his surroundings. "The place looks wonderful, Vicky. You've done some redecorating."

"Yes, a bit here and there. Nothing major." Considering the low-slung modern architectural marvel he and Nancy called home, Victoria thought tartly, this probably looked strictly potato-patch to him.

Steve halted suddenly, staring into the living room. Victoria's gaze followed his and fell on the sight that doubtlessly had captured her ex-husband's attention. The coffee table—two goblets with dregs of wine in each, the cardboard pizza box, Grant's pipe resting beside it and two pairs of shoes on the floor, one definitely masculine. She cleared her throat nervously. "Now what's this about some papers?"

Steve turned to her, his eyes speculative, but he said nothing. Reaching inside his suit jacket, he withdrew some folded papers. "I ran across these old stocks issued in both our names. My broker advises me to unload them quickly, so I need you to sign. . . ."

Victoria almost snatched them out of his hand. "All right. Do you have a pen?"

"No, I'm sorry, I don't. I left it in the car."

The nearest pen was in the desk in the living room. Although the last thing Victoria wanted was for Steve to enter the main part of the house, she had no choice but to step down into the living room. Dismayingly, he followed without waiting for an invitation. "Then I'll get one," she said, hurrying for the desk. Bending over it, she found the spot on each of the certificates where she was supposed to sign. Behind her, Steve was speaking.

"Yes, these places have really skyrocketed in value. You were smart to buy it from me when you did, Vicky."

Victoria wanted to say, "It was either buy it or find myself out on the street." She wanted to scream, Get out of here and stop calling me Vicky! The name sounded too intimate. She scribbled furiously.

"Yes, they can't help but increase in value with each passing year. We're thinking of doing something similar in another part of town, and the pre-development price will be considerably more than you paid— Oh, good morning."

Victoria's heart plummeted. She didn't have to turn around to know Grant had put in an appearance. Embarrassment flooded her, and she wished she were anywhere else on earth at that moment. That Steve should catch her in such a compromising situation seemed the height of mortification. She hated herself for caring, for even giving it a thought, but she couldn't help it. Right or wrong, she had always strived for perfection in his eyes.

"Good morning," she heard Grant's familiar baritone voice say. There was nothing she could do but raise tremulous eyes to him. He was wearing only faded jeans, was bare-chested and barefoot. His eyes were foggy from sleep, his hair tousled, dark stubble on his chin. No one past the age of twelve would think for a minute he'd been sleeping in the guest room. So much for Victoria's short-lived role as a modern woman, unashamedly involved in a passionate love affair. She felt like a teenager whose father had caught her smooching on the living-room sofa.

She cast a sidelong glance at Steve. The slight quirk to his mouth suggested...what? Amusement? Censure? A bit of surprise that proper Victoria had cast off her inhibitions and lured this hunk into her bed? Was he wondering what Grant saw in her? All that and more, she guessed, and felt her face color deeply.

Never had she thought it was possible for one's life to pass before one's eyes in a blinding flash, but in that eternal moment she relived every single second of the pain of a year ago. She and Steve had been in this very room when he had dropped the bombshell. "I'm sorry, Vicky, I want out. There's someone else." Even now she shuddered at the recollection. She knew with finality that she could never go through that again.

Across the room Grant studied her. He didn't need to ask who their visitor was. One look at Victoria's stricken face told him ex-hubby was paying a call. He scrutinized the visitor with unabashed jealousy. Good-looking guy, he supposed, if you liked the pretty type. And he had sure knocked the props out from under Victoria.

Damn him! Why now? Another hour or so and he would have spirited Victoria away to Arroyo Grande, sparing her this, sparing him this. She was valiantly trying for courage and failing miserably. A sense of impending disaster enveloped him like a shroud.

Hurriedly Victoria glanced back at him. Their gazes locked. Hers telegraphed her humiliation, and his flashed her an apology. *Had I known, I would have stayed out of sight,* they said.

That brought her to her sense. Why should Grant apologize? Why should she feel guilty? Grant had far more right to be here than Steve did. It was none of Steve's business if she had a dozen lovers, and he would be a fine one to pass judgment. At least she wasn't an adulteress. Giving herself a little shake, she defiantly lifted her chin.

"Steve, I'd like you to meet Grant Mackenzie," she said with deceptive calm. "Grant, this is my— this is Stephen Bartlett."

It would have been ludicrous for the two men to lope across the expanse of the living room to shake hands, so neither made a move. Grant propped his shoulder against the doorjamb. "How do you do," he said simply.

"Nice to meet you, Mackenzie."

"Steve had some papers for me to sign," Victoria said weakly, wondering why she felt she needed to explain. She handed the stocks to Steve with a ridiculous flourish. "Here you are."

It was an awkward tableau. Silence lay over the room. They looked like three actors in a play who had simultaneously forgotten their lines. Predictably, it was Steve who recovered first. Stuffing the papers back into his breast pocket, he affected an air of amiability. "Thanks, Vicky. Well...I've really got to be running." Already he was moving toward the door. "Oh, by the way, I'll be selling these stocks at a loss. . . ."

Dear God, did he honestly think she cared anything about the money? "It makes no difference to me." Her tone was brittle.

Steve looked relieved. "Well, you folks have a nice day."

"Same to you," Grant said, while Victoria followed her ex-husband to the door like a sleepwalker, mumbled an incoherent farewell and closed it behind him. *I could kill him for doing this to me,* she thought miserably. Steve's untimely appearance had thoroughly spoiled the day, just how she wasn't sure. For two days, she suddenly realized, she had forgotten the past. For the first time since the divorce she had lived only for the present. Now everything came rushing back—the disbelief, the sense of betrayal, finally the pain.

Fate, Kismet, whatever had sent Steve to this house this morning had sent him to remind her what could happen to a person who loved too much. And behind her was a man who could destroy her all over again, if she let him. She was going to have to back off, take a careful look at this. When she turned around, Grant's eyes impaled her.

"Coffee should be ready," she said quietly.

Grant nodded, a heaviness settling on his shoulders, weighting him down. He knew what she was thinking, and he felt a sickening lurch in the pit of his stomach. The day that had been filled with such bright promise was disintegrating before his eyes. "I think I'll shave first."

IT WAS SOME TIME before Grant appeared in the kitchen. When he did he was freshly shaven, fully dressed and carrying his suitcase and shaving kit. Victoria moved from stove to table in jerky movements. "Good heavens, you're all ready to leave, and I've done nothing! I'll hurry—"

"No hurry, Victoria. I...think it's best that you don't come with me."

She stopped in her tracks and turned widened eyes on him, aware of ominous undercurrents in the air. "Are you serious?"

"Completely." It hadn't been an easy decision to reach. Grimly staring at his face in the steamed-up bathroom mirror as he shaved, all he had seen was Victoria's face, her miserable expression as she had confronted her ex-husband. It was too much, and he was in no mood to pretend it wasn't.

He set down his luggage and ambled into the room, going to the cupboard to take down a cup. He walked to the coffeepot and poured. Victoria's eyes never left him. It occurred to her that he knew where she kept everything; he moved around her house as though he belonged in it, would always belong in it.

"Oh, Grant, if you mean about Steve, that was nothing. I was just surprised— I mean, I haven't seen him in ages, and...."

His shoulders drooped in a way that made him look older than his years. At the moment he felt about eighty. An unwell eighty at that. "I know I'm not the first man in your life, Victoria, but right now I want to be the only one...and I'm not."

"That's ridiculous!"

"Is it?" He propped his hip against the counter, sipping morosely from the cup.

"Of course it is. You...you can hardly blame me for...well, for anything. It was a bit embarrassing, if you want the truth. It was so obvious we were, er, cohabiting."

Grant laughed without mirth. "And that bothered the hell out of you, not because you were caught in a compromising situation, but because it was Pretty Boy who did the catching. You're still hung up on him. You've still got a lot of exorcising to do, love."

"And you don't, I suppose. What about Helena? What if she had stumbled in on us this morning? How would you have felt?"

"I don't know, but I seriously doubt I would have looked as though I'd been struck by lightning. And kindly leave Helena out of this!"

"Why? Grant, I know it's so much harder when we've both been married before. I know you must wonder about Steve and me, just as I wonder about you and Helena."

"I've told you all you need to know about my marriage."

"And you know all you need to know about mine," she said a little frantically. "Steve is remarried; he has a son. He's part of the past."

Leisurely Grant set his cup on the counter and crossed the room to her. "He'll never be part of the past, Victoria, as long as he's still in there." A finger poked meaningfully just below her left breast. "I can't handle that."

"It was just a surprise, that's all," she said feebly. "Can't you understand that? Why must you have everything right now? Give me time, Grant, to get used to us...."

"I guess I'm too possessive, too jealous," he said with a sad sigh. "I couldn't live with you, knowing he was still lurking in your heart, your thoughts. Even if we lived at Arroyo Grande, we would naturally spend time here in Corpus, what with your mother here and all. I'd always be worried you might run into him, afraid you'd go to pieces if you did. Not many men could live with that, me least of all. No, I want him gone before I move in."

"You're being unfair."

"Perhaps."

"I...I see nothing wrong with my going to Arroyo Grande as planned, with our spending the rest of the week together and...just seeing what happens."

Grant's face was taut and earnest. "Simply continue our affair, you mean? Bed and board but no long-term lease. That might satisfy you, but it won't satisfy me. I can't bear loving you and knowing you love someone else."

"I'm not sure I do."

"But you're not sure you don't."

Victoria faltered before saying, "Grant, I told you I care for you deeply, and that in itself is a milestone for me. You are the only man except—"

"Except Steve?" he prodded. "I want no exceptions."

"You said you would accept whatever I could give. You said there was no hurry."

"That was before I saw your reaction to him."

"Am I supposed to apologize for having loved the man I married?" She despised the high-pitched quality to her voice.

"Not at all. And I'm not going to apologize for wanting you to myself."

"What is it with you, that marriage is all you'll accept? Don't my feelings for you count for anything?"

"I want more." The words were precise, clipped.

A feeling akin to panic swept through Victoria. She didn't want to lose him, but honesty compelled her to admit she wasn't sure, not yet. Maybe she was being terribly selfish, wanting to enjoy him without making a commitment. How would she feel if the tables were turned? How cruel to accept a man's love without returning it, without qualification. One of the most painful aspects of Steve's unfaithfulness had been the knowledge that his affair with Nancy had been going on for a long time, that he had accepted his wife's love while loving someone else. Victoria was sure she could never be guilty of such dishonesty. No, she didn't blame Grant. He wasn't the one being unfair; she was.

"I thought you understood how I feel about. . . failing again. I couldn't bear it. I have to be sure. I need more time."

"Take all the time you need, Victoria, but do it on your own. I can't stand making love to you, then wondering how I'm doing afterward. I thought, hoped I could be patient, hoped I could wait it out. I can't."

He made a move toward the door, and Victoria had to stop herself from reaching for him. If there was to be any future for them, she would have to "exorcise" Steve, and Grant couldn't help her do that.

"I'll. . . miss you," she said tremulously.

He made a halfhearted attempt at a smile. "I hope so. Now maybe you'd better tell me how to get to your mother's house. I need to pick up Rita and hit the road."

She gave him succinct directions, but when he bent to retrieve his luggage, she choked back a sob. "Aren't you even going to kiss me good-bye?"

Slowly he straightened, turning to her. His eyes sparkled like pitchblende diamonds. He held out his arms, and she stumbled into them. He laid his palm against her cheek, laced his fingers into her hair and bent his head to capture her lips with his own.

It was a poignant farewell. Though Victoria clutched at him, Grant, with great constraint, kept the kiss tender and undemanding.. She hungered for more, but he gave her only a taste before breaking their embrace and stepping away from her. Victoria forced herself to stand erect and give him a small smile.

"I'll...be in touch," she said, refusing to turn this into a final goodbye.

"I hope so...but only if you can tell me what I want to hear. I don't want any phone calls just to chat or garbage like that. Clear?"

She nodded briefly. "Will you tell Rita goodbye for me?"

"Of course."

And she stood mutely, listening as he crossed through the front of the house. The precise click of the front door as it closed behind him sounded so final, triggering a rush of tears.

The tears turned to choking sobs some minutes later when she returned to the bedroom, to be greeted by the sight of the crumpled bed where they had made unbridled love. Throwing herself on it, she clutched at the pillow Grant had used. It smelled of him.

She wondered if something askew within her—a cell, a gene, a chromosome gone haywire—was the source of her inability to commit herself to Grant. Something was definitely missing.

FOR THE NEXT FEW DAYS Victoria drifted around her house, lethargic and apathetic, beginning projects and abandoning them moments later. Her "vacation" stretched interminably ahead of her. She thought of Grant incessantly and harbored the faint hope that he would swallow his pride and call her. When he didn't she turned pettish and resentful. If he cared for her as much as he claimed he wouldn't be able to stay away. Twice she had come within a whisker of telephoning him, but common sense intervened in the nick of time. What could she tell him? He didn't want to hear from her unless she could say, "I love you unreservedly and I want to get married now!" She wanted to be with him; she wanted him to hold her, to make love to her, to make her feel desirable—but signing that long-term lease? She still wasn't sure she could do that.

Her uncertainty was reinforced when she turned on the local five o'clock news to see Steve being interviewed. His firm was designing a major new industrial complex, and the cooing female reporter was slavering all over him. But it was neither Steve nor the interviewer who arrested Victoria's attention. Rather, it was the sight of Nancy Bergman Bartlett sitting quietly at her husband's side—mousy as ever, and Good Lord, pregnant again! And Steve was the one who hadn't wanted a family. "Not now, Vicky," he had said. "Maybe never. I'm not too sure I want kids."

*He apparently meant he didn't want kids by me,* Victoria thought bitterly, and her sense of inadequacy returned, stronger than ever. Without Grant's presence to assure her of her attractiveness, her desirability as a woman, the feeling fed on itself.

Rachel couldn't help, though she tried. Her mother had telephoned only minutes after Grant, minus Victoria, had stopped to pick up Rita. Victoria, naturally, had told her the whole story. Rachel was sympathetic, but what could she do? "I really liked that man, Victoria. There's something so genuine about him, earthy and real."

"You're not making me feel a bit better, mom."

"I know. It's a shame, but as long as you have doubts, you're wise to shy away from a commitment," was the best her mother could do.

So Victoria lived vicariously through her dreams, which had become exquisite torment. In those dreams she could feel Grant's soothing warmth, his mouth, his hands touching all those secret places. She could find release from the doubts plaguing her.

The days plodded on.

"YOUR VACATION didn't do you a helluva lot of good, Victoria," Chuck Singleton said bluntly. "You look tired."

Victoria smiled cheerlessly. "I'm tired, all right. Tired of doing nothing." Her first week back at work had been dull, dull, dull, and this second week had begun no more eventfully.

"Well, I'll fix that. You and I are going to a burg called Parker's Crossing, where we'll rendezvous with representatives from Texas Parks and Wildlife, the county health department, a couple of guys from the Audubon Society, to say nothing of the mayor, a congressman and a U.S. senator."

"I'm impressed. This sounds like something big. What does it involve?"

"Birds," Chuck replied laconically.

"Birds?"

"Yep. A mess of them. Egrets—twenty thousand, to be exact. It seems that on their journey southward the feathered creatures have taken an unusual liking to Parker's Crossing. Unfortunately, the feeling isn't mutual. The citizens are disgusted, fed up, a hair trigger away from an uprising, and they're demanding the government do something now. However, those birds are protected by the Migratory Waterfowl Act, so you and I are going to get up there and tell the good people of Parker's Crossing what will happen if they harm so much as a feather of one of the little dears' heads."

## CHAPTER FOURTEEN

PARKER'S CROSSING was a pleasant little farming and ranching town of some seven hundred souls, all of whom seemed to have turned out for the meeting in the town square. To a person they were angry. The atmosphere was noisy and hostile.

Personally, Victoria didn't blame them. The rookery the birds had established on the outskirts of town was, to put it mildly, a filthy mess. Bird droppings, feathers and broken eggs littered the area; a cloud of ammonia hung in the air. Victoria and Chuck had visited it with a man from the county health department—she wasn't anxious to return soon. The townspeople were outnumbered thirty to one by these unwelcome visitors, and they didn't know what to do about it.

The "authorities," Victoria and Chuck among them, didn't either—not yet—but they did know the law. They knew what the citizens of Parker's Crossing couldn't do, and their mission that morning was to spell it out for them. They had appointed Victoria their spokesperson, apparently feeling her job at the nuts-and-bolts level put her "closer to the people." The congressman, whose name Victoria couldn't remember, hoisted her up in the bed of a pickup, handed her a megaphone, and it was all hers.

It took some time to get the crowd silenced. "Ladies and gentlemen, please!" she shouted. "May I have your attention please!" She was forced to repeat this plea several times before the din subsided somewhat. She took a deep breath and began. "First let me introduce myself. I'm Victoria Bartlett with U.S. Fish and Wildlife. As you know, the Department of the Interior is fully aware of your problem. Our scientists will be working with state and local officials to seek nonlethal means of discouraging the birds from remaining—"

A collective groan went up. That wasn't what the crowd wanted to hear at all. "It seems to me," a man shouted from the rear, "that the government cares more about those birds than it does for people! I say shoot 'em! We won't have to kill many before the others leave." The crowd roared its agreement.

"Folks, please. You must understand the seriousness of what you're proposing. The egrets are protected by international treaties with Canada and Mexico, as well as by federal and state laws. Anyone caught harming them will end up in court."

"In other words, the birds go where they damn well please."

"That's about the size of it," Victoria admitted. "But as I said, we are studying nonlethal means of getting rid of them."

"Such as?" someone wanted to know.

"Some measures that have been discussed include the use of scarecrows, or imitating the egret's distress cry. Almost any sort of violent noise might frighten them off. Perhaps we can discharge blanks—"

Another collective groan. "That'll take forever!"

"And I am assured by experts that the egrets will eventually leave and go on to Mexico."

A woman in the front spoke up. "How do those birds know when they get to Mexico? Maybe they think this is Mexico!"

"Those birds stink!"

"They're making my asthma worse!"

"I say we kill them and pay the fine!"

"Yeah, I'd rather be out a few bucks than dead!"

Victoria's head was beginning to pound. Her eyes flew to Chuck, who simply shot her a thumbs-up gesture. Mildly encouraged, she continued. "Ladies and gentlemen, I am sure none of you wants to be on the wrong side of the law. And the birds pose no threat to public health."

"Says who?"

"The man from the health department assures me—"

She tried to explain, but was drowned out by an irate citizen who yelled, "Anyone who says those birds don't breed disease is an idiot!"

"My neighbors moved away because of those birds, but I'm too old to move!" someone else cried.

"Please, folks, the government sympathizes with the problem, and we are working diligently...."

And so it went, over and over, until the representative from the Audubon Society came to her rescue, and Victoria gratefully relinquished the floor. Half an hour later the citizens dispersed with pinched faces, clearly unappeased. Victoria and Chuck began the drive back to their Corpus Christi office.

"I thought you handled that very well, Victoria," Chuck complimented.

Behind the wheel of the government car, Victoria pursed her lips. "I didn't do a damned thing, and you know it."

"Ah, well, what could you do, really, besides informing those people of the law?"

"Frankly, my sympathies are with them. How would you like to have that rookery in your backyard?"

"I wouldn't, but the law is the law."

"Chuck, do you ever feel...useless? As if you're drawing a salary and not really doing anything?"

"Nope, never do because I'm a realist," Chuck said simply. He stretched his legs in front of him. "I thought the fellow from Audubon was quite eloquent."

"And the elected officials quite silent," Victoria observed.

"Did you expect anything else? They could hardly advocate breaking the law, but they weren't about to jeopardize votes. At least you and I had a cut-and-dried mission."

"I just wish there was something we could do for those folks back there. Maybe there's some loophole in the Migratory Waterfowl Act...."

Chuck snorted. "I doubt that. The egrets have something going for them; they're cousins of the blue heron, and the Audubon Society was founded to save the heron from extinction. You can't touch one of the little suckers without taking on the society." He shifted in the seat to study her intently. "Victoria, did it ever occur to you that you might not be cut out for law-enforcement work? You might be happier in Research, the fact-finding arm of the service."

"I didn't mean to imply I'm not all for our wildlife laws—I am," Victoria was quick to amend. "Like most of us who get involved in this work, I've come to look upon wildlife as sort of an oppressed minority. But people have to be considered, too. I felt the same way in Reyes County. In some ways I could sympathize with the stockmen—and I don't mean ones like Martin Rumbaugh. I think some of them are misinformed about the dangers eagles represent, but they're sincere. The people of Parker's Crossing are sincere, too, and that rookery was disgusting."

"Oh, someone will come up with a way to help them one of these days. There's very little Enforcement can do. No wildlife laws have been broken yet. You have to be patient. Didn't you learn that with the eagle episode? Nothing came of that, did it?"

She smiled ruefully. "Not much." Not much, except she had met a man who had further confused her already tangled emotions. She was still smarting from Grant's continued silence, convinced he was being too one way about their relationship. A part of her mind wanted him to be unable to stay away from her, but she remembered how obstinate he was.

Another more sensible part recognized that Grant's feelings doubtlessly mirrored some of her own. Falling in love left one open to possible rejection, and Grant would despise exposing himself to such weakness. . . just as she did.

She sighed. Affairs of the heart could be so perverse. It had occurred to her more than once that she and Grant probably weren't well suited, so it might be best to let the thing die a natural death. Yet the thought invariably brought on such a feeling of anguish, such a sense of loss. She didn't want to let go of Grant. . . and apparently she couldn't let go of her memories of Steve.

She thought Grant was a complicated one! Emotionally, she was a mystery even to herself.

IT WAS INCHING TOWARD five o'clock when Victoria and Chuck returned to the office, which was deserted. While Victoria filed her report and got ready to go home, Chuck casually sifted through the day's memos. She was starting for the door when he detained her. "Here's a message for you, Victoria."

She paused. "For me?" she asked expectantly,

unable to stifle the hope that Grant might have finally called.

"Someone named Sally Anderson phoned. Wants you to call her back."

Victoria's heart leaped. "Sally?" She took the slip of paper from Chuck's hand. On it was written a phone number, along with a note not to telephone until after nine o'clock, when the café would be closed.

Seeing the look on her face, Chuck asked, "Is it important?"

"It might be. It just might be."

Victoria thought nine o'clock would never come. After leaving the office, she hurried home, made a duty call to Rachel, prepared a quick supper, did some laundry, and still she paced until the appointed hour. Alive with expectation, she placed the call.

"Hello," said a sweet feminine voice on the other end of the line.

"Sally...? Victoria."

"Oh, Victoria.... I'm glad you called. I don't know if this will do you any good or not, but— have you got a minute?"

"I've got plenty of them."

"Well, last Saturday a friend of mine and I were invited to a barbecue at Martin Rumbaugh's ranch. When Joe and I got there— Joe Wentworth, he's my friend. He's with a construction company that's developing some ranchettes near here. Anyway, when we got to the ranch we discovered almost everyone in the county had been invited—quite a shindig—and Martin had a helicopter there, offering rides to anyone who would go up.''

"Was it a Dawson helicopter?" Victoria asked anxiously. The old gut feeling was stirring.

"Yes, the same one that used to be kept behind Miller's.''

"Was Frank Oakley piloting it?''

"Yes. That's what I wanted to tell you. As the afternoon wore on and everyone got tanked up on beer, Rumbaugh announced he was holding what he called an 'eagle roundup.' Said he would pay a hundred dollars for every eagle that was killed. Oakley and his partner took up anyone who wanted to try it.''

"I don't believe it!" Victoria gasped. A hundred dollars for something irreplaceable.

"Victoria, it was disgusting! Joe was furious. He doesn't have any ties to Reyes County or to Martin Rumbaugh, and he couldn't believe what he was seeing. They must have shot a dozen or more. After it was all over, everyone who had killed one lined up in front of the helicopter with the dead birds on the ground to have photographs taken.'' She paused. "Joe took one.''

Victoria's heart missed a beat. "Do you have it?''

"Sure do. I figured you might want it.''

"Oh, Sally! Do you have any idea what this means?''

"To tell you the truth, no. But I knew it would be important to you.''

"Sally, tell me exactly what the photograph shows, down to the last detail."

"Well, just a minute. . . ." There was a pause while, Victoria assumed, Sally studied the photograph. "The helicopter's in the background, and there are fourteen men lined up in front of it. Rumbaugh's in the center. Everyone but Rumbaugh is holding a rifle. They all have stupid grins on their faces. And. . . there's a pile of dead birds at their feet."

"Can you read the helicopter's ID number?"

"Hmm. . . some of it. But I can sure read Dawson Helicopter Service on the chopper's door."

Victoria's mind was racing. She knew wildlife laws, but she wished she knew more judicial law. Would that photograph be enough to get a grand-jury hearing? "Sally, whatever you do, put that picture in a safe place. Would you be willing to testify in court, to identify the people in it and to state you were a witness—"

"Oh, hey, Victoria, you really want your pound of flesh! That could ruin me in this town. Look, the picture is yours, with my blessing, but don't ask me to go to court and identify those people. Most of them are customers of mine."

Victoria groaned. "Sally, I'm not sure that photograph will be enough."

"You can't ask me to do that! I live here! I have to get along. I wouldn't have called you except I remembered your saying that if I ever called, it would be confidential. No one would ever know. . . ."

As difficult as it was for Victoria to understand how Martin Rumbaugh could have become such an intimidating influence in Reyes County, she could sense the real fear in Sally's voice. No good could come of pressuring her now; she would try to persuade her later. The most important thing was getting hold of that photograph, showing it to Chuck, who would then decide whether it warranted contacting the U.S. District Attorney. And Victoria wasn't sure she was willing to trust either Sally or the U.S. Mail to get the photograph to her.

Besides, she needed to talk to Sally in person. At her persuasive best, she just might be able to talk the woman into turning state's evidence. Failing that, she might find someone else who had been at the barbecue and would be willing to testify. Sometimes the mere mention of a grand jury could magically restore faulty memories. "All right, Sally, forget testifying. You put that picture in a safe place, and I'll drive to Kierney in the morning to get it."

"Oh, Lord, I'm beginning to wish I hadn't said a word," Sally moaned. "Look, Victoria, I don't want you to come anywhere near this café. Nothing personal, you understand, but your name is mud around here."

"I don't believe this! Sally, you can't begin to imagine the importance of that photograph. It's something real, concrete—hard evidence. Do you think it's right that Rumbaugh does as he pleases, with total disregard for the law?"

There was a long pause. At last Sally sighed. "No, of course I don't. All right, Victoria. Tell you what—I'll find someone to watch the café for me tomorrow evening, and I'll meet you at Arroyo Grande at six o'clock. How's that?"

Grant's place. She couldn't.

"Victoria, did you hear me? I'll meet you at Grant's. It's the perfect place, the only place. We can both slip in and out without anyone knowing we were there."

Quickly Victoria cleared her fogged brain. She needed this woman's trust, so they would have to meet wherever Sally felt secure. That was the essential thing right now, not some foolish qualms about seeing Grant again. "All right, Sally," she said calmly. "Six o'clock tomorrow at Arroyo Grande. And...thanks so much."

"Yeah." Sally laughed ruefully. "I just hope I've done the right thing."

An overwhelming excitement possessed Victoria as she hung up the phone, though the feeling was mixed with dread. How she longed to see Martin Rumbaugh squirm, to make him pay for mocking the law. But it was dishonest to pretend that was the sole source of this surge of exhilaration. Seeing Grant again—that was the real source of the excitement, and the dread.

## CHAPTER FIFTEEN

THIS WAS A LEGITIMATE REASON to return to Arroyo Grande, her mind kept telling her, not some fabrication. Grant would be as interested in seeing justice served as she was. After all, it had been his indignant phone call to Chuck that had started...everything.

Only God knew what she was letting herself in for. Two weeks with no word from him. Maybe, away from her, he had discovered he didn't want her as badly as he had thought. And why did that tear at her heart so? Hadn't she been the one who wanted no commitment? Wasn't she still uncertain? All he wanted was for her to tell him she loved only him, and there was no way she could do that, not yet.

Victoria took a moment to almost despise Steve for doing this to her, for making it impossible for her to accept another man's love, even if that man had an impatient, jealous nature. She desperately wanted a reunion with Grant, even knowing it would only confuse her more and further complicate her life.

She picked up the telephone again to call Chuck at home. She supposed she should call Grant, too, but she knew she wasn't going to.

DRIVING UNDER THE MASSIVE WOODEN ARCH with Arroyo Grande Lodge painted on it, Victoria experienced a peculiar sense of coming home. It had been, what? Only a little over three weeks since she had last been here, yet she felt as though she had been away for years and was happily coming back. Knowing she was only minutes away from seeing Grant again had her insides churning with anticipation. He would have to be glad to see her, too, wouldn't he?

It had been raining, light winter drizzle, but now the clouds were beginning to disperse; small drops of sunshine touched the tops of the cedar hills. Smoke puffed out of one of the lodge's chimneys. Victoria parked behind Grant's pickup, proof positive he was inside, and hurried into the familiar warmth of the lobby.

There was no one around. She could hear sounds coming from upstairs, other muted sounds from the kitchen. Maria and Mrs. Guilford were no doubt busy with their work. Rita wouldn't be home from school yet. If Grant was in the lodge, he would be in his office. She stared down the hall as if it were the Last Mile. Nervously smoothing at her dress, she moved forward. All of the doubting and mulling over and reconsidering during the long trip here came down to this—walking quietly down the hall and tapping on his office door.

She heard his gruff summons, "Come in," and she opened the door.

He was sitting behind his desk, feet propped up on it, reared back in his swivel chair. His pipe was clenched between his teeth, and he was wearing the dark-rimmed reading glasses that were so flattering to his rugged good looks. She had only a split second to scrutinize him, for he looked up almost immediately, his dark eyes locking onto hers. A curious weakness overtook her; she felt numb.

Grant had been expecting Jake, but the moment the door opened he was assailed by the flowery smell that was so uniquely Victoria. Of course, he could have been fantasizing, something he frequently did of late. Even when his eyes took in the woman who held such a stranglehold on his heart, he couldn't be sure he wasn't fantasizing. The fantasy moved, shifted from one foot to the other, and he knew she was real.

"Victoria?"

"Hello, Grant." Her smile was shy, apprehensive, lovely.

The glasses and pipe were discarded as he got to his feet. With a glad cry he crossed the room and took her in his arms. He didn't have to ask why she was here; there could only be one reason. She had decided.

It was touching, Victoria thought, that he didn't sweep her into his arms and kiss her passionately, but only held her close to him, as though he was trying to reassure himself she actually was there. She smiled against his chest, and her arms went around him.

This was exactly the response she had hoped for. If it hadn't been forthcoming, she didn't know what she would have done. Oh, he did feel so good, strong and comforting, and she was so glad to be with him. What was it that held her tongue in check, prevented her from telling him what he wanted to hear? Plaguing doubts intruded on this warm reunion.

He stepped away from her slightly, only far enough to stare down at her. "Victoria," he groaned. Gently he touched her face, then laced his fingers through her hair. He bent his head, and the kisses came in rapid-fire succession, robbing her of breath. With delight she fed on the taste of his mouth, the sweet flavor of his tongue as it intimately explored the moist cavern of her mouth.

Finally they parted. "Grant," she said, half laughing. "You leave me breathless."

"Victoria, if only you knew what I intend doing to you...but perhaps you can guess. If I wake up in a minute and discover this is a damned dream, I'm going to kill myself. Stand back and let me look at you."

He held her at arms' length, feasting his eyes on her. She was wearing a simple shirtwaist dress in a soft shade of turquoise that perfectly complemented her exquisite coloring. In all the world, he thought, there was only one woman who wore clothes with such flair. "That color is perfect on you, do you know that?"

Of course she knew it. Few women could reach her age without knowing what worked and what didn't. Turquoise in all its many hues was her best color, but it surprised her somewhat that Grant would even notice what color she was wearing. "Thank you," she simply said.

"Love, why didn't you call me to let me know you were coming?"

"I thought perhaps Sally would."

He frowned. "Sally?"

"Yes, I'm to meet her here at six o'clock. Oh, Grant, you'll be so excited when you hear the news! Sally has a photograph—"

"Photograph?" He didn't understand what she was saying to him.

She nodded and excitedly told him about Sally's evidence, all the while sensing the reason for the sudden change in his mood. She had never seen a darker expression on that face. When she finished speaking, his arms dropped to his sides.

"That's why you're here? On business?"

"Well. . . partly."

Grant's high hopes crashed at his feet, and he uttered a harsh laugh. "Well, I guess that takes me down a notch or two. I foolishly assumed you had come to see me."

"I did, of course." She reached for his hands, holding them tightly. "If I hadn't wanted to see you, I could have arranged to get the photograph another way. Of course I wanted to see you."

Roughly he flung her hands away. "That's not what I meant. I thought you had come to make the commitment."

Victoria's body sagged. Of course that would be his immediate reaction. She had disappointed him, the last thing she had wanted to do. She should have telephoned first, prepared him, but this was a fine time to be realizing that. "Oh, Grant, why is that the only thing that's important to you? Can't you just be glad I'm here?"

His disappointment was acute; he could practically taste it in his mouth. And he reacted the way he always did when faced with the unfaceable—with outrage. "No!" he barked.

"No? You're being too obstinate!"

"Perhaps."

"I don't understand you!"

"Apparently not, but I thought I had made it perfectly clear I didn't want to see you until—"

"*You* didn't want! I seem to hear a goodly amount of what *you* don't want! What is it with you that—"

"What is it with you, Victoria? Don't you know how it drains me to see you again, knowing you'll be here today, gone tomorrow? What am I supposed to do, allow you to drift in and out of my life as you see fit, dropping little crumbs of affection along the way?"

Victoria's hands flew to her throbbing temples. "That's the way you see it? Grant, why must you be so pigheaded about this? Why must you have everything or nothing?"

"Because I love you, goddammit!"

"And I think I love you, but how am I ever to know if you won't let me get near you? It seems to me we should—" Oh, Lord, she didn't know what they should do. "Grant, some people have relationships that last for months and months, even years before they make the total commitment. What possible good does it do to stay away from one another? We should be together, talk to each other—"

"And make love, I suppose," he snapped. "Great! You've got the hots for me and want me to serve as an outlet for your frustrations. No, thanks! You're too damned liberated to suit me, lady."

Victoria seethed; her face flushed crimson. "You're coming dangerously close to getting your face slapped!"

"Go on if it'll make you feel better."

"I felt fine until you started barking at me! I was absolutely dying to see you again. Why can't you enjoy that? Why can't you be glad there's someone who cares for you and wants to be with you and—" Her voice broke, and she took a deep breath to restore her composure. When she spoke again it was in a slow, measured tone. "I'll tell you why. Because you're afraid to be with me without a legally binding document. You're every bit as afraid of rejection and failure as I am. The difference is that I admit it, and you won't. Pray, tell me what good a certificate of marriage does. Did it keep Helena with you? Did it keep Steve with me?"

They stood facing each other, perhaps two feet separating them. The air seemed to crackle and hiss. Grant's hands were clenched at his sides. Victoria felt drained, exhausted, desperate, as though she were engaged in mortal combat. *Why must it always be like this between us?* she wondered. Why were they saying these awful things to each other? Some reunion. Five minutes together, and already they were snapping. It made no sense. *They* made no sense. Yet events kept propelling them back to each other.

For several long wordless moments they glared at each other. Then Grant expelled a struggling sigh. He had overreacted, as usual. It was his worst failing, a weakness he despised. Why did he allow Victoria to frustrate him so? What was there about this sweet, wonderful woman that turned him into a monster? "You're right, of course," he murmured at last.

"Grant...." Victoria closed the space between them. Slipping her arms around his waist, she laid her head on his shoulder and rubbed his back sensitively.

For a moment he remained motionless, made no move to touch her in any way. Finally, slowly, his arms went around her. "That's right, Victoria, rub that irresistible body against me, turn me into a mindless idiot...."

"Grant, that's not what I'm doing. Stifle that masculine pride of yours for once. Enjoy this feeling. It's so warm and tingling, so lovely. I've missed you so much."

"Warm and tingling, is it? More like hot and explosive." And he pressed her against him to prove it. Victoria gasped, lifting her mouth to his.

At that moment the door to the office flew

open, and Rita dashed in. Victoria and Grant bolted apart.

"Daddy, I—" She stopped, wide-eyed. "Victor-ia!" she screeched, flying across the room to throw her arms around Victoria in an exuberant hug. "When did you get here? Why didn't you tell us you were coming? Oh, daddy, isn't this great...Victoria's here!"

Over the top of Rita's head, Victoria's eyes challenged Grant. *Is it?* they asked. He met her gaze steadfastly. "Yes, hon," he said. "It's great."

THE PHOTOGRAPH Sally Anderson gave her turned out to be a good piece of incriminating evidence; it would be even more so with Sally's testimony, Victoria told her.

Sally's face twisted. "Oh, Victoria, I've thought about it, honestly I have, but—"

Just then the man who had accompanied Sally to Arroyo Grande stepped forward. Joe Wentworth was a pleasant, quiet man of about thirty, nice looking in an unspectacular way, and it was obvious to Victoria that he was quite fond of Sally. "I'll be glad to help you any way I can, Ms Bartlett," he said. "I understand Sally's position, but I couldn't care less what people around here think of me, and I never saw anything as revolting as that sight at the Rumbaugh ranch. You know, it never occurred to me that a person could actually witness a gathering of eagles like that. I've got a couple of young nephews, and I'd like to bring them out here sometime, so they can see it, too. There might not be any of those birds left when they're grown. Yes, it will give me great pleasure to testify.''

Triumph swept through Victoria. ''I don't know how to thank you, Joe,'' was all she could think of to say.

''Well, this calls for a drink!'' Grant said, getting to his feet. ''Sally, you and Joe stay for dinner, okay?''

They were soon joined by Jake, Roy and Sam, and for the remainder of the evening Victoria and Grant had no opportunity to exchange more than small talk. But at the dinner table she noticed his eyes resting on her more often than not, sending her messages loud and clear. He wanted her, and there was a long lovely night stretching ahead of them. Anticipation left Victoria trembling. She was reminded of their first night together in Corpus Christi, when he had so artfully seduced her with those eyes.

*Am I so terribly wrong,* she wondered, *to want him the way I do and still steer shy of a commitment? Grant won't wait for me forever. If I reach for him one day, maybe he'll be gone.*

## CHAPTER SIXTEEN

GRANT MOVED METHODICALLY through the silent
lodge, switching off lights and checking door
locks. The evening had been a busy one, and it had
taken everyone an uncommonly long time to call it
a day. Perhaps it had only been his imagination,
though...and his impatience for night. He might
have insisted that Sally and her friend Joe stay for
supper, but he certainly hadn't insisted on everyone's lingering over coffee and chitchat for hours.
Victoria, he thought, had been unusually animat-
ed, and Rita had hung on her every word. For a
while he had thought he was going to have to carry
the kid off to bed.

Even Jake and the boys had seemed in no hurry
to leave, whereas normally they scurried away the
moment the evening meal ended. Again, it might
have only seemed that way to him.

Victoria had gone to Rita's room twenty
minutes earlier—he knew because he had checked
his watch: and he hadn't wanted to follow so soon
behind. She had to be pleased, he mused. With
Sally's photograph and Joe's offer to testify, Victoria had her case. Yes, she would have to be
pleased, and he was experiencing ambivalent feel-

ings about that. He both admired and loathed her work. Caring for her the way he did, he regarded her job as a rival. He wanted to be the only thing that mattered to her. If that was chauvinistic, so be it—though he would never want to stand in her way professionally.

He locked the front door, then walked soundlessly down the hall, his heart pounding viciously. The place was different when Victoria was in it. Ridiculous, he knew, but true nevertheless. Tonight there would be an end to his loneliness, for a while at least.

For a while—that was the stickler. Each time they were together he found it harder and harder to let her go.

Light welled from under the door to Rita's bedroom. Grasping the knob, he opened it and stepped inside. The bed had been turned down; only a small bedside lamp illuminated the room. He closed the door behind him and locked it just as Victoria emerged from the bathroom.

A soft smile curved her mouth. Without taking her eyes from him, she reached behind and flipped off the bathroom light, watching as he went to sit on the edge of the bed. She joined him, sinking beside him and taking his hand in hers. He simply stared at her for a moment, then leaned toward her and gently captured her lips with his. When their bodies parted, the look she gave him was almost shy.

"You don't seem surprised to see me," he said huskily.

"Did you think I would be? You were sending out some pretty smoldering messages over the meat loaf tonight."

"And receiving a few in return."

Her lashes dipped for a second. "I think... there's probably something basically wrong with my wanting you the way I do," she admitted.

"But there's nothing you can do about it, is there?"

"Apparently not. You bring out something in me I didn't even know existed." Her voice was soft and breathy.

Grant's eyes moved over her hungrily. She was wearing some sort of dressing gown—floor-length, long-sleeved, pristine white with a scooped neckline trimmed in lace, so like Victoria. During those two halcyon days he had spent with her in Corpus Christi, he had learned of her fondness for soft lacy things next to her skin. She had drawers full of the stuff. Dear God, he knew so much about her...and so little. To think he had once despised soft, feminine things, for they had reminded him of Helena. No longer. Had he seen this gown in a store he would have thought of Victoria. On anyone else the garment might have been demure; on her it screamed sensuality. The fabric clung seductively to her appealing lines. Beneath it, two soft mounds rose and fell, their shadowy, puckered tips pointing enticingly toward him. Gently he fingered the lace. "Lovely," he murmured.

"Thank you."

"Is it new?"

"No, I've had it some time."

"How long?"

"Less than a year, Grant." At no time had she worn the gown with Steve, which is what she thought Grant wanted to know.

"I guess you're pleased with everything that happened this evening."

"Yes."

"What now?"

"We'll doubtless get Rumbaugh and a whole bunch of other people into court." Victoria's hand inched up his shirtfront, and her fingers flicked the first button out of its hole. "Let's talk about it later, okay?"

"Okay." He reached for her, drawing her into the comforting circle of his arms. She curled against him, her head against his shoulder, and lifted her face to his. Their mouths fused perfectly, pliantly. One of Grant's hands slipped around to hover above her breast for a second; it closed over the flesh. His thumb teased the bud to hardness.

"Grant," Victoria whispered against his mouth. "I can't believe the way you make me feel—brand-new, unused."

"I wish we both were, Victoria—brand-new, I mean. I wish no one else had ever touched either of us. Then maybe—"

"Hush, lover, hush. Don't talk. Just kiss me."

Her mouth, eyes, throat felt his kiss, but it wasn't enough to assuage the terrible ache growing inside. With trembling fingers she fumbled at the buttons of his shirt. "Would...you like me to undress you?"

"Please. I...I don't seem to be able to move."

Deftly she jerked the shirt free of his jeans, finished unbuttoning it and slipped it off his shoulders and arms. Her hands wandered luxuriously over the broad expanse of his chest, pausing to finger the thick mat of dark hair before traveling down to his belt buckle. Once she had undone the belt she unsnapped the jeans, but Grant's hands covered hers, detaining her.

"Darling, a man always takes off his boots before his pants."

"Oh, of course. I guess I knew that."

Quickly she got to her feet and turned her back to him, swung one leg over the one he offered her. As she presented him her backside, her gown rode up to midthigh. Firmly clutching his leg between her knees, she grasped the boot at the heel and toe, tugged, and it thudded to the floor. Repeating with the other, she felt Grant's stockinged foot pushing against her bottom. The boot soon joined its mate on the floor.

"This is an unnerving sight, Victoria." Grant's voice was deep and throaty, and Victoria could feel his hands roaming over her firm, round buttocks. Grasping her hips, he pulled her up to his lap, to the aching center of him. With one hand he parted the hair at the nape of her neck and kissed her gently. The touch of his lips on the sensitive area spun a kaleidoscope of new emotions through her body.

Slowly both his hands moved up her sides and around. Each cupped a full breast, pulling her back so that her shoulder blades were pressed against him. Victoria's lips formed a small O of astonished pleasure as he continued to kiss and sip at her neck. Her skin hummed and tingled.

"Your socks," she said breathlessly, slithering off his lap to kneel at his front. The gown billowed and fell in soft folds in a circle on the floor around her.

Grant's mind reeled and stumbled, intent on nothing but the lovely creature at his feet and the pounding arousal in his loins. When she had dispensed with his socks, she tugged at his jeans. He raised his hips to facilitate their removal.

She tossed them to one side in a heap near his boots. Then, still kneeling on the floor, she wrapped her arms around his legs, turned her lips to the inside of his thigh and kissed him. Groaning his desire, expending a valiant effort at self-control, Grant filled his hands with the lustrous softness of her hair and closed his eyes, sucking in a ragged breath.

She kissed one thigh, then the other, and her hands inched upward to his hips. Intoxicated with passion and joy, Grant could stand it no longer. He slid his hands under her arms, lifted her up, stood with her and hastily pulled the gown over her head.

"You're too slow, love...or I'm too impatient." He stripped out of his undershorts in a flash. Carefully he guided her back on the bed, taking a moment to savor her exquisite body before covering it with his own. Her legs wound sleekly around him. Passion surged through them. There was nothing to do but give in to the tumult raging and storming inside them, to drown it quickly in Grant's possession.

It was their sacred love ritual all over again, hasty though it was. Abstinence had made him avaricious. His hands roaming over her satin skin, Grant quickly brought her to the pinnacle of pleasure; there would be time for finesse later. This time there was a desperation, a pulsating urgency to their lovemaking that transcended anything they had known before. He gloried in the whimpering voice that echoed his name over and over again. Stroking rhythmically, he watched her face and knew the second she had ecstasy within her grasp.

Victoria bit her bottom lip. She slid her hands down his hard, lean torso to hold him more tightly to her as the golden fire began spreading through the lower part of her abdomen. The ensuing explosion seemed to go on and on and on. Grant gathered her to him tightly, and she felt the shudders racking his body. A soft smile touched her lips as she realized they had reached the summit together.

THERE WAS PLEASURE to be found in the quiet aftermath, pleasure as intensely satisfying, in its ways, as the union preceding it. Victoria stretched languorously beside Grant, enormously content. As before, the force of their union staggered her.

And as before, her abandonment amazed her. Grant had unearthed a taproot of sensuality in her she hadn't known existed. Whether she was moved by unbridled lust or something more profound she wasn't sure.

"Before you, I thought I was frigid," she confessed.

She felt the rumble of laughter in his chest. "Well, I think that's something you can stop worrying about."

Gradually strength returned to her limbs, and she propped herself on one elbow, smiling down at him. "I want to bury my face in that forest on your chest."

"Be my guest."

Smiling, she did just that while he idly played with her lustrous hair. "Grant, am I really too liberated for you?"

"Probably, given my inherent caveman instincts," he said facetiously, but quickly sobered. "Any man over thirty who claims he harbors no 'me Tarzan you Jane' tendencies is lying. Am I too chauvinistic for you?"

"Probably, but most men over thirty are."

"Your ex-husband?"

"Definitely."

"Your father?"

"Oh, God, the worst! Mom was his resident slave. Fat lot it got her."

Moments ticked by. He asked, "Do you have to go tomorrow?"

"I should. The wheels of justice grind slowly,

and I need to start them rolling.'' She wrapped her arms around his naked middle, gently rubbing his rib cage. She felt rather than heard him sigh.

''We're doing this all backward, you know. In those old movies it's always the hero who flits in and out of the heroine's life, driving her nuts. And all the while she's begging him to give up that awful job of his and settle down with her.''

Victoria laughed lightly, continuing to rub her cheek against him.

''I need you, Victoria,'' Grant said finally. ''Rita needs you, too. She's a different girl when you're around. You put a light in her eyes that I certainly can't.''

She closed her eyes. ''Please don't put it that way. Please don't. As though I'm depriving the two of you....''

''You are.''

''You're trying to make me feel guilty,'' she accused.

''Maybe.''

''That's unfair!''

''Isn't everything fair in love?''

''No!''

More silent moments. Then.... ''Victoria,'' he said gravely, ''I'm going to ask you to do me a favor.''

''Yes?''

''I want you to see Steve.''

She frowned and raised up to look at him. ''What?''

''Perhaps I should rephrase that. I don't want

you to, but I think you should. I mean it. Arrange a meeting with him or something. Have lunch together.''

''Nancy would take a damned dim view of that. Besides—'' she tried to laugh, but the sound had a hollow ring ''—I don't have anything to do with married men.''

Grant couldn't have been more serious. ''Then ask for an appointment at his office. I'm sure you can think of something if you set your mind to it.''

''I'm sure I could, too, but why on earth would I?''

He wasn't looking at her; he was staring at an obscure point on the far wall. ''You've got to do something to break his hold on you. Maybe if you talk to him awhile you can get rid of all those memories of the good times. . . .''

''It's not the good times I remember, Grant,'' she said soberly, lying back down, unsure what she was saying was the unvarnished truth. ''I never think of the good times. They don't haunt me at all.''

''Then what is it?''

''The hurt when it ended. The sense of absolute betrayal.''

''I'd never do that to you, love.''

''How do you know you wouldn't? I didn't think Steve would, either. I trusted him completely. I thought he was the best friend I had in the world.'' Her voice cracked with bitterness.

''I know it hurts, Victoria. I, too, know all about betrayal.''

"Maybe. . . maybe I'm not the only one haunted by ghosts, Grant. Don't you have a few of your own?"

"No," he said decisively. "Mine are gone."

"Are you sure? If you didn't still harbor bitterness and resentment, wouldn't you—" Victoria hesitated, not sure she had the right to say it "— wouldn't you allow Rita to see her mother?"

She felt him tense, heard him suck in his breath, but the reaction was brief. "My ghosts are gone, Victoria. The moment I let you into my heart I was free of them. And once you let me into yours you'll be free, too."

Which didn't really answer her question, she noted. "Grant, it would be so easy to tell you what you want to hear. Everything seems so clear-cut and uncomplicated when I'm lying here with you. But I'd only be fooling myself, and I know you don't want me to be dishonest. Seeing Steve again. . . what possible good can come of that?"

"Something might," he insisted. "Will you do it? Promise me?"

Victoria thought about it, tried to envision calling on Steve at his office, having a long talk with him. She wasn't sure she could do it, had the strength to do it. She had been bitter for so long.

But perhaps Grant was right. She had to do something about this uncertainty or let this relationship with Grant die, and right now that was something she couldn't seriously contemplate. She stirred in his arms, leaned over him. "I promise you I'll try to see Steve, if you'll do something for me in return.''

"Anything.''

"I want you to see Helena, or at least talk to her.''

Grant's expression darkened. "That's preposterous!''

"Is it? There's not a nickel's worth of difference in our situations, Grant—only that you've been divorced longer, and you have a child. Seeing her will make you remember everything. I know. Then and only then you can be sure you're ready to try again.''

"I've rearranged my thinking for you, and still you want more!''

"I have to be sure. And you should be, too.''

His sigh was deep. "So you see Steve, and I see Helena. What if one of us decides against. . . us?''

Victoria lay back down and caressed his cheek with her fingertips. "It's. . . thanks for the memories, I guess.''

"So still we wait?''

"Please be patient with me. I'll. . . know when things are right.''

"What if 'things' are never right?''

"Isn't it better to discover that now rather than later?''

"Together we can make things right, Victoria.''

"Grant, I don't want us to have to make them right. I want them to be right.''

Grant contemplated the ceiling and reflected on the complexities of human nature, particularly the female mind. It was so fascinating in its contrariness; what ordinary man could hope to comprehend it? He wanted to demand, Love me exclusively or get out of my life! But he couldn't risk issuing an ultimatum to Victoria, because he wanted her so.

He was awfully old, he thought, to have found, only now, someone whose presence was essential to his happiness. No one, not even Helena, had ever made him feel this way, and he was quite prepared to believe no one ever could again. It might be his very age that made him so impatient. He was so acutely aware of the passing of time.

He would get nowhere trying to rush her. She wanted time, time he was loath to allow her, yet living without Victoria was not something he intended doing. He would just have to be patient; he didn't know what else he could do. "Just don't wait until it's too late for us, Victoria."

An ominous chill ran up her spine. How would she know when the point had been reached?

Slipping a forefinger under her chin, he tilted her head up. "We're together now. Troubling things can wait. Let's just make love."

"Again?" A relieved giggle escaped her lips; their mood had been much too somber, and they had so little time together. "Oh, Grant, you're positively decadent."

"Hmm...."

"Do you suppose it could be dangerous—to your health, I mean—to make love too much?"

He chuckled heartily. "I never heard of anyone

dying from it. But it might be a good way to go, in the throes of ecstasy. I die a little every time. . . . ''

"I know, I know," she whispered.

"You, too?"

"Of course. Men don't have a monopoly on it, you know."

Grant grew solemn. "I don't want to have to say goodbye to you in the morning, Victoria."

"Why? It's not really goodbye."

"Are you sure? I never am. I don't even want to watch you drive away. I'll just steal away and go commune with some squirrels or something until I'm sure you've gone."

"I suppose you don't want me to call, either."

"The only phone call I want from you, Victoria, is the one telling me you're coming here to stay."

An obstruction lodged in her throat. "All right. I'll leave early."

"Try to say goodbye to Rita before you go."

"I will."

He brought her face down to within inches of his. "But for now, there's still tonight."

DRIVING AWAY from Arroyo Grande the next morning was the hardest thing Victoria had ever done. At some point during the night Grant had gotten up and gone to his own room. She awakened in the hour just before dawn, dressed hurriedly and drove away before the rest of the household stirred, forgetting her promise to say goodbye to Rita. She never wanted to say goodbye to either of them again. Speeding down the lonely country road, watching the sunrise in the rearview mirror, she was certain she had never felt lonelier.

TWO NIGHTS LATER, when Victoria was certain she would go mad if she spent another evening alone in her house, she paid her mother a visit.

"How was dear Rita?" Rachel asked.

"Fine, mom, and she sends her love. You certainly made an impression on her."

"She's a darling. Rather reminds me of you at that age. Inquisitive, enthusiastic, brighter than average." Rachel paused. "How was her father?"

Victoria grimaced. "He wants me to go talk to Steve. That will be the magic restorative, according to Grant. All I have to do is have a cozy chat with my ex, and all my problems will vanish."

"I think the man's absolutely right, Victoria," Rachel said firmly. "That's what you should do— see Steve, talk to him. You should have done it long ago, instead of crawling off in a corner and licking your wounds."

"What, pray, shall I say?"

"Anything. Ask him why he left you."

"Oh, mom!"

"Ask him. It'll surprise him so much he won't have time to think of a lie. His answer might be enlightening. And I'll go Grant one better. I'd like to suggest that you see your father, too."

Victoria was stretched out on a chaise longue in her mother's cavernous bedroom, watching Rachel primp at the dressing table. Her daughter sighed in exasperation. "Mom, I wouldn't know what to say to either one of them."

"Nonsense. Something would come to you." Slowly Rachel turned on the stool to glance fondly at her daughter. "How can you possibly hope to love someone else when you're so filled with resentment toward the only two men you've ever been close to?"

Victoria studied her fingernails; finding a chip in one, she began to pick at it. "Correction, mom...I've been close to three men. I'm very close to Grant. Sometimes I feel closer to him than I ever did to Steve."

"Three men," Rachel muttered. "Twenty-seven years old and you've been close to three men, one of them your father! How awful! When I married I had had dozens of boyfriends."

Victoria was lost in thought and scarcely heard her mother. "Of course there are other times when I feel as though he just dropped down from another planet and we're trying to communicate through sign language. If he weren't so hardheaded about a commitment, I think we could have a fantastic relationship."

Rachel smiled. "Did it ever occur to you that Grant might consider you a little 'hardheaded,' too?"

Victoria lifted her chin. "All I'm asking of him is time to let the relationship grow. He wants me to sign on the dotted line. I'm not ready to do that yet, and I should think you could sympathize.

You've not been able to, either, and you and dad have been divorced eight years."

Rachel turned back to the mirror to rearrange an already perfect coiffure. "I was too old."

"Garbage!"

"I had already lived a twenty-year marriage. It was enough."

"More garbage! You were scared to death of failing again, just as I am."

Rachel didn't deny it. "Of course. Steering clear of commitments is the easy way out. If you don't attempt a relationship, how can you fail? I'll tell you one thing, Victoria—I've been lonely more often than I haven't these past eight years. There might have been something missing with Dan Graham, but he had plenty going for him, too, and my life would have been richer had I accepted his proposal. That's something for you to think about."

Victoria sat, her head thrown back on the chaise's cushioned surface, her mouth a hard line. "I asked Grant to see his ex-wife, too."

That made Rachel start. "Why on earth did you do that?"

"For the same reason he wants me to see Steve, I guess. I want him to be sure."

"Oh, Victoria," Rachel sighed. "You want an iron-clad, money-back guarantee! None of us can have that, dear. You may live to regret sending Grant to see that ex-wife."

Victoria's stomach lurched. "Mom, I came over

here this evening to avoid spending it in that cold, empty house of mine—and you're doing your best to depress me!''

"No, I'm doing my best to make you face life as it is, not as you want it to be! You always lived something of a fairy-tale existence, Victoria. The total idealist. I often had the nagging suspicion you were born into the wrong century. Marrying the only man you ever dated, for heaven's sake! Who does that sort of thing anymore? You missed out on so much. I should have insisted...."

"I wouldn't have listened. You know that."

"No, you wouldn't have. You always had a mind of your own, too." Rachel sighed dramatically. "You were convinced you and Steve had the absolutely perfect relationship. No one does, and if you took a long, hard, objective look at your marriage, I think you would come to recognize its flaws."

Victoria's eyes narrowed. "For instance?"

"For instance, Steve's self-engrossment. We all need a little humility. Steve has none."

"I thought you adored Steve, mom."

"I did—do! Well, perhaps 'adore' might be a bit much, but I always liked Steve very much. Of course, I don't think as much of him as I once did, and it's not because he divorced you. It's the adultery angle. If I live through two dozen so-called sexual revolutions, I'll never condone adultery. A little anger would do you a world of good, dear."

"Oh, I've been angry—furious—livid!"

"But more at yourself than at Steve, right?"

Victoria opened her mouth to deny that, closing it quickly when she realized how astute her mother was. For all the ranting and railing she had done, she had mostly ranted and railed at herself for not being able to make the marriage work. Rachel was right about something else: she had considered hers and Steve's relationship perfect. She hadn't been able to shake the notion that if a "perfect" marriage could fail, what chance would a not-so-perfect one have?

Victoria pushed back her hair, clearly agitated. "Well, mom, you've certainly given me plenty of food for thought."

"I hope so, dear." Rachel set down her hairbrush and turned to her daughter with the air of one who has said all she intends to on that subject. "So tell me the results of this latest trip, Victoria."

Victoria snapped out of her private thoughts. "It was very fruitful. Very fruitful. A piece of hard evidence in the form of a photograph, and an eyewitness who's willing to testify. Chuck was so pleased. I honestly thought he was going to hug me. We're meeting with a federal attorney in the morning."

THE ATTORNEY WAS ROGER DAVENPORT, an intensely serious bespectacled young man who was undertaking the case with enthusiasm. Legislation regarding wildlife resources was new to him. His interest was genuine. And since Chuck's knowledge of the subject was vast, Victoria found it fascinating to discuss the situation with the two men.

It was midafternoon when the attorney finally snapped his briefcase shut and declared, "Well, I'm going to the grand jury with this, and if we get a trial—which I'm almost sure we will, or I wouldn't be going to the jury—I'm going to need an expert on eagles. I'm talking Foremost Authority with capital letters."

Chuck nodded. "I'll ask around."

"I want to know everything there is to know about the birds. Our prosecution will go with the fact that there's a law stating an eagle cannot be killed. Obviously an eagle has been killed. We have them dead to rights on that one, so I expect defense to counter with the ranchers' rights to protect personal domain, something a jury might very well sympathize with. I'm going to have to know exactly what threat the birds pose to the stockmen."

"Right!" Chuck said emphatically.

Roger Davenport stood up. "I'll be in touch as soon as I know something. It's been a pleasure meeting both of you. Good day, Ms Bartlett."

"Goodbye, Mr. Davenport."

"Nice man," Chuck said when the lawyer had departed.

"Yes, very pleasant."

"I have a feeling we struck it lucky when we drew him. Where can we find him an eagle expert?"

Victoria frowned thoughtfully. "Well...you could call my father," she said hesitantly.

"Your dad?"

"Dr. Adam Carpenter. He's a biology professor and something of an expert himself. I'm sure he'll know whom we should contact."

"That's great. Will you ask him?"

Victoria nibbled her bottom lip. "Well, I—"

"Victoria," Chuck said with his customary lack of patience. "What's with the hesitation?"

She sighed. "My dad and I seldom talk, and it's been months since I've seen him. My folks are divorced, you see, and dad is constantly yammering away to mom about my never calling him."

Chuck nodded understandingly. "All right, I'll call him."

"No, no, I will. I've been giving some thought to seeing him again soon. It's past time, and this would be a perfect excuse." She stared at the opposite wall beyond Chuck's shoulder. Steve, too, she thought. She might as well do it, stop licking her wounds, stop wringing every drop of misery out of problems. What it would accomplish she wasn't sure. Perhaps by talking to Steve and her father she could get some insight into the deterioration of two seemingly ideal marriages. Once she understood why, once she had pinpointed the pitfalls, she might be willing to try again.

She missed Grant, or thought she did. Maybe she simply missed the wondrous things he could do to her. If that was all they had together—the physical part, the lust—it seemed a pretty flimsy foundation on which to build a solid marriage.

*Marriage.* Even the word was scary. And *divorce* was even scarier.

Chuck cleared his throat loudly; Victoria's head snapped around. "Sorry, Chuck. I was lost in thought."

"So I noticed." Idly he tapped the desk top and pursed his lips, not looking directly at her. "Victoria, forgive me for getting personal, but...is there something you'd like to talk to me about?"

"What? Oh—no."

"You haven't been yourself since, well, since you got back from your vacation. I wondered if something was troubling you."

"It's...personal."

"Obviously." He paused, looked at her with a faint smile and added, "Grant Mackenzie called me yesterday after you left for the day."

Her eyes widened. "Who?"

"Grant Mackenzie. You remember him, don't you?" His sly smile, his tone implied he was sure she did.

"Of course. What...what did he want?"

"Hard to say. He rambled on about several inconsequential things, then asked how things were going, specifically how you were. When I hung up I had the distinct feeling that was the whole purpose of the call."

*He might have called me,* Victoria thought pettishly. *What does he hope to accomplish with this silent routine? Why isn't he turning himself inside out wooing me?*

Chuck's eyes were intent. "Is Grant the problem?" he finally asked.

She laughed nervously. "Why on earth would you ask that?"

"I know Grant."

"If it is, Chuck...I'll work it out."

"Just wanted you to know I make a good listener. I've been sort of a Father Confessor around here for years, so I've had a lot of practice." Chuck drummed on the desk for a few seconds, waiting to see if she might confide in him. When she didn't, he cleared his throat and added, "You know, Victoria, if whatever's troubling you doesn't get worked out, there's a lateral transfer to the Albuquerque office available. No promotion, but sometimes a change of scene does wonders."

"Trying to get rid of me?" she teased.

"Not at all! Just trying to help you. You could spend a year in Albuquerque, then come back here."

Victoria was deeply moved by her supervisor's compassion. "Thanks. I'll keep that in mind."

Victoria left Chuck's office filled with steely determination. This inner conflict had to be dealt with. If it had played such havoc with her behavior that even her supervisor had noticed, it had to be resolved. Grant deserved that much. If she discovered she couldn't make the commitment, she needed to tell him. . . soon. Her indecision was unfair to him and unworthy of her. The moment she got home she would telephone both Steve and Adam and ask if she could see them within a few days.

And if that didn't help. . . well, she just might think seriously about Albuquerque.

# CHAPTER SEVENTEEN

THE PANELED OFFICE reflected the personality of
the man who occupied it, Victoria thought for the
hundredth time in her life. Quiet, dignified, taste-
ful. There had been a time when she had loved
bringing her friends to this room, had loved showing them what an important man her father was.
That had been so long ago. Now Adam had a new
secretary, and his office had new drapes and
carpet. These irrelevant observations served to remind her of the length of her estrangement from
her father.

She had made the appointment over the phone
through Adam's secretary, who had assumed Victoria Bartlett was one of Dr. Carpenter's students.
Apparently Adam hadn't known she was coming
until she was announced. To her relief, as surprised as he was, he didn't jump up to hug her or
anything like that, although his pale face and
astonished eyes gave away his confusion. On the
surface, however, he managed to maintain his
characteristic poise, and he looked, Victoria
thought, positively wonderful. He had always
been a handsome man, tall, straight and trim, and
he still was. She could only wonder at what cost he

kept that lean body. The "salt" in his dark hair only enhanced his distinguished good looks. It was widely rumored that the majority of Dr. Carpenter's female students fell a little bit in love with him.

"Well, Victoria...this is a surprise, I must say."

"I'm sure it is. I'm not keeping you from anything important, am I?"

"Of course not! What could be more important than a visit from my daughter? You're looking unusually lovely, my dear."

"Thank you, dad. How have you been?"

"Oh, fine, just fine. Surprisingly few aches and pains for a man who's on the shady side of fifty."

It came to Victoria with something of a shock that her father was almost fifty-five. That was a long way from being old, of course, but she still thought of him as a much younger man. "How is Martina?" she asked politely, not really caring.

"Martina is fine. I'll tell her you asked about her. She'll be so pleased."

Victoria doubted that. The few times she had been around her father's second wife she had been treated with nothing more than cool courtesy and indifference. But then, she thought in all fairness, Martina might have sensed Adam's daughter's hostility toward her. Victoria had never been very good at hiding her feelings, particularly the more unkind ones.

"Victoria, you'll have lunch with me, won't you?" Adam asked. "I have a conference at two o'clock, but I'm free until then."

Victoria hesitated. Two hours with her father was more than she had bargained for. What could they possibly talk about for two hours?

But her hesitation was brief. "Of course. I'd love to."

"I try to keep up with news of you through Rachel. Your mother tells me you've become quite involved in your work. I was most interested in the Parker's Crossing incident. I understand you were there."

"Yes, I was there, and to be honest with you, if I were a citizen of that community I might have a hard time deciding which side of the law I was on. The rookery is foul."

Adam nodded solemnly. "I've read the newspaper accounts. The uninformed seem to think this concentration outside Parker's Crossing is unusual, but actually, gregariousness is an outstanding feature of Ciconiiformes' behavior. Some of the assemblies are enormous. For example, a single African lake hosts over a million of them at one time. So I hardly think the twenty-odd thousand outside Parker's Crossing are noteworthy."

*Ever the professor!* Victoria thought, though not unkindly. To have such facts on the tip of one's tongue was remarkable. Adam Carpenter was precisely the sort of authority they could use. She leaned forward with great interest. "Why Parker's Crossing, dad? Why have the egrets chosen to congregate there? Any ideas?"

"It's cattle country, right?"

"Yes."

"There's your answer. That particular species of Ciconiiformes are dependent on livestock infested with insects, their basic food. Since humans raise livestock, the birds colonize near humans, often to said humans' great distress."

"You mean, it's the ready availability of food, not the particular countryside, that's the main attraction?"

"I would have to think so."

Victoria sat back, her brow furrowing. "Well, it's an interesting piece of information, something I'll pass along. I doubt anything will come of it, but you can never tell. And as long as we're on this subject, I'd like to tell you about another case I've been working on...."

As briefly as possible she told Adam about the Reyes County eagle incident, concluding with, "So now we're going to trial, and the federal attorney wants an eagle expert, someone with impeccable credentials. I was thinking perhaps you would be a good choice."

"No, not me, Victoria, but I have just the man for you. His name is Robert Barrett, and he's tops in his field. He wrote *Twilight of the Eagle* a number of years ago. The book was instrumental in raising public awareness of the plight of our national bird. Perhaps you read it."

Victoria shook her head. "Read it, no, but I've heard of it, and of Dr. Barrett, too."

"Bob's a wonderful gentleman, knowledgeable and quite a talker. He's done very well on the lecture circuit. I'm sure he'd love helping you. He lives near San Antonio now. I'll get his phone number for you.''

Victoria was twice as relaxed as she had thought she would be; the meeting with her father was going quite smoothly. They soon left his office to drive to a nearby restaurant for a lunch of shrimp gumbo. Glancing around the place, Victoria remarked on how long it had been since she had visited this particular restaurant. ''I had forgotten all about it, but I seem to recall our eating here frequently years ago.''

Adam nodded. ''It was one of Rachel's favorites. For years, whenever she got in the mood to cook, she tried to duplicate this gumbo. She always claimed she never came close, but it tasted the same to me.''

Adam's mentioning her mother's name brought Victoria to the question she had been wanting to ask all along. ''Dad,'' she said quietly. ''You and mom. . . the divorce. How did it happen?''

Adam appeared completely taken aback for a moment. Victoria supposed she had been rather blunt, but she hadn't been able to find a tactful way of broaching the subject. Recovering, he put his hand to his mouth and coughed lightly. ''I'm not sure I can give you a pat answer to your rather startling question, Victoria. I can't say this happened, then that happened, so we divorced. It was more complicated than that.''

''I'm sure it was, and I wouldn't ask except. . . except that knowing, understanding might help me make a big decision in my own life." She paused, drawing in a deep breath. This was difficult for her, having never found it particularly easy to talk to her father, not as she could to Rachel. Adam was such a learned, scholarly man. Though unaware of the fact, he had always possessed the unfortunate knack of making Victoria feel gauche and a little stupid. But how could she expect him to confide in her if she couldn't open up with him? "You see, dad, there's this man...."

Once she got the first hesitant words out, she found it surprisingly easy to tell Adam about Grant. She divulged no really intimate details of their relationship; what father would want to hear them? But she explained her instant attraction to him, Grant's desire for marriage and her doubts and fears. "I could never go through another divorce, never! When Steve asked for his freedom, I was stunned. You might think it impossible to live with a man and not know something was amiss, but... I didn't! I'm afraid I behaved horribly—raging, storming, threatening—all the while angry at myself, so sure I had done something wrong. I kept remembering how I felt when mom told me the two of you were splitting up. For a long time I felt that was somehow my fault."

Victoria wondered if she had gone too far. The expression on her father's face was ghastly. Taking a handkerchief out of his hip pocket, Adam mopped his brow and seemed to be struggling for words. "Good Lord, Victoria, you had absolutely nothing to do with what happened between Rachel and me. Where do kids get these outlandish ideas?''

"I was no kid, dad,'' Victoria reminded him quietly. "I was nineteen and, I thought, pretty levelheaded. Now I realize my reaction wasn't all that unusual. I've been told children often feel guilty when their parents split up. The divorce was hard on me, in some ways harder than my own. I think if I knew why those two seemingly wonderful marriages failed, I might be able to decide if I'm willing to try again.''

Adam cleared his throat. It wasn't going to be easy for him. She didn't think she had ever seen him nonplussed, but he was now. "Well, Victoria,'' he said finally, "the simplest thing I can tell you is that sometimes when two people live together for a long time, they grow apart, and sadly, they don't realize it until it's too late. In the early years of our marriage, I was preoccupied with getting ahead in the world of academia, and Rachel...well, Rachel had you. She was the most devoted mother I've ever known. Looking back, I can see we never had any coinciding interests, and that was my fault. When I wasn't teaching, I was either writing or attending a seminar or giving a lecture somewhere, and I disdained the academic social life, which Rachel would have loved. I was determined to get ahead on my own merit, not because my wife was a fantastic hostess or rot like that. So...Rachel had to find her own diversions.''

Victoria nodded. "Room mother, scout leader, chairman of the school's yearly carnival—all anyone had to do was call mom."

Adam's eyes grew vacant and distant. "One day you were grown, and Rachel's main reason for being was gone. Unfortunately, I was practically a stranger to her, so she threw herself into volunteer work. We scarcely ever saw each other. We were more like longtime friends who happened to share a house. And, too...."

"By that time you had met Martina," Victoria prodded.

Adam sighed. "Yes. You must believe me, Victoria. I never meant things to snowball the way they did. A...relationship with another woman was the furthest thing from my mind. Throughout my marriage to your mother I was the picture of fidelity."

As difficult as it must have been for her father to tell her these things, it was doubly difficult for Victoria to hear them. Her parents had always seemed perfectly happy and content to her, but then, in the way of offspring, she had hardly scrutinized them. She had taken it for granted they would always be there, like the sun in the morning and the moon at night.

Now that she thought about it, Adam had scarcely ever been around. She had seen more of her grandfather, Rachel's father, than she had her own. It had seemed only natural that a busy, important man wouldn't be home very often.

Her parents had seldom gone anywhere together, just the two of them, nor did they have the same friends. Guests in the Carpenter home had invariably been Rachel's socialite friends, people she had known all her life, and Adam had never seemed really comfortable with them. Odd to only now be realizing that.

*Well, it wouldn't be like that with Grant and me,* she thought decisively. *I would be as involved in Arroyo Grande as he is, and I could be of enormous help to him. It would be so different with us.* Or would it? What did she really know about Grant, other than the fact that he was moody, possessive, and that his eroticism could drive her out of her mind?

Now she was embarrassed and wishing with all her heart she hadn't brought up her parents' marriage. "Please, dad, you don't have to—"

"No, no. If you're to understand, you should hear everything. I'm not sure how long Rachel knew about Martina before everything came out. A long time, I suspect. Too long. The damage had been done. I had grown too attached to Martina, so I couldn't break it off, and in all truth, Rachel never asked me to."

Victoria's brows lifted in surprise. "Never?"

Slowly Adam shook his head. "Not once."

"If she had... would you have...?"

"It's useless to speculate on what I might have done. Rachel would never have taken me back, Victoria. Her pride had been crushed, and she was bitter. Things would never have been the same again."

Yes, Victoria could understand that. Given the chance, would she have taken Steve back? Probably—and lived with suspicion the rest of her life. The marriage would never have been the same, doubtless would have died a slow painful death instead of a quick one.

"Tell me, dad. What attracted you to mom in the first place?"

The faintest hint of a smile touched Adam's mouth. "That's an easy one to answer. I thought she was the prettiest thing I'd ever seen, and I had never met a real socialite. I was just a high-school biology teacher, working on my master's degree so I could teach at college level. The doctorate came later, as did the books. An acquaintance of mine who moved on the periphery of Rachel's exalted social circle wangled an invitation for me to some party, and that's where I met her. I guess I was smitten from the beginning. I couldn't believe such a gorgeous creature could be interested in me. The people she introduced me to, the parties we attended—it was a new world to me. I was enchanted, temporarily. I'll admit something to you, Victoria, that I've never admitted to anyone else: I always stood a little in awe of Rachel and her crowd."

Not the answer Victoria had wanted at all. She had wanted Adam to tell her how much he had loved Rachel, and he couldn't have lived without her. "And Martina?" she ventured boldly, fully aware she had no right to ask.

Adam didn't falter; apparently he had become

inured to his daughter's forthrightness. "I felt. . . comfortable with Martina, not at all out of my element. She adored me, and adoration from another human being is almost impossible to resist."

Victoria felt a little sickened by the revelation. That was the reason her father had married a woman twenty years his junior—to bask in her adoration? How shallow and superficial! And his reasons for marrying Rachel hadn't been particularly admirable. She wished she hadn't asked. She wasn't a bit better off.

CHUCK HAD GIVEN HER THE DAY OFF for her to speak to her father, so the moment Victoria dropped Adam off at the campus she drove straight to her mother's Ocean Drive mansion, alive with questions. She confronted a somewhat surprised Rachel. "Is that true, mom? Would you not have taken him back under any circumstances?"

"Is that what Adam said? Very perceptive of him, I must say."

"You didn't answer my question."

Rachel calmly buffed her nails and gave her daughter's question some thought. "Perhaps if you had been much younger. . . perhaps then I would have, for your sake."

"But since I was nineteen and engaged to Steve. . . ."

"No. I wouldn't have taken him back. My pride was involved, and I knew I would never trust him again."

Victoria sank into a chair and regarded Rachel evenly. "I don't understand the two of you! If only you had talked to each other!"

Rachel smiled. "Communicate, you mean. The answer to everything. I tried, Victoria, honestly I did, but for such a learned, erudite man, your father was remarkably nonverbal around me. I often yearned to go sit in on one of his classroom lectures, just to hear him put a long string of sentences together. He does it so beautifully on paper, although I don't understand half of what he writes in those books."

"You mean you never heard dad in front of a class?"

Rachel shook her head. "I often told him I'd like to, but he said I would only make him nervous."

Victoria sighed. "Mom, I'm going to ask you a question you probably aren't going to like."

"Ask it, dear. If I really don't like it, I won't answer it."

"Why didn't you confront dad the moment you learned about Martina?"

Rachel shrugged. "Pride again, I suppose. I thought the thing would burn itself out, so I stuck my head in the sand and waited. I knew the moment it was out in the open my life with Adam, as I had known it, would be over."

"How long did you know about the affair before it came out?"

"A long time."

"Are we talking weeks, months?"

"A year."

"Dear God!" Victoria blurted out. "You let the thing pass the point of no return. If you had screamed, stormed—if you had nipped it in the bud...."

Rachel's icy glance silenced her. "Victoria, perfect hindsight is something with which we're all gifted. A pity it's so worthless."

Feeling properly chastised, Victoria softened her tone. "One more question, mom, and I'll shut up. What attracted you to dad in the first place?"

Rachel smiled slightly. "First, his looks, of course. Then, I thought he was the smartest man in the world. He was so distinguished and intellectual compared to the other men I knew. I was never very bookish, and I guess I thought I could absorb some of his intelligence by osmosis, and I was flattered to death that such a brainy man could find me interesting. I always stood a little in awe of him and his intellectual friends. You know, he never wanted to take part in any of the faculty social activities, and I often wondered if he was a little ashamed of me."

Victoria rubbed her eyes tiredly. She couldn't remember ever feeling so low-down, miserably sad. It had all been so unnecessary. If Adam and Rachel had spilled their innermost thoughts, the divorce might never have happened. But what possible good would be served by telling her mother Adam had never been ashamed of her, that he had been awed by her, just as she had been by him? The divorce was a fact of life, and the marriage could never be repaired. By the time Martina had come on the scene, the damage had already been done.

It was pitiful, really. Not once had either of her parents mentioned the word "love." Victoria wondered if she was an incurable romantic, thinking everlasting love should be one of life's pounding forces? Was it unrealistic of her to want to be able to lose herself in another human being—the way she felt when she was with Grant?

With Grant. Merely thinking of the way he made her feel sent a hot, explosive sensation coursing through her veins. Her ideas, her attitude had certainly gone through an abrupt change in a little over a month's time. But was it love, the kind that lasted forever, through good times and bad, transcending many of the mundanities of life? Did that kind of love even exist?

She didn't know. . . and there was something else she had to do before she could hope to know.

"Well, Victoria, did the visit with your father help you make up your mind about Grant?" Rachel asked suddenly.

Sometimes Victoria had the eerie feeling her mother could read her mind. "No, not really."

"Did it—how should I put it—have any lasting impact on you? It's been some time since you talked to Adam. How do you feel about him now?"

"Oh, that he's not the great strong idol of my youth or the ogre of the past eight years. I guess I see dad as just a person, with strengths and weaknesses, good points and bad, like the rest of us."

Rachel nodded. "Good. Idols are terribly fragile creatures, destined only to fall off their pedestals. Are you going to see Steve?"

"Yes, I'm meeting him for lunch tomorrow. It seemed the best way. I could tell my request almost floored him, and he pumped me for the reason behind it. I couldn't very well tell him I wanted to discuss our marriage. I'm sure he's about to choke with curiosity." Victoria pursed her lips. "I wonder if he's told Nancy."

VICTORIA SPENT most of the following morning in Chuck's office with him and Roger Davenport. The meeting was so interesting that she was late arriving at the restaurant where she was to meet Steve. He was probably steaming, since he was Mr. Punctuality himself. She shed her light coat in the foyer, then approached the maître d'. "Stephen Bartlett's table, please."

"Of course. Right this way."

Oddly, Victoria had never felt calmer in her life. Perhaps the stimulating morning, envisioning the look on Martin Rumbaugh's face when he received his subpoena, listening to Roger Davenport spell out their plan of attack was responsible for her mood. Maybe the strange premonitory sense that her inner confusion was about to be resolved was having a positive effect. Whatever the reason, she was in control when Steve rose to greet her.

"Hello, Vicky. How nice you look!"

Remembering the way she'd looked the last time he'd seen her, she could well imagine her smart gray suit was quite an improvement. "Thank you, Steve. Sorry to keep you waiting, but the morning was especially busy."

"No problem. I've been happily nursing a martini." Steve waited for her to slide into the curved booth before sitting opposite her. "Would you care for a cocktail?"

"No, thanks."

"Then we'll order now," he said, signaling the waiter.

"I think I'll just have the soup and salad."

Steve ordered a rather substantial meal, and while he was explaining to the waiter exactly what he wanted, Victoria's eyes swept around the elegant restaurant. It was precisely the sort of place Steve would choose, she reflected—expensive and exclusive. Her ex-husband liked the best of everything, be it clothes, jewelry, cars, liquor, food, and he enjoyed them with the casual air of a man long accustomed to fine things. Yet as he himself had often joked to their friends, it wasn't until he married into the Carpenter family that he "could finally live the way I was always meant to live." The remark had always got a laugh, but Victoria had hated it, feeling it implied he had married her for her money.

Once she had gone so far as to tell him just that, only to have him explode. "Don't be ridiculous, Vicky! What's the matter with you? It's a joke, and everyone knows it is!"

"How about finding another one," she had fumed. "I don't find that particular one amusing."

"You're awfully touchy."

"So are you!" Her reaction, she supposed, had been uncalled for, but it had frightened her to death to think the Carpenter name and money had been irresistible to him.

Whatever had made her remember that?

The waiter scurried away with their order, so there was nothing for Steve to do but fold his arms on the table and look at her expectantly. He was uncomfortable, Victoria could tell. When she met his gaze squarely, his discomfort increased, so she did her best to put him at ease.

"How are Nancy and the baby?" she asked pleasantly.

"Fine. We're . . . ." He hesitated.

"Expecting again. Yes, I know. I saw you on television the other night. That's an impressive project your firm is undertaking."

She thought he relaxed somewhat. "Yes, and we hope for great things from it, but I don't ever anticipate having the same enthusiasm for a project that I had for Bartlett Square, since it was my first big job. You know, you could pick up a tidy profit if you ever decided to sell the house."

"I'm sure I could, but as long as I'm in Corpus I want to keep the house. I've become so used to it. It's really home to me."

"Ah, yes, it always was your house, wasn't it? All our friends referred to it as 'Victoria's house.' I thought that rather odd, since I was the one who designed it and paid for it, yet it forever remained 'Victoria's house.'"

She tensed, and a vague frown creased her forehead. Steve had said it with a smile, but Victoria knew him too well—the smile was not genuine, and his tone was laced with sarcasm...or something less definable. "Well," she said too brightly, "I think women are always more closely identified with a home."

"Perhaps," Steve said noncommittally. "So tell me, how's work?"

"Unusually interesting right now." Succinctly she told him about some of the work she was involved in, although she didn't for a minute think he was genuinely interested. She concluded the account only when she spied a familiar face across the crowded restaurant. "Oh, Steve, isn't that Arthur Keller, the builder, over there?"

Steve shifted in his seat, then turned back to her. "Yes, it is."

"I haven't seen him in ages. Do you still do business with him?"

"Occasionally."

"I was always very fond of him, because he's the one who asked you to design Bartlett Square."

"Hmm. He asked me in order to score points with you."

Victoria flushed slightly. Again the sarcasm. She was at a loss to understand it. "That's not true, and you know it," she insisted. "He thought you were an extremely talented architect."

"Vicky, I don't believe you're really that naive. Arthur Keller always had an eye for you."

"Well, if he did, he was much too much the

gentleman to let me know it. Besides, he's married." Her tone was gentle, but the meaning was clear. *Not everyone is an adulterer.* "I thought you liked Arthur. You always insisted I invite him to our parties."

"He was useful to me, and I knew he would never miss an opportunity to show up at one of 'Victoria's parties.' No one did. You were the hostess with the mostest."

It was not a compliment, although it, too, was said with a smile. Victoria was receiving some unpleasant vibrations from this man she thought she knew so well. Intently she watched him over the rim of her water glass.

Fortunately, at that moment their food arrived, so conversation while they ate was confined to innocuous local gossip. Marriages, babies, divorces—more of the latter than anything, it seemed. Amazing how out of touch with the old crowd she had become, she who had once been at the center of everything. Hard to believe that who was doing what with whom had once seemed so important to her.

She feigned rapt attention and made all the appropriate remarks, but her mind whirled. A nagging something prickled at her brain. There was a hard, cynical edge to Steve's manner, and that wasn't typical of the Stephen Bartlett she had known. Unless he had had more than one martini. He could be brutally frank when gin had oiled his tongue.

"Do you still have to do a lot of entertaining?"

she asked, not really caring, but she had to do something to keep the conversation alive. "Does Nancy enjoy it?"

"Nancy pretty well keeps to the house. She shuns the limelight. Any entertaining I do is of the stag variety at the club. It works much better that way. I score all the points. I don't have to wonder if I'm getting the commission because of my talent, not because my wife can charm the birds out of the trees."

Victoria's eyes narrowed. Where had she heard something similar recently? From her father, of course! And something her mother had said leaped to the forefront—something about "Steve's self-engrossment." Coming from a middle-class background, he had always been hungry to better himself, but Victoria had preferred to refer to that admiringly as "ambition." Now she was viewing his ambition with more critical eyes.

Steve took a few more bites of food before asking casually, "What did you want to see me about, Vicky?"

Slowly Victoria put down her fork. Earlier she had thought she knew exactly what she was going to say to him. She had planned to calmly and dispassionately ask him why, from his point of view, their marriage had failed. She no longer needed to. Everything was slipping neatly into the compartments of her mind; in a flash of insight she had her answer. Steve had been jealous of her!

It was ludicrous, but true. While she had been

busting her fanny to further his career, to charm his friends and business associates, to be the perfect hostess, the perfect helpmate, she had been alienating him. She had thought them to be equal partners; he had considered her a rival—she now knew it as surely as if he had admitted it. It was a stunning revelation.

In the early days of their marriage, when Steve's career had taken off like a rocket, he had been the first to give her some of the credit. But later? Later resentment had set in. She just hadn't wanted to see it.

Victoria had always wondered why Steve, who was such a handsome man, had turned to an average-looking woman like Nancy. She wondered no longer. Nancy would adore him and never give him any competition. With Nancy he could be the star of the show.

The amazing thing was that Grant had correctly assessed the situation from the beginning. Victoria had to suppress a ridiculous urge to laugh out loud. But she knew the laugh, if she had allowed it, would have been more like a mournful cry. She had wasted a precious year of her life wondering where she had failed, when she hadn't failed at all. She had been too successful, and Steve's ego hadn't been able to take it. Abruptly everything she had ever felt for this man melted into pity. How awful to have to live with such fragile self-confidence.

What a fool she had been. Never having known anyone else, she had considered Steve the perfect husband. She had turned herself inside out trying to please him. If he told her she was too possessive, she believed him. If he criticized what she was wearing, she changed, even when her instincts told her the clothes were perfect. Come to think of it, he had criticized freely. When everyone else at one of their parties was raving about the food, Steve always found something wrong with it. No wonder she had felt at fault when the marriage split up. She had lived with and accepted criticism for years.

She thought of Grant, and a faraway look came to her eyes. She didn't regret the time she had wasted with Steve half as much as the time she had lost with Grant. Oh, he wasn't perfect; who was? Certainly not she. He growled and snarled, and she was quick to snap back. He had moods that could only be wondered at. She didn't suppose she would ever fully understand him, or was meant to. But he possessed a strong sense of his own worth; he knew who he was and what he wanted. And no man on earth could make her feel more a woman than he could. In a rush of emotion, she remembered the feel of his hands and mouth, all the wondrous sensations when she was in his arms. . . .

Oh, Lord, she wanted to see him, had to see him! She loved him. She must! He was the one she wanted to be with. At that moment it seemed inconceivable that she could have given Steve a second thought once Grant had entered her life. Grant was twice the man Steve was.

"Vicky?" A mildly impatient voice across the

table snapped her out of her reverie. "What did you want to see me about?" Steve asked again.

"Huh? Oh, well, I'm thinking of...getting married."

A barely perceptible widening of the eyes was Steve's only reaction. "Oh? That fellow I met at your place? The one with the...chest?"

A giggle bubbled up in Victoria's throat. "Yes, the one with the...chest."

"Congratulations." Unspoken but implied was, *What does that have to do with me?*

She looked down at her half-eaten lunch, which was no longer appetizing. All she could think of was getting out of that restaurant, back to the office and a telephone. "Ah, if I do, I'll be leaving Corpus, and—there are some boxes in the attic!" she exclaimed, relieved to have thought of something—anything.

"Boxes?"

"Yes, cartons actually, and I think they're yours."

Steve frowned and shook his head. "I don't think so. I'm almost sure there's nothing of mine in the attic."

"Oh, well, perhaps not." She shrugged her handbag strap onto her shoulder and glanced at her watch. "Gosh, Steve, I hate to eat and run, but—"

"You've scarcely eaten a thing!" he protested.

"I really wasn't very hungry, and I can't believe how the time has flown. I've got to be on my way.

There's so much going on at the office right now, and—"

"Vicky, what the devil's the matter with you? I know you didn't ask me to meet you for lunch just so you could tell me there are some boxes in the attic. You could have told me that over the phone."

Quickly she got to her feet. "Believe me, Steve, you told me everything I wanted to know. Thanks for the lunch, and I'll be seeing you around sometime." As she turned to leave, something suddenly occurred to her—something so utterly senseless and petty it defied logic, but something she couldn't hold back. She whirled to face a perplexed Steve.

"By the way, Steve, there's something I always meant to tell you...."

"Yes?"

"I despise being called Vicky!" And she scurried away from the booth, leaving her ex-husband to stare after her in bewilderment.

Outside the restaurant, Victoria paused. Steve probably thought her half crazy, but who cared? She felt a little crazy, a little disoriented, totally exhilarated. The March day carried with it the first hint of spring. She inhaled deeply and experienced a wild urge to laugh and cry and sing all at the same time. It was so nice to be free, free to finally commit herself to Grant, who loved her so.

## CHAPTER EIGHTEEN

THE AFTERNOON plodded along interminably, even though Victoria's spirits were soaring to majestic heights. Her first impulse had been to place the call to Grant from the office, charging it to her home phone. Then she thought better of it. The mere prospect of hearing that deep rich voice again brought high color to her cheeks; it would be best if she heard it in private.

There was so much she wanted to say to him; she wondered if she would know where to start. And she imagined his reaction, the things he would say to her. The prospect left her tingling with excitement. She wanted to say those things, hear those things when there was no one else around.

So she waited. Somehow she managed to go through the motions of staying busy, but her eyes strayed to the clock too often, and uncharacteristically, she was one of the first to leave when five o'clock finally arrived.

Not even the rush-hour drive to her house could dampen her enthusiasm. Everything had changed, and she had never been happier or more certain of herself and what she wanted. The burden Steve had represented—the misery, the guilt, the sense of inadequacy—was gone, lifted from her shoulders. Free at last to love again, she planned to do just that: to love Grant with all her heart and soul, mind and body.

There were some drastic changes on the horizon, and she was anxious to start her brand-new life. She wouldn't be able to get away to Arroyo Grande, not now while so much was going on at work, but she was sure Grant would gladly come to Corpus Christi for the time being. Wasn't this what he had been wanting all along?

She fairly flew through the front door of her house. Memories of the last time, the only time she and Grant had been here together flooded her mind. Her heart palpitated wildly, and her fingers were trembling as she dialed his number. She had no idea what she would say when she got him on the phone. Perhaps "I love you" would do.

She didn't get the chance. "Oh, hello, Victoria," Mrs. Guilford said. "No, Grant isn't here. He left for Houston this afternoon."

"Houston?" Victoria gulped in dismay. Damn! If she had called from the office she might have caught him. "Well, when do you expect him back?"

"Can't say for sure, dear. He said he had no idea when he would be back."

How quickly unbridled spirits could be reined in, Victoria thought. He had gone to see Helena, after all. Funny...she had rather imagined he wouldn't. An uneasy feeling stirred in the pit of her stomach.

She gave herself a shake. She was being absurd. She had wanted him to confront the past, bury it, so the two of them could begin with a clean slate. She needed no better proof that his feelings were sincere. He was doing something he obviously dreaded simply because she had asked him to. Soon it would all be over, and they would be together again, permanently this time.

"Do you happen to know where I can reach him in Houston?"

"He's staying at the Warwick. Shall I get the number for you?"

"I can get it, thanks."

"I'll be sure to tell Grant you called in case you miss him."

"Please do that. Is Rita around, by any chance?"

"I think so. Let me see if I can find her."

There was a lengthy wait before the familiar girlish voice came over the line. "Victoria! I was thinking about you today."

"How are you, honey?"

"Fine. Please don't ask me how school is."

Victoria laughed lightly. "I wanted to talk to your father, but Mrs. Guilford tells me he's in Houston."

"Yeah, he left this afternoon while I was in school. He only decided to go yesterday. Jake drove him to San Antonio, and he was flying on from there. I can't imagine why he wanted to go. He always said he'd never go near the place."

"Well, I'm sure it must have been very important."

"Yeah, I guess so. Oh, Victoria, I hope you come to see us real soon."

"I hope so, too, Rita. In fact, I'm counting on it."

"I'll tell daddy you called."

"Thanks. I'd appreciate it."

"Will you say hi to Rachel for me?"

"Of course. You take care of yourself."

"You, too, Victoria. Bye."

"Goodbye, honey."

Victoria immediately dialed directory assistance and got the hotel's number, then dialed it. Grant didn't answer the ring, so she had him paged without results. An hour later she tried again, and again just before going to bed. Still no Grant. This time she left a message. Hanging up, she slowly sank to the bed, disappointed but resigned. As soon as Grant got her message he would call, and it would be every bit as exciting then as it would have been tonight.

TWO DAYS PASSED with no word from him, then three and four. Victoria refused to telephone the Houston hotel again. She had left a message. That was all she could do. She and Chuck were in and out of the office that week, mostly out, and the other agents were in the field, but the automatic-answering device was always activated when the office was empty. If Grant called, she would know about it.

Finally she could stand it no longer. Swallowing her pride, she telephoned the hotel one more time, only to be told Mr. Mackenzie had checked out.

"Would you mind looking in his box to see if there's a message he inadvertently didn't receive?" There was none, and the desk clerk was quite certain Mr. Mackenzie had received all his messages; he had given them to the gentleman himself.

Victoria was swamped by despair and bewilderment. Why hadn't Grant returned her call? Perhaps he had been in a rush to catch a plane or something. That had to be it. No doubt he planned to call when he returned to Arroyo Grande.

He didn't, not that day, or the next, or the next. Victoria became a slave to Alexander Graham Bell's invention, worse than any schoolgirl waiting to be asked for a Saturday-night date. Whether at home or at work, she found herself staring at it, willing it to ring, unable to believe it wouldn't. Her mind refused to entertain the notion that he wouldn't get in touch with her at all.

She made excuses. The message she had left at the hotel could have been lost or misplaced, put in the wrong box. Perhaps Rita and Mrs. Guilford had forgotten to tell him she had called the lodge. Victoria came within an inch of telephoning Arroyo Grande again, going so far as to dial the area code before common sense took over, and she slammed down the receiver. Rita wouldn't forget to tell him—of that she was sure.

When a week had passed with still no word from him, Victoria was finally forced to admit Grant wasn't going to call, not now, not ever, and the reason for that was somehow connected to his visit to Houston. . . and Helena. Seeing her again, remembering the nasty divorce might have caused him to think twice about trying marriage again. Or maybe some old feelings had begun to stir. He had once been smitten with the beautiful Helena. Both of them would have matured and mellowed. And they had a daughter who would be a powerful bond. Falling for his ex-wife would be the one thing Grant would find almost impossible to tell her. That possibility was like a knife slicing through Victoria's heart.

Oh, why had she insisted he see her again?

It was the hardest thing she had ever endured. The ordeal with Steve paled by comparison. Victoria tried reminding herself just which one of them had wanted to move cautiously. Had Grant had his way, they would either have been married by now or rushing headlong toward it. She tried congratulating herself on being so sensible. How much better for it to end now, instead of in two or three years. Most of all, she tried convincing herself that having survived one emotional crisis in her life, she would survive this one, too.

This kind of thinking would sustain her for a while; then she would ache from the loss of something she now supposed she had never really had. She persisted in going over in her mind every word Grant had ever said to her, every touch, every kiss, every heated moment of passion—a depressing pastime and a worthless one. It only reminded her of how much he had once wanted her, of how he no longer did.

She might have coped better, she rationalized, if Grant had broken it off in a more civilized manner. Simply not returning her calls, when he must have known damned well why she had called, was unconscionable and cowardly. Surely he didn't fear being confronted by hysterical feminine tears. Surely he knew her better than that, she thought, weeping helplessly nevertheless.

Briefly she summoned up anger. *The third time!* The third damned time in her life that a man she had trusted had let her down. She was beginning to think herself the world's worst judge of men's characters. Grant Mackenzie hadn't turned out to be the man she had thought he was. He was moody and unpredictable, and she was better off without him. They were handy clichés. She managed to cling to these thoughts for several days, to plod through a normal existence and hide her inner turmoil from her co-workers.

One day a package arrived in the mail. Opening it, she saw the weaving Rita had been working on when Victoria had first arrived at Arroyo Grande. A note accompanied the artwork. "Victoria," it said. "I just finished this, and since you liked the colors so much, I thought you might like to have it. Love, Rita."

That did Victoria in. It seemed the bottom, the absolute rock-bottom point, from which there could be no rising. All her defenses crumbled, and she was engulfed by misery, self-pity and regret. Clutching Rita's gift to her chest, she sobbed uncontrollably. *We could have been happy, the three of us,* she thought. *I would have made sure Rita's talent was nurtured. I would have been good for Rita and Grant, and they would have been good for me.* She cursed herself for her uncertainty, cursed Steve for helping to create it in the first place, and ended up cursing Grant for ever telling her he loved her. And she wondered if she was doomed to a life of disappointment and disillusion.

However, she had her wits about her enough to write Rita a short note, thanking her for the lovely gift. Victoria concluded the note with, ''Rita, there's little chance I'll be returning to Arroyo Grande. In fact, I may soon be moving to Albuquerque. But please know I love you, and we'll stay in touch forever. I promise.'' Mailing the note seemed to signal the end of something that had hardly begun.

Victoria operated in a haze of depression for days afterward. But her indomitable spirit prevailed, and abruptly she turned a corner. *Look at yourself, Victoria,* her mind scolded. *Here you are again, crying in loneliness and despair. Haven't you gotten a bit smarter? Haven't you learned anything?*

Well, she had learned plenty, and she was getting smarter by the minute. She had lost, but she had lost before. She was lonely, but she had been lonely before. She would cope. And as she told Rachel—no man was ever going to do this to her again. Not ever.

MEANWHILE, EVENTS IN THE EAGLE CASE were moving at breakneck speed. Victoria got caught up in trial preliminaries, and she thanked God more than once that she had her work. It enabled her to temporarily forget what she perceived to be Grant's dishonesty and disloyalty. Once the subpoenas had been served, an astonishing number of the accused entered pleas of guilty and paid their fines. Frank Oakley, the helicopter pilot, was among them. During the pretrial hearing, he revealed what Victoria had long suspected—paying pilots a bonus for killing an eagle was common practice, and the helicopter companies involved always knew about it.

Only the attorneys representing Martin Rumbaugh and Morgan Dawson staunchly denied any wrongdoing on their clients' parts. In the end, the rancher and the owner of the helicopter company were indicted by the grand jury and would stand trial.

The trial was scheduled for the first week in April, only two weeks away, a swift stroke of luck for the prosecution. There was a vacancy on the court docket, and the judge assigned to the case was booked on a Caribbean cruise in late April, so he was less than receptive to the defense attorney's attempts at a delay. Roger Davenport couldn't believe their good fortune.

Victoria was present when the grand jury handed down the indictments, her first face-to-face confrontation with Martin Rumbaugh since the day at his ranch. When the proceedings were over, the rancher made a point of speaking to her. The smile he gave her was icy and insolent.

"Well, Ms Bartlett, are you pleased with yourself for having raised such a big fuss over such a *little* thing?"

"It's no 'little thing,' Mr. Rumbaugh. Far from it."

Still, she was disturbed by the stockmen's general attitude, and she spoke to Chuck about it.

"Dawson acts a little nervous," she commented. "But Rumbaugh and his cronies are treating the whole thing as a joke."

"They might not be smiling so broadly when it's all over," Chuck said. "We've got 'em dead to rights."

"Maybe," she mused. "But I've heard several stockmen's organizations have raised a considerable amount of money to pay their legal fees, and those groups have a lot of influence in the state. You know Rumbaugh will pack the courtroom with his supporters."

"So? I have faith in the system."

"So do I . . . though it wouldn't hurt to have a few rooters on our side. Courtroom sentiment might sway the jury in a close decision."

"Victoria, you've forgotten we have the distinguished Dr. Barrett on our side. He's told me more about eagles than I wanted to know. Defense can't come up with a single allegation about the threat the birds pose to livestock that Dr. Barrett can't refute.''

"Chuck, I'm not worried that we don't have an airtight case. It's just that I hate to see this thing pass without notice. A little publicity would go a long way toward preventing incidents of this kind. The general public needs to be aware that, one, wildlife legislation exists, and two, the laws are enforced.''

"I couldn't agree more, Victoria. What are you getting at?''

"Well, Chuck,'' she said with a grin. "With your permission I'd like to write a few letters to some interested parties.''

Chuck shrugged. "Have at it.''

"I'll let you have a look at them before they're mailed.''

She spent the remainder of the afternoon drafting a letter, then typing copies of it to send to the Audubon Society, Friends of Animals, the National Wildlife Federation and the Sierra Club, asking them to send representatives to the trial. Their presence, she felt, might offset the considerable influence the stockmen would have. What she mostly wanted, however, was to turn the trial into enough of an event that the media couldn't ignore it.

IN SOME NEBULOUS WAY Victoria had always imagined a courtroom to be the scene of constant high drama. She wasn't prepared for the snail's pace, it seemed to her, at which the trial progressed. She had been excited and nervous about her own testimony, but her turn on the witness stand was cut-and-dried. Under Roger Davenport's careful questioning she clearly recounted the details of her investigation, and no one could have been more surprised than she was when the defense attorney said, "No further questions, Your Honor." The defense was a little harder on Joe Wentworth, but not much. It all served to perplex Victoria.

She was bitterly disappointed by the mix of courtroom spectators, as well. Almost to a person they were friends, families and colleagues of the defendants. A partylike atmosphere prevailed. No one took the prosecution seriously. Apparently her letters had done no good.

Worse, Roger Davenport was concerned. The lawyers for Rumbaugh and Dawson weren't proceeding according to plans. Defense was basing its entire case on the moral character of the defendants, on what upstanding, law-abiding citizens they were. Not one word was uttered concerning the stockman's right to protect his livestock. No one accused the eagle of being a threat to sheep. Roger called Frank Oakley to the stand, but he wasn't cross-examined, even though Victoria thought the pilot's testimony was the most startling yet. Dr. Robert Barrett was standing at the ready, just itching to take the stand, but Roger could use him only to refute an accusation made by the defense, and no such accusation was forthcoming.

The defense attorneys harped on Rumbaugh's and Dawson's outstanding contributions to the state and their communities. Every cent either man had ever given to charity was duly noted. In Rumbaugh's case especially, the contributions were impressive. A steady parade of well-known citizens—congressmen, philanthropists, doctors, even a popular film personality—all claimed to know Rumbaugh and Dawson well. All declared each man to be the salt of the earth.

Over coffee during a short recess, Victoria, Chuck and Roger fumed. "Damned if I don't expect the president to show up any minute to tell us what a great guy Martin Rumbaugh is!" he muttered.

"What are they trying to do?" Victoria asked.

"Simple. They're trying to make the jury forget why the men are really on trial."

"Will it work?"

The lawyer shrugged. "Who knows? I've seen cases...one in particular. A very wealthy man was accused of murdering his ex-wife's lover. The district attorney had what I thought was an excellent case. But the defense attorney very skillfully tried the wife instead. She was a beautiful woman with rather lax morals—at least that's what the defense strongly implied. Before it was all over, the jury's sympathies were entirely with the accused, and he was acquitted. Frankly, I think he was guilty as sin."

"Reassuring endorsement of our judicial system, Roger," Chuck said with an undaunted grin, getting to his feet. "I think we're due back in court."

As the three of them walked down the corridor to the courtroom, Victoria lagged behind, deep in thought. She reflected sadly that, should Rumbaugh and Dawson be acquitted, a great deal of time, effort and money would have been expended on absolutely nothing. Apparently they weren't even going to get any publicity out of all this.

Absently she glanced up...and stopped short. Ahead of her a man walked with a loose and easy gait. He was wearing jeans, dusty boots, a plaid shirt. His hair was very dark, almost black, and his shoulders were broad. Knowing full well it wasn't Grant, she stared at him nevertheless. In spite of her resolve, she could never get him out of her thoughts for long.

Each day that passed strengthened her belief that Helena must be back in the picture. It was the only explanation. She tried to be glad for him, for Helena, especially for Rita, who would benefit from a mother's influence, even that of an unconventional one. Victoria tried...but nothing worked.

The man ahead of her stopped in front of a door, opened it and disappeared from view. She hurried to catch up with Chuck and Roger. Forgetting for a moment that she was bitterly disappointed in him, cut to the quick, she wondered where Grant was right that minute, what he was doing. Did he ever think of her, and more important, why hadn't he called to say goodbye?

GRANT STEPPED OUT of the Ford pickup and stretched. The sun was lowering in the western sky; the warmth of the bright spring day was quickly being replaced by the cool of the evening. God, he was tired! It was good to be home. The past weeks had been exhausting, but fulfilling, and he felt the satisfaction and contentment that came from having at long last smoothed out some important rough edges in his life. He retrieved his luggage just as Jake McGrath got out of the driver's side of the truck.

"Much obliged, Jake. Thanks for driving all the way to San Antonio to get me."

"Don't mention it, boss. Didn't want you having to take the bus. Sure you don't want to drive in to Kierney with me and the boys for some of Sally's good cooking? With Mrs. Guildford and the young'un gone, that big old place is gonna be kinda lonesome."

"Won't bother me a bit. I'm going to take a shower, open a can of chili and just relax. You guys enjoy yourselves, and thanks a helluva bunch for minding the store. I didn't expect to be gone so long."

Hoisting his suitcase and slinging his garment bag over his shoulder, Grant clomped up the porch steps of the lodge, taking note of the Closed sign on the front door. Each year during the school spring break he gave the household staff a week off. Mrs. Guildford always went to visit her daughter on an east Texas farm, and since the daughter had three teenagers, Rita usually accompanied her. They both looked forward to the break, and Grant realized it was a refreshing change for Rita to be around kids her own age, ride horses, go on hay rides and the like.

But it made an empty house. The lodge had all the warmth of a tomb when he was the only one in it. The first thing he did was build a fire in the fireplace; its cheerful crackling helped dispel some of the dreary gloom pervading the big room. He deposited his luggage in his bedroom, stripped and headed for the shower. For a few moments he emptied his mind, concentrated only on the needles of water stabbing at his skin and the steam enveloping him. Then he dried briskly, knotted a towel around his waist and made for the front of the lodge, where he mixed a Scotch and soda. Carrying it with him, he walked back to the bedroom and idly began dressing. There, in absolute peace and solitude, he mulled over the events of the past few weeks.

The ramifications of the trip still seemed unreal. There would be changes in Rita's life, if she wanted them. Changes in several lives, in fact, his own included. All he could do was hope he had made the right decisions for everyone concerned. At least his motives had been honest and unselfish. For the first time in a while he had been full of protective concern for others.

Well, perhaps for himself, too. Now, at last, he was free of old doubts and confusions, ancient grievances. He hoped the trip had done some good. He certainly felt good.

Taking a hefty swig of his drink, he switched on the television set standing in one corner of the room. He was in time for the five o'clock state and local news. He hadn't seen television or read a newspaper in weeks.

Immediately a handsome face filled the screen, and a perfectly modulated masculine voice filled the air. Grant stepped into a clean pair of jeans, zipped and buttoned them, reached for his shirt and shrugged into it. He was buttoning it when something the newsman said arrested his attention. He paused to listen.

"Today marked the fourth day of what has come to be known as 'The Reyes County Eagle Trial,'" the newsman said. "What began as an inauspicious event was suddenly turned into a cause célèbre when representatives from various national conservationist organizations began gathering at U.S. District Court. . . ."

Grant sank to the edge of his bed and watched with great interest. The camera panned the front of an imposing courthouse, then swept over the throng of people collected on either side of the steps. Some were carrying placards. He could read one: Eagle Killers Belong in Jail! The young woman carrying it was grim-faced, determined to get the placard in plain view; the cameraman was only too happy to oblige her.

The camera switched to the street in front of the courthouse. A long black automobile pulled to a stop at the curb, and a group of men got out. Grant immediately recognized Martin Rumbaugh.

The rancher was accompanied by a burly man dressed in a Western-style suit and three other men who wore dark business suits and carried briefcases.

The newsman identified them for the audience. "Defendants in the case, Martin Rumbaugh of Kierney and Morgan Dawson of Kerrville, arrived with their team of attorneys—they were greeted by a chorus of boos and cheers. Feelings are running high in the trial, and local police have had their hands full keeping the demonstrations orderly."

Grant's eyes were riveted on the screen as the camera moved in for a closeup of Rumbaugh. The rancher exuded bravado, smiling and waving to the crowd. Dawson looked more subdued. A zealous newsman shoved a microphone in front of Rumbaugh, but one of the attorneys quickly intervened. "No comment," he mumbled, and hurriedly ushered his clients up the steps.

The anchorman's commentary continued. "It now seems certain that neither Rumbaugh nor Dawson will ever take the witness stand, much to the disappointment of the prosecutors and the conservationists. In that case, speculation has it the trial will soon go to the jury, possibly as early as tomorrow."

The camera returned to the street just as another automobile pulled up to the curb, and four figures emerged. "Arriving shortly after the defendants were the other principals in the case," the commentator reported. "Roger Davenport, the prosecuting attorney, told Channel 5 News that he remains confident of a guilty verdict, and reiterated the point that killing an endangered species carries a much more severe penalty than does the illegal taking of game animals. With him was Charles Singleton, senior agent with U.S. Fish and Wildlife in Corpus Christi. Close behind were Joe Wentworth, the prosecution's chief witness, and Victoria Bartlett, the Fish and Wildlife agent whose investigation led to the indictments of Rumbaugh and Dawson.''

Grant's hand, holding the drink, was on its way to his mouth when his eyes zeroed in on that fantastic mane of chestnut hair. Victoria came on the screen, and someone stuck a microphone in front of her.

The off-screen commentary continued. ''Ms Bartlett spoke to reporters today. Responding to criticism from some quarters that the trial is much ado about very little, she had this to say.''

''On the contrary, this trial carries immense importance. Had there been wildlife legislation a century ago, many species would not now be extinct or in trouble. I think the public's general attitude is undergoing a marked change. People are beginning to look on wildlife not only as game but as a necessary part of our environment. We all suffer when someone flouts the law regulating our endangered species.''

''Mr. Davenport seems confident of a guilty verdict, Ms Bartlett,'' the reporter said. ''Do you agree?''

''Yes, I do.''

Then she was a blur rushing past, but the camera-man followed her progress up the courthouse steps. Grant watched the movement of her hips, the slight swaying of her skirt, the shapely calves below, and a knot formed in the pit of his stomach.

She had probably been so busy with this trial that she hadn't given him a thought, but he hadn't been able to get her out of his mind. Seeing her again, if only on a television screen, was devastating, and a part of him cursed her for being able to stay away from him. Quickly he got to his feet and switched off the set.

There was one of life's rough edges that hadn't been smoothed—his endless desire for Victoria Bartlett. Damn, why couldn't he have fallen for an uncomplicated woman who needed him and wanted nothing more than a home and babies? It seemed to him he hadn't known a moment's peace since Victoria entered his life.

Needing something to do, he left his bedroom and wandered through the lodge, stopped to mix another drink, to fill and light his pipe before continuing on to methodically check all the rooms. In his office he riffled through the mail that had accumulated in his absence, but there appeared to be nothing requiring his immediate attention. He walked across the hall to Rita's studio. Her loom was standing there, rewarped and ready to go. He wondered when she had finished that piece she had been working on, and he took a moment to marvel at his daughter's talent, something he had come to accept, even to admire.

He missed Rita, and he missed Victoria. He projected the image of a loner, but he was finally admitting, as he approached middle age, that he wasn't meant to live alone.

Grant sauntered into the workroom and glanced around. Rita was a tidy kid. Helena's studio had always been a disaster area, but this was pin-neat. He walked to the drafting table and studied the graph-paper drawing. Her next project, he supposed. While admiring it, his eyes happened to fall on a small envelope lying next to it. He picked it up, noticing it was addressed to Rita in a neat feminine script. When he saw the return address in the upper left-hand corner, his chest constricted sharply. Without considering the rightness or propriety of his actions, he pulled out the note inside and read it.

Apparently Rita had sent something to Victoria, and this was her thank-you note. It sounded very Victoria-ish, all sweet and proper, he thought with a smile, and the handwriting seemed like her, too. He read on—until two lines fairly leaped off the paper to hit him between the eyes: "... there's little chance I'll be returning to Arroyo Grande. In fact, I may soon be moving to Albuquerque."

Grant's heart all but stopped. He read those lines three times before he accepted what they said. Albuquerque? Why? A promotion? Did that damned job mean so much more to her than anything he could offer?

Albuquerque! Not halfway around the world, but still a damned sight farther from him than

Corpus Christi. Grant didn't think anything had ever hit him so hard. So she had decided...and not in his favor. It was over. But when and how had she planned to tell him? Perhaps she hadn't meant to at all. Perhaps she simply intended moving out West and letting the thing die a natural death.

He took a long pull on his drink; it settled heavily in his stomach. Being a realist, he had told himself all along this could happen. Each day she stayed away from him had increased the likelihood of her staying away forever. He had thought he was prepared for it. He wasn't. A sense of loss that was something like death overwhelmed him.

For most of his thirty-five years he had known only one way to get what he wanted—reach out and take it. The advantages of wealth had made taking pretty easy, and there were those who would have said he had coasted through life. Up until now they might have been right. But he couldn't take Victoria, not unless she wanted to be taken. Now, to his everlasting regret and consternation, the one thing he wanted most in life seemed to be furthest from his reach.

Grant replaced the note in its envelope, put it back where he had found it and left the studio. Draining his second drink, he mixed another. Hell, he might as well get drunk. Otherwise, this was going to be one long night.

# CHAPTER NINETEEN

"COURT'S RECONVENING. Jury's coming in!" Word was passed along the courthouse corridor, and there was an instant flurry of activity.

Reacting like prizefighters at the sound of the bell, Victoria, Chuck, Roger and Joe moved toward the courtroom. Victoria glanced anxiously in the lawyer's direction.

"That didn't take long," she commented.

"Sure didn't," Roger agreed.

"Is that good or bad?"

"Never can tell," the attorney answered blandly.

Victoria heaved a sigh. "Roger, I'll bet you're one heck of a great poker player."

They soon had their answer. The foreman of the jury, at the judge's command, stood and intoned, "The jury finds the defendants guilty as charged." Astonished gasps, some of approval, others of dismay, filled the air. Then there was an eerie sort of silence, broken only by the sound of a woman's quiet sobbing. Later, someone told Victoria and Chuck the weeping woman was Morgan Dawson's wife.

Guilty as charged! It took some moments for

that reality to sink in. Victoria's faith in the judiciary system was instantly renewed. For all the defense attorneys' distracting tactics, even though they had skillfully kept both Rumbaugh and Dawson off the witness stand so they couldn't perjure themselves, the seven men and five women had listened to the evidence and voted accordingly. It should have been heartening, gratifying, and it was...in a way.

The heavy fines and suspended jail sentences handed down by the judge, however, amounted to little more than a slap on the wrist. Victoria faced Chuck indignantly.

"That's nothing!" she fumed. "Rumbaugh and Dawson will pay their fines and be on their merry way. That's hardly more than pocket change to them."

"That's not the point, Victoria," Chuck said in his maddeningly sensible way. "The point is the law was tested, and the law won. We got a helluva bunch of good publicity out of it, thanks to you, and the whole episode might cause others to think twice before shooting something there's too few of to begin with. Do you suppose Rumbaugh still thinks it's a law 'that can't be enforced'?"

"I wonder if he and Dawson will appeal."

Chuck grinned. "If I were those two I think I'd go on back home and lie low. The American public has an attention span of, at best, six weeks. Two months from now no one will remember this ever happened."

"Oh, Chuck, how you discourage me!"

"What did you want, Victoria? A penitentiary sentence? Maybe a public flogging in the town square? This is it; this is the way it works. Win one here, lose one there, maybe raise a little public awareness along the way." He paused and touched her briefly on the arm. "Like I said... maybe you're not cut out for law-enforcement work. Unfortunately, by the time we become involved with animals, they're usually dead."

"Maybe you're right." Victoria sighed heavily, unable to understand her gloomy mood. Of course Chuck's attitude was the reasonable one. The trial, from their standpoint, had been tremendously successful.

Media coverage had been extensive and favorable. She had never imagined she would see the day when killing eagles would be front-page news. Roger Davenport, to his own astonishment, had become something of a cult hero with the conservationists. Martin Rumbaugh looked, if not chastised, a bit subdued. And Morgan Dawson appeared to be in a state of shock. Dawson's troubles were only beginning, since the state was investigating his company's procedures. Yes, it had been very successful, and it had been her baby.

So why this letdown? Instead of exhilaration over a job well done, Victoria felt an empty kind of despair, a sense of loss, of abandonment. And she thought she knew the source of that. For weeks there had been something to occupy her mind, something besides Grant and his treachery.

Now there would be too many lonely nights with nothing to do but think and regret.

She wasn't going to let that happen. Admittedly, she had been harboring in her sentimental mind the faint hope that Grant would still call, that there was some good explanation for his silence, but she had to stop hoping. Too much time had passed; it was over.

It was decision time—time to sit down, take stock of her future and decide what she should do. She thought a drastic upheaval in her life would be in order, a definite move in another direction. The transfer to Albuquerque, for instance. Or she might see if there was a position available in Research. She thought she might like the kind of work Grant did.

Oh, God! She had to stop thinking about him. Looking back on a mistake was one thing; dwelling on it, dissecting it was another. She was going to do something. Never again would she simply sulk in a corner and lick her wounds.

"What d'ya say, Victoria?" Chuck's jubilant voice interrupted her thoughts. "Want to come have a celebration drink with us?"

She glanced up to see Chuck, Roger and Joe hovering over her. With them was Dr. Robert Barrett, whose testimony had never been needed but whose interest in the case had kept him in the courtroom from beginning to end. All four men were grinning broadly, and she would have given anything if she could have joined them in their exuberant mood. "If you don't mind, fellas, I think

I'll beg off. Thanks just the same. Have one for me.''

Joe shook Victoria's hand. "Will you be coming to Reyes County again anytime soon, Victoria?"

"No, Joe, I don't think so."

"Well, that's too bad. I'm thinking of settling down there, buying one of the ranchettes when we get them finished."

Victoria looked at him with some surprise, and he chuckled. "I guess that sounds pretty crazy, huh? What with this trial and all, I haven't exactly endeared myself to some of the county's most prominent citizens, but that sort of thing doesn't bother me much. I have endeared myself to Sally Anderson, and...well, we're thinking about getting married."

"Oh, Joe!" Victoria exclaimed. "I'm so happy for both of you. When it happens, will I get an invitation to the wedding?"

"You bet! Take care of yourself, Victoria."

"You, too, Joe."

Victoria got to her feet and approached Roger Davenport, who was beaming with well-earned satisfaction. "Roger, anything I could say now would be redundant. You know how grateful Chuck and I are to you."

"I wouldn't have missed it for the world, Victoria," the lawyer said enthusiastically. "Who knows, I just might turn out to be an expert on wildlife legislation. And I certainly intend keeping in close touch with you and Chuck."

She moved on to speak to Dr. Barrett, to apologize for wasting his valuable time. The distinguished gentleman dismissed her apology with a wave of his hand. "Never a waste of time, my dear. One, I finally got to meet Adam's delightful daughter, and two, I've been approached by a national magazine to write an article on the trial. So you see, my time in this courtroom was well spent."

A final round of goodbyes followed. Then Victoria watched the men meld into the crowd spilling out of the courtroom. Now that the trial was over, it all seemed to have happened so quickly.

She waited until the room had emptied before leaving. Out on the street in front of the courthouse, the television cameras were rolling, and anyone who cared to was being asked to comment on the trial. Victoria wanted no part of it. She had had her fill of being interviewed. She would catch the media's account of the trial on the late news. Finding a side entrance, she slipped away unnoticed.

It was Friday afternoon, a long weekend stretched ahead, and by the time Monday morning rolled around she would have decided what she was going to do. For now she didn't want to decide anything, didn't want to think about anything. She especially didn't want to go back to that solitary house, to eat dinner alone, to stare at a telephone that never rang. She would pay Rachel a visit. She might even spend the night at her mother's house. If there was anyone who could snap her out of the doldrums, it was Rachel.

She was only blocks away from Rachel's when something occurred to her. Damn! She had to go home; she'd forgotten the plumber. She had awakened to a sluggish kitchen sink that morning and had considered herself fortunate to have found a plumber who would accommodate himself to her hours. He had promised to be there at four-thirty, and it was that now. Braking, she quickly reversed direction. Pray he would wait for her. In her present mood, a stopped-up sink might be more than she could cope with. She would go to her mother's later.

Two men were sitting on her doorstep when she arrived home. Victoria wheeled into her driveway and got out of the car. She was almost upon them before she realized one of the men was no plumber. He was well-dressed, wore a big Stetson low on his forehead and was...chomping on a pipe. Stopping short, she gave herself a little shake. Too many times during the past weeks she had seen someone she thought was Grant. Her hallucinations were almost an affliction.

She hurried on toward the men, her high heels clicking loudly on the sidewalk. At the sound, the two men stood and turned to her.

VICTORIA DID A DOUBLE-TAKE; her heart pounded frantically in her chest. *Grant!* Could it be? It had to be. No one else wore his hat that way or had such broad shoulders. For a minute she thought she had stopped breathing altogether, and for one wild second she had the urge to flee, to run from

him and what she was sure he was here to tell her.
But some deeper source of courage pushed her
ever closer.

"Good...afternoon," she said, ostensibly to
both men, but her eyes were riveted on Grant. He
stuffed his unlit pipe in his pocket and met her
gaze steadfastly. His mouth was set in that implacable line she remembered too well.

"Victoria," he said huskily, touching the brim
of his hat with his forefinger.

Victoria's insides were a whirlpool of agitation.
What right did he have to stand there looking so
handsome after giving her the most wretched
weeks of her life? She had mentally chastised him
for not having the decency to break it off with her
in person or on the phone. Now she wished he had
written her a damned Dear Jane letter.

"Hullo, ma'am," the other man said. "Pete
Carson from Triple-A Plumbing and Sewer Service. Havin' a little trouble with the kitchen
sink?"

"Yes, yes, I am." She fumbled in her handbag
for her keys. "Come in, please...both of you. I
do thank you for waiting, Mr. Carson."

"I was about ready to leave, but then your
friend here showed up, so we've been havin' us a
chat."

Victoria pushed open the front door and
stepped inside; Grant and the plumber followed.
"The kitchen is right this way, Mr. Carson," she
said, hurrying across the living room and casting a
backward glance over her shoulder at Grant.

"Well, now, let's see what the problem is," Pete Carson said, heading for the sink.

"Will you be needing me, Mr. Carson?"

"I don't think so."

"I'll be in the living room if you do."

"Sure, ma'am."

Taking a deep breath, Victoria turned and retraced her steps. Grant was standing in the middle of the room, looking every bit as uncertain and uncomfortable as she felt. There were dark circles under his eyes, which tore at her heart. He must have spent some sleepless nights worrying about this confrontation. Magnanimously she gave him A-plus for guts. This couldn't be easy for him. *Play it cool, Victoria,* her inner voice warned. Spare him the tears and yourself the humiliation.

Her tongue skimmed nervously over her bottom lip as she approached him. Her chest was heaving, but she was powerless to control it. "You. . . look tired."

"I got drunk last night," he growled.

Ah, yes, she thought. Man's age-old method of screwing up courage. She waited for him to say something else, waited until it seemed she would erupt into a million pieces. "Wh-what are you doing here?" she finally managed to ask.

Something about the defiant way she was holding herself told Grant some very complicated thoughts were churning in that fascinating head. He decided in a split second to approach the thing head-on. "Obviously I came to see you. I've driven for hours with a granddaddy of a hang-over, I might add.''

"Why?"

"Because I'm not going to let you off the hook so easily.''

Victoria frowned. "What? What are you say-ing?''

He reached for her. His fingers closed around her upper arm. "It came to me last night in the mid-dle of my fifth Scotch and water. I'm not going to let you skip out on me without an explanation. You're going to have to say it to my face, love.''

"You're talking in riddles.''

"I'll admit I was a fool. I'll admit I made it too easy for you.''

"I don't have the slightest idea what you're talking about!''

"I read the note.''

"Note? What note?''

"The note you wrote to Rita telling her about Albuquerque. Why there, Victoria?''

"Why not?''

"Stop answering all my questions with ques-tions!'' he barked, forgetting he had vowed there would be no snarling. "Weren't you going to tell me?''

She lifted her chin higher. "Why should I?''

"Say, ma'am, how long's it been since this drain has been reamed out?'' Carson appeared from the kitchen.

Victoria whirled. "What? Oh, I don't know. A year, I guess.''

"That's not too bad. You're lucky. Some folks can't keep those drains open more'n a few months. Those garbage disposals do it. Bad for drains, but I guess I shouldn't complain, huh? They keep us in business." He headed for the front door while Victoria and Grant stood awkwardly watching him. "I'll get my rooter out of the truck. You happen to know where the main sewer line is?"

"No—no I'm sorry, I don't."

"That's okay," the plumber said pleasantly. "I'll find it."

The moment the door closed behind the man, Grant twirled Victoria around to face him. "Why should you?" he sputtered in disbelief. "I ought to wring your lovely neck! How can you ask that, Victoria? All right, you might not have been ready to settle down with me, but dammit we had something! Almost from the beginning I opened up to you, told you I loved you, and you pay me back this way. I can't believe you would move away without even telling me."

Tears scalded her eyes. "Why should I tell you when you didn't even return my phone calls?" She hadn't meant to say that. It sounded so pettish and hurt.

Grant stepped back, his brow furrowing. "Phone calls? What phone calls? I never heard a word about any phone calls."

Victoria eyed him suspiciously. "You didn't?"

"Not a one. Victoria, love...you mean you called me? When?"

"Weeks and weeks ago. I thought. . . Helena, I mean."

"Helena? What on earth does she have to do with anything?"

The front door flew open, and Carson entered carrying the rooter machine. "This won't take long, unless, of course, you got more problems than I think you have."

Victoria and Grant simply stood staring at each other, transfixed, as the plumber hauled the cumbersome machine through the living room and into the kitchen. Just before disappearing, he halted. "You haven't got an ice machine draining into that sink, have you?"

With some effort Victoria shifted her attention back to the plumber. "Honestly, I don't know a thing about the plumbing in this house, Mr. Carson. The refrigerator has an ice dispenser."

"Naw, that won't be a problem, but some folks have those fancy under-the-counter ice machines that drip water all day long, and if it's hooked up to the sink's drain you can have big trouble. All that grease and ice. . . you can imagine."

"Yes," Victoria said weakly. "It sounds like a problem."

"Well, this will only take a jiffy."

"Lord, I hope so," Grant muttered.

Victoria turned back to Grant. "I. . . assumed you and Helena had—"

"What in hell made you think that?" he boomed, understanding all too well the incredible thing she was trying to tell him.

"I saw Steve, the way you wanted me to, and afterward I called you. You had gone to Houston, so I telephoned the hotel and left a message. You didn't call back, so I called again, only to be told you had checked out. I thought you would call when you got home, but you didn't, and I—"

In the middle of her spiel the plumber started up the rooter machine. The ensuing racket was deafening and made conversation almost impossible. Grant took Victoria by the arm and propelled her toward the sofa, pulling her down with him.

He raised his voice. "Love, I didn't go back to Arroyo Grande after I checked out of the hotel. In fact, I wasn't the one who checked out at all. A fellow who works for Jordan did it for me."

"Jordan? Your brother? You saw Jordan, too?"

"Admittedly I went to Houston to see Helena, at your insistence, remember. I wanted to be able to tell you I'd done it. I spent maybe a couple of hours with her. It was mainly Jordan I wanted to see."

Hope was beginning to bubble inside Victoria like champagne. Could all of this have been a misunderstanding, a mix-up in signals? Messages undelivered, hurt feelings, misconceptions? Could she dare dwell on such a delightful prospect? Grant looked so sincere, almost contrite, adorably humble. "Why? What prompted you?"

"It's a long story, love, and as soon as that guy turns off that blasted machine I'll try to tell you about it!" he shouted. "But I never got a message from you, believe me! Surely you didn't think I would ignore it if I had.''

"I didn't know what to think," she shouted back. "I tried to make excuses for you. I tried to convince myself you could have missed my message at the hotel, but I was sure Rita or Mrs. Guilford would tell you I was trying to reach you.''

"Rita and Mrs. Guilford are in east Texas right now. I haven't spoken to either one of them in ages.''

"Oh, Grant...." Victoria was shouting, sobbing and laughing at the same time. "You mean you came here today when you didn't even know I had called?''

"Victoria, I came here today because—" In the kitchen the machine stopped, and Grant's voice boomed through the suddenly quiet house. He immediately lowered it. "Because I saw that note you had written to Rita, telling her you were moving to Albuquerque, and losing you, after waiting for you for so long, was something I knew I couldn't let happen. I just had to come here today and make you see...."

She felt as giddy as a teenager. He leaned toward her earnestly, his eyes begging her to understand, begging her to believe.

"I hadn't really decided to take the transfer," she admitted. "I don't know why I put that in the note. I was feeling pretty awful about then, abandoned and unloved. Maybe—" she glanced down at her hands, then back at him "—maybe subconsciously I was hoping she would tell you and you would discover you didn't want to let me go.''

Grant slapped his knee. ''Oh, hell, Victoria! If you'd used half your brain you would have known I wouldn't want you to go away. I want you with me! I love you, goddammit!''

''I was so afraid you had seen Helena again, and. . . you know.''

''What the devil goes on in that unknowable brain of yours, love? Helena is as big a fruitcake as ever. Nice enough, I suppose. A little different. No, real different. She'll never grow up. And after knowing you, hell, I couldn't stand her more than a couple of hours. There's only one like you, babe. . . .''

''Well, that just about does it, ma'am.'' Carson put in another appearance. He deposited his machine in the middle of the living room. ''But I'm going to check all the other drains while I'm here.''

''That won't be necessary, Mr. Carson,'' Victoria murmured without taking her eyes off Grant.

''Won't take but a minute. Might save you another call.'' The plumber walked into the bedroom wing, and Victoria and Grant were soon treated to the sound of water running in sinks, the shower, the bathtubs, toilets flushing.

''I suppose one must admire him, but God in heaven, that man's caught up in his work.'' Grant clutched Victoria's hands a little frantically. ''Victoria, listen to me. I'm going to let Rita visit her mother part of the year, if Rita wants to, that is. Helena and I both agreed it was up to her."

"Oh, Grant, it's so good that you did that. I know it can't have been easy."

"We even got some lawyers into it, and I spent most of my time with them. I did what I should have six years ago—I worked out a fair and equitable property settlement. Helena didn't want that big house, et cetera, but she didn't know how to get rid of it. I was hardly at the hotel at all, so I finally asked Jordan to have someone check me out and settle the bill. I guess your message just got lost in the transition."

Victoria tenderly placed a sympathetic hand on his arm. "How was it . . . seeing them again?"

He shrugged away what she knew must have been a traumatic event. "The past is now in the past, where it belongs. Once the business with Helena was settled, Jordan and I took off for the old family place in the hill country. It's pretty rustic. No telephone, no television. We went hunting, fishing, got gloriously drunk on a couple of occasions. It was good for both of us."

Victoria closed her eyes and felt the most marvelous loosening taking place inside. "Oh, Grant, and all that time I thought you'd changed your mind, decided you didn't want . . . ."

"Love, how could you have ever doubted? You should have kept calling and kept calling until you reached me."

Her smile was weak. "I'm the original doubter, don't you know that by now? You and I were doing exactly what my parents did—not communicating with each other.''

''My fault, I'm afraid. I know now that staying away from you was the worst way to handle it. I should have been wooing you, for God's sake! I should have bombarded you with phone calls, letters, flowers. I knew the doubts you had. I should have worn down your resistance, instead of sulking because you could stay away from me.'' He paused and frowned, remembering something. ''Victoria, you saw Steve. How...was it?''

She gave him her brightest smile. ''Grant, it was the most, the most...disburdening thing I've ever done. He's not the man you are, darling. Not nearly the man.''

Grant's eyes widened. ''Darling! You called me darling! I don't think you've ever done that before.''

''Haven't I? I should have, because I love you.'' She looked deeply into his eyes and knew it was true.

His face registered absolute joy. ''That's something else I've never heard you say.''

Victoria lifted radiant eyes to him. Their faces inched closer together.

''All the drains are flowing good, so I'm finished now.'' Victoria jerked back, looked up to see Pete Carson standing nearby, brandishing a bill. ''Let's see now...that'll be forty-two-fifty.''

''Oh! Well, I'll, ah, write you a check.''

She started to get to her feet, but Grant detained

her. Muttering something under his breath, he stood up, reached into his hip pocket and withdrew his billfold. "Here you are, Mr. Carson. This should take care of it."

"Well, gosh, I'm afraid I don't have change for a fifty, sir. Most folks pay with a check."

"That's quite all right. You keep the change and buy yourself a six-pack or something," Grant said heartily, impatiently guiding the man toward the front door.

"I've got to get my machine," the plumber reminded him.

"Oh, yes, you do, don't you? Here, let me give you a hand." With seemingly little effort, Grant lifted the machine and carried it to the front door, where he relinquished it to the plumber. Pete Carson started out, then turned and peered past Grant's broad shoulders.

"I'll give you a little tip, ma'am. If you wanna keep those drains open you ought to pour a couple of quarts of boiling water down 'em once a week or so."

"Thank you, Mr. Carson. I'll remember that," Victoria said, stifling a giggle as Grant rolled his eyes toward the ceiling.

Finally, at last, the plumber was gone. Grant closed the door behind him, breathed a relieved sigh and turned and spread his arms. "Now, dammit!" he said gruffly. "Come here!"

Victoria was across the room and in his arms in a flash.

VICTORIA SANK MORE DEEPLY into the warm comfort of the frothy bathwater just as Grant stepped into the brimful bathtub. "How long does it take to get married?" he asked.

"Not long," Victoria said. "Monday I'll give Chuck my two weeks' notice, and once that's been served I'm all yours."

"Just think, Victoria. You'll never get your government pension."

She giggled.

"Scoot over," he commanded.

"Somehow I never figured you for the bubblebath type," Victoria cooed, flicking him playfully with water.

"Ordinarily I'm not. A brisk invigorating shower is more my style, but...ahh, this feels good." He stretched a leg on either side of her and pulled her on top of him. Their bodies bobbled buoyantly in the fragrant, steamy water. "I think this must be the biggest bathtub I've ever seen. And these mirrors! It has all the sedate dignity of a French bordello."

"I designed it!" she exclaimed in mock indignation. "And I certainly don't know what a French bordello looks like. How come you do?"

He grinned. "It looks like what I imagine a French bordello would look like," he amended.

"This bathroom was a bit of whimsy on my part. Almost sybaritic, isn't it? I should have opened champagne, lit candles, burned incense, turned this into a real event!"

"It's quite an event as it is. You tempt me beyond belief...."

Smiling sensuously, she locked her hands behind his neck and slithered her legs along the length of his, sending him an erotic message all her own.

Grant groaned. "This is a side of you I haven't seen before, Victoria Bartlett."

"Oh, there's a lot you don't know about me, Grant Mackenzie. But you'll have years and years to find out... everything."

"Right now I want to find out if you're waterproof."

"Grant!"

His searching hands began exploring her under the water, moving up and down her back, over her bottom and down her thighs. "Mmm, you seem to be." Languid at first, his hands became more urgent, until Victoria arched her neck in a sigh, then bent her head and found his mouth with hers.

Grant's hands tantalized her. They moved to her waist, lifting her up and out of the water slightly. He shifted her to one side, and his mouth captured one rosy nipple, sipping on it gently. He repeated the process, shifting her to the other side. Victoria sighed and squirmed, hungering for him. Never again would she be able to do without him. If Grant didn't come to her periodically with these permutations of love she would wither and die, like a plant deprived of water and sunlight.

Then she was gliding back into the water, her water-slick torso moving easily along his. Her hips settled against his, into that familiar niche. Victoria caught the rhythm of his movements and followed them—instinctive, primitive, gracefully erotic in the water as they could never have been in bed. Slowly, so slowly, Grant guided her, lifting and bringing her down to accept his thrust of possession. Water lapped at her chin, tickled her earlobes, churned and surged from their passion and sloshed over the tub's rim. It had cooled considerably, but not enough to dampen the white-hot flame that was surging through her veins. Her insides felt like molten lava.

Grant's lovemaking was skilled and insistent. He knew exactly how to please her, exactly what words to say. He persisted in pleasuring her until finally, lost to control, she gave herself up to their storm of passion, and repeating his name in a choked whisper, she allowed the spasms to overwhelm her.

Together their bodies shuddered as the long crescendo of fulfillment began. Familiar guttural sounds came from deep in Grant's throat. Finally, they collapsed so completely that it was up to Grant to keep her head above water; the sweet aftermath of passion left her limp.

For what seemed hours but could have only been minutes, they clung languorously together. Then Victoria felt his strong arms lifting her up and out of the water; the sudden chill on her wet skin brought her to her senses. Grant wrapped a thick velour towel around her and rubbed gently.

"I...I thought I was drowning," she confessed breathlessly.

"You were," he said with a smile. "In love."

When she was thoroughly dry she returned the favor. Each of them wrapped snuggly in a towel, they went to lie on her bed. Long moments of contentment passed before Grant propped himself on one elbow to look down at her. "Is the trial over?"

"Uh-huh."

"What was the verdict?"

"Guilty as charged."

Grant's eyes widened. "I'll bet Rumbaugh damned near split a gut over that one!"

"He looked a trifle subdued."

"Are you finished with that cops-and-robbers stuff, Victoria?"

"Yes. From now on I'm going to play nursemaid to harlequin quail and golden-cheeked warblers and things like that."

"Good. It's about time." Smoldering eyes raked her up and down. "Damn, you're gorgeous!"

"So are you."

"I am not now, nor have I ever been gorgeous!"

"Gorgeous is in the eye of the beholder. Believe me, you're gorgeous!"

Grant traced the outline of her bottom lip with his forefinger. "I know I have no right to ask you about the meeting with Steve, but in my he-man fashion, I'm itching to know."

Victoria smiled knowingly. "Just as I'm dying of curiosity about your meeting with Helena."

"I guess none of it is really important, is it?"

"Not in the least. You and I are here together. That's the bottom line. That's what's important. But I'll tell you one thing—you had Steve pegged correctly right from the beginning."

"How's that?"

"Steve thought—it sounds absolutely ridiculous, but he thought I was in competition with him."

"Ah." He nodded.

"Grant, you never did tell me what prompted you to see Jordan again."

"Oh, I was sulking around the lodge, getting little work done, feeling sorry for myself because you could stay away from me, wondering if you had seen Steve again, if you ever would...and it dawned on me that I was a fine one to insist you do this and that, when my own life was so full of loose ends." He smiled down at her. "That's about it. Nothing very dramatic."

"Grant, did we come close to losing it altogether?"

"No," he said firmly. "When I read your note to Rita I decided what I had to do. I knew I had to come to you, no matter what. Then I got here and found that damned plumber."

"You'd better be glad that 'damned plumber' was here. If he hadn't been, I would have been at my mother's house."

"I would have found you at Rachel's, Victoria. I would have found you in Albuquerque, Atlanta or Albany. I would have found you."

"Yes," she murmured thoughtfully, "I guess you would have. I have all the confidence in the world in you." She curled her arms around his neck and settled comfortably into the sweep of his shoulder, so happy she thought she might explode. "You can do anything you set your mind to."

She heard the rumble of laughter deep in his chest but didn't see the slightly wicked grin crossing his face. "Right now," he growled, "my mind is set on. . . ." Deftly his fingers loosened the knot holding the towel around her breasts. It fell away, revealing the satin-smooth body that could turn him almost crazy with desire.

"Grant! Again? You're positively insatiable!"

Loosening his own towel, he moved over her. "Guilty as charged."

## CHAPTER TWENTY

"VICTORIA!" RITA SQUEALED, racing through the front door of Arroyo Grande Lodge. Setting down her suitcase, she gave Victoria an enthusiastic hug. "I'm so glad you're here! I thought you guys were never going to get married."

Victoria laughed. "Well, we did. A week ago."

"Did you go somewhere on your honeymoon, after all?"

"No, we spent it at the lodge. We came here right after the ceremony."

"Yuck!" Rita grimaced. "From your mom's house to here. That's not very romantic."

Victoria grinned, remembering the glorious, love-filled two weeks they had spent at her Corpus Christi house before the wedding. Chuck had thoughtfully kept her close to the office during her final two weeks with the service. Grant had amused himself while she was at work, and had been patiently waiting for her every afternoon when she got home. She remembered the feeling of excitement inside her each time she had opened the front door and called, "I'm home!" It had been the best honeymoon imaginable.

"Well, your father felt he had to get back. So

let me look at you. How was your visit with your mother?''

Rita grew serious. "Interesting," she said. "She took me to an art gallery that's showing her work. She seems to be getting pretty famous, and I think she kinda liked taking me around and showing me off to her friends."

"That's great, Rita. I'm glad it went so well."

"And Helena— She told me to call her Helena, which was a relief, 'cause I would have felt silly calling her 'mother.' Anyway, she was really nice about my weavings, and she told me I should stick with it, 'cause there aren't many people around who do that sort of thing anymore."

"So you should. I'll see to it that you do."

"And she says when I get older, if I want, she'll introduce me to some people who can do me some good, whatever that means."

Victoria paused, carefully choosing her words. "How did you and your mother...get along?"

"Oh, okay. Helena's...different. Oh, I mean she's nice as can be, but she's just different. And she doesn't know much about teenagers. She asked me if I wanted a peanut-butter-and-jelly sandwich, for Pete's sake! I haven't eaten one since I was a kid. And she assumed I wanted to go out for hamburgers every other night. I finally had to tell her I like pizza better than hamburgers, and that I like pot roast and meat loaf and roast chicken and all sorts of things. I even like broccoli!''

Victoria laughed and hugged Rita ferociously.

For all Grant's claims about being uptight over the parenting business, he had done a good job. Rita had her head on straight. Watching her grow up, Victoria thought, was going to be one of the delights of her life. "So you had a good time. That's great!"

"It was fun, and I guess I'll go back to see her, but what I really want is to stay here with and you daddy." Rita pulled away slightly and lifted shining, inquisitive eyes on her. "Victoria, are we really going to get a house? When Jake picked me up at the airport in San Antonio, that's the first thing he told me."

"Oh, yes, Rita, we are! Isn't it exciting? Grant feels you and I should have a real home, not just live here at the lodge. Do you remember Sally Anderson's friend, Joe? Well, his company has developed a dozen ranchettes near here, only about five miles away, as a matter of fact, and your father and I looked them over a few days ago. Oh, Rita, they're lovely!

"The one we picked out has four bedrooms, three baths, a heavenly kitchen. The people who are buying them are from all sorts of places. We've already met some of our neighbors and like them very much. The family on our right has four kids, one of them a girl about your age. It will be a real neighborhood."

Rita looked puzzled. "But what about Arroyo Grande?"

"Your father and I will work here every day, but we'll live at the ranchette. Each house has five acres, so we can have a garden, a swimming pool, keep a couple of horses.''

Rita's eyes brightened even more. ''Victoria...do you suppose daddy would buy me a couple of lambs?''

''Lambs?''

''Yes, so I could grow my own wool. I'd take care of them, I swear I would! I'd learn to shear, then wash, dye and spin the wool before I weave it. Victoria, that's the Total Navaho Experience! I've studied all about it, all about the old designs handed down for hundreds of years. I could be a real artist!''

Victoria stood a little in awe of this young girl, her talent and ambition. She and Grant didn't have a ''weekend artist'' on their hands. There might even be some genius lurking behind that winsome face. ''Of course, honey, of course,'' she said. ''I'll tell your father, and I'm sure he'll do it.''

''If you ask him, Victoria, I'm sure he will, too,'' Rita said with an impish grin. ''I always knew he liked you. Everything's been so different since you came along. Daddy's different. It's...nice.''

''I'm glad you think so, Rita, because I think it's nice, too.''

Rita picked up her suitcase. ''Well, I'm going to put my stuff in my room and go find Mrs. Guilford and Maria. They'll want to know all about my trip. See you later.''

''Later, honey. It's good to have you home.''

Just then the front door flew open, and Grant stepped inside, followed by a very familiar face. "Victoria, look who just dropped in—literally."

"Chuck!" Victoria exclaimed delightedly. "What on earth are you doing here?"

Her former supervisor grinned. "Oh, I wanted to pay a call on the newlyweds, and there's something I want to show you."

"Show me?"

Grant held out his hand to her. "Come on, love. Chuck's being very mysterious about this, but apparently there's something he's itching for you to see. We're going to take us a little trip."

Victoria was intrigued...but less so when she saw their mode of transportation. Parked in a clearing some distance from the lodge was a helicopter. Victoria clutched her husband's arm. "Grant! I don't have to go up in that thing, do I?"

He grinned down at her. "Of course. Come on, I'll be with you. You won't be afraid if I'm with you, will you?"

She tried to give him a brave smile, but it came across looking as sick as she felt. "I...guess not."

She clung to him for dear life as the chopper lifted off the ground, her body rigid, her eyes wide with fright. "Loosen up, love," Grant said, patting her hand. "Relax."

She despised her fear of flying, but there didn't seem to be anything she could do about it. It was bad enough in a jumbo jet, but this machine

looked so flimsy. She quite imagined that when it
crashed—which it surely would—it wouldn't fall
gradually to earth; it would just drop straight
down—plop! While Grant and Chuck chatted casually about a number of things, occasionally
leaning forward to look down at the ground, Victoria kept her eyes riveted on the young pilot. *If he
doesn't look concerned,* she thought grimly, *I
won't be.*

They had been airborne for perhaps thirty
minutes, long enough for Victoria's insides to
have calmed somewhat, when the vehicle descended in a swoosh. Victoria clutched Grant again.
"Must he do that?" she cried frantically, and her
husband gave her a sympathetic if somewhat
amused glance.

"I want you to look at something, Victoria,"
Chuck said, gesturing toward the ground. "Down
there. What do you see?"

Summoning up every bit of courage she possessed, she leaned forward just far enough to look
out of the aircraft. "I see...houses," she croaked.
"And ground. The ground's a whole lot farther
away than I wish it were."

"You're not paying attention," Chuck said.
"Doesn't anything look familiar?"

Victoria frowned and looked again. "I don't
know. Is that...is that Parker's Crossing?"

"Sure is. Now, look at this...." Chuck tapped
the pilot on the shoulder. He nodded and made
another swooshing maneuver that sent Victoria's
stomach surging into her chest.

"Look down there and tell me what you see."

"Well, not much of anything, to be honest."

"For sure you don't see twenty thousand egrets, do you?"

Victoria looked at Chuck with surprise. "Is that the rookery? What happened? It looks so clean."

"We passed along the information your dad gave you. After a lot of haggling and grumbling, the farmers and ranchers who live near the rookery instituted a pesticide program to make the area as insect-free as was humanly possible, all paid for by government funds and private donations. Deprived of food, the egrets made an early, hasty exit northward, and we cleaned up the mess they left behind."

"But what's to keep them from coming back next year?" Victoria wanted to know.

Chuck rubbed his chin. "We're studying that now, and we'll come up with something. Right now the citizens of Parker's Crossing are happy, and none of the birds were harmed. I thought you would be pleased."

Victoria sat back, leaning comfortably against Grant's shoulder. Yes, she was pleased. Parker's Crossing was just a tiny incident in the continuing struggle to maintain wildlife resources in the face of encroaching civilization, but it was something. "Thanks for showing it to me, Chuck."

Chuck addressed his next question to Grant. "How's Martin Rumbaugh these days?"

"Fat and sassy as ever," Grant said. "But his day's coming. The county's changing rapidly,

Chuck. Lots of new people moving in, people who couldn't care less who Martin Rumbaugh is or how long his family's been here. You can almost feel his influence eroding.''

Chuck turned around to speak to the pilot, and Grant squeezed Victoria's hand. "Why, Victoria Mackenzie, I think you've almost got a smile on your face. Could it be that your fear of flying is abating somewhat?''

"I'll tell you when we land—if we do.''

"Oh, we'll land all right," Grant teased. "What goes up must come down.''

"Yes, but I want us to come down on purpose!''

Grant laughed and hugged her, then held her tightly throughout the journey back to Arroyo Grande. Victoria melted against him, awash in the contentment his presence always brought her. Never could she have imagined such happiness. And there was so much in store—the work she and Grant would do, moving into the new house, meeting new people, nurturing Rita's talent....

The helicopter settled gently to earth. Grant hopped out and held out his arms to Victoria. Waving goodbye to Chuck and the pilot, they stood and watched as the aircraft again lifted off.

"Well, what do you know, we made it!" Grant grinned in mock astonishment. "Isn't that amazing? I'll tell you, it was touch and go there for a minute!''

Victoria shot him a look of disgust, then smiled. "I knew all along it wouldn't crash.''

"Oh? You could have fooled me, what with all that clutching and grabbing. My arm feels like it's been mauled by a lion."

"That chopper wouldn't have dared crash. Not now I have you."

"I suppose you're going to live under a lucky star from now on, or some such nonsense."

She slipped her arm around his waist, and together they strolled toward the lodge. "Somehow, Grant—" she smiled wistfully "—it seems I've already begun."

"Well, I'm real proud of you for getting in the thing, love, when I know how you feel about flying. I think such a show of bravery deserves a present. Let me buy you something. What do you want?"

"Nothing," she said decisively. "I have everything."

"Now, Victoria, there must be something you want," he persisted, grinning down at her.

"Well, now that you mention it—I'd like to talk to you about a couple of lambs. . . ."

**November's other absorbing
HARLEQUIN *SuperRomance* novel**

**PERFUME AND LACE by Christine Hella Cott**

On an urgent cross-Canada blitz to promote her
line of fragrances, Camille Beesley was shadowed
by a vaguely enticing spy. By the time she hit
Toronto, the man had taken definite shape—and
action! Professor Jacob Darleah was like a fine
essence, the first refreshing tang supported by a
lingering sensuous impression. . . .

He was lecturing in ancient remedies; his itinerary
just happened to coincide with hers. He said. Back
home in Vancouver, he was concocting more than
ointment in her lab late at night. . . .

Yet when Camille needed loving, she went to him,
but all she could trust about Jacob were his feelings
for her.

A contemporary love story for the woman of today

These two absorbing titles
will be published in December
by

# HARLEQUIN
## *SuperRomance*

## A DREAM TO SHARE by Deborah Joyce

Eden Sonnier was making her mark. As an interior designer, she was on the brink of success. Then she met Nicolas Devereaux.

Suddenly Eden was full of doubts. Nick had a way of making her examine her goals. Was success enough? What about a husband and a family? Each time Eden thought she knew what she wanted, Nick's tender, triumphant lovemaking confused her even more.

The only thing they didn't question was their deep abiding love. But their love had a price—and one of them would have to pay much more than the other.

## BELOVED STRANGER by Meg Hudson

As an anthropologist, Sara Westcott had come to San Francisco to research the Russian community, not to fall in love. Then she met Alexei Varentsov.

Alexei was an enigma in so many ways. He spoke little of his past and never of the future. Sara's mind held a thousand reservations—what if he were a spy, a fugitive—but her heart was immediately lost to this strong, gentle man.

She would live for the moment and not think of the inevitable—the day she would wake up and find Alexei gone . . .

These books are
already available
from

# HARLEQUIN
*SuperRomance*

MORE THAN YESTERDAY Angela Alexie
LITTLE BY LITTLE Georgia Bockoven
SONG OF THE SEABIRD Christina Crockett
DELTA NIGHTS Jean DeCoto
WHEN MORNING COMES Judith Duncan
MOUNTAIN SKIES Sally Garrett
CHAMPAGNE PROMISES Meg Hudson
THE RISING ROAD Meg Hudson
SILVER HORIZONS Deborah Joyce
THE GENUINE ARTICLE Pamela M. Kleeb
THE AWAKENING TOUCH Jessica Logan
THROUGH NIGHT AND DAY Irma Walker

If you experience difficulty in obtaining any of
these titles, write to:

*Harlequin SuperRomance*, P.O. Box 236,
Croydon, Surrey CR9 3RU

## Look out this month for

### NO SAFE PLACE   *Barbara Bretton*

For too long, Stefanie Colt had skated on thin ice. Unable to walk the streets of New York without casting nervous glances over her shoulder, unable to contemplate her responsibilities at work without feeling a cold dread, Stefanie felt that her memories were slowly consuming her. It was only a matter of time, Stefanie knew, before she became totally paralyzed by fear.

Helping people like Stefanie was more than Dan O'Conner's business—it was his obsession. He knew of no other way to exorcise his own very private demons. . . .

### ADAM AND EVA   *Sandra Kitt*

St. John was everything Eva Duncan had been promised. Almost. Lush, warm, exotic and spectacularly beautiful, it was not quite the picture of serenity and tranquillity it was cracked up to be. That was Adam Maxwell's fault. If he had confined his ill humour to her, Eva could have tolerated the neighbouring marine biologist. But having flown down to the island with his adoring young daughter, Eva bristled whenever she heard him ordering the child about.

For his daughter's sake, someone had to stand up to this man. Gathering her courage, Eva was determined to do just that, despite the consequences!

### SOMEONE ELSE'S HEART   *Zelma Orr*

Over the years, Andy Timmons had developed a sixth sense for danger. A pilot in her family's Colorado-based charter service, Andy discovered that her keen instincts enabled her to chart a course around pea-soup fogs and treacherous winds—and thus avoid mishap.

Andy's instincts told her to give Scott Rawlins a wide berth. Scott, who soon became a regular customer, didn't like flying, and his loud misgivings were enough to distract any pilot. Unable to avoid Scott, Andy tried to ignore him, but it was just not enough to avert catastrophe!

# 2 BOOKS FREE
## Discover
## Harlequin SuperRomances
### Sensual and Spellbinding, Dramatic and Involving...

Strong stories with unpredictable plots. . .
fascinating characters. . . gripping suspense. . .
exotic locations. By becoming a regular
reader of Harlequin SuperRomances
you can enjoy FOUR superb new titles
every other month and a whole range of
special benefits too:
your very own personal membership
card, a free monthly newsletter packed
with exclusive book offers, competitions,
recipes, a monthly guide to the stars,
plus extra bargain offers and big
cash savings.

**AND an Introductory FREE GIFT for YOU.
Turn over the page for details.**

**Fill in and send this coupon
back today and we'll send you**
# 2 Introductory
# SuperRomances yours to keep
# FREE

At the same time we will reserve a
subscription to Harlequin SuperRomances
for you. Every other month, you will receive
the FOUR latest novels by leading Romantic
Fiction authors, delivered direct to your door.
You don't pay extra for delivery. Postage and
packing is always completely Free. There is
no obligation or commitment — you only
receive books for as long as you want to.

**What could be easier? Fill in the coupon below and return it to
HARLEQUIN, FREEPOST, P.O. BOX 236, CROYDON, SURREY,
CR9 9EL.
Please Note:- READERS IN SOUTH AFRICA write to
Harlequin S.A. Pty., Postbag X3010,
Randburg 2125, S. Africa.**

# HARLEQUIN PRIORITY ORDER FORM

**To:- Harlequin, Freepost, P.O. Box 236, Croydon, Surrey, CR9 9EL.**

Please send me my 2 SuperRomance titles absolutely FREE. Thereafter please send
me the four latest SuperRomances every other month, which I may buy for just £6.00
postage and packing free. I understand I may cancel my subscription at any time,
simply by writing to you. The first two books are mine to keep, whatever I decide. I am
over 18 years of age.

Please write in BLOCK CAPITALS.

Signature _____

Name _____

Address _____

_____ Post code _____

**SEND NO MONEY — TAKE NO RISKS.**

*Please don't forget to include your Postcode.*

Remember, postcodes speed delivery. Offer applies in UK only and is not valid
to present subscribers. Harlequin reserve the right to exercise discretion in
granting membership. If price changes are necessary you will be notified.
4SR  Offer expires Dec 31st 1985.                                    EP13F